Formerly writing as ~~T~~ ~~. Alexande~~ ~~. Kay~~ is ~~.~~ *TODAY* bestselling author of more than fifty novels of contemporary romance and women's fiction. She lives in Houston, Texas. To learn more about her, visit her website at www.patriciakay.com

Initially a French/English teacher, **Emma Darcy** changed careers to computer programming before the happy demands of marriage and motherhood. Very much a people person, and always interested in relationships, she finds the world of romance fiction a thrilling one and the challenge of creating her own cast of characters very addictive.

Sophie Pembroke has been dreaming, reading and writing romance ever since she read her first Mills & Boon novel as a teen, so getting to write romance fiction for a living is a dream come true! Born in Abu Dhabi, Sophie grew up in Wales and now lives in Herfordshire with her scientist husband, her incredibly imaginative daughter and her adventurous, adorable little boy. In Sophie's world, happy is for ever after, everything stops for tea and there's always time for one more page.

The Billionaire's New Year Gift

PATRICIA KAY
EMMA DARCY
SOPHIE PEMBROKE

MILLS & BOON

First Published in Great Britain 2019
by Mills & Boon, an imprint of HarperCollins*Publishers*
1 London Bridge Street, London, SE1 9GF

THE BILLIONAIRE'S NEW YEAR GIFT © 2019 Harlequin Books S. A.

The Billionaire and His Boss © 2008 Patricia A. Kay
The Billionaire's Scandalous Marriage © 2007 Emma Darcy
The Unexpected Holiday Gift © 2016 Sophie Pembroke

ISBN: 978-0-263-27995-5

1219

MIX
Paper from
responsible sources
FSC™ C007454

This book is produced from independently certified FSC™ paper to ensure responsible forest management.

For more information visit: www.harpercollins.co.uk/green

Printed and bound in Spain
by CPI, Barcelona

THE BILLIONAIRE
AND HIS BOSS

PATRICIA KAY

This one's for Gail, with a huge thank-you for all the years of encouragement and friendship.

Prologue

Mid-July, The Hunt Mansion

Harrison Hunt, founder and CEO of HuntCom, sat behind his enormous mahogany desk in the library of the behemoth he called home and looked from one to the other of his sons. "Four sons and not a marriage among you." He shook his head in obvious dismay. "I've never thought much about my legacy, nor about having grandchildren to carry on the Hunt name. But my heart attack made me face some hard truths. I could have died. I could die tomorrow."

His face was grimly intent as he continued. "I finally realized that left to your own devices, you four never *will* get married, which means I'll never have grandchildren. Well, I don't intend to leave the future of this family to chance any longer."

His eyes bored into theirs. "You have a year. One year. By the end of that time, each of you will not only be married, you will either already have a child or your wife will be expecting one."

Alex Hunt stared at his father. He couldn't believe what he was hearing, and he could see from the expressions on the faces of his brothers that they felt the same way. Was this a joke? Had that heart attack Harry'd had affected his brain?

"And if any one of you refuses," Harry continued flatly, ignoring the disbelief in their faces, "you'll all lose your positions in HuntCom…and the perks you love so much."

"You can't be serious," Gray, the oldest at forty-two, finally said.

"I'm deadly serious."

J.T., two years older than Alex at thirty-eight, broke the brief, shocked silence. "How will you run the company if we refuse to do what you want?" He reminded their father of the expansions taking place in Seattle and in their Delhi facility. "Construction delays alone would cost HuntCom a fortune."

But Harry didn't budge. He said it didn't matter about the current projects, because if they didn't agree to do what he was demanding, he would sell the entire HuntCom empire, including the ranch Justin loved so much, the island that was J.T.'s passion, and the foundation that meant so much to Alex. Gray cared about everything. He'd been second-in-command to Harry ever since graduating from college and he fully expected to move into the president's spot when Harry finally retired.

"Before I die," Harry continued relentlessly, "I mean to see each of you settled, and with a family started. I want you married to decent women who'll make good wives and mothers." He paused for a moment, then added, "And the women you marry have to win Cornelia's approval."

"Does Aunt Cornelia know about this?" Justin, who was the youngest brother at thirty-four, asked in disbelief.

Alex also had a hard time believing their sensible honorary aunt would go along with such a nutty scheme.

"Not yet," Harry admitted.

Alex knew his relief was shared by his brothers. When Cornelia learned about Harry's plan, she'd put a stop to it. In fact, she was the *only* one capable of talking Harry out of anything. He would listen to her.

"So," Justin said, "Let me see if I've got this straight. Each of us has to agree to marry and produce a kid within a year—"

"*All* of you have to agree," Harry interrupted. "All four of you. If one refuses, everyone loses, and life as you've known it—your jobs, the HuntCom holdings you each value so much—will be gone."

Muttered curses followed this pronouncement.

"And the brides have to be approved by Aunt Cornelia," Justin said.

If the situation hadn't been so surreal, Alex would have laughed. If Cornelia'd had to approve *Harry's* brides, Alex's and his brothers' lives would have been very different.

Harry nodded. "She's a shrewd woman. She'll know if any of the women aren't good wife material."

Alex looked at Gray, whose expression was furious.

Ignoring their incredulity, Harry went on. "You can't tell the women you're rich, nor that you're my sons. I don't want another fortune hunter in the family. God knows, I married enough of them myself. I don't want any of my sons making the same mistakes I made."

That's for sure, Alex thought. Every single woman Harry had ever married had been a gold digger. And Alex's mother was probably the biggest gold digger of them all. As always, thoughts of his mother produced feelings of bitterness. Alex shook it off. Long ago he'd decided dwelling on the subject of his mother was counter-productive.

"I don't know about my brothers," Justin finally said, "but my answer is that you can take my job and shove it. Nobody tells me who to marry, or if I'll marry, or when I'll have kids."

Harry's expression changed. For a moment, Alex actually thought his father's feelings had been hurt. But hell, what did the old man expect? He was treating them like chattel. As though their feelings didn't matter at all. Did he think they'd just lie down and take it? After all, they *were* his sons. But no one had *ever* told Harry what to do.

"So be it," Harry said, his voice hardening. He looked around. "What about the rest of you?"

Alex nodded. "I'm not my mother. You can't buy me."

Although the brothers all agreed, Harry didn't back down. His last words before leaving them were, "I'll give all of you some time to rethink your positions. You have until 8:00 p.m. Pacific time— three days from now. If I don't hear from you to the contrary before then, I'll tell my lawyers to start looking for a buyer for HuntCom."

"Son-of-a-bitch," Justin swore softly as the door closed behind Harry.

"He's bluffing," Gray said. "He'd never sell the company." His cell phone rang and he glanced at the caller ID before tucking it back in his pocket. "Even if he does hold the controlling interest." Gray was referring to the fact that their father held fifty-one percent of the stock in HuntCom, so even if all four of them plus their Aunt Cornelia voted no to a sale, Harry's wishes would prevail.

"I don't see it happening, either," J.T. said. But there was doubt in his voice.

"I don't know," Justin said slowly. "Cornelia says Harry's been different since his heart attack."

Alex hated to admit it, but he agreed with Justin. Even if Harry hadn't had that heart attack, he was a stubborn man. When he made up his mind about something, it was impossible to sway him.

"Different how?" Gray asked dubiously. His cell phone rang again and he glanced at it impatiently.

"She says he's been moody, a word I found it hard to believe the old man even knows."

"Then maybe he *is* serious," Alex said, frowning.

"We're in the middle of a buy-out." Gray shrugged into his jacket. "There's no way he'd consider selling the company until it's finished and that might be months away. He's bluffing."

"How can you be sure?" Alex asked. "What if you're wrong? Do you want to take that chance? Lose everything you've worked for over the past eighteen years? I know I sure as hell don't want to see the Hunt Foundation shut down…or run by someone else." For years now, Alex had headed the foundation, the philanthropic arm of HuntCom. For Alex, it was more than a job. It was his passion, his raison d'être. As far as he was concerned, the best thing about being a Hunt was the ability and means to do some good in the world.

The brothers continued to discuss Harry's ultimatum, but since they weren't getting anywhere, they finally decided to call it a night.

"I'll see you at the office tomorrow," Gray said to J.T. as they all moved toward the door. "We need to go over the figures for that possible plant in Singapore."

Alex walked with his brothers down the hallway and out of the house to the parking deck, which was halfway up the hillside overlooking Lake Washington. Every time he came here, he marveled at the beauty of the place. Across the lake, the lights of the Seattle skyline shimmered.

Not that Alex wanted to live in a place like this one. Who the hell needed a mansion, anyway? Even when all four of them had lived with Harry, they'd rattled around in the place. And now that their father was alone except for the servants, it seemed ludicrous to have a place this large. But Harry seemed to need the trappings of wealth.

Alex continued to think about his father's edict as he drove his silver Navigator back to the city where he kept an apartment downtown near the Hunt Foundation offices.

By the time he'd gotten home, fixed himself a drink and a salad and warmed up some leftover chicken piccata that he'd made two days earlier, he was completely convinced that he and his brothers had done the right thing in turning down their father's deal. It was simply too manipulative. Too cold and calculating. Besides, he was now beginning to think, like Gray, that Harry was bluffing.

Sure, he was stubborn, but Alex had a feeling Harry was counting on the fact his sons knew how stubborn he could be to convince them that he meant what he had said. But Alex also knew his father had worked far too long and too hard to build his empire to ever give it up.

No.

He'd never sell everything. All they had to do was wait him out, and he'd back down.

So when Alex and his brothers were conferenced

into a call from Justin the following evening and
Justin said he thought they should take the deal,
Alex was shocked, even though Justin explained
why he thought so.

"I went to see Cornelia," he said. "And she feels
there's a strong possibility Harry's threat to sell the
company is real. She said she's been growing in-
creasingly worried about him since his heart attack.
She confided that Harry seems uncharacteristically
introspective and that on several occasions he's told
her all he wants is for us to be married and to have
children. Cornelia says she's afraid Harry feels a
need to right his wrongs and is getting his fiscal and
emotional affairs in order in preparation for dying."

"So you're willing to let him choose your *wife?*"
Alex said to Justin in disbelief.

"No," Justin said. "I'm willing to convince him
that's what's happening, but I'll do the choosing. I
spend half my time in Idaho, not Seattle. I'll marry
someone acceptable to him and set her up in a home
in the city and then I'll go back to Idaho."

"You think that'll work?" The question came
from J.T.

"Oh, yeah," Justin drawled, cynicism lacing his
tone. "The second she realizes she's married to a
Hunt and has a generous allowance, she'll gladly
live in Seattle while I live wherever the hell I want.

I'll write off the cost of keeping her and the kid as a business expense."

"Damn, Justin," Alex said. "That's cold." Not to mention dishonest. But Alex didn't say that. He knew his brothers all thought he was too idealistic, that he simply didn't understand the cold realities of the world.

"Not cold. Practical," Justin said.

"You know this won't work unless all of us are in," Gray said.

"I know," Justin said. "And it won't work for any of us unless we come up with a contract that ties Harry's hands in the future. We'd have to make sure he can never blackmail us like this again."

"Absolutely," J.T. put in. "If he thinks he can manipulate us with threats, he'll do it again in a heartbeat."

"So if we do this, we are going to need an ironclad contract that controls the situation," Alex said, thinking out loud.

"If all Harry had threatened us with was loss of income," Justin said, "I'd tell him to go to hell and walk. But I'm not willing to lose the ranch. What about the rest of you?"

Alex finally broke the silence that followed his question. "If it was just money, I'd tell him to go to hell, too. But it's not, is it?"

"It's about the things and places he knows matter most to us." J.T. sounded grim.

"Part of Harry's demand was that the brides not know our identities until after we're married. How are you going to find a marriageable woman in Seattle who doesn't know you're rich, Justin?" Gray asked.

"I've been out of state for most of the last eighteen months, plus I've never been as high-profile as the rest of you," Justin said.

"Yeah, right," J.T. scoffed. "There isn't a single one of us who hasn't had our picture in the paper or a magazine."

"But not as often as Harry," Gray said. "He's the public face of HuntCom. I've got to give the old man credit, he deflected as much publicity from us as he could."

"True," Justin agreed. "So how about it, Gray? Are you in?"

Alex knew Gray could be as stubborn as Harry. "Face it, Gray. Harry holds all the cards."

"He always has." Gray sighed audibly. "This totally sucks, but if we can come up with a way to tie Harry's hands in the future, then I guess I'm in."

By the time they finished their call, Alex was already thinking of ways he could fulfill his part of their strange bargain and begin his own hunt for Cinderella.

Chapter One

Six weeks later...

Alex looked around his new apartment with satisfaction. This place, with its nondescript decor and discount-house furniture, was a far cry from his pad in the city, but he didn't mind. He didn't need fancy digs. Never had. The only reason he lived where and how he did was because it was expected of him in his position as the director of the Harrison Hunt Foundation.

Thinking about the foundation, he frowned. He'd

put out every fire, assigned as many tasks as he could to others and taken care of everything else he could think of before telling his staff he was taking an extended leave of absence. And he knew his assistant, Martha Oliver, affectionately called Marti by all who knew her well, could be trusted to handle ninety-nine percent of anything else that might come up.

But it was that other one percent that worried Alex. Still, he was only a ninety-minute drive from downtown Seattle, and in an emergency, Marti could reach him on his cell and know he'd come as soon as possible. In fact, she'd been texting him religiously, keeping him up to date on everything. Alex made a mental note to give her a hefty bonus when this situation was finally resolved and he was back to work. Which, he hoped, would be soon.

He knew there was no reason to worry. Things would be fine while he was gone. He reminded himself that all he had to do was quickly find a suitable woman to marry, and he might not have to be away from the foundation for long at all.

Alex was not arrogant or vain. But he wasn't unaware of his appeal. All his life he'd been told he was good-looking and wherever he went women made eye contact and flirted. So if he found someone who interested him and that he felt his father and his

Aunt Cornelia would approve of, he suspected all he'd have to do was go through the motions women expected from a suitor.

After he and his brothers had decided to go along with Harry's edict, Alex had given considerable thought to his strategy in the campaign to find the kind of wife he wanted. What he'd decided was he would never be able to do so while continuing to work at the foundation. He needed to go somewhere he wasn't known and he needed to be working at an ordinary job with ordinary people.

Then he thoroughly researched Harry's various holdings and narrowed them down to the one where he thought he might not stick out like a sore thumb. He told his father he wanted a position at their distribution center in Jansen, an hour and a half drive from Seattle—just south of Olympia. He already knew most folks in Jansen watched Portland television stations and read the Portland newspaper, so they'd be unlikely to recognize him from any of the publicity photos tied to the Hunt Foundation. And if anyone *did* recognize him, he'd simply say he was always being mistaken for one of the Hunt brothers.

Alex didn't think he had to worry. He had always tried to keep a low profile. He hated society bashes and disliked the club scene. If not for the foundation and its work, he doubted anyone would ever recognize him as belonging to the Hunt family.

Today would be the true test, though, because in less than forty-five minutes, he would begin his new job at HuntCom's main distribution center.

New job.

New apartment.

And new name.

He'd also decided that for the duration of his "hunt" he would be known as Alex Noble. It would be different if he were going to go to work somewhere that wasn't associated with HuntCom, but at the distribution center there was no way he could be Alex Hunt without someone questioning the coincidence of the shared name.

So he'd decided on Noble, which was the surname of a previous stepfather. Alex's mother, Lucinda Parker Hunt Noble Fitzpatrick, was on her third marriage and Alex had once cynically figured it wouldn't be her last, although he'd finally conceded that maybe Terrence Fitzpatrick was the real deal. He and Alex's mother had recently celebrated their twenty-fourth wedding anniversary.

There were things about Terrence Alex didn't like, namely his penchant for thinking money could solve any problem, but he'd done one thing right. He'd given Alex a much-loved younger sister, Julie, although Terrence was doing his level best to spoil her with the enormous amounts of money and gifts he lavished upon her.

Thinking about Julie and her recent escapades, Alex frowned. He wished he could get through to her, but she laughed off his concern, telling him he was "stodgy" and "old-fashioned" and had forgotten what it was like to be young.

Her scorn, even though delivered with affection, had hurt. Alex didn't think he was stodgy. He was just sensible and practical. So he didn't worship at the altar of money and power. Did that mean there was something wrong with him? He guessed in his little sister's crowd, it probably did.

He was still thinking about Julie when he pulled into the employee parking lot at the HuntCom Distribution Center. But when he emptied his pockets and passed through security, he deliberately put her out of his mind. Today he couldn't afford to be distracted by Julie or anything else. He would need all his wits about him to pull off a successful masquerade.

It took an hour to fill out necessary paperwork and watch an orientation film in the human resources department, but by nine o'clock—he was on the first shift which began at eight in the morning—the HR manager's assistant, who made a point of telling him her name was Kim, walked him down to the gigantic storage center, which was a beehive of activity.

Alex couldn't help grinning when a young girl with purple spiked hair whizzed by them on roller blades. At his quizzical look, Kim said, "That's Ruby. She's also a picker."

Alex frowned. "Picker?"

"Sorry. Merchandise rep. Same job you're going to do. You know, *pick* the merchandise from the shelves so it can be shipped to the company or person who placed the order."

"Ah." It amused Alex to think what his colleagues at the foundation would say if they could see him now. Most, he knew, were in awe of him. After all, he was one of the mighty Hunts. They respected him, because he worked as hard or harder than they did, and they knew he cared about the work they were doing, but they still couldn't manage to treat him the way they treated the others on staff. To them, he was out of their league.

"I'm sure you'll be great at the job," Kim said, giving him an admiring glance.

Alex wasn't interested; he'd seen her wedding band. So all he said was, "Hope so."

She led Alex toward a cluster of several people who seemed to be arguing about something. When they spied him, the conversation abruptly stopped and a young woman—a very *attractive* young woman, Alex noticed—with wildly curly red hair tied back with a navy-blue ribbon and dressed in snug jeans and a white blouse open at the throat, broke away from the group and strode toward them. Very blue eyes filled with intelligence gave him a quick assessment before turning their intensity on Kim.

"Um, P.J.," she said, "this is Alex Noble, the new member of your crew. Alex, this is P.J. Kincaid, the floor supervisor."

Alex wondered if P.J. had adopted initials in lieu of her first name for the same reason J.T. had adopted his, because she hated her given name. J.T. had said Jared was a sissy name and he would kill anyone who insisted upon using it.

"Hello," P.J. said, thrusting out her right hand. "Welcome to HuntCom."

Alex took her hand and gave it a firm shake. Hers was just as firm. "Hello," he said.

"Good luck," Kim said. She smiled at him, then turned and walked off.

When Alex's attention returned to P.J., her eyes met his squarely. Something about their steady scrutiny disturbed Alex. Did she suspect something? He forced himself not to drop his gaze.

"I'm told you have experience," she said.

Yes, that was definitely a hint of doubt in her voice. Deciding brevity was his best bet, Alex nodded. "Yes, I do."

"And you worked...*where*...before?"

Sticking to what it said on his fake résumé, Alex answered, "At a warehouse in Sacramento."

She looked at him thoughtfully. "What kind of products?"

"Household appliances."

Her eyes remained speculative. "Why'd you leave?"

He made his voice light. "Couldn't very well commute from here."

She nodded, but instinct told him she wasn't completely buying his story. "You've completed all your paperwork?"

"Yes."

"Had your physical and drug testing?"

"Yes." That wasn't true, but on paper, it said Alex had done so and passed.

"So...you ready to go to work?"

"Yes, I am."

Turning, she gestured to one of the men in the group still gathered nearby. "Rick."

A dark-haired, dark-eyed man Alex judged to be in his late twenties or early thirties walked toward them. Like P.J. and Alex and almost everyone Alex had seen so far, except for the employees of the HR department, he wore jeans. His black T-shirt hawked a Red Hot Chili Peppers concert.

"Rick," she said, "this is Alex Noble. You'll be training him." Meeting Alex's eyes again, she said, "Alex, this is Rick Alvarado. He's been with the company seven years and can answer any questions you might have."

The two men shook hands. Rick's eyes were friendly. Alex liked him immediately and sensed he could turn out to be a friend.

"Follow me," Rick said. "I'll give you a tour of the place so you can get a general idea of where everything is stored." He kept up a running commentary as they headed down the nearest aisle. "You know much about the company, Alex?"

Alex nodded. "Quite a bit. I researched it when I knew I was going to be working here."

"So you know old man Hunt started out by coming up with a new software and things escalated from there?"

Alex nodded.

"Now we manufacture just about everything in the computer field," Rick continued. "We have over three thousand products that we ship from this location."

"That many?" Alex said, although he'd already known this.

"Keeps us hopping 24/7. We run three shifts. Eight to four, four to twelve, twelve to eight. Lots of the guys like the afternoon and night shifts, but me, I like days. 'Course, I work the other shifts anytime they need extra hands, 'cause it's overtime, and with three little girls and a wife who likes to give those old charge cards a workout…" He laughed. "I can always use the money."

"Three little girls, huh?"

Rick grinned. "Yeah, we had 'em pretty close together. My oldest is eight, the youngest is four." Pulling a wallet from his hip pocket, he took out several photos. "I'll only do this once," he promised, handing Alex the pictures.

Alex smiled at the likenesses. All three girls had curly dark hair and dark eyes. "They sure are cute."

"Yeah," Rick said proudly. "They're good kids, too. Maria, she's been a stay-at-home mom, but in September Jenny, she's the youngest, starts school, so Maria's going to go back to work."

"What does she do?" Alex asked politely.

"She's a preschool teacher. She'll be teaching at Jenny's school."

By now, they'd stopped in a densely stocked aisle. "You don't have to remember everything I'm gonna show you," Rick said. "I'm just giving you an overview. You'll get a diagram of the place and a product list showing where each of the different products can be found. It'll take you a while, but after a couple of weeks, you'll be an old pro at this."

Alex hoped so. The last thing he wanted to do was fuel that doubt he'd seen in his new boss's eyes. He was going to have a hard enough time of it remembering to keep in character without worrying about keeping *her* happy, too. "This place is huge. Do we fill orders from all over or just in certain areas?"

"The center's divided into four quadrants," Rick said. "Our unit fills orders for Quad B. I'll show you. We'll walk the whole quad. Actually, you'll probably want to become familiar with all the quads eventually."

"Why is that?"

"Sometimes certain products sell heavily, like when we're running a special promotion or something, and you might be asked to fill in at one of the other quads."

Alex nodded. That made sense. "Does P.J. supervise all the quads?"

Rick nodded. "Yep. She's the boss. Only one higher than her here is Steve Mallery, the GM."

Just then, the girl with the purple hair skated by.

"Ruby," Alex said.

Rick laughed. "You know about her, huh?"

"The clerk who brought me down from HR told me her name."

"Ruby looks like a punk rocker with those tattoos and all the body piercings, but she's okay. She's one of our best pickers."

"I admit I was surprised to see the roller blades."

"A couple of the kids use them. Wish I could skate. I'd wear 'em, too. You can sure get around faster. But I'd probably kill myself. Or if not that, break a leg or something."

"I know what you mean," Alex said, although he prided himself on being physically fit. Still, he wasn't a skater. Never had been.

Rick smiled and turned his attention back to the merchandise. "Okay, Alex, lesson number one. Here's how we stock the products...."

Frat boy.

It was the first thing P.J. thought when she was introduced to Alex. What was *he* doing there? All P.J.'d had to do was look at him to know he didn't belong. He was too good-looking and way too polished. His hands alone told the story. No calluses. No rough skin. Clean, manicured nails. Long, elegant fingers.

And then there were his teeth. P.J. always noticed people's teeth, for they indicated class and financial status more than anything else. And Alex's teeth were gorgeous—straight and white. Obviously, they'd been well cared for.

She wondered if he'd once held a top-level job, maybe lost it due to drugs or alcohol. *Or maybe he's a corporate spy, sent here to find out if we're doing a good job. If* I'm *doing a good job.*

The thought was sobering. It also pissed her off. Because P.J. worked hard, harder even than her crew. She had to. She was a woman supervising mostly men. She constantly had to prove herself.

Geez, if corporate wanted to know what was going on here, all they had to do was talk to Steve, or better yet, be above board and come and observe the center openly. They'd soon see what a tight ship she ran.

Well, she'd keep a close eye on Alex Noble. And if he *was* a spy, she'd soon find out. In the meantime, she wouldn't trust him as far as she could throw him. And yet, even as she was telling herself all of this, she couldn't deny the frisson of attraction she'd felt when they shook hands. Acknowledging this, she was infuriated with her body's betrayal.

What's wrong with you? Alex Noble was so not the kind of man she wanted in her life. Ever since she was old enough to know better, she'd envisioned herself with a man who held the same beliefs she did: say, a union boss or champion of migrant workers. Someone she could respect and admire for his ideas and not how well he filled out a pair of jeans.

Certainly not for his sexy dimples or his thick, wavy hair or his dark-chocolate eyes.

Dark chocolate!

Had she *really* thought that?

But even as she chastised herself for the gushy term, she knew it applied. His eyes really had reminded her of dark chocolate. Sweet, melt-in-your-mouth dark chocolate. The kind of eyes a woman could lose herself in. Just remembering the way he'd looked at her gave her a funny feeling in her stomach.

Oh, man, Kincaid, you've been celibate way too long. You really need to get laid.

"P.J."

P.J. jumped.

"You looked like you were miles away. I called your name twice."

The speaker was P.J.'s best friend at work—Anna Garcia. Actually, for the past six years, Anna had been P.J.'s best friend, period. P.J. smiled at the pretty brunette. "What's up?"

"We having lunch together today?"

"Sure."

"Great. Want to eat in the cafeteria or outside?"

"It's a nice day. Let's eat outside." When the distribution center had been built, HuntCom had made sure the area surrounding was beautifully landscaped and that there were pockets of trees and flower beds interspersed with walkways and areas with picnic tables. Employees were urged to use the grounds on their breaks, although the smokers grumbled that there were too few places for them to indulge in their habit. Although P.J. didn't admire many corporate titans—she'd grown up around too many of them—Harrison Hunt actually seemed to care about his employees.

Be fair. So does Dad.

Well, yes, her own father also treated his employees fairly and sometimes even generously. But he and Harrison Hunt seemed to be the exceptions.

After Anna had headed back to the mailing center, which she supervised, P.J. printed out the newest batch of orders that had come through in the past hour. After sorting them, she handed the orders for Quads A, C, and D to Chick Fogarty, her assistant, to distribute, then walked toward aisle 24, where they stocked some of the peripherals in their inventory. She knew this was where Rick would have started Alex's training.

Sure enough, the two men were standing in front

of the section where the eighteen different mouses they sold were stored, and although P.J. stood well back as she watched, she could hear Rick naming them as he pointed out how they were arranged by model number.

"I can't believe there are so many different kinds," Alex was saying. "Do we really sell all of them?"

"Yeah, we do," Rick answered. "Hey, I personally have three at home. A wireless, a basic USB plug-in, and a mini for when I travel. You got a computer?"

Alex nodded. "Yeah. I bought myself a laptop last year."

"One of ours?"

"Uh, no. I guess I shouldn't say that too loud."

"Not if you don't want the boss lady to hear." Rick glanced over at P.J. and grinned. "'Course, it's too late. She already did."

Alex whipped around.

P.J. almost laughed at the guilty expression on his face. Walking over to them, she said, "It's okay, Alex. Buying a Hunt computer is not a prerequisite for working here. However, we do give a hefty discount to our employees, so if you decide to upgrade or buy something else in our product line, you'll save quite a bit of money."

Deciding Rick had everything under control, P.J. handed him half the stack of new orders. "You can get started on these whenever you feel Alex is ready."

Rick gave her a salute. "Okay, boss."

Alex's eyes met hers briefly before he looked away. And once again, P.J. felt that unwelcome spark of awareness and attraction.

She frowned. Damn. She had to get control of herself and quit acting like a silly teenager.

Quickly striding away, she decided the best thing for her would be to give Alex Noble a wide berth. A really wide berth. On the other hand, that wouldn't be the best thing for HuntCom.

In fact, she should probably keep a close eye on him these first few weeks. Make sure he was actually doing the job he'd been hired to do.

But for the rest of the morning, she kept her distance. She would quiz Rick later, see what he thought. Maybe she was just paranoid about Alex because he was so attractive. Face it, she chided herself, you've been exposed to too many good-looking, self-centered, arrogant men in your lifetime and now you think they're *all* like that.

Maybe Alex Noble would prove to be the exception.

Yeah, right.

But P.J. wasn't going to hold her breath.

Chapter Two

"I thought there was a hiring freeze."

P.J. made a face. "Yeah. That's what I thought, too." She and Anna were just finishing up lunch.

Anna popped the last bite of her tuna-fish sandwich into her mouth, then wiped her mouth with her napkin. "But Jimmy said you've got a new picker."

P.J. nodded.

"So what's the deal?"

"You tell me."

"Me?" Anna laughed. "You're kidding, right?"

"Well, you usually hear all the gossip, so I

thought if anyone would know what's going on, you would," P.J. pointed out. That was the other thing about Alex Noble—maybe even the most important thing—the fact he'd been foisted on her without any warning.

"I haven't heard a word," Anna said. "Not a peep." She reached for a plastic bag filled with cut-up apple.

P.J. polished off her turkey sandwich, accompanied by a handful of potato chips—she was a junk-food addict, much to her mother's chagrin. "Not even from Ben?" Ben Garza was the HR Director and he'd had a thing for Anna for a while.

Anna made a face. "I've been avoiding Ben."

P.J. refrained from saying something trite like *you could do worse*. She knew how sick she was of people trying to pair her off with guys who didn't interest her in the slightest. Still, she almost felt sorry for Ben. He wasn't the best-looking guy in the world, but he had a good job and he seemed really decent. But Anna simply wasn't interested. She'd gone out with him twice and told P.J. that the thought of going to bed with him actually turned her stomach.

"So what's he like?"

"The new guy?"

Anna laughed. "Yes, P.J., the new guy."

P.J. frowned and finished chewing and swallowing before answering. "I don't know. He doesn't seem to belong here."

"What do you mean?"

"He's too good-looking. Too…sophisticated or something."

Anna chewed thoughtfully on a piece of apple. "Tina said he's a hunk."

"Tina? When did *she* see him?"

"She snuck down to your area earlier this morning. Said she wanted to check him out." Anna grinned. "We don't get that many eligible guys here. *Handsome* eligible guys. Every woman in the place is going to be checking him out. Maybe they already have." Anna's grin turned sly. "So if you want him, P.J., you'd better stake your claim early."

"*Want* him? I have absolutely no interest in Alex Noble. Believe me, he's not my type."

"What's wrong with him?"

"I told you. He's too good-looking." The truth was, Alex looked like he belonged in her sisters' crowd. The country club, golf and tennis crowd. The Armani crowd. The kind of men P.J. had wanted to get away from.

"Tina says he looks like Colin Firth."

"Who the hell is Colin Firth?" Irritation made P.J.'s voice increase in volume.

Anna looked at her as if she'd suddenly grown two heads. "You mean there's a female alive on this earth who doesn't know Colin Firth?" Her voice was laced with astonishment.

"What is he? A movie star? You know I don't pay attention to those people." In P.J.'s opinion, movie stars were only a cut above rock stars, and P.J. considered them the armpit of the universe, with no redeeming social value whatsoever.

Anna sighed. "Honey, Colin Firth is way more than a movie star. He's the most gorgeous guy to come along in years. He's British and has one of those upper-crust accents that is sooo sexy. He also has dreamy dark eyes, he's tall, and he lives in a villa in Tuscany." She sighed again. "Unfortunately, he's married."

P.J. rolled her eyes. Honestly, even sensible Anna could be an airhead at times. "Alex Noble isn't *that* good-looking."

"No? Well, with your ideas about men, I don't think I can trust your judgment, P.J. I think I'll have to have a look myself."

P.J. abruptly stood and began clearing up her trash. "Oh, for God's sake. Come and drool all over him. I certainly don't care. Just make sure you don't distract him from his work."

"Somebody certainly is testy all of a sudden," Anna said, giving P.J. a knowing look.

P.J. knew she'd overreacted, and for the life of her, she didn't know why. All she knew was, she was heartily sick of the subject of Alex Noble.

Alex was beat.

He'd thought he was in great physical shape. Hell, he worked out three times a week at the gym and played tennis at least three times a week. But he had a soft job at the foundation, mainly sitting on his butt. And today, for the first time since he'd spent a summer building houses with Habitat for Humanity, he'd done physical labor, with lots of stretching, kneeling and lifting. He'd used muscles he hadn't even known he had. So by the time four o'clock rolled around, he was more than ready to leave.

Other than that, he was satisfied with how the day had gone. He found it interesting seeing how many orders came through during his shift and how much work was involved in filling them and getting the merchandise shipped out. Although before he started this job, he'd studied the numbers associated with HuntCom and its myriad arms, actually seeing all the products they manufactured and sold was a real eye-opener.

Whether you worshiped at the altar of money and power or not, you had to admire what Harry had accomplished. It wasn't as if he'd come from money.

Just the opposite, in fact. Alex's Hunt grandparents had been squarely middle-class. His grandfather Hunt owned a small hardware store; his grandmother had been a stay-at-home mom.

And Harry had been a too-tall, just-this-side-of-weird, geek.

Yet look what he'd accomplished. He'd developed ground-breaking software that had changed the personal computer industry practically overnight and followed that by designing cutting edge hardware that was as good as or better than anything else on the market.

Now he was worth billions.

And he employed thousands of people.

Alex had met a couple of dozen of those people today. Among them several attractive women. Two of those women seemed promising as far as his bride hunt went—one worked in the mail room, one was a picker from a different quad—although he'd have to know more about both of them before he could make any kind of decision. After all, he was talking about the future mother of his children.

Too bad P.J. Kincaid didn't have a more agreeable personality, because she was definitely the most intriguing of the women he'd met. But she hadn't even made his short list. He didn't have time to win over someone who obviously didn't like him.

She'd certainly made no secret of her feelings. In fact, as the day wore on, she'd seemed to be more suspicious of him rather than less, even though he'd worked hard and given her no cause to look at him the way she had.

What was her problem, anyway?

Why did she seem to always be watching him?

Alex knew she'd asked Rick about him, because he'd seen the two of them talking and Rick kept glancing Alex's way the whole time. In some ways, this amused Alex, because Rick was obviously not the cloak-and-dagger type. In other ways, it didn't amuse Alex at all.

Alex didn't think P.J. could possibly know who he was or why he was there, so why was she acting so weird? Was it because *she* hadn't hired him? Did she resent the fact he'd been presented to her as a fait accompli? Alex grimaced. He'd bet that was it. She felt he'd been pushed on her. Well, in that case, maybe he could change her mind about him.

Question was, did he want to?

The minute P.J. closed her apartment door behind her, she began stripping off her clothes. Today more than any other, she felt the need to get outside and work the kinks out. She could hardly wait to put on her running clothes and shoes and hit the park.

A scant ten minutes later, she was in her bright-blue Miata convertible—top down, breeze ruffling her hair—and heading for the Jansen River and the park that had been built along its banks. Washington State looked beautiful in late summer, she thought, with its riot of colorful flowers and lush green lawns. People complained about all the rain they got, but without the rain, the landscape would be as brown as California's. As she drove along, idly enjoying the scenery, her mind once again drifted to her new employee.

Just as Anna had predicted, throughout the afternoon, at least half a dozen women from different departments at the distribution center had come, on the flimsiest of excuses, to check out Alex Noble.

One of them, Carrie Wancheck, a twenty-one-year-old who worked in payroll, hadn't even bothered with an excuse. She'd grinned at P.J., saying in a stage whisper, "I just wanted to see the hunk everyone's talking about."

"He's too old for you," P.J. had snapped.

Carrie's smile was knowing. "I like older men. They're usually the best lovers."

P.J. had had to force herself not to say anything else, because she realized it might sound as if she were jealous or something. Jealous! Nothing could be farther from the truth. She had absolutely *no* interest in Alex Noble. None. Zero. Nada. But she knew how the women at the center could be. If you said you weren't interested in someone, they immediately thought you were lying. Especially when the man in question was as attractive as Alex Noble.

So she'd kept quiet and silently fumed instead. *Dammit.* She needed this kind of distraction in her department like she needed a hole in the head. If they were going to palm off a new employee, the least they could have done was make him homely.

And the women in her own department were the worst of all! Even Ruby, who was only nineteen and a year out of high school, had hung around Alex to the point where P.J. had to say something to her. P.J. had wanted to add that she didn't think a man like Alex would be interested in a kid with purple spiked hair, five earrings on each ear, and a rose tattoo down her right arm, but despite her appearance, Ruby was a nice kid, and P.J. liked her, so she just sighed and told Ruby to get back to work, then watched the girl skate away.

She was so engrossed in thinking about Alex Noble and the disruption he'd caused today that she almost passed up the entrance to the park.

Hitting the brakes, she managed to slow down in time to turn onto the driveway. Five minutes later, settled into a nice easy jogging rhythm, she finally managed to put Alex Noble and the rest of the irritations of the day out of her mind.

Just as he had taken off his clothes and was heading into the shower, Alex's cell phone rang. He thought about ignoring it, then sighed, reached for it and looked at the caller ID. It was his sister Julie.

"Hey," he said. "I hope this doesn't mean you're in trouble again."

"Hey, yourself," Julie said, her voice filled with amusement. "Why would you assume I'm in trouble? Can't I just call to say hello?"

"Yes, but you rarely do."

"Now Alex…is that nice?"

Alex chuckled. Deciding this call might take awhile, he grabbed a towel from the towel rack and, tucking the phone under his chin, wrapped the towel around himself, then sat on the rim of the tub to continue the conversation. "So if you're not in trouble, what's up, Jules?"

"I called to invite you to my birthday bash."

"That's right. You *have* got a birthday coming up soon."

"Don't pretend you forgot."

Alex smiled. They both knew he never forgot her birthday. In fact, he'd already bought her gift—

earrings and a matching bracelet designed by a local artist who worked in silver and semi-precious stones. The moment Alex had spied the pair set with deep-blue tourmalines, he'd known they were perfect for his sister, whose eyes were an exact match. "So where's the party going to be?"

"Well, believe it or not, it's going to be at the house."

"That's certainly different." Usually Julie's parties took place at one of the many clubs she and her friends frequented.

"Mom insisted."

"And bribed you how?"

Julie laughed. "I want a new car."

"A new car?" Alex said in disbelief. "Your Mini Cooper is only two years old."

"I know, but I'm tired of it."

Alex mentally shook his head. He remembered how Julie had wheedled when she'd wanted that car. "So what do you want now?"

"I saw this really gorgeous black Lotus—"

"Lotus! Geez, Jules, you're talking, what, sixty thousand or more?"

"Daddy can afford it."

"That's not the point. You don't need a car like that."

"Need has nothing to do with it."

Alex sighed. She was so damn spoiled. There was no doubt in his mind that his stepfather would buy her the Lotus.

"Anyway, will you come to my party?"

"When is it?"

"On my birthday. It's a Friday, so that works out great. Seven o'clock. You can bring a date, too, if you want."

"No date."

"But *you'll* be there, right?"

"I'll be there."

"Mom'll be happy."

Alex grunted. His mother had been attempting for a long time to get back into his good graces, but no matter how she tried to make it up to him, Alex found it almost impossible to forget that when he was only two years old, she'd given custody of him to Harry.

Hell, every single one of Harry's wives had sold out for money. Although he and his half-brothers rarely talked about it, Alex couldn't help but think Justin, J.T. and Gray had been just as affected by their mothers' abandonment as Alex had. Because what else could you call it when your mother took money in exchange for giving sole custody of you to your father?

At least Alex, as the next to youngest, had only had to get used to one stepmother—Justin's mother—and she hadn't lasted all that long. Gray, on the other hand, had gone through three stepmothers, all of whom had a short shelf life with Harry. No wonder Gray was so mistrustful of women.

It was pretty sad, but the only stable female influence in their lives was their Aunt Cornelia. And she wasn't technically their aunt at all, even though they'd referred to her that way all their lives. She was actually the widow of Harry's best friend, and it was Alex's private belief that Harry had been in love with Cornelia for years.

As Julie continued to chatter excitedly about the car she coveted, Alex wondered if it would do any good for him to talk to his stepfather about her. Alex didn't want his sister to turn out like their mother, and indulging her the way her father did wouldn't encourage her to be any different.

But as much as he wanted to do something, he knew he'd better not. Terrence would get his hackles up if Alex said anything to him. No sense causing any more tension in the family.

When Julie wound down, they said their goodbyes—Julie exacting one more promise from Alex that he'd be at her party—and Alex tossed the towel he'd been wearing onto the towel rack. He started to step into the tub when he suddenly changed his mind. Even though he was tired, he knew he'd feel better if he got some *real* exercise today. Something to unkink his muscles and blow the stink off. After that he could come home and shower and crash with a beer and dinner.

Twenty minutes later, dressed in shorts, a Coldplay T-shirt Julie had given him along with their newest CD, and his cross-trainers, he pulled into Jansen Park. Although running wasn't his favorite activity, in the absence of a tennis partner, it would do. He still hadn't found a gym to join, but he hoped to remedy that soon, too.

He was about halfway through his run when one of the runners coming toward him from the opposite direction looked familiar to him. As she got closer, he realized it was his boss, the prickly P.J. Kincaid.

Well, well.

His gaze took in the riot of red hair inadequately held back by a sweatband, her perspiration-soaked white T-shirt that had molded to her rounded breasts, the navy-blue running shorts that showed off her nice firm butt, and her long, shapely legs with their well-defined calf muscles. Prickly or not, she sure was easy on the eyes.

He knew the exact moment when she realized who he was. Her eyes widened, her nice, even rhythm faltered, and she nearly stumbled.

Recovering quickly, she stopped, and when her breathing had slowed enough to speak, she said, "Hello, Alex."

"Hi." Alex mopped his brow with the towel he'd thrown around his neck.

"So you're a runner, are you?"

Damn, those blue eyes of hers were unnerving. "Not much of one, I'm afraid."

She shrugged. "You're here."

"I need the exercise. You run here a lot?"

"Every day."

No wonder she looked as good as she did. "How far does this trail go?" he asked to distract himself from just how good she looked.

"If you go all the way around, it's exactly five miles." Now her gaze held a challenge. "You plan to do the whole trail?"

"I thought I would," he said, although he hadn't planned anything of the kind.

"Good." She looked at her black sports watch. "Well, I'd better get going. I'm meeting my sister for dinner at seven and if I don't hurry, I'll be late." She gave him a wave as she set off. "See you tomorrow."

Alex couldn't help it.

Instead of continuing on his way immediately, he watched her. Yes, she certainly did have a nice butt. In fact, it was one of the nicest butts he'd seen in a long time. It would fit very nicely in a man's hands.

And those legs!

Alex couldn't stop himself from imagining those legs twined around a man when making love.

It was at that moment Alex decided maybe he'd forget about playing tennis and joining a gym. Maybe running here in the evenings was a much more sensible choice.

Chapter Three

P.J. wanted to turn around and look back in the worst way. Yet the last thing, the very last thing she wanted was for Alex Noble to think she was interested in him like the rest of those silly women at work.

Because she wasn't.

Not at all.

But, she thought grudgingly, she had to admit he was good to look at. Idly, she wondered how tall he was. At least six-two or six-three, she imagined. P.J. had always had a thing for tall men. Maybe that was because at five-seven she was on the tall side herself. And the rare times she got dressed up, she liked wearing three-inch heels. She also liked looking up when she was with a man. No Katie Holmes–Tom Cruise thing for her!

Will you stop it? Alex Noble is not in the running as an escort or anything else. Remember that. He's an employee. Your employee. So even if you were interested—and you're not!—you don't date employees.

Ever.

Yet no matter how many times she told herself to stop thinking about Alex, she couldn't seem to wipe the image of him in those shorts and that T-shirt that defined his well-developed pecs out of her mind.

She thought about him all the way back to her condo. She thought about him as she took a quick shower. She thought about him as she dressed to meet Courtney. And she was still thinking about him as she walked into Mackey's Bar and Grill in beautiful downtown Webber—which was halfway between Seattle proper and Jansen—at exactly one minute to seven.

Courtney was already there and had secured a booth. She grinned at P.J. and stood to give her a hug. Courtney had inherited their mother's blond hair and green eyes, whereas P.J.'s coloring came from her Grandmother Kincaid. As always, Courtney looked bandbox perfect in creamy linen cropped pants, a short-sleeved black silk summer sweater, and black espadrilles. P.J. couldn't help but notice the beautifully manicured toenails and fingernails sporting a summery shade of coral. In contrast, P.J.'s own nails were unpolished and desperately needed work. And her jeans and T-shirt weren't exactly the latest fashion, either.

That's what happens when there's no man in your life, an insidious little voice said. *You forget to pay attention to yourself.* She couldn't even use the excuse of her job, because most of the women at the center paid a lot more attention to their appearance than P.J. did.

She and Courtney had barely said their hellos and how-are-yous when their waiter approached. "What can I get you to drink?" he asked, looking at P.J.

"What have you got on draft?" she asked.

He named the brands.

"No Black Sheep?" P.J. had a weakness for good English ale.

"No, sorry."

"Okay. I'll have a Guinness." She smiled at her sister after he'd left to fill her order. "What're you drinking?"

Courtney made a face. "Ginger ale."

Thinking her sister wasn't having a beer because she had a fairly long drive back to Mercer Island where she and her husband had bought a new home the year before, P.J. said, "One beer should be okay. I mean, you're going to eat before you get behind the wheel again."

Courtney hesitated, her gaze sliding away briefly before returning to meet P.J.'s. "That's not why I'm not drinking," she finally said.

"Well, what then—?" P.J. stopped abruptly. She fought against feelings she'd thought she'd conquered long ago. Yet here they were again, still hurtful, still unworthy of her, especially considering how much she loved Courtney. "You're pregnant again?" she asked softly.

Courtney nodded. "Three months."

"Three *months!* And you've kept it a secret this long?" P.J. was proud of herself. She sounded just the way she wanted to sound—happy for Courtney and nothing else.

"I wanted to wait till I'd passed the first trimester." Courtney's eyes searched P.J.'s. P.J. knew Courtney was worried about how her news would affect P.J.

Reaching across the table, she took Courtney's hand. "Are you happy about this?" Courtney and her husband already had three kids—a boy, ten, and two little girls, seven and four.

Courtney nodded. "I am. Brad…well, he wants another boy in the worst way."

P.J. refrained from rolling her eyes or saying what she thought about Brad and his *wants*. In her opinion, her sister's husband was a neanderthal. P.J. wouldn't have put up with him for a minute, let alone the twelve years Courtney'd been married to him. For one thing, he didn't believe in women holding jobs outside the home.

For another, he was constantly saying things like, "Honey, you wouldn't understand that even if I *did* explain it," when Courtney asked him about anything to do with his job. You'd think he was a rocket scientist, for God's sake, when he was a lawyer.

Courtney was every bit as smart as he was, probably smarter, P.J. thought. Yet she seemed contented with Brad. His put-downs didn't seem to bother her at all. In fact, she didn't even seem to notice them.

To each his own, P.J. thought. Better her than me.

"Well, if you're happy, then I'm happy for you," she said now. "Congratulations."

"Thanks." Courtney sipped at her ginger ale and eyed her sister over the rim of her glass.

P.J. knew she wanted to say something. To prevent yet another conversation about P.J.'s situation, she hurriedly asked, "Do Mom and Dad know?"

"Not yet."

"You mean, you're telling *me* before you told them?"

"You're my favorite sister, you know that."

They smiled at each other, and P.J. forced herself to remember how lucky she was. She might not ever be able to have any children of her own, and she might have repudiated her family's money and her status as an heiress, but that didn't mean she didn't love her parents and siblings. And she absolutely adored her nieces and nephews—Courtney's three and soon to be four, Jillian's two, and Peter's two.

P.J. told herself it didn't matter if she couldn't have kids, because she had no intention of getting married, anyway. She'd known long ago she wasn't cut out for marriage. In fact, she couldn't imagine subjugating herself to a man...*any* man. Just the idea of a man telling her what she could and couldn't do set her teeth on edge.

And she certainly wasn't cut out for homemaking. Hell, she couldn't even boil water, let alone cook. And as far as cleaning went, forget that, too. One of her indulgences was a once-a-week maid service, and even if she had to give up food, she intended to keep that.

Well, maybe that was an exaggeration. She liked

food too much, especially carbs. In fact, she'd never met a carb she didn't like. That was the biggest reason she forced herself to run five miles every day. So she could keep eating all those fries and pasta and pizza and still keep her figure.

Yet, even as she told herself all of this, she knew she might have been willing to give the marriage thing a try if not for her probable inability to have children. Providing, of course, the right man should come along.

You can always adopt.

Maybe, she thought. But there again, it would take the right kind of man. And lately, she'd begun to think he didn't exist.

Plenty of single women adopt.

P.J. had actually considered adoption. In fact, she'd given some serious consideration to adopting an older child—one of the ones considered hard to place since everyone seemed to want babies. And maybe one of these days she'd finally get around to doing something about it.

By now the waiter had brought P.J.'s beer and the sisters had placed their orders—P.J. a steak sandwich and fries, Courtney the house specialty of coconut-crusted shrimp salad.

"P.J., you eat entirely too much junk food," Courtney said mildly as their waiter walked off.

"I know. That's why I run."

"Do you ever eat a salad?"

"Sure."

"How often, once a month?"

P.J. grinned. "You know me too well." After taking a swallow of her beer, she said, "So you're due in…mid-February?"

Courtney nodded. "February fourteenth, to be exact."

"At least it's not Christmas day." P.J.'s birthday was two days before Christmas and she'd always hated that. "Just don't name him Valentino or something like that."

Courtney snorted. "Like Brad would let me."

To keep from saying something snide about Brad, P.J. said, "So what else is new?"

"Let's see. Um, Melissa McKee is getting a divorce."

"You're not serious!"

"Melissa's the one who told me."

"That's a shame. I thought she and Rod had a good marriage."

"Hey, he'll be eligible now…" Courtney's eyes were speculative.

P.J. knew what she was thinking. "Forget that," she said quickly. "He's not my type. But he'll have no shortage of women lining up to be the next Mrs. McKee, I'm sure of that."

Rod was a very wealthy man as well as a good-looking one. P.J. wasn't sure what he did. Something in commodities trading, she thought. He probably had no social conscience to speak of. Definitely not her type.

Thinking that, she couldn't help remembering she'd said the same thing about Alex Noble just today, that he was not her type, either. Something in her expression must have alerted Courtney to the direction of her thoughts because her sister said, "Wait a minute. Are you dating someone?"

"What makes you ask that?"

"You had a strange look on your face."

"Oh, I was just thinking about a new guy who started working for me today. Anna—you've heard me talk about her—said something about him and I told her he wasn't my type, either."

"Why'd she say something about him?"

P.J. shrugged. "He's kind of a hunk. If you like that type."

"And what type is that?"

"Oh, you know, tall, dark, handsome." P.J. smiled in spite of herself.

"And you don't like that type." Courtney shook her head, laughing. "You're one of a kind, you know that?"

Just then the waiter came with their food, and the sisters fell silent until he was gone again.

Courtney began to cut up her salad. She speared a piece of shrimp and some lettuce leaves, but before putting them into her mouth, she said, "Maybe you should give this new guy at work a chance. Who knows? You might actually like him."

"Who said he's interested in *me?*" P.J. poured a mound of ketchup next to her fries and dipped one in.

Courtney gave her a look. "You're a very pretty, very sexy woman. Of course he'll be interested in you." She forked another bite of salad into her mouth. Then she grinned. "That's if you can keep your mouth shut."

P.J. glared at her sister. But she couldn't hold the expression and was soon laughing. "Yeah, that *can* be a problem," she admitted. She'd run more than one guy off by expressing her opinions, which were almost always diametrically opposed to theirs.

"So tell me more about this guy," Courtney said when their laughter subsided.

"No point. I'm not interested in him. And even if I *were*, which I'm *not*, he works for me. I don't date guys who work for me. It wouldn't be a good idea."

Courtney nodded. "Yeah, you're probably right. Conflict of interest or something." She studied P.J. for a minute. "Are you sure it's not the baby thing stopping you? Because if it is, lots of guys don't want kids."

P.J. sighed. "I know that." She wanted to add that any guy who didn't want kids was probably not the kind of guy she'd want to be with, anyway, but she didn't. Courtney would just feel bad if she said something like that.

"Do you? Seems to me you throw up all kinds of excuses to keep men at a distance, and I can't help thinking that's the real reason."

P.J. shrugged. "It's not. But I can't help thinking about it. I mean, what if I start dating someone and really like them and they like me? Then I tell them I can't have kids? Is that fair?"

"Well, you can hardly tell them *before* you go out with them," Courtney pointed out. She made a face. "It *is* a problem, isn't it?"

P.J. nodded, then made a face. "Let's change the subject, okay? I'm awfully tired of this one. Tell me what Jillian and Peter are up to. I haven't talked to either one in weeks."

"The phone works both ways, you know."

P.J. started to laugh. "If my eyes had been closed, I would have sworn that was Mom talking."

The expression on Courtney's face was priceless. But then she joined P.J.'s laughter, and for the rest of evening, they kept their conversation lighthearted.

Alex had just finished his dinner—a really excellent omelette—and before settling in with the new

T. Jefferson Parker book he'd bought, he decided to check his messages on his home phone. He didn't really expect there to be anything important, but he'd better check, anyway.

The first two were invitations he wasn't interested in accepting—he'd ask his secretary to send his regrets—the third was a hangup, and the fourth was from Georgie—short for Georgianna, the oldest of Cornelia's four daughters.

The message started with, "Hey, Alex, where the heck *are* you? I called your office but the call was routed to Marti and she said you're taking a leave of absence? Holy cow, has *hell* frozen over? I've hardly ever known you to leave your precious foundation for a *vacation*, let alone a leave of absence. Call me! I need to talk to you. Smooches."

Alex chuckled. He loved Georgie. Too bad he felt toward her the way he felt toward Julie, because if not, she'd have made a perfect wife.

Punching in the code for her cell, he waited for her to pick up. Instead he got her voice mail. "This is Georgie. Leave a message and I'll call you back soonest."

At the beep, he said, "Hey, girl. It's me, Alex. Call me if you get this message before eleven. After that I'll be racking up Zs. Oh, and I've got a new cell." He gave her the number, then said, "If you don't get home early enough to call back tonight, wait till after four tomorrow, okay?" Not wanting to explain any further, he broke the connection.

Her call back came a little after ten.

"A leave of absence, a new cell, don't call after eleven, don't call during the day...what in the *world* is going on?" she said.

"And hello to you, too," Alex said, grinning. He laid his book on the coffee table, then got up and stretched.

She laughed, the sound low and warm and contagious. "C'mon, quit stalling. Have you joined the CIA or something?"

"Nothing that drastic."

"Well, where *are* you?"

So Alex explained. When he was finished, there was silence for a long moment. Then she said, "I cannot believe this. I especially can't believe my mother went along with it. I mean, Alex, this is the craziest scheme I've ever heard."

"Maybe not that crazy."

"What do you mean, not that crazy? This is the twenty-first century, not the eighteenth." Her voice was indignant. "And giving you a *time* limit? It's blackmail, that's what it is."

"Yes, I guess it is, but—"

"But nothing. I'm going to have a serious talk

with Mother. I always knew she was blind as far as your father is concerned, but this is the limit."

Alex couldn't help grinning at Georgie's anger on his behalf. She was nothing if not loyal. "Calm down, okay? I admit, I was ticked off at first, but I'm actually okay with it now." An image of P.J. and the way she'd looked in the park earlier flashed through his mind. "I think it might work out well."

"Wait a minute. Are you saying you've found somebody already?"

He laughed. "I wouldn't go that far. But there are some possibilities."

"So you're saying you're no longer free to meet me for lunch during the week?" Georgie worked for an ad agency in downtown Seattle, and they'd fallen into the habit of meeting for lunch at least once a week.

"No, afraid not."

"How about dinner?"

"Dinner I can do."

"How about tomorrow night?"

"Where?"

She named a restaurant they'd frequented in the past. Luckily it was on the Portland side of Seattle, so Alex wouldn't have as much traffic to contend with.

"It'll have to be an early night, since I'll have a long drive back," he said.

"How early?"

"Seven?"

"That's doable. I'll see you then. Oh, and Alex?"

"Yes?"

"Despite what you said, I'm *still* going to give Mother a piece of my mind!"

Chapter Four

By the end of his first week, Alex felt like an old pro at his job. He knew where the most popular products were located without having to look at his diagram, and even when he did have to look, it didn't take him long to find what he needed, get it off the shelf, and fill the order. In fact, he worked almost as fast as Rick did.

"You're doing a great job," Rick said, clapping him on the back late Friday afternoon. They'd both been asked to stay until five because of a huge order that had come in right before their shift was about to end. "You filled as many orders as I did today."

Alex smiled. "Thanks."

Even P.J. gave him a compliment, saying, "You've caught on fast, Alex."

It was absurd how pleased he was by their praise, especially P.J.'s. Maybe she was beginning to trust him. She didn't seem to be watching him as much as she had those first few days.

He'd been watching her, though. He couldn't seem to help it. And the more he watched her, the more intrigued he became, and the more he entertained the possibility of her as a potential wife.

She had just walked by the aisle where he was working when Rick approached from the other end. Alex hoped the younger man hadn't seen him staring at P.J.

But Rick's gaze was guileless. "Hey man, it's quitting time."

Alex looked at his watch. It was after five. The time had gone so fast that afternoon, he hadn't realized how late it was.

"I wanted to tell you that we usually stop off at Jake's for a couple of beers on Fridays," Rick said. "Want to come?"

"Who's we?"

"Just a bunch of us from the different departments. Mostly singles."

Alex wondered if P.J. would be there. "Okay,

sure. Sounds good. Uh, does the boss usually go, too?" He inclined his head in the direction of P.J.'s office.

"Sometimes. Not always. But even if she *does* show up, she's pretty low-key when she's there. She doesn't act like the boss or anything."

"That's good," Alex said for Rick's benefit.

"Some of the guys stay and eat," Rick said as they walked out to the parking lot together. "Jake's has great fried shrimp and onion rings, but me, I gotta get home. Maria's mother is visiting and she said she'd babysit tonight if me and Maria want to catch a movie or something. Maria's all excited." He grinned. "Thing is, we don't get out much."

Alex had seen Jake's Grill on his drive back and forth to work. Located on River Street, it was only about five minutes from the distribution center. Although it had been raining earlier in the day, the sun had broken through the clouds by the time he reached the five-year-old red Ford pickup truck he'd purchased to conform with his new status in life.

He grinned as he unlocked the driver's-side door. He actually liked the truck. Hell, he might even keep it when this masquerade was over.

After getting in, he rolled down the window. He also liked fresh air. In his capacity as Managing Director of the Harrison Hunt Foundation, when he wasn't sitting on his butt in the office, he spent a lot of time traveling to various facilities. That was the hardest part about his job at the distribution center—having to be indoors all day long.

The drive to Jake's was short. When he got there, the parking lot was already half-full, even though it was early by most standards. He parked the pickup, locked it and strode toward the entrance.

The inside of Jake's sported dark woods, dart boards on the far wall, and long tables rather than booths. Alex smiled at the player piano cranking out "The Entertainer" and the pretty waitresses in their short black skirts and white blouses. He saw there was also a juke box and some video games on the far wall.

Spying Rick at a long table near the bar, he walked over to join the HuntCom group. He'd met most of them already. A quick glance told him if P.J. was coming, she hadn't made it yet.

"Hey, Alex," Rick said. Sliding his chair over, he made room for Alex to join them. "You know everyone?"

"I don't believe *we've* met," said a striking blonde sitting on the other side of Rick. "I'm Carrie Wancheck. I work in payroll."

"Alex Noble," Alex said, leaning over to shake her hand. "I've seen you around." He was almost certain she was one of the women who had checked him out during his first couple of days on the job.

She was very pretty, but too young for him, nearer his sister's age than his. He guessed she was probably in her early twenties. He knew a lot of men who had married women fifteen and twenty years younger than them—in fact, the older the men, the more they seemed to like young women. But he wanted someone who wasn't a kid. Someone with ideas, who maybe read the newspaper and had opinions on more than fashions and movies.

Someone like P.J.

The thought came unbidden, almost surprising him. Yet he knew it had been brewing for a while.

"So how do you like working at HuntCom?" Carrie asked.

"I like it fine."

She smiled. "And we certainly like having you."

Her tone left no doubt that she was flirting with him. "Thanks," he answered casually. "It seems like a good place to work."

"You want a beer?" Rick said, pushing his chair back and standing.

"Yeah, but I can go get it. Or wait for the waitress to bring me one."

"Okay. Enjoy. I've gotta get going or Maria will kill me."

There were good-natured mutters of "henpecked" and "who wears the pants in your family, Rick?" as he headed for the bar.

The moment he was gone, Carrie slid over onto his vacated seat. She smiled up at Alex. "So I hear you're from Sacramento?"

"Not from Sacramento. I was born in the San Diego area."

That was actually true. Alex's mother had been visiting friends in La Jolla when her water broke—three weeks early—and she gave birth to Alex there. Without Harry's presence, as she had bitterly said more than once.

"I worked in Sacramento before moving here, though." Alex felt he could carry this myth off without tripping himself up because he'd spent a couple of weeks in Sacramento in the course of doing the foundation's work.

"What made you come to this area?"

"My brothers all live around here." *Now why did he say that?*

"Brothers?" Her eyes met his coyly. "Are they all as good-looking as you are?"

Alex was saved from having to answer by Rick's reappearance. "Hey," he said to Carrie. "You stole my seat."

She grinned. "Yes, I did."

He made a face at Alex, handed him his beer—
Miller on tap—and sat in her old seat.

"You guys want to hear a joke?" said one of the
men on the other side of the table.

"Is it clean? There are ladies present," someone
else—Alex thought his name was Mike—said.

"Ladies?" the jokester countered, laughing. "I
don't see no ladies."

"Hey, watch it," Carrie said.

"Oh. Didn't see you there, Carrie," he answered
with a mock frown.

The banter continued and Alex was able to turn his
attention away from Carrie without being rude, but
when Rick got up a few minutes later, saying he had
to leave, she put her hand on Alex's arm and leaned
closer.

"I know a much quieter and nicer place where we
could have some privacy." Her smile was suggestive.
"And they have much better food."

Alex was taken off-guard and for a moment and
couldn't think how to answer her. "Thanks, Carrie,
but I have to be going myself."

She pouted. "Oh, *do* you? Darn. I was really
hoping to get to know you better."

And Alex had been hoping to have dinner *there*,
with the others, especially if P.J. should show up,
but now there was no way he could. *Damn.* He'd

have to figure out a way to head little Miss Carrie off at the pass. She wasn't even being subtle about her intentions. But she was definitely too young for him, no matter how pretty and sexy she was. More important, he couldn't imagine his aunt approving of someone like her, even if he *were* interested.

After draining his beer, he stood. "Have a good weekend, everyone. I've got to be going, too."

"Sure you won't change your mind?" Carrie asked.

Alex just shook his head and said his goodbyes, making a quick exit.

As he drove home to his apartment, he wondered if J.T. and Gray were faring any better than he was in finding a suitable candidate to be the next Mrs. Hunt. Justin, of course, had already found his—the mother of his year-old daughter, Ava. A daughter Justin'd had no idea even existed, because Lily, Ava's mother and Justin's former lover, had never told him about her after their breakup.

Alex smiled thinking of Ava. He hadn't met his niece yet but he'd seen a photo of her, and she was a winner. With her dark hair and dimples, she was clearly a Hunt. In fact, she looked exactly like Justin. And from the look on Harry's face when he'd seen that photo, she'd already captured *his* heart.

For a moment when Justin had told them about Lily, Ava's mother, Alex had hoped Harry would drop the challenge for the rest of them. After all, he had his much-coveted grandchild now. But no such luck. Harry had only said the rest of them had better get busy.

Alex knew he'd have to make up his mind soon. Pick one of the women he'd met or make an effort to meet someone new. It was already entering the second week of September and he needed a bride *and* a baby on the way by next July.

What would Harry do if one of the brides wasn't pregnant by July? Hell, there were no guarantees. Surely the old man would be fair. If they'd fulfilled their part by marrying suitable women, surely Harry would give them some leeway on the pregnancy question.

But what if he didn't?

What if, after finding brides, they ended by losing their stakes in Harry's empire, anyway?

P.J. was just about to walk out the door when her cell phone rang. Checking the number, she saw it was her brother.

She pressed the talk button. "Hey, Peter, what's up?"

"Nothing much. Just haven't talked to you in a

couple of weeks and thought I'd better see if you were still alive."

Why was it Peter always made her feel guilty? "I've been busy. For some reason, lots of people have decided they need Hunt products this month."

"So business is good?"

"Very good."

"And you still like that...job?"

"I still like my job." Peter asked the same questions every time they talked. It was as if he couldn't believe anyone could possibly enjoy the kind of work she did. He was always telling her she was wasting her education, not to mention her brain. His lack of respect for what she did used to make P.J. mad. Now she just patiently gave him the same answers and ignored his jabs.

"Allison said to tell you hello. She's looking forward to seeing you at Dad's birthday dinner next week."

P.J.'s father would turn seventy the following Saturday and they were celebrating with a big family dinner at her parents' home.

"I still haven't figured out what to buy him," she said. "He has everything. What're you and Allison giving him?"

Peter laughed. "You're not going to believe this."

"What?"

"A guitar."

"A guitar!"

"It was Allison's idea."

P.J. was laughing now, too. "Did he *say* he wanted a guitar?"

"Nope. But you know how he is. A total workaholic. Allison said he needed something to do that was relaxing and fun. A hobby of some kind. So we settled on a guitar. I mean, he used to like Dylan. I actually heard him listening to Dylan's music once."

P.J. was still laughing. "Maybe I should arrange for him to have some lessons."

"That's a good idea."

"Think so? Okay, then. I will." Somehow she didn't think her father was going to be pleased, but she had to hand it to Allison and Peter. They had guts.

"So what are you doing tonight?" Peter asked. "Got a hot date?"

P.J. snorted. "Yeah. Sure. Actually, I was just getting ready to join some of the guys from work at a local pub."

"I won't keep you then. See you next week, okay?"

They said their goodbyes, and P.J. finished clearing off her desk, then headed out the door. Fifteen minutes later, she walked into Jake's Grill. Quickly scanning the crowded room, she spied the group from HuntCom.

Even as she told herself she wasn't looking for him, her gaze traveled around the group to see if Alex was there. When she didn't see him, she told herself she wasn't disappointed. If anything, she was relieved.

But she knew she was lying.

"Hey, P.J. 'Bout time you got here." This came from Mike Fields, who worked out at the docks.

Everyone scooted their chairs to make room for her, and P.J. grabbed an empty chair from another table and squeezed in between Carrie Wancheck and Chick Fogarty.

She motioned to a nearby waitress. "I'll have a bottle of Beck's, Jessie."

"Sure thing, P.J."

Carrie nudged P.J.'s arm. "You just missed Alex."

P.J.'s traitorous heart skipped a beat. "Alex who?"

"Oh, c'mon, P.J. Alex Noble. Your new *sexy* employee. Don't tell me you haven't noticed."

"Oh. Him."

"Yeah, him. I tried to persuade him to go to Costello's with me, but he had to leave."

P.J. pretended indifference. "Maybe he had a date."

Carrie frowned. "Think so?"

"A man like him? I don't see him sitting home on a Friday night."

"Shoot. You're probably right. Well, I'm not giving up. Guys like Alex don't come along every day."

"You know, Carrie, he really *is* a lot older than you are. And you don't know anything about him."

"He's gorgeous, he's well-spoken, he smells good, and he has a fantastic smile. I mean, those *dimples!*" Carrie sighed. "The only thing he *doesn't* have is money."

P.J. refrained from rolling her eyes. "How do you know that?"

"Oh, please. As if he'd be working as a picker if he *did*. I mean, come on, P.J."

Not for the first time, P.J. wondered what her co-workers would think if they knew about her and her family. Then again, she knew what they'd think. It was the reason she'd decided to use initials instead of her first name, which was Paige, when she'd come to work for HuntCom.

P.J. wanted to be treated like everyone else, and if they'd known she was the daughter of Peter Prescott Kincaid and—until she'd repudiated it—heiress to a multimillion-dollar trust fund, there was no way she'd be one of the guys the way she was now.

"Well, money or not, he's still too old for you," P.J. said.

"He's not *that* old. I'm guessing he's in his early thirties."

"Thirty-six." P.J. had checked his application.

"So? That's only fifteen years older than me. Big deal."

"He might have an ex-wife and ten kids."

"Oh, please," Carrie said, rolling her eyes.

P.J. could see that nothing she said was going to head Carrie off. She had set her sights on Alex, and she wasn't going to be persuaded otherwise.

And why should you care?

She *didn't* care. As a thirty-year-old, more experienced woman, she just felt she should look out for the younger women at work, that's all.

But even as she told herself this, P.J. knew she was lying to herself. For some reason, Alex Noble intrigued her. More than intrigued her.

Admit it, you're attracted to him.

Even though there was something about him that just didn't add up and even though she'd told Courtney she didn't believe in dating an employee and even though she knew there'd be no future in it—how could there be, given her situation?—she knew if Alex Noble were to ask her out, she would want to say yes.

But it would be madness. Absolute madness. Dating Alex Noble would do nothing but cause trouble for her.

So, regretfully, even if he *were* to ask her out, she would have to say no.

Chapter Five

Now that he was almost home, Alex wasn't sure he really wanted to go there. So what *did* he want to do? He was hungry, but he didn't feel like stopping at any of the restaurants he'd seen and eating by himself. Nor did he feel like cooking tonight, although cooking was one of his passions.

Normally he loved cooking for himself, and he never minded eating alone. But tonight…tonight he wanted company.

Oh, hell, admit it. You're lonely.

He wondered what his brothers would say if he

ever admitted this to them. They all seemed perfectly happy to be single. Well, maybe not Justin anymore. Now that Lily, the mother of his child, was back in his life, he seemed different. Alex knew without being told that calling Lily when he first knew he had to find a bride quickly was one of the best decisions Justin had ever made. It was obvious that he cared about her. Alex didn't know the background of the two of them—only that they'd been lovers at one time.

But J.T. and Gray? They were stereotypical, self-possessed and self-absorbed bachelors—J.T. with his island and Gray with his business interests.

Alex had always known he was different from his brothers, and this deep-seated loneliness had always isolated him even more. Part of Alex knew the loneliness would only be assuaged by having someone to share his life, someone who loved him unconditionally. He also knew he probably wouldn't feel this way if he'd had that kind of love from either his mother or Harry.

Don't go there.

Alex forced himself to stop thinking about what he didn't have in his life. Long ago he'd made up his mind that he wasn't going to feel sorry for himself. Instead, he would build the kind of life he wanted with the kinds of people he wanted to be around, and he would be content with that. But no matter how many times he'd reinforced his goals, he couldn't seem to erase that bone-deep loneliness that always seemed to be waiting for him anytime he lowered his guard.

Tonight was one of those nights.

In an effort to put off the time when he'd have to face his empty apartment, Alex decided to stop at the bookstore he'd noticed in a shopping center a block over from his street. He was just about out of reading material and he knew Greg Isles had a new book out, one Alex was looking forward to reading.

After killing three-quarters of an hour and spending more than a hundred bucks on books, Alex's stomach began to grumble. Time to head home. But as he walked out to the parking lot, he spied a Thai restaurant he hadn't noticed before. He loved Thai food and hadn't had any in weeks.

Abruptly changing his mind about going home, he switched direction and headed for the entrance to the restaurant.

Alex finished some really excellent hot and sour soup and an order of crispy egg rolls and settled back into his booth to wait for his entree. He was glad he'd decided to eat at the restaurant rather than getting takeout. Even though he was alone, he felt better here than he would have in his empty apartment.

He sipped at his Singha beer and idly watched the other diners: an Oriental family of four with exceptionally well-behaved young boys, a college-age couple who were obviously lovers, a middle-aged couple who kept smiling at each other, and a table of four seniors who were laughing and talking like old friends.

Alex felt wistful as he watched.

A moment later, the bell on the front door jangled as a new customer walked in. Alex looked up. Blinked. And looked closer. Yes, that was definitely P.J. approaching the hostess. He watched as she picked up one of the takeout menus and studied it.

In his second impulsive act of the evening, he slid from the booth and walked to the front.

She looked up at his approach. The expression that flitted across her face—which she quickly banished—gave Alex the distinct feeling she was as pleased to see him as he was to see her.

"Hey, P.J.," he said.

"Hi, Alex."

"You placing a takeout order?"

"That's the plan."

The hostess, a pretty girl who looked about seventeen, looked curiously from one to the other.

"How about joining me instead?"

P.J. hesitated, and for a moment, Alex thought she was going to refuse. Then she smiled. "Actually, I wouldn't mind company. I'm really not much in the mood to eat alone."

"Good. I'm not, either."

He led her to his booth and waited until she slid in across from him before taking his seat. The pretty hostess had followed them and she handed P.J. a menu. "I'll send your waiter," she said before leaving them.

P.J. glanced at the menu, then set it aside. "So how are you liking your job now that you've been with us a while?"

Alex was glad he could answer truthfully. "I'm enjoying it a lot."

"That's good. I confess, I'm surprised."

"Surprised? Why?"

"You just don't seem the type to be working at the center."

"What type is that?"

She leaned back, a smile teasing the edges of her mouth. "I had you pegged for a college man. You seem much better suited to a white-collar job."

"I could say the same about you."

"Oh, really?"

Alex returned her smile. "Yes, really."

"Well, you'd be wrong. My job suits me perfectly."

"You certainly do it well."

Once again, that pleased expression flitted across her face. "Thank you."

"You're welcome."

Just then, their waiter approached.

"I'll have what he's having," P.J. said, pointing to Alex's bottle of beer.

"And I'll have another," Alex said.

"I also want the pad thai," P.J. said.

Alex grinned. "I already ordered some. Want to get something different and we can share?"

"Sure. How about the green curry chicken?"

"Great."

Once the waiter had gone, P.J. settled back again and said, "So where were we?"

"Saying neither one of us looks the type to be working in a big warehouse." Alex figured he might as well be up-front about her comment. No sense pretending it hadn't been said.

She studied him thoughtfully. "*Did* you ever go to college?"

"Yes."

"And?"

"And what?"

"And…did you get your degree?"

Keeping to his promise to himself that he would tell the truth whenever he could, Alex said, "Yes, as a matter of fact, I did." He didn't think he needed to add that he'd also gotten a master's degree.

"So what happened?"

"I didn't like the business world." Alex still didn't like the business world. Thank God he didn't have to be a part of it.

"I didn't like the business world, either," she said.

"What did *you* study in college?"

"What makes you think I went to college?"

"Oh, c'mon, P.J. It's as plain as the nose on your face. You're obviously well educated."

She shrugged. "On my father's recommendation, I was in public relations. I hated every minute of it."

Alex chuckled. "How long did you last?"

"Oh, I got my degree. My parents would have disowned me if I hadn't. But when I decided to take an entry-level blue-collar job at HuntCom, my father went ballistic." She smiled crookedly. "He still doesn't understand me."

Alex thought about Harry. Maybe *all* fathers were destined not to understand their children. Harry certainly was batting zero. "So how did you end up at HuntCom?"

"Through a friend of a friend."

Alex would have liked to question her further, but

their waiter had just walked up with their beers. A moment later, he returned with Alex's pad thai.

"Dig in," he said when the waiter left.

They ate companionably for a few minutes, then P.J. said, "I apologize if I gave you a hard time at first."

"You didn't give me a hard time."

"Yes, I did."

He grinned around a fork full of food. "Okay, you did. But that's okay. You were just doing your job."

She looked at him for a long moment. "I was worried you might be a spy," she confessed.

"A spy!" Alex laughed. "What kind of a spy?"

"You know. A corporate spy. Somebody sent to see if I was doing a good job or something."

Something in those blue eyes of hers told Alex she might still harbor that suspicion. "Listen, P.J., I swear to you, I am *not* a spy."

She nodded.

Alex started to say he was just a regular guy who wanted to do a good job, but that wasn't really true, was it? When and if she found out who he *really* was, she would remember how he'd looked her in the eye and lied to her. And even though Alex wasn't sure how he felt about P.J. Kincaid or whether she'd ever assume more importance in his life than she did at this moment, he didn't want her to think ill of him. *Damn.* This pretending to be someone he wasn't was more complicated than Alex had envisioned it being.

"Here comes our curry chicken," she said, saving him from having to say anything more.

After the waiter finished serving them and had walked off once more, P.J. said, "You have any family around here, Alex?" She spooned some rice onto her plate, then helped herself to the curry.

He nodded. "My brothers all live in the area, and my parents are in Seattle. What about you?"

"My family all live around here, too." She took a bite. "Umm, that's good."

Alex liked the way she enjoyed her food. He got tired of women who never seemed to eat anything but salad. "Their food is good."

"Yeah, I get takeout here about once a week." She grinned. "If you're interested, I know all the great takeout places in Jansen. I know a fantastic pizza place as well as the best Italian restaurant in town."

"Actually, I like to cook."

"You're kidding."

He shook his head. "Nope. Cooking is probably the thing that gives me the greatest pleasure." Next to his work at the Hunt Foundation, but of course, he couldn't say that.

"I can't even boil water." She laughed. "Once I burned the coffee."

Alex laughed, too. "Cooking's easy. If you can read, you can cook. You just follow the directions."

She rolled her eyes. "That's easy for you to say. You like it. Believe me, I've tried. Not only am I a terrible cook, but I hated it. I mean, why bother when you can get food like this?" She waved her fork at the serving dishes. "Are you going to eat the rest of that pad thai?"

"No, I'm full."

"Oh, good." Reaching for the platter, she scraped the remainder of the noodle dish onto her plate.

Yes, a *very* healthy appetite, Alex thought. He wondered if that appetite extended to other areas of her life. Somehow he imagined it might. P.J. seemed like the kind of woman who would thoroughly enjoy sex.

As if she knew what he'd been thinking, a faint flush crept into her cheeks as their eyes met and held.

She was the first one to look away, and Alex knew he'd flustered her.

"That was great," she said, putting down her fork and lifting her napkin to her mouth.

"Yes," he said. "Thank you for joining me." He motioned to their waiter.

"Are you finished?" the waiter said.

"I think so, unless the lady wants dessert?"

P.J. shook her head. "No, just the check."

The waiter said he'd be right back.

"I don't want an argument over the check," she said. "I'm paying for my share."

"No, you're not," Alex said. "I invited you to join me, it's my treat."

"Look, Alex—"

"I insist," Alex said.

P.J. argued a few more seconds, then finally relented.

The waiter returned, laying a leather folder by Alex. Alex reached back and pulled his wallet out of his back pocket. Opening it, he automatically reached for his platinum American Express card, but at the last second, he remembered that he wasn't Alex Hunt tonight, he was Alex Noble, and he took out his new Visa card instead. Close call, he thought, as he slipped the card into the leather folder.

When he looked up, P.J. was watching him. Damn. Had she *seen* that card? If she'd been looking at his wallet when he'd opened it, she probably had. Worse, she would have seen that he had several platinum cards. What would she make of that information?

I'm going to have to remember to be more careful. She's way too observant.

The waiter came by again and picked up the folder. P.J. excused herself to go to the ladies' room and was gone when the waiter returned. Alex took care of filling in the tip and signing the charge slip, then went to the front of the restaurant to wait for her.

When they walked outside, the sun had set and there was now a decided chill in the air.

"Summer fades fast in this neck of the woods," Alex said.

"Yes," P.J. agreed. She stopped next to a little blue Miata. "Thank you for dinner. I enjoyed it."

Alex smiled. "My pleasure."

She opened the driver's-side door. "See you Monday."

He waited till she'd gotten into the car before walking to his truck. Would Cornelia like P.J.? Alex wondered. He thought she would. In fact, there were things about P.J. that reminded him of Cornelia. Not that they looked alike. Although Cornelia was a tall woman and so was P.J., that was the extent of their physical similarities. Cornelia was more delicately built and in her youth had had pale blond hair whereas P.J.'s coloring was more vivid. But both were strong-willed, intelligent and independent.

Yes. Cornelia would approve of P.J.

Alex smiled as he climbed into his truck. He had a feeling Georgie would, too, even though she still remained adamant that this whole bride hunt was ridiculous and had followed through on her promise to tell her mother exactly what she thought.

Not that Georgie's objections had made any difference to either Cornelia or Alex.

He wasn't a hundred-percent certain, but he was beginning to believe he might have found the woman he wanted.

P.J. pulled into the circular drive in front of the stately home where she'd grown up and cut the ignition. Reaching for the small gift bag that contained a couple of oldies CDs and the gift card for a dozen guitar lessons with the best instructor she could find in the Seattle area, she got out of the Miata and walked up to the massive oak front door and rang the bell.

"Miss Paige, you know you can just come on in," Carmelita, the family's long-time housekeeper said as she opened the door. "You're family." Leaning over, she kissed P.J.'s cheek.

P.J. inhaled the scent of talcum and gave Carmelita a hug.

"Everyone's back in the solarium," Carmelita

said. "You go on and join them. I'll have Marianne bring you some lemonade."

P.J. headed for the dome-topped, semicircular room that overlooked Puget Sound. As she approached the solarium, she heard the cheerful noises of her rapidly expanding family.

"Paige!" her mother exclaimed as P.J. walked into the room. Getting up, Helena Kincaid held out her arms. Hugging her mother was vastly different from hugging cushiony Carmelita. Helena, like most women in her social class, was reed-thin and smelled of the most expensive beauty products on the market. Although dressed casually, there was no mistaking the designer slacks in a soft fawn wool or the meticulously crafted cream silk blouse as anything but the best money could buy.

"Darling, it's so good to see you," her mother said, releasing her and holding her at arm's length. "I do wish you'd buy yourself some decent clothes, though." She eyed P.J.'s denim skirt and white T-shirt with distaste.

P.J. had learned to ignore her mother's critiques. "Well, *you* look lovely, Mom," was all she said. Then she turned to greet the rest of her family.

Jillian, younger by three years, grinned at her. The grin said she was glad P.J. was the object of their mother's scrutiny instead of her. As they hugged, she murmured, "She's in rare form today."

"Thanks for the warning."

After that, P.J. got hugs in quick succession from Matt, Jillian's husband; Courtney and Brad; her father; Peter and his wife, Allison; and then all the nieces and nephews she could corral.

"So what's new, Paige?" Allison asked after the men had wandered off to the den to watch the Mariners game.

"Same old, same old," P.J. said. "Thanks, Marianne," she said to the maid, who had brought her a tall glass of the homemade lemonade she was famous for.

"Any new men in your life?" Allison continued. Her dark eyes were filled with lively curiosity.

P.J. gave her sister-in-law a dark look. Why was it that one of the first questions out of everyone's mouth had to do with men?

Allison laughed. "I take it that's a no."

P.J. shrugged. "Take it any way you like."

Allison raised her eyebrows. "Hear that, Courtney? Jillian? Sounds like maybe there *is* a new man on the horizon."

P.J. tried not to think about Alex but she couldn't help it. And thinking about him made her blush. Oh,

God, she'd give anything not to have the pale skin of a redhead. Skin that showed every single emotion.

"Tell us everything," Jillian said excitedly.

Hell and damnation. I don't need this.

P.J. made a face. "There is no new man. I don't know what you're talking about."

"Well, *something* made you blush," Jillian said.

"*Are* you dating someone, Paige?" her mother said.

"No, mother, I'm not."

"You know, Paige, you aren't getting any younger."

P.J.'s eyes met Courtney's. Courtney's eyes sparkled, and it was obvious she was trying hard not to laugh.

"Mom, please…"

"Well, it's true," Helena said. "And there's absolutely no reason for you to still be single. Why, even Liliana Fox is engaged, and no one thought she'd *ever* find a man. You're just too picky, that's all. When I think about Douglas…" Her voice trailed off in despair.

Douglas Sloane Bryant was the son of P.J.'s parents' oldest friends, Liz and Oliver Bryant, and at one time, he and P.J. had dated. This was before P.J.'s medical problems, before she knew she could probably never have any children of her own. Of course, her mother *still* didn't know it, and if P.J. had her way, she never would. That's all she needed—unsolicited medical advice from her mother. In fact, the only person in her family who did know was Courtney, and that's how P.J. wanted to keep it.

At the time P.J. had dated Douglas, if she'd given him any encouragement at all, he would probably have produced the obligatory diamond ring, but even though she'd liked him as a friend, there was absolutely no passion between them and no sense pretending otherwise.

Plus he worked in his father's business. As the Chief Financial Officer. And he was totally into status. He and his wife—he'd married last year—had built a six-thousand-square-foot home on Bainbridge Island. Now who needed six thousand square feet?

"And how you expect to meet anyone suitable working in the kind of place you do," her mother droned on, "is beyond me. If you'd only stop being so stubborn and—"

"I told you, Mom," P.J. interrupted. "I have no interest in meeting someone *suitable*…or in getting married. And I'm tired of people harassing me."

Her mother sniffed. "As your mother, I feel I have a perfect right to—"

"No, Mom," P.J. interrupted again, "you *don't* have a right to continually berate me about getting married. I have a right to make my own choices."

"Yes, well, if your choices were sensible…"

P.J. sighed. What was the use? Her mother would never change. "Tell you what, Mom. If I meet someone *suitable*, you'll be the first to know. Okay? And in the meantime, let's just drop the subject. Otherwise, I'm going to just leave Dad's gift here and take off." So saying, she got to her feet.

"Oh, Paige, sit down," her mother said. She sighed dramatically. "Fine. I won't say another word." She made a motion as if she was turning a key to lock her mouth. "Happy now?"

P.J. grinned. "That's two words, Mom."

Their laughter broke the tension, and for the remainder of the afternoon, no more was said about P.J. or her personal life.

Chapter Six

Monday turned out to be Alex's busiest day at the HuntCom Distribution Center since he'd begun the job. There was barely time to breathe, let alone take a break. And lunch consisted of a sandwich gobbled in ten minutes. He was in the middle of filling a large order for an office supply store in Portland when his cell phone vibrated.

"Dammit," he muttered. Checking the caller ID, he saw it was J.T. He almost let the call go to voice mail, then decided it must be important because J.T. rarely called him.

Alex pressed the talk button. "Hang on." Moving away from the noise of a nearby forklift, he said, "There must be a problem if you're calling me at work."

"'Work' is eighty miles north of here," J.T. said. "What you're doing is…what *are* you doing, anyway?"

Alex laughed. "Filling orders."

"Right. Look, there's no problem. I just need to talk to you. I'm over at the expansion site."

"You're in Jansen?"

"Yes. I just finished a site inspection with the construction foreman. Which warehouse are you in?"

Alex lowered his voice. "Don't come over here. If somebody recognizes you, they might recognize me. I get off at four. Meet me at my place at four-thirty."

"Where's that?"

Alex gave J.T. directions. "Don't be surprised by the place. It's not what you're used to," he said in warning. That was an understatement, he thought after they'd hung up. He'd seen Gray's place in town and he figured J.T. and Justin probably lived in places just as luxurious when they happened to be in the city—which wasn't often. That was one of the reasons Alex hadn't seen either place—the other being that unfortunately, he and his half-brothers weren't close, something Alex was beginning to hope might change one of these days.

On the dot of four-thirty, a knock sounded at Alex's front door. He opened it and smiled at J.T. The brothers weren't close, yet there was a bond that couldn't be denied.

"Hey," J.T. said, stepping in.

"Hey, J.T."

J.T. glanced around. "When Gray said you'd taken a job at the warehouse as a cover for this bride thing, he didn't mention that you'd moved in with the masses."

Alex laughed. "When in Rome …"

"In Rome, they at least live with some color." J.T's thoughtful frown moved from the breakfast bar that separated the small kitchen from the living area. He took in the beige sofa, nondescript coffee table and black leather recliner, which formed what there was of Alex's seating area. "You could seriously use some art here," he observed. "Did the furniture come with the place?"

Alex shook his head. "I bought it at a discount store. If anyone from the plant comes over, I don't want them to suspect anything."

"Any luck there? Meeting an appropriate woman, I mean?"

Alex gave a guarded shrug. "I've only been there

three weeks," he said evasively. He wasn't ready to talk about P.J.

"Then you've spotted a prospect?"

"It's too soon to tell. I don't have much of a liquor supply," he added, not bothering to be subtle about the change of subject. Alex wasn't ready to talk about P.J. to anyone. "About all I can offer you is a beer." He nodded toward the kitchen. "Do you want one?"

J.T. grinned. "Let me guess. You bought it on sale, $3.99 for a twelve-pack."

Alex smiled sheepishly. "There are a few things I still splurge on. I have Beck's or Black Sheep."

"Surprise me."

"So," Alex said as he swung open the refrigerator door. "Why'd you want to see me?"

"I need some advice."

Alex turned from the refrigerator, a bottle in each hand and one eyebrow arched. "From me?" He couldn't remember the last time one of his brothers wanted his advice.

From where he remained on the other side of the bar, J.T. frowned. "You're the only person I know who knows anything about fund-raisers."

"What makes you think I know about fund-raisers?"

"Hell, Alex. You go to them all the time. And you have to raise money for the foundation somehow."

"That shows how little we know about what each of us does," Alex informed him. "You're right about one thing. I've attended a lot of fund-raisers for different charities or organizations, but the Harrison Hunt Foundation doesn't raise money that way." He popped off the caps with a bottle opener and held a bottle out for J.T. "We use the interest from Harry's money to fund our causes." And occasionally they accepted donations from other parties, but that wasn't relevant, so there was no point in bringing it up. "What is it you want to know about them?"

"The short version is that I want to help someone raise some money."

"And the long version?"

J.T. tipped up his bottle and drank. Alex wondered if he wanted to buy time before answering, because there was something about his expression that seemed wary.

"This bride-hunt thing," J.T. finally said. "Because of Harry's rules, I can't just write a check. Or," he added with a half-smile, "go to my brother and ask the foundation to do it. If I did that, I'm afraid she'd figure out the money had something to do with me." The smile died. "If she did, I could tell her I just happened to know someone with connections, but I don't want to raise any red flags."

Curious now, Alex rounded the counter and

pulled out a bar stool. Motioning for J.T. to take the other, he said, "You've found a potential wife?"

J.T. frowned. "How'd you get that from what I just told you?"

"You're talking about helping a woman. You said you can't because of Harry's rules. I'm not the math genius in the family, but it's pretty much one plus one, J.T."

"I've found a woman with the potential to be a wife," J.T. said. He hesitated. "But the woman I want to help is her assistant. Her grandmother lives in this home that's going to have to close if the director can't come up with about fifty grand."

Both of Alex's eyebrows lifted this time. "That's not the kind of money you can raise selling calendars. You need an event, and a corporation or two to underwrite it. Like I said, we don't organize fundraisers, but I know people who do."

He thought for a moment. "One of women on the foundation board chairs an annual luncheon and fashion show that makes a mint for the Seattle Opera Guild. Maybe your girlfriend's assistant could do something like that in Portland."

"Think she'd be willing to talk to Amy?"

"Amy's the assistant?"

J.T. nodded.

"I can't imagine that she wouldn't."

J.T. seemed relieved. "Let me run this by Amy, then. If she thinks it's something she can handle, I'll get back to you."

"Sure. Not a problem." Alex drank some of his beer. "You hungry?"

"Getting there."

"I'm starving. How about I throw something together for us to eat?"

"What did you have in mind?"

"Paella," he said, heading back into the kitchen. "I picked up shrimp and sausage at the market last night. That sound okay?"

"You can make paella?"

Alex just shook his head and laughed. J.T., Justin, and Gray were all intelligent, successful men. But their idea of cooking was limited to grilling steaks or chicken.

"Then it sounds great," J.T. said.

As Alex began his preparations with J.T. watching, he tried to remember the last time he'd shared a meal with one of his brothers, and he couldn't.

Harry's bride-hunt idea might be unconventional, perhaps even crazy, but it had accomplished something unexpected. It had brought Alex and his brothers closer together.

And for that, Alex was grateful.

* * *

J.T.'s visit had got Alex thinking, and he'd decided he really needed to find out more about P.J. before he made any kind of move—for two reasons. One, even though she seemed to be exactly the kind of woman he wanted, and it was hard to believe she was hiding anything, only a fool would take someone on face value, and he wasn't a fool. Two, if she was already spoken for, he'd have to look elsewhere for his bride.

The first thing he did was Google her. Several items with either the initials *P.J.* or the name *Kincaid* came up, but those didn't apply. Then he saw an article that had appeared in the *Seattle Times* about someone named Paige Jeffers Kincaid.

He clicked on the article, dated April of the previous year. It was a write-up about Peter Prescott Kincaid, CEO of Kincaid Industries, whose ancestors had made fortunes in lumber and shipbuilding. Paige Jeffers Kincaid was one of Peter Kincaid's daughters. At the time the article was written, she was twenty-nine years old.

Alex frowned. Could P.J. be Paige Jeffers Kincaid? The age was about right. Too bad there wasn't a picture with the article.

He went back to the Google home page and entered *Paige Jeffers Kincaid*. Several items appeared and he scrolled down until he found one with a picture.

The picture accompanied an article about Paige Kincaid's graduation from a private girls' high school where she'd been valedictorian of her class.

The picture showed a fresh-faced, serious-looking P.J. Alex stared at the photo for a long time. The article called her an heiress. "Heiress to a great fortune," it said. "The third of Peter Prescott Kincaid's four children," it said, "who will be attending Stanford in the fall."

At first, he was indignant. What the hell was she *doing*, pretending to be an ordinary woman working at an ordinary job? Before long, though, amusement supplanted the indignation. She was doing exactly what he was doing. How could he be angry with her? He'd be willing to bet every single thing she'd told him had been the truth.

Well, well, well. This changed everything. And yet, did it? After all, if Alex *did* marry P.J., no one could ever accuse her of wanting his money.

So now he knew half of what he needed to know. And he'd just bet Rick could supply the other half. He decided the first chance he got, he would quiz Rick about her.

It was Wednesday before he got the chance. The two of them were eating lunch together in the cafeteria and Rick mentioned something P.J. had said earlier. "Hey," Alex said after he'd finished telling the anecdote, "I've been meaning to ask you. What's P.J.'s story?"

Rick, who had just taken a huge bite of his burger, chewed and swallowed before giving Alex a knowing grin. "I knew you liked her."

"I'm just curious about her. You have to admit, she's not exactly the kind of woman you'd expect to find in a warehouse."

"Yeah," Rick agreed. "I figured out a long time ago she comes from a different background than most of the women at the center. More educated." He looked at Alex speculatively. "Kinda like you."

"Me?"

"It's obvious you're a helluva lot more educated than the rest of us, Alex. Lotta the guys been wondering what you're doing at the center."

Alex winced. And here he thought he'd been fitting in so well.

"It's no big deal," Rick continued. "Most of 'em figure you got your reasons for working there. Hell, we all got our reasons. Anyway, I think P.J.'s family probably has some money or something. She pretends she's like the rest of us, but you can tell she comes from a privileged background. I mean, even the way she talks is different, you know? Something must have happened, though," Rick added, "because here she is."

"Happened with her family, you mean?"

"Yeah. Maybe they don't get along."

Alex nodded. Yet on the night he'd met her jogging she'd mentioned having a date with her sister for dinner and the other night at the Thai place she'd said her family all lived in the area. She hadn't sounded as if they were estranged or anything. On the other hand, she might have felt she didn't know him well enough to mention any problems they might have. He certainly hadn't said anything about *his* family. "Does she ever talk about them?"

Rick shook his head. "One time she just said they didn't see eye to eye."

That could have been a reference to the differences she'd mentioned regarding her job choice. Or it could be something deeper. *Maybe she's got a mother like mine.* "How long has she worked for the company?"

"She started about six months before I did. In fact, we worked on the same team for a while."

Alex wondered if Rick had resented the fact P.J. had been promoted to a supervisory position and he hadn't.

"But it was obvious from the beginning she wouldn't stay a picker for long," Rick said. "She's too smart."

"Did you mind that? That she got promoted and you didn't?"

"Me? Hell, no. I don't want to be in management. Nothing but headaches managing people."

Alex smiled. Rick was right. In fact, managing the staff at the foundation was Alex's least favorite part of the job. Thank God for Marti. She was a jewel when it came to getting people to do their jobs without resentment or problems.

"P.J.'s a good boss. Lots better than I would have been," Rick said.

"Wonder why she's not married," Alex commented, keeping his voice casual as he got to what he really wanted to know.

"Now *that* I can answer." Rick grinned. "She doesn't believe in marriage. Said there's no way she's ever gonna let some man order her around."

Alex chuckled in spite of himself. That sounded like P.J. "Think she means it?"

"I've never known P.J. to say anything she doesn't mean."

The words were hardly out of Rick's mouth when a voice behind Alex said, "Who's taking my name in vain?"

Alex turned around. P.J. stood there, hands on her denim-clad hips, a mock frown on her face.

"We were just sayin' what a great boss you are, boss," Rick said.

P.J. rolled her eyes. "Yeah, right."

"We *were*," Rick insisted.

"Is that true, Alex?" she said.

"Scout's honor," Alex said, raising his right hand.

She fought against the smile, but lost. Soon all three were laughing. "Well, next time you have to fill out one of those surveys about our department, make sure you remember to say that," she said. "Maybe they'll give me a big raise." Then she waved goodbye and left them to their lunch.

"She's a good sport," Rick said.

Alex nodded. He admired the way she treated her employees. She was professional, but she was also friendly. He could tell they respected her. He wondered what they'd think if they knew her background.

"She's also a really nice person," Rick added.

"Seems to be," Alex said.

"No, I mean *really* nice. She's helped out a couple of the people here. Financially, I mean. One of the girls in the shipping department, her little boy was sick and the girl either needed to stay home and take care of him or hire someone to do it and either way, she couldn't afford it. P.J. heard about it and she made sure Evvie was taken care of."

"Taken care of…how?"

"She started a sick-day pool. You know, she convinced the powers that be to let any employee who wanted to to contribute some of their sick days to

Evvie so she could stay home and not lose pay. And P.J. contributed the most. Plus I heard she also gave Evvie some money."

The more Rick talked about P.J., the more Alex admired her. It seemed to him that she had exactly the same kinds of values he had. In fact, he couldn't imagine finding another woman more suited to him.

She was the woman he wanted.

Now all he had to do was convince her she really *did* want to be married.

"Hey, Alex, you have any interest in poker?" Rick asked later that afternoon.

"I love poker. Play every chance I get." He'd actually started a poker night with a couple of the guys who worked for the foundation.

"Well, a bunch of us play twice a month, and we're supposed to play tomorrow night, but Chick, who's one of our regulars, can't make it. Wanna fill in?"

"Sure, that'd be great."

"It's at Wayne's house. He'll give you directions."

When Alex walked into Wayne Crowder's house the following evening, the first person he saw was P.J. He could see she was as surprised as he was, even though she tried to disguise it, just as he did. Alex wasn't sure if he was glad or not. Having her there would be a distraction, and Alex took his poker seriously.

Wayne brought Alex a beer and he joined the others at the table. They were playing in the dining room of the small bungalow, and Wayne had set out bowls of nuts, pretzels and chips.

Alex noticed a high chair in the corner but no sign of a child or a wife. What he'd seen of the house was homey and had a woman's touch, so he figured there must be a female in the equation.

"Let's get started," Rick said. He began to shuffle the cards as the others dug out their money.

"What do you guys play?" Alex asked.

"Texas hold 'em," Wayne said.

"My favorite," Alex said.

"You play much poker, Alex?" The question came from Jim.

"Whenever I get the chance."

Rick explained the rules. "No one's allowed to lose more than twenty dollars. Once your twenty bucks is gone, you gotta just watch."

The first hand was a dud for Alex. Dealt the three of hearts and nine of spades, he immediately folded.

P.J., on the other hand, had a pair of jacks in the hole and when the river card was a third jack, the pot was hers.

"That was nice," she said as she scooped up her winnings.

"For you, maybe," grumbled Jim.

Alex smothered a smile. Most men hated losing to a woman. A lot of women might have made a disparaging remark, saying something like, "Oh, I was just lucky," but not her. She grinned happily, quite obviously pleased with herself.

Of course, considering her background, it didn't surprise him that she had so much self-confidence or that she wasn't falsely modest. It was funny how now that he knew who she really was, he could see evidence of it in everything she said and did.

Rick dealt the next hand. Alex's hole cards were the two red kings. Wayne folded immediately, throwing his cards down in disgust. P.J. bet the minimum and Jim called. Then it was Alex's turn. He had decided not to raise, because he didn't want to give his hand away. He'd wait and see what happened with the flop. "Call," he said.

The flop consisted of the Queen of Spades, the deuce of clubs and the eight of diamonds. P.J. again bid the minimum and Jim raised. Alex called again, and P.J. threw her money in, staying with the hand.

When the turn card was another eight, Jim couldn't disguise his excitement. Alex figured he probably had two eights in the hole. He almost folded, but then threw in his money. He'd stayed this long, he might as well see what the river brought. What it brought was the Queen of Hearts. Disgusted, Alex finally folded. He was certain Jim had a full house.

But to his amazement—and Jim's shock—after two more rounds of bidding and raising, P.J. revealed her hole cards to be the two missing queens.

That hand set the tone for the night. Alex was a good player—a very good player, in fact—yet he was outplayed by P.J., who was not only skillful but lucky, and who ended up the night's big winner.

"See why we're considering making this a men-only night?" Rick said, half-jokingly. "She cleans us out every time."

P.J. grinned. "Better not try it. I have ways of re-taliating, you know."

As they got ready to leave, there was the sound of a car in the driveway, and a few minutes later the back door opened. A pretty dark-haired woman holding a sleeping child walked into the dining room.

"Hey, Lauren," chorused the men.

Lauren smiled and said hello. Her gaze moved to Alex.

"Honey," Wayne said, "this is Alex Noble. He works with us. Alex, my wife, Lauren, and that's our rug rat, Billy, sleeping on her shoulder." Wayne's smile was proud. "He was a year old last week."

"Hi, Lauren," Alex said. "Nice to meet you."

By now, P.J. had gotten up and walked over to where Lauren and the baby stood. "Wow, he's grown," she said softly, touching his silky dark hair. Her smile was tender as she peeked at him. "He gets cuter every day."

Lauren smiled and Wayne beamed. "And smarter," Wayne said.

"And more demanding," Lauren said. "He actually thinks he runs this household."

P.J. chuckled. "And I'd be willing to bet he does."

Wayne made a face.

"Well," Rick said. "We'd better be going. Let you people get to bed."

As Alex drove home, he kept thinking about P.J. How she'd looked that night—her face flushed with excitement, her hair tumbling out of its clips, her eyes sparkling. He thought about how they came from similar backgrounds and spoke the same language. He thought about how smart she was and how good with people and what a wicked game of poker she played. But mostly, he thought about how she'd looked and acted toward little Billy. It was obvious she loved kids.

That was a huge factor to Alex, because even if

Harry hadn't made having a child part of the challenge he'd issued, Alex definitely wanted children. In fact, he wanted lots of them.

And from what he'd seen tonight, it looked as if P.J. felt exactly the same way.

Chapter Seven

Alex walked up the flagstone driveway toward the laughter and noise of his sister's birthday party. He'd much rather have gone to Jake's tonight with the rest of the guys from work, but he'd promised Julie he'd be here.

When he reached the wrought-iron gate, he stood for a moment before opening it and entering. Even then, he didn't head toward the merrymaking, but took a few minutes to observe the crush of guests gathered on the back veranda and around the pool. There were about forty people there, he estimated, most of them his sister's friends. Looking around, he spied Julie, who looked spectacular in a form-fitting black strapless dress, laughing and talking to a group of young people about her age. Suddenly, as if she felt his gaze, she turned.

"Alex!" she cried. "You made it!"

Beaming, she rushed to his side. Putting his arm around her, he kissed her cheek. "Hello, birthday girl."

Her blue eyes shone with excitement. Julie loved nothing better than a party. And a party in her honor was the best of all possible worlds.

Alex handed her the small, silver-wrapped box he carried. "Happy Birthday."

"Thank you! Oh, I love presents." Taking his hand, she led him toward her friends. "C'mon. I want to introduce you."

Alex knew it was useless to protest, so he let himself be led. Six pairs of eyes turned his way.

"This is my gorgeous brother, Alex," Julie said. "Alex, these are…" One by one, she named them. "Crystal, Russ, Scott, Madison, Penn and Phoebe."

The girl named Phoebe, a truly spectacular blonde, gave him a seductive look from under long eyelashes.

"Gorgeous is right," she murmured.

Alex would never get used to the boldness of Julie's crowd. The girls didn't seem to care what they said or how they said it. If they wanted something, they went after it, no holds barred.

Not waiting for Alex to answer, Phoebe slipped her arm through his and said, "He's mine."

The others laughed.

Gently but firmly, Alex removed her arm. "It's nice to have met all of you, but I have to go say hello to my mother." Directing his smile at all of them, he said, "Excuse me."

Shaking his head mentally, he headed toward the house. It was a moment before he realized Julie had hurried after him.

"Alex, wait up!" she said.

He turned around, stopped so she could catch up to him.

"You broke Phoebe's heart," she said as she reached his side.

"I seriously doubt that."

"I've been telling her about you for weeks." Although her tone was scolding, her blue eyes—the same shade as the tourmalines in his gift—were amused.

Alex looked down at her. "Not interested, Jules."

"Why not? Phoebe's beautiful and sexy and rich in her own right. Plus she's my best friend."

"For one thing, she's too young. For another, she's not my type."

"Too young? She's twenty-five! And how could she not be your type? Most men would die to have Phoebe."

Alex wasn't in the mood to spar or to justify his reasons for not wanting to get involved with the model-like Phoebe. "Aren't you going to open your present?" he said instead, for Julie still held his gift.

"Later. I'll put this on the table with the rest of them."

Alex knew his sister was punishing him for not going along with her matchmaking scheme. Or maybe she just wanted to ensure he'd stay at the party for a while.

"Mom's probably over there," Julie said, pointing to the area on the other side of the pool where there were several umbrella-topped tables.

Alex and Julie headed that way. Sure enough, his mother sat at the nearest table along with Julie's father and another older couple. At their approach, Terrence touched his wife's arm, and Lucinda turned around.

Her face lit up, and she rose. As always, she looked beautiful. Tonight she wore an emerald silk pants outfit with wide legs. Her dark hair was swept up, and sizable diamond studs twinkled in her ears.

A small woman with a trim figure, she didn't look her fifty-eight years and could have easily passed for someone in her early forties.

As always, Alex felt himself tense as she rushed forward and put her arms around him. Because he was essentially kind and because he did love her, even as he knew he would never be able to trust her, he returned her embrace, saying, "Hello, Mother."

"Oh, Alex, it's so good to see you." She drew back and looked up into his eyes. "You look wonderful."

"You look very nice yourself." He heard how stiff he sounded and wished he could be more generous toward her. But the habits of a lifetime were hard to break, especially when the underlying reason for his feelings hadn't changed.

"Thank you for coming," she said softly, her dark eyes liquid in the deepening light. Her dimples flashed briefly when she smiled.

Alex had inherited his height from Harry, but everything else came from his mother: dark hair, dark eyes, dimples. Julie, on the other hand, looked more like her father than like Lucinda, with her blue eyes, five-foot-eight height, and larger bone structure. The only trait of Lucinda's she bore was the dark, almost black, hair.

"Come meet our friends, darling," Lucinda was saying. She took Alex's hand and led him forward.

"These are Spencer and Deanna Steele. My son, Alex Hunt." There was no denying the pride in her voice as she introduced them.

Alex shook hands with Spencer Steele, a powerful-looking man with gray hair and an enviable physique. He smiled at Deanna Steele, a lovely, cool-looking blonde who had remained seated. He then turned to his stepfather. "Hello, Terrence."

"Glad you could make it, Alex," Terrence said.

"Alex just met Phoebe," Julie said, addressing the remark to the Steeles. Turning to Alex, she said, "Spencer and Deanna are Phoebe's parents." Her eyes twinkled mischievously.

Alex decided he would not let his sister get to him. "You have a very beautiful daughter," he said graciously.

"Yes," Deanna said, "we think so." Her gaze was speculative.

They made polite conversation for a few more minutes, and all the while Alex was wondering how long he'd have to stand there before he could make his escape.

"What do you do, Alex?" Spencer Steele asked.

"I'm the CEO of the Harrison Hunt Foundation."

"Really?" Deanna Steele said. "And you like working for the foundation?" There was just the faintest hint of surprise in her tone.

"It's all I've ever wanted to do."

She nodded, and he wondered what she was thinking.

"You don't have a drink," Terrence said, saving him from further questions. "C'mon, I'll show you where the bar is."

"I can do that, Daddy," Julie said.

"Now, sweetheart, you have other guests to attend to," Terrence said. "I'll take care of Alex."

Alex realized Terrence wanted to talk to him, so he gave Julie a smile and said, "I'll be right back."

Terrence put his arm around Alex's shoulder. "We set up the bar in the cabana."

Once they were out of earshot of Julie and Lucinda, Terrence said, "I'm going to have to make a trip to Singapore next week, Alex. Be gone about ten days."

Terrence was in the import/export business and frequently traveled abroad, especially to the Orient.

"I was hoping you'd keep an eye on the girls for me."

"Oh?" This was a first. "Something I should know?"

"It's not a big deal, just…" His voice trailed off.

By now they'd reached the bar and Alex ordered a vodka and tonic. Terrence waited until he'd got his drink and they'd moved away before saying anything else.

"Look," he said, leading Alex toward the back of the cabana where it was relatively quiet and no one else could hear their conversation. "Julie's been acting funny the past couple of weeks. I'm worried that maybe she's messing with drugs."

Jesus, Alex thought. "Have you said anything to her?"

Terrence shook his head. "I don't want to accuse her of something that might not be true."

"I'm not afraid to. I'll talk to her."

"It's not that I'm *afraid* to," Terrence protested. "I just…I trust my little girl."

Then why the hell are you asking me to keep an eye on her? Alex wondered if Terrence had any idea how contradictory he sounded. "Even sensible people can be led astray by the wrong kinds of friends."

"Her friends all come from the best families," Terrence blustered.

Alex raised his eyebrows.

Terrence had the grace to look sheepish. "I know, I know. That doesn't mean they can't get into trouble."

"No, it doesn't." Alex sipped at his drink thoughtfully. It would be hard to keep an eye on Julie now that he was working in Jansen, which wasn't exactly close to the Queen Anne area where Julie lived with her parents. "I'm in the middle of a big project right now that's keeping me out of town most of the time, but one way or another, I'll keep tabs on Julie."

Terrence huffed a breath. "Thanks, Alex. I really appreciate that."

"I love Julie, too," Alex pointed out. "And I don't want her to get into trouble…or hurt herself."

"I know."

Alex made himself a promise as he and Terrence moved to rejoin the others. He would not only keep tabs on his sister, he would sit her down and talk to her.

In fact, he'd start tonight.

P.J. couldn't believe how disappointed she was that Alex hadn't shown up at Jake's. She wished she could ask Rick why, but of course, she couldn't.

She wondered if he was seeing someone. If maybe he had a date tonight. The thought bothered her a lot more than it should have.

It's just your ego that's smarting. You were sure he was interested in you, and obviously, since he hasn't made a move to ask you out, he's not.

You should be glad. You've dodged a bullet. This is the best thing that could have happened…or not happened. Considering you've decided there was nowhere for a relationship with Alex to go, anyway.

Yet no matter how many times she told herself

all of this, she couldn't stop wondering where he was tonight.

And with whom.

It was nearly eleven before Julie opened her gifts, and by then Alex knew it was going to be impossible to talk to her that night. Resigned, he watched her indulgently as she squealed and exclaimed over each offering. He'd say one thing for her. She might be spoiled and pampered, but she wasn't jaded. He smiled wryly, remembering the Lotus. Well, maybe not totally.

"Oh, Alex, they're *gorgeous!*" she said upon seeing the tourmaline-set silver bracelet and earrings he'd given her. Coming over to where he stood, she kissed him. "Thank you," she said softly. "You always know what I'll love."

Love for her warmed him. Funny how she had so easily crept into his heart whereas he had always felt an off-putting distance with his brothers. Not for the first time, he wondered why that should be so. Perhaps it was being raised by a succession of nannies and the impersonal atmosphere of Harry's mansion. Or maybe it was simply Harry himself, so absorbed in his business and his money that he couldn't give much face time to his sons.

After Julie finished opening her gifts, Alex pulled her aside.

"I'm beat," he said. "I'm going to head out."

"You're *such* a party-pooper," she said, pouting. "We're all going to Twist, and Phoebe's going to be *so* disappointed if you don't go with us."

"You know how I feel about the club scene."

Julie just shook her head. "Twist isn't a club. It's fun. You'd like it."

Alex smiled. "I've been there. I'll pass."

"Honestly, you'd think you were ninety instead of just thirty-six. You keep saying you're not stodgy, but I'm having a hard time believing it."

Alex shrugged. "Actually, I was hoping we could get together for a while tomorrow. There's something I want to talk to you about."

Julie frowned. "You sound serious. What's up?"

"I'd rather not get into it tonight. How about having lunch with me tomorrow?"

"Just as long as it's not too early. I'm not like you. I don't turn into a pumpkin at the stroke of midnight."

"Some of us *do* work for a living," he said mildly.

"Tomorrow's Sunday."

"You know what I meant."

They made arrangements to meet at a small seafood restaurant Alex liked that wasn't too far from the house. Alex suggested one o'clock, hopefully ensuring that Julie might be on time. Then he said his goodnights to everyone and headed back to Jansen.

The next day, promptly at one, Alex walked into the restaurant and secured a window table for two. As he'd expected, Julie hadn't made an appearance yet.

Alex ordered a glass of iced tea and the seafood appetizer the restaurant was known for—cold shrimp and crab in a spicy cocktail sauce—and settled in to wait.

Twenty minutes later, he had eaten most of the appetizer, and Julie still hadn't shown up. Sighing, he whipped out his cell phone and hit the speed dial number for her cell.

"I know, I know," she said when she answered. "Sorry. I slept through the alarm—I didn't get home till almost dawn—but I'm on my way now. I'll be there in ten."

Alex just shook his head. It was pointless to be angry with her. Since he knew she was always late, he should have just waited and arrived thirty minutes later himself.

When she walked in—as promised, ten minutes later—he marveled at how fresh and pretty she looked. That was the advantage of being young. Late hours didn't start to show until you were a lot older. Wearing a bright-yellow dress, long hair gleaming in the sunlight-filled restaurant, she resembled a younger version of Catherine Zeta Jones and drew admiring glances from the other diners. One man sitting alone at the bar stared at her so intently Alex was certain he was going to get up and try to talk to her. In fact, he leaned forward, putting one foot on the floor. But when Julie headed for Alex's table, waving and giving him a wide smile, the man relaxed back in his seat again.

Alex stood to greet her, giving her a kiss on the cheek.

"This has got to be a record," she said, "seeing you two days in a row." Her perfume, something light and flowery, drifted around him.

He pulled her chair out and she sank gracefully into it.

"You look awfully pretty today," he said, sitting again himself. "Hard to believe you got so little sleep."

She took her napkin out of her water glass and put it on her lap. "Thank you. Now that I've reached the ripe old age of twenty-two, I'm trying to take better care of myself."

Alex couldn't have hoped for a better opening. "Funny you should say that, because that's what I want to talk to you about."

Something in his expression or tone must have alerted her to the fact this might be a discussion she wouldn't enjoy, because she frowned.

Just then their waiter approached, so Alex didn't continue.

After she'd ordered something to drink, the waiter left them to study their menus.

"Well?" Julie said. "Are you going to tell me what's going on or am I going to have to guess?"

"Why don't we decide what we want to eat first? Otherwise we'll keep getting interrupted."

She looked as if she wanted to protest, but finally she just sighed and picked up her menu.

After placing their orders—Alex opted for the fried scallops, his favorite, and Julie ordered the crab quiche—Alex leaned forward and said, "Terrence talked to me last night. He's worried about you."

"Why?"

"He's concerned that you might be involved with drugs."

"What?" She looked aghast.

Alex studied her. Julie was a good actress, but he didn't think her reaction was fake. She looked genuinely shocked.

"Geez," she said. "You'd think he'd know me a little better than that. I know why he thinks this, Alex, but he's wrong."

"Why does he think it?"

"Because Penn—you met him last night, the really tall one with the sort of reddish hair?—was busted at a party where they were doing coke. But I don't do drugs. I never have. They scare me."

Alex felt tremendous relief. Her voice rang with conviction, and he believed her. "I'm really glad to hear that."

"Did you really think I might be involved in that scene?"

"I didn't know what to think. I only knew that Terrence is concerned enough to ask me to keep an eye on you while he's gone."

"Where's he going now?"

"Singapore. Didn't he tell you?"

She shrugged. "He might have. He travels so much, I lose track of what he's doing."

She stopped talking as their waiter appeared with their food.

Once he left them alone again, Alex said, "What happened with your friend Penn?"

"What do you mean?"

"Was he charged? You said he was busted." He forked one of his scallops.

She grimaced. "Yes, he was charged with possession."

"And what happened?"

"I don't know. His dad's pulling some strings, I think. You know his dad, actually. Senator Pennbridge?" She ate some of her quiche.

Alex just shook his head. Why should that information surprise him? It happened too often, in his opinion. Kids with rich parents rarely paid the price for their foolish or unlawful behavior.

"I'd feel better if you didn't run around with him anymore."

Julie put her fork down and drank some of her iced tea. "But Alex, he's my friend. I like him."

"He sounds like a bad influence to me."

"He's learned his lesson. That bust scared the hell out of him." Picking up her fork, she resumed eating.

"For now maybe," Alex said skeptically.

"I told you. I don't do drugs. Now will you quit worrying? And will you tell Dad to quit worrying, too? I'm not a child. I don't need a keeper."

Alex figured he knew how parents must feel when their kids got older and they couldn't supervise their every moment as they did when they were little. You just had to trust that you'd taught them right and they'd be okay. Julie might be spoiled, but she was basically a good girl. She'd probably be just fine. Anyway, what choice did he have but to trust her?

As if she'd read his thoughts, she smiled and said,

"Now, c'mon, Alex, quit looking so serious and let's enjoy our food."

Alex had always known when to fold. Returning his sister's smile, he nodded and turned his attention to his lunch.

Normally, P.J. really enjoyed her weekends, but for some reason, this weekend she felt restless.

She did her laundry, cleaned her condo then took a long, leisurely bath and washed her hair. These activities should have made her feel virtuous and proud of herself. Instead, they left her wishing she had somewhere to go, something fun to do and someone to do it with.

Here she was, thirty years old, single, and with nothing better to do on a Saturday night except watch a movie on DVD and order in a pizza. She'd be willing to bet Carrie Wancheck wasn't sitting home alone tonight. Or Alex, either.

Now why had she thought of those two, practically in the same breath?

Oh, you know why.

Was it possible that Carrie had accomplished her mission of catching Alex's interest? She hadn't been at Jake's the night before, either, and when P.J. had casually asked about her, one of the guys said Carrie had bragged that she had a hot date. *A sleep-over date,* he'd said, and the others had all laughed knowingly.

What if that hot date had been with Alex? Although it was the last thing she wanted to think about, P.J. couldn't help imagining the two of them in bed together. Carrie had a fantastic body—toned and slender, with curves in all the right places. What man wouldn't desire her?

The idea of the two of them together made P.J. want to throw up. And that made her even more disgusted with herself. Why did she care anyway? *You don't want him. So what's the problem?*

But even as she told herself this, P.J. knew exactly what the problem was. She *did* want him. And unfortunately, what she'd imagined to be a corresponding interest from him had turned out to be just plain normal friendliness on his part. Because if he'd been going to make a move in her direction, he'd darned sure have done it by now.

Really disgusted with herself now, she decided that once and for all, she would wipe Alex Noble out of her mind. Not only that, she would stay away from him at work as well as after work. If that meant she would have to give up going to Jake's, so be it. She needed some new interests in life, anyway. In fact, instead of just giving lip service to some of the areas that interested her, it was past time to put some of those interests into action. Like volunteering at a women's shelter. And getting involved in politics.

It was a good thing she had that management meeting in Seattle this week. She needed to get away. Maybe after a week of meetings, she'd have her head back in the game again.

And nowhere near Alex Noble.

Chapter Eight

The week went fast for Alex. They were extremely busy at work, and it felt as if he'd no sooner had lunch than it would be time to punch out.

After work, he always ran his five miles in Jansen Park. He kept hoping he'd see P.J. there since Chick Fogarty had told them she was in management meetings in Seattle this week. But she didn't come to the park, or if she did, she came earlier or later than he did.

Because he was curious, he gave Gray a call and found out the meetings would be over by noon on

Thursday. While he had Gray on the phone, he asked him how his bride hunt was going. As always, Gray was noncommittal.

"What about you?" he asked.

"I'm working on it," Alex said.

After they'd hung up, Alex wondered if P.J. would be back to work on Friday. He hoped so. Now that he'd decided Miss Paige Jeffers Kinkaid was the perfect candidate for his bride hunt, he was determined to make some forward progress in his campaign to win her.

On Friday morning, as he entered the quad, the first person he saw was P.J. sitting at her desk. She looked up when she heard his footsteps. "Good morning."

"Good morning," he said, smiling down at her. She looked great in a short-sleeved sweater the same blue as her eyes. It hugged her breasts and Alex couldn't help noticing the faint outline of her bra. "How were your meetings?"

She shrugged, not meeting his gaze. "Fine."

Alex started to say something else, but she'd already turned her attention back to her computer.

Alex frowned as he walked away. She certainly wasn't very friendly this morning. He wondered if something was wrong. And if so, if it had to do with him. Could she have found out who *he* was? But he didn't have time to think about her for long because only minutes later the morning orders began pouring in.

Again, the day went by fast. He barely saw P.J. When he passed her desk, she always seemed to be somewhere else, and she wasn't around at lunchtime, either. And when he did see her, she never stopped to talk, not even for a few minutes. By the end of the day, he had the distinct feeling she was purposely avoiding him.

When Rick asked if he was planning to go to Jake's after work, Alex said yes. He hoped P.J. would be there, too. If she was, he was going to make it his business to talk to her.

She was still at her desk when he and Rick left, and Alex was glad when Rick said, "Hey, boss, you goin' to Jake's?"

She looked up. Her gaze met Alex's for an instant before resting on Rick. After hesitating a moment, she shrugged. "I don't know."

"Ah, c'mon, boss," Rick cajoled. "Do you good to go. You've been uptight all day. Those meetings must've done you in. We'll see you there, okay?"

Alex wondered if she'd show up. He'd almost given up after an hour went by and she didn't appear. And then suddenly, there she was. She looked tired, not her usual lively self at all. Something must be wrong. Maybe whatever it was had nothing to do with Alex at all. Maybe the week had just been a rough one for her. He wished there was an empty chair near where he was sitting, but even though he'd tried to sit at the far end of the table where there was room for a few more, Rick wouldn't hear of it and had insisted Alex come and join him and Wayne and Jim, who were all sitting together.

The good thing was, Carrie Wancheck wasn't there. In fact, the only female to join the group that night was Ruby.

P.J. walked over to the bar, got herself a beer, then sat at the far end where Alex had initially wanted to sit, too.

Damn. She hadn't even acknowledged his presence, just gave a nod and general "hello" to everyone. Soon she was engaged in a conversation with Buddy Willis, one of the pickers from Quad A. Alex might have been worried at the intimate way they were talking, but Buddy couldn't have been more than twenty, way too young for P.J. After a few minutes, Ruby drifted down to that end of the table and joined them.

Rick nudged Alex. "Ruby's got the hots for Buddy."

Alex smiled. "What about him?"

Rick grinned. "I think he's into her, too."

About six, Rick said he had to go. Soon after that, the other married men left one by one. By six-thirty, only Alex, two of the dock workers, Buddy, Ruby and P.J. were left and finally Alex was close enough to P.J. to actually talk to her.

"While you were gone we had a really busy week," he said.

"I noticed."

"We missed you, though." He nudged Ruby. "Didn't we?"

Ruby grinned. "You might have. I didn't."

P.J. laughed. "Ruby tells it like it is."

"No, seriously, boss, we *did* miss you," Ruby said. "Things never go as smooth when you're not there."

"You don't have to flatter me," P.J. said. "I'm planning to give you a raise."

Ruby squealed. *"Really?"*

By now the two dock workers had decided they were ready to eat and waved the waitress over. Alex waited to see if P.J. was going to order, saw that she was, and placed his own order for a cheeseburger and fries.

After the waitress left to turn in the food orders, the two dock workers got up to play a game of darts. Alex wished Ruby and Buddy would find some-thing to do so he could have P.J. to himself, but they sat there and dominated the conversation, which now centered on video games. At one point when they were arguing the merits of two different war-type games, Alex caught P.J.'s eye and he could see she was as bored as he was. He winked, and for the first time that day, he got a smile.

Once the food came, and the two dock workers returned to the table, the talk turned to the less-than-stellar season the Mariners were having.

"Damn games are too expensive," one of the dock workers grumbled. "Pretty soon only rich people will be able to afford big-league sports."

Alex felt a guilty pang at the thought of the HuntCom sky box. He could go to a game any time he wished and sit in comfort, yet he rarely went. He made a mental note that when this charade of his was over, he would invite some of his co-workers from the distribution center to a game or two.

After they'd eaten, the dock workers got up to play another game of darts and Ruby and Buddy decided to have a game of pool.

"Well," P.J. said after they'd left the table, "I really should be going."

"Me, too," Alex said, although he had no reason to leave. But if she was going, he also had no reason to stay.

They paid their tabs, said goodbye to the others,

and walked outside together. The late September evening had already cooled considerably, and P.J. shivered. Alex wished he'd worn a jacket. He'd have given it to her.

"Where's your car?" he asked.

She pointed to far end of the parking lot.

"I'll walk down there with you," he said.

"It's not necessary—" she began.

"I know, but I'll come anyway."

When they reached the car, she went to the driver's side, pausing before inserting her key. "Have a good weekend."

Alex didn't intend to let another weekend go by without asking her out. "Wait, P.J.," he said as she started to unlock the door.

She looked up. It wasn't completely dark yet, and in the half light of dusk, it was hard to read her expression.

"I was wondering…if you're not busy tomorrow night…would you like to have dinner with me?"

"I…" She licked her lips. "Thank you, but I don't think so."

Alex had not expected her to say no. For a moment, he stood there awkwardly. Faint sounds of music came from inside Jake's, and somewhere nearby a car backfired.

"Look, Alex, I really like you, and I'm flattered you asked, but I just don't think it's a good idea to date someone who works for me."

Damn. He hadn't even thought of that. She was right. In normal circumstances, it *wasn't* a good idea. Of course, their circumstances were far from normal. The fact that he wasn't who he was pretending to be was something she couldn't know. And she certainly had no idea he knew *her* real background.

"I hope you understand," she said.

What could he say? "Sure, I understand."

How was he going to get around *this* obstacle? he wondered. Maybe he couldn't. Maybe he'd have to find someone else to fulfill Harry's challenge. But dammit, he didn't want to.

When P.J. got into her car, Alex waved and walked toward his truck. He was just unlocking it when he heard the whine of her starter. The sound was unmistakable. Her car wouldn't start.

Hurriedly, he got into his truck, started it and drove down to where she still sat futilely trying to get the Miata's engine to catch.

He set the brake, then climbed out of the truck and walked to her side of the car. She lowered the window.

"I'll give you a jump," he said.

"You have cables with you?"

"Yep. I was a Boy Scout."

"Be prepared," she said, smiling.

Her car started on the first try.

"Let it run a few minutes. Then I'll take the cables off," he said. Once he was sure her car wasn't going to die on her, he unhooked the cables and lowered her hood. "I'll follow you home, make sure you get there okay."

"Oh, Alex, that's totally unnecessary," she said. "I'll be fine."

"I'll follow you." His tone left no room for argument.

"All right. Thank you."

She lived fairly close to Alex's apartment complex. When they reached her building she put her window down and when he pulled up next to her said, "Would you like to come in for coffee or a glass of wine?"

"Sounds good." Which was an understatement.

"You can park in one of the visitor slots in front," she said. "I'm going to go park in back. My unit is 112."

Alex parked the truck, found unit 112, which was located at the far end, and sat on the low stone wall bordering the front walkway. He wondered why she had invited him to come in. He'd have thought after refusing his invitation to go out with him, she would simply have thanked him and said goodnight.

A few minutes later, her front door opened. She smiled, standing back to let him in. When she closed the door, she leaned back against it, and their eyes met. For a long moment, their gazes held. Without conscious thought, Alex reached for her. There was no hesitation on her part. As if she, too, knew there was no use fighting what they both were feeling, she simply stepped into his arms and raised her lips to meet his.

P.J.'s head spun as the kiss went on and on. Part of her, the tiny part that was still capable of rational thought, was shouting, *What are you doing? This is madness!* But the rest of her, oh, the rest of her, was reveling in the thrilling sensations flooding her body. Desire, something she hadn't felt in a long time, ignited every inch of her flesh.

One kiss became two, two became three. Soon kissing wasn't enough. She wanted more.

And more.

When Alex's hands slid under her sweater she shivered. When they found her breasts, she moaned. When he unhooked her bra, she never said stop. When he raised her sweater to get it off, she finished the job herself.

Then she reached for his belt buckle. The only sounds in the room were the ticking of the grandfather clock that had belonged to her grandmother

Marjorie, the muted hum of traffic from the highway nearby, and their frenzied lovemaking.

They never even made it to the bedroom, which was both a good and a bad thing. The good thing was she stopped thinking and just let delicious sensation take over. The bad thing was she stopped thinking and just let delicious sensation take over. It had been a long time since she'd felt this way.

Maybe she'd *never* felt this way.

Later, she never remembered exactly what happened. She only knew that her clothes ended up scattered over the floor along with his, that they didn't even seek the relative comfort of the couch but fell to the carpet.

Alex touched her and kissed her, finding every hidden place that yearned to be touched and kissed. And just at the point where P.J. thought she could stand it no longer, he thrust into her, pushing deep and hard, then deeper still. She reveled in the heat of him and cried out again and again as she crescendoed to a climax, and seconds later, he buried his face in her neck and muffled his own cry as he shuddered with his own release.

Afterwards, they lay twined together as their hearts gradually slowed.

It was only then that sanity returned.

P.J. sat up. Spying her sweater she grabbed it and

put it on. She didn't look at Alex. Couldn't. What must he think of her? She'd been wanton tonight.

"P.J." he said softly. He caressed her arm. "You're not sorry, are you?"

Oh, God.

"Because I'm not."

Of course not. You're a man. You have nothing to lose.

"I'm…only sorry about not having a condom. Truth is, I never even thought about a condom. I didn't think about anything…except you." Taking her hand, he turned it palm up and kissed it.

P.J. shivered and finally turned to look at him. Her heart thudded as their gazes met. She forced herself to keep her eyes trained on his face instead of sweeping down his magnificent body.

And it *was* magnificent.

Alex Noble was one of the finest male specimens she'd ever seen. Just thinking about how fine he was made her want him all over again.

"Don't worry," she forced herself to say in as normal a voice as possible. "I'm on birth control pills." The moment the lie was out of her mouth, she was sorry she'd said it. But what *should* she have said? *Don't worry, Alex. I probably couldn't get pregnant if I tried, because my insides are totally screwed up. So you're safe.*

Sure, the doctors had said there was a slim—very slim—chance she might be able to conceive, but they hadn't held out much hope. In fact, the last specialist she'd seen had said in all honesty he would put her chances at about ten percent, if that. And the older she got, the slimmer that percentage became.

At any rate, she had no intention of discussing her health issues with Alex…or any man, for that matter. After all, it wasn't as if he'd asked her to marry him. All they'd done was have great sex.

You just keep telling yourself that, P.J.

"That's good," Alex said. "But I wanted you to know that I believe in safe sex."

Hell's bells, she hadn't even thought of that. *Of course not. You weren't thinking, period.*

Seeing the look on her face, he said, "I'm clean. I promise you. You're in no danger."

She nodded.

"I wish you'd say something." Leaning over, he kissed her cheek, then nuzzled her ear.

Oh, God. If she didn't get up and away from him, she'd succumb again, she knew she would. She could already feel herself weakening. "What do you want me to say?" Even her voice sounded weak. What in the world was wrong with her? She never let a man get the upper hand. But here she was acting like some kid with her first big crush instead of a thirty-year-old, experienced, fully independent woman who should know better.

"Say you'll go out with me tomorrow night," he said softly. His hand inched up under her sweater again, finding her bare breasts. When his thumb rubbed the nub of the one closest to him, P.J. fought with herself for all of about three seconds, then relaxed into him and turned her face for his kiss.

A long time later…a *very* long time later…after the most satisfying and wonderful sex P.J. could ever have imagined, she finally lay sated and resigned to her fate. She knew what she was doing was crazy and stupid. She knew one of these days she'd be very sorry and probably have to pay a price for her lapse in judgment. But at that moment, she really didn't care.

"So what do you say? Is it a date?" Alex asked lazily.

"Yes," P.J. said. She could feel his smile, even though she didn't look at him.

"I'll pick you up at seven."

"Okay."

"And P.J.?"

Sighing, she finally turned her head to meet his eyes.

He smiled. "Wear something sexy. You *do* own a dress?"

For just a second, P.J. bristled. Then she grinned. "I've got a dress that'll knock your socks off."

"I can hardly wait."

Alex whistled all the way home.

P.J. was incredible. Somehow he'd suspected she would be. But suspecting and actually experiencing *how* incredible were two distinctly different things.

He smiled, remembering.

Yes. P.J. Kinkaid, alias Paige Jeffers Kinkaid, heiress to a fortune, who obviously believed in working for a living, was the perfect candidate for his Cinderella. Beautiful, smart, sexy, generous, kind and passionate.

What more could he want?

Courtney gave P.J. a quizzical smile. "Okay, spill. What's going on?"

At P.J.'s request, the sisters had met for coffee at a Starbucks near where Courtney lived.

P.J. drank some of her latte before answering. "Remember the new guy who came to work for me? The one I told you about when we had dinner together three weeks ago?"

Courtney grinned and broke off a piece of her muffin. "I knew this had to be about a man."

P.J. blew out a breath. "I don't know what to do."

"About what? Has he asked you out?"

"Yes, but that's not it."

Courtney stared at her. Lowering her voice, she said, "Uh-oh. You've done it, haven't you?"

P.J. didn't even pretend not to understand. Glumly, she nodded.

"What's wrong? Was it awful?"

"No, just the opposite, in fact. It…it was fantastic."

Courtney sighed and ate some of her muffin. "You lucky dog. Tell me everything."

So P.J. did, starting with how she'd tried to ignore Alex and ending with how they'd had sex. Twice. "On the *floor*, no less!" she said in a fierce whisper.

Courtney sighed again. "Sounds absolutely wonderful to me." Her voice was wistful. "I can remember when Brad and I used to have unplanned, sweaty and wonderful sex. That was sans kids, of course."

Sans kids. *I'll always be sans kids.* For some reason, the thought hurt. Really hurt. That surprised P.J. She'd thought she was long past the pain of knowing she would probably never have a child of her own.

"So what now? Are you in love with him?" Courtney asked eagerly.

"I don't know how I feel. I'm certainly in lust with him."

"Well, that's a good start. Are you seeing him again?"

P.J. nodded. "Tonight."

"Is he taking you out or are you just going to cut to the chase?"

"We're having dinner together. But I was halfway thinking I should call him and cancel."

"What? Why?"

"For all the reasons I gave you before. Number one, this relationship can't go anywhere. And number two, he works for me."

"Wait a minute…why can't it go anywhere?"

"You know why…marriage is not for me."

"So? You can just live together. And as far as the job thing goes, find another job. Jobs are a dime a dozen. But trust me on this, Paige. Great guys are hard to find. No, not hard. *Impossible!"*

P.J. stared at her sister as though she'd lost her mind. "Quit my *job?"*

"I would. Shoot, P.J., if you've found someone special and he could be 'the one' what's a job compared to that? Besides, you and I both know you don't need to work." She finished off the last bite of her muffin and wiped her mouth with her napkin.

"I *like* working."

"Okay, fine. You like working. But it doesn't have to be there, does it? Dad can set you up with any kind of job you want."

"I don't want any favors from Dad."

Courtney rolled her eyes. "You are the most stubborn person I've ever known. Dad would love to have you working for him."

P.J. was sure her sister was right. But she'd put in more than seven years at HuntCom. She was respected there, not for being the daughter of the owner as she would be at one of her father's facilities, but for her intelligence and hard work. She didn't want to leave HuntCom. "There's something else…" she finally said.

"What?"

"I don't really know anything about Alex."

"Like what?"

"Well…he obviously comes from a classy background. So why is he working a blue-collar job? He's got to be hiding something."

"Paige, listen to you. *You're* hiding something."

P.J. frowned. "I know, but I have a damned good reason. I don't want to be treated differently than my coworkers, and they *would* treat me differently if they knew about the Kincaid money."

"So? Maybe *he* has a damned good reason, too."

"What if he's hiding something bad?"

"Like what?" Courtney said again.

"I don't know. I just—" She broke off. "Something doesn't seem quite right with him."

"Have you asked him why he's working there?"

"Yes."

"What did he say?"

"He admitted he'd gone to college but didn't like the business world."

"P.J., this guy sounds perfect. In fact, he sounds just like you!"

P.J. made a face. "I'm not sure he told me the truth."

"But…what other reason could he have for doing the kind of work he's doing?"

"He could be a spy."

"A spy!"

"Yeah, a spy. Corporate spies exist, you know."

"Do you really think that?"

"I don't know." The truth was, P.J. didn't know *what* she thought. "I Googled him, you know."

Courtney smiled. "And?"

"Nothing. Well, there were Alex Nobles, but none that matched him."

"That doesn't mean anything."

"I know, but still…"

"You want to know what I think?"

P.J. nodded.

"I think you're scared."

P.J. wanted to deny this, but she had a sinking feeling her sister was right. The truth was, Alex was dangerous to her well-being. It was as if he'd gotten into her brain and rewired it or something. Hadn't last night proven that? Just being near him had messed with her mind to the extent she'd behaved in a way she'd never have imagined herself doing.

Courtney drained her latte and stood up. "I've got to go. But I have one last thing to say. If you push Alex away because you're scared, then you're not the woman I thought you were."

And with that, she blew P.J. a kiss, and walked out of the coffee shop.

Chapter Nine

Alex decided to go for broke. After doing a bit of research, he called and made a reservation at the River Lodge, which stood on a rise overlooking the Jansen River a few miles north of town. Supposedly, the Lodge was one of the nicest restaurants around and famous for its great seafood and tender steaks. And on Friday and Saturday nights, a combo played live music. It sounded perfect and romantic, just what he wanted. After all, he didn't have a lot of time to woo P.J. Harry's deadline was only nine months away.

Alex also made the round trip into downtown Seattle and unearthed one of his favorite outfits: custom-made dress pants in a shade of soft gray, a dark gray silk T-shirt, and a black cashmere jacket. The clothes were expensive, but if she happened to comment, he could sheepishly admit that he occasionally splurged on good clothes.

On the way back to Jansen, he stopped at a florist's shop. The florist—a pretty woman about fifty with bright green eyes—asked if she could help him.

"I'd like a bouquet of flowers. Roses, probably."

"For a woman?"

"A special woman," Alex said.

"What color is her hair?"

Alex blinked. "Her hair? It's red. Actually, kind of a red-gold."

"Then I suggest peach roses." So saying, she walked to a large cooler and removed a container.

The moment Alex saw the color, he knew they were perfect.

"Have a wonderful evening," the florist said after Alex had paid for the flowers and was leaving.

"I intend to," he said, smiling.

He left his apartment at six-forty-five and arrived at her condo ten minutes later. The florist had talked him into letting her put the flowers in a vase instead of taking them to P.J. in a box. "You'll be glad you did," she'd said. "Otherwise, your special lady will have to find somewhere to put them and she might not have a tall enough vase."

Holding the vase in one hand, Alex rang P.J.'s doorbell with the other. She opened the door on the second ring.

Holy cow. He was stunned by how she looked. She wore a short black sleeveless dress with a high neck, paired with strappy black heels. Her curly hair was swept back and held in place by a black velvet hair band, and diamond studs sparkled in her ears.

Gorgeous.

There was no other word for it. She looked gorgeous.

"Wow," he said.

She smiled. "I clean up good, huh?"

"That's an understatement."

She stood back to let him in. "So do you." She gave him an appreciative once-over. "Nice threads."

"Thanks." He handed her the flowers. "I hope you like roses."

"I love roses, and these are just beautiful. Thank you."

He could see her pleasure was genuine, and it made him feel good. He tried to remember the last time he'd spontaneously bought flowers for a woman and couldn't. In fact, he couldn't remember the last time he'd looked forward to being with a woman. Most of his social life consisted of obligatory attendance at some black-tie affair.

When she turned to place the vase on the small credenza in her entryway, Alex's breath stopped for a moment. Her dress plunged in a deep V in the back—almost to her waist—exposing smooth porcelain skin. Skin he knew would warm to his touch.

He could feel himself becoming aroused and had to force his thoughts away from that skin and how it had felt last night. "You'll need a wrap," he said. "It's already cooling off."

"I know." She reached for a black knit shawl lying on a needlepoint-covered chair next to the credenza and wrapped it around her shoulders. Picking up a small silk bag that had been under it, she gave him a bright smile. "I'm ready."

As they walked out into the already darkening evening, Alex could smell her perfume—something light and clean—just the kind of fragrance he would have imagined she'd wear. When they reached his truck, he helped her in. Her legs looked fantastic in those heels. He wondered if she knew how fantastic. "I'm sorry I don't have a nice car for the occasion."

"I like trucks," she said with a smile.

"Hey, what happened with your car?" he asked after he had walked around and gotten into the driver's seat.

"My neighbor gave me a jump this morning, and I took it to Sears for a new battery."

"Good."

She shifted in the seat, which caused her skirt to ride up another inch or so. Yes, those were definitely gorgeous legs. In fact, he was having a hard time keeping his eyes on the road.

"Where are we going?" she asked.

He smiled. "It's a surprise." Turning to her, he added, "Want to listen to music?"

"What're my choices?"

He thought about his CDs. "Sheryl Crow, Martina McBride, Michelle Branch, Beyoncé, James Taylor, the Beatles, Coldplay…I've even got some classical stuff, if you prefer that."

She started to laugh. "That's the strangest mix of music I've ever heard."

He grinned sheepishly. "I've got eclectic tastes."

"I *guess*."

"So what'll it be?"

"Martina McBride."

He inserted the CD. The first song was "My Baby Loves Me," and within moments, P.J. was tapping her fingers on the console between the front seats and humming along with the music. When the song ended and the next one began, she said, "We're going to the River Lodge, aren't we?"

"Yes."

He could feel her eyes on him. Turning to meet her gaze, he saw the speculative look. "What?" he said.

"You're just full of surprises, aren't you? How'd you know about the Lodge?"

"The Internet. I just searched on restaurants and that one seemed to fill the bill." Now he wondered if he'd made a mistake. He couldn't afford to make her suspicious again, now that she seemed to finally trust him. First he needed to get a ring on her finger. "I wanted to take you somewhere nice."

"The Lodge is very nice," she said softly. "I haven't been there in a long time."

It suddenly hit him how much he wanted to please this woman...and keep pleasing her. Maybe his father's plan was unorthodox, but it sure seemed to be working. This was the first time in years— maybe the first time ever—that Alex had felt this way about a woman. Usually, he was counting the minutes until he could escape.

"The drive is coming up right around this bend," she said. "It'll be on your left." She smiled when he glanced her way. "It's kind of hard to see if you've never been there."

An understatement, Alex realized. On his own, he would have passed it up. Only a small sign marked the turn, and in the dark, it was almost impossible to see.

The drive climbed uphill for about one hundred yards, then turned to the left through a stand of tall pines. Finally they came to a rustic building surrounded by trees and bordering the Jansen River to the right. The trees were strung with tiny white lights and reminded Alex of Tavern on the Green in New York.

He surrendered the truck to the valet parking attendant and, hand on her elbow, escorted P.J. through the front entrance and into the restaurant. A pretty hostess with long black hair and a brilliant smile greeted them. Alex gave his name—almost saying *Hunt* before he caught himself—and they were promptly ushered to a table by the window. The river beyond was a dark ribbon with patches of moonlight shining upon it.

Alex looked around. He'd been in some high-end restaurants over the years, and the River Lodge compared favorably in ambiance. Now if the food lived up to its touted excellence, he'd be a happy man.

About thirty tables ringed a small dance floor. In the corner was a tiny elevated stage with a grand piano next to it. Either the combo providing music for the evening hadn't started yet or they were taking a break.

"The musicians start playing at eight," P.J. said.

A lighted candle flickered in a cut-glass holder in the middle of their table. Her face, reflected in the candle's glow, seemed younger and softer than it normally did. Maybe that's because she was more relaxed. She smiled at him. "This is nice."

"It is." He wished he could tell her about some of the places he'd been, some of the places he'd like to take her...but that would be too dangerous.

Just then their waiter approached, and the next few minutes were taken up with ordering drinks. After he left to place their orders at the bar, Alex said, "I've been looking forward to this all day."

She didn't answer for a long moment. When she did, she prefaced it with a sigh. "I don't know, Alex. I keep thinking this is a mistake."

"A mistake?" He couldn't have read her wrong. She'd been just as turned on last night as he'd been. She certainly hadn't resisted.

She met his gaze squarely. "You work for me. Remember?"

Reaching across the table, he took her hand. Her fingers were slim, the nails unpainted but nicely shaped. "I'll make you a promise, P.J. If my working for you turns out to be a problem, I'll find another job."

Before she could answer, their waiter arrived with their wine. Alex reluctantly let go of her hand. They didn't talk as the waiter served them a plate of some kind of pâté and a basket of warm French bread.

Once he was gone, she said, "I couldn't let you do that, Alex. It wouldn't be right." Worry clouded her blue eyes.

"Why don't you let me be the judge of that?" He reached for his wineglass. "Let's not have any more talk about anything serious. Let's just dedicate tonight, our first real date, to enjoying each other's company and having a wonderful time."

She hesitated, then picked up her glass and clinked it against his. But the worry didn't leave her eyes.

Alex vowed then and there that from tonight on, he would make sure that worry was gone…and stayed gone.

There was something about dancing that was so sexy and erotic. If a girl felt even a smidgen of attraction for her partner, she was probably a lost cause once he took her into his arms and led her around a dance floor. And if the music was soft and romantic and the partner a great dancer—well, it was no contest.

P.J. knew that she and Alex would end up in bed together at the end of this perfect evening. She could tell herself whatever lie she wanted, but the bottom line was, her body would rule. In fact, sex with Alex was all she could think about as they danced and ate their superb dinners and drank the mellow wine.

By the time they were ready to leave, she was so turned on, she wasn't sure she could wait.

For the ride home, Alex unearthed a CD, and as the understated elegance of the singer's vocals filled the cab, the tension and delicious anticipation of what was to come pulsed like a living thing between them, and P.J. knew Alex was feeling exactly the same way she was.

When they reached P.J.'s condo, he parked in front and they walked together to her front door. The very air seemed to shimmer in expectation.

When Alex reached for her keys, she gave them up without a word. They stood so close, she wondered if he could hear her heart beating. After he unlocked the door and pushed it open, P.J. stepped inside knowing he would follow.

The small hurricane lamp on the credenza in the entryway gave off a soft glow, illuminating the roses in their frosted vase. Their fragrance filled the air. P.J. turned and their eyes met. As the grandfather clock began to chime the hour, he reached for her and pulled her close. When he lowered his head, she raised hers and gave herself up to his kiss.

A long time later, after making love, sleeping for a while, then waking and making love again, they lay together spoon fashion in P.J.'s bed.

"We fit together nicely," Alex said, lazily cupping a breast and nuzzling the back of her neck.

"Ummm," P.J. murmured noncommittally, although she'd been thinking the same thing.

"You're not going to let our work situation make a difference between us, are you?"

"Depends how things go." But she already knew she wouldn't. Because if she made their jobs an issue, she'd have to give him up, and she didn't want to. Of course, if it became a situation where she could no longer do her job or he could no longer do his, she'd have to rethink her decision.

But for now, at least, she intended to enjoy being with Alex…and not worry about tomorrow.

The next few weeks went by swiftly. Alex kept his promise to keep tabs on Julie, but was relieved when Terrence returned home from his business trip and Alex no longer felt quite as responsible for her.

He and P.J. spent a lot of time together. He took her to movies, they went out to dinner, they fell into the habit of running together after work, and one Saturday afternoon and evening they attended a festival at the local Catholic church.

"I love Ferris wheels," P.J. said as they stood in line waiting their turn to ride.

Alex smiled down at her. She looked like a kid in her jeans and flip-flops with her hair pulled back in a ponytail.

"I almost came to this festival last year," she continued.

"Why didn't you?"

She shrugged, the smile fading. "No one to go with."

The way she said it made Alex feel tender toward her. She acted so tough most of the time, but he suspected the toughness was a facade to mask deeper feelings.

Maybe she's lonely, too.

Most people, he'd discovered, presented a face to the world that was not necessarily their real face. He certainly did. No one who knew him socially or in the world of philanthropy would ever guess at the emotions he kept hidden. Even his half-brothers probably had no idea what he was really like, just as he had little idea what made *them* tick.

"Well, you've got me now," he said, putting his arm around her.

Their eyes met, and Alex could tell she wanted to say something—was actually on the verge of saying something—but just then the line began to move and the moment was lost.

Later that night, Alex awakened to the sound of rain hitting the roof. P.J. was still sleeping soundly. He smiled as he watched her. She looked delectable. There was no other word for it. Her hair tumbled over the pillow, her sleep shirt—which she'd put back on after they'd made love—had ridden up, and her really gorgeous backside was visible. It was all he could do to keep from caressing it, but he knew if he did, he'd wake her. He resisted the temptation. They had all day tomorrow to enjoy each other. He was just drifting back to sleep when his cell phone rang. Groaning, he picked it up off the bedside table and looked at the caller ID.

Julie.

The digital clock on P.J.'s side of the bed read 4:43 a.m.

"Damn," he muttered, pressing talk and getting out of bed as quietly as he could. "This had better be important," he whispered, moving toward the hallway.

"Alex," Julie cried. "I've…I've been arrested!"

"What? Why?"

"I didn't *do* anything, but they won't listen to

me. They hauled me down here to the police station just like a common criminal!"

"Calm down. *Why* were you arrested?"

"It was a drug raid. I—I was at Sandpipers and some of the kids were doing coke and stuff."

"Jesus, Julie." Alex pushed his hair back from his forehead in frustration.

"Well, I wasn't *part* of it. I was just *there*. They had no right to arrest me! Oh, God, I don't want Mom and Dad to know. Can you come?"

He sighed. "Yes, I'll come. Where, exactly, are you?"

After she told him, he said, "It'll be an hour, hour and a half before I get there."

"Okay," she said in a small voice. "Thank you, Alex."

By the time Alex had dressed and gathered his stuff, P.J. was stirring.

"You leaving already?" she said sleepily, sitting up in bed.

"I have to." He walked around to her side of the bed, leaned down, and kissed her. "I probably won't get back before noon."

Her brow furrowed. "Is something wrong?"

"I just got a call from my sister. I've got to drive to Seattle and bail her out of jail."

P.J.'s eyes widened. "What happened?"

"It was a drug bust at a club. Look, I've got to get going. I'll call you later, okay?"

She nodded. "Be careful driving."

He made it to the precinct where Julie was being held in record time, but even so, it was almost six-thirty before he walked in. It took another thirty minutes before he was allowed to see her.

She sat on a bench in a holding cell, along with a dozen other young people. Alex gritted his teeth when he recognized the infamous Penn, who sat with his head in his hands. He looked up when Alex and the duty cop approached. Alex nodded in the boy's direction, even as he wished he could pound some sense into him and the others. He did notice that the beautiful Phoebe wasn't part of the group. So, obviously, she was smarter than Julie.

"Alex," Julie said, getting up and coming toward him. Her mascara was smudged, her blouse wrinkled and dirty, her face pale and exhausted-looking. A lone tear rolled down her face as her blue eyes met Alex's.

Alex reached through the bars and took her hand. The duty cop unlocked the cell and let Julie out.

"Fifteen minutes," he barked after taking them to a small, windowless room with a table and several chairs. "Then she's gotta go back till bail is set."

"When will that be?" Alex asked.

The cop made a show of looking up at the large, ugly wall clock. "Lemme see, it's seven-ten. Judge Winkle won't be in chambers till nine. So that means at least two hours, prob'ly more."

"Two more hours!" Julie said.

"Yeah, cutie. It's no fun here, is it?" With that the cop left them.

"Alex," she cried, the tears starting in earnest now.

He let her cry for a while. Just held her in his arms and rubbed her back and made comforting sounds. When she finally stopped, he handed her a clean handkerchief. "Sit down, Julie. Tell me what happened."

"I told you. We were just at Sandpipers and—"

"Who's we?"

"Me, Bits, Crystal, Logan, Phoebe—"

"Phoebe? I didn't see her back there," Alex said, interrupting her again.

Julie rolled her eyes. "She ran. The cops didn't see her, I guess."

"Who else was there?"

"Russ, Terri, and Penn. You met some of them at my birthday party."

"Penn's the one who was busted before for drugs. The one your dad was worried about. The one I told you to stay away from."

She hung her head. "Yes."

Alex sighed. "Hell, Julie, when are you ever going to learn?"

"But I wasn't doing anything. I was just there. It's so not fair. Couldn't they give me some kind of test or something? Did they have to arrest me?"

"Haven't you ever heard that old saying that you're known by the company you keep?"

The tears began again. "Daddy's going to kill me."

"He should, but I doubt he will."

"I don't want him to know. Please don't tell him. You won't, will you?"

"On one condition."

Her eyes, so big, so blue, so frightened, perpetuated the myth that she really was as naive and sweet as she appeared to be. But Alex knew better. Sure he loved her. And yes, he wanted to protect her, especially from her own bad judgment, but she was already too wise in the ways of the world and far too sophisticated and indulged for her own good. Right then he was torn between feeling sorry for her and wanting to turn her over his knee and give her the spanking she should have had many years ago.

"What's the condition?" she asked.

"You have to promise me nothing like this will ever happen again."

"It won't! I promise."

"Because if it does…" He paused to let his next words sink in. "I'm not going to come to the rescue."

She nodded solemnly. "I understand."

"I hope so."

A few minutes later, the same duty cop came back. He opened the door without knocking, said, "Time to go, Missy." His pale eyes met Alex's gaze. "You can wait out front."

It was almost ten o'clock before bail was set. By then Alex had drunk half a dozen cups of bad coffee and had a whale of a headache. The only good thing was that because this was a first offense for Julie, it only cost Alex a thousand dollars to get her released.

"Where's your car?" he said as they claimed her belongings—a leather shoulder bag and a black leather jacket.

"I didn't drive last night."

"Okay. I'll take you home."

As they walked out the front door into the morning sunshine, a photographer, who had been sitting on the concrete wall bordering the building, jumped up and snapped a couple of photos before Alex could react.

"Oh, God," Julie said. "Now Dad will find out for sure."

"Maybe you should just tell him yourself."

Julie, too miserable to be aware of anything except her own situation, slumped into the passenger seat of Alex's truck and never even asked why he was driving it instead of his Navigator.

"You want to stop and have some breakfast on the way?" Alex asked.

Julie shook her head. "I'm not hungry. Just pull into the drive through at the first Starbucks you see and get me a giant latte, okay?"

It was eleven-thirty before he finally dropped Julie at the house. She insisted he let her out at the foot of the drive so no one would see him. "They expected me to spend the night at Phoebe's," she said.

"Like I said, if I were you, I'd tell them the truth."

She nodded, leaned over and kissed his cheek. "Thanks, bro," she whispered.

"I'll call you later."

"Okay."

He watched until she disappeared around the bend of the driveway, then took off.

It was only as he was driving back to Jansen that he remembered he hadn't called P.J. as he'd said he would. He flipped open his cell phone, ready to make the call, then wondered what he was going to say. Could he afford to tell her the whole truth?

Damn, he hated this subterfuge. Above all, he

wished they could be completely honest with one another.

Soon, he thought. If things between them continued to go well in the next few weeks, he should be able to tell her the truth about himself by Thanksgiving.

And with luck, they might even be married by Christmas.

Chapter Ten

After Alex left, P.J. tried to go back to sleep, but hadn't been able to. Finally, at five-thirty, she gave up, got up, showered, pulled on clean jeans and a warm sweater, then padded barefoot into the kitchen to make a pot of coffee. Peering out front, she saw that the Sunday newspaper had been delivered.

She slipped into an old pair of clogs and unlocked the front door. The early-morning air was crisp and cold after the night's storm, but it was supposed to warm up to the sixties this afternoon. She hoped the weatherman had been right. She and Alex had talked about going bike riding today, and it would be more pleasant if the weather was warmer.

She wondered if Alex would still want to go. She also wondered about his sister. Funny he had never mentioned her before. Of course, he hadn't talked about his family much at all. When asked, he'd said he had brothers who lived in the Seattle area and once, when she'd pressed a little, he'd said his parents were divorced. Although she'd been intensely curious to know more, she hadn't wanted to press too hard because he might press back, and she absolutely did *not* want to talk about her family if she could help it.

Oh, she'd told him she had two sisters and a brother and a total of seven nieces and nephews, but she'd changed the subject as soon as she could. Maybe one day she'd tell him about her family— who and what they were—but it was too soon. And perhaps pointless. Whether or not she came clean with Alex about her background would depend on what developed with their relationship.

Oh? And what happened to "this relationship can go nowhere?"

P.J. purposely ignored the little voice inside her that persisted in reminding her just how naive she'd been. And yet, had she really? Hadn't she always known, down deep, that a casual relationship with

Alex wasn't possible? From the beginning, she'd been far too attracted to him. In fact, he should have been wearing a sign that said Danger Ahead. *Oh, hell, Kincaid. He was wearing the sign. You just pretended not to see it.*

As the morning wore on, as P.J. fixed herself some scrambled eggs and toast, as she read the paper, as she tidied her condo, she kept looking at the phone and wondering where Alex was now and what he was doing. She wished he'd call as he'd promised. Didn't he realize she was concerned? Worried?

A little after one the phone finally rang. Dropping her magazine, she rushed to answer it.

"Still want to take that bike ride?" he asked.

"If you do."

"Good. I'll be there in fifteen minutes."

"Park in back, by the garage. Easier to load the bikes that way."

When he arrived, P.J. could see he'd stopped at his apartment to shower and change clothes before coming to her place. "Are you sure you still want to go?" she asked. "You look tired."

"I am, but I need the fresh air."

"Have you had any lunch?"

"I grabbed a sandwich at the apartment."

She was dying to ask about his sister, but something held her back. "Okay, then. Let's get the bikes."

Ten minutes later, bikes in the bed of the pickup, they headed out to the park. They'd briefly toyed with the idea of driving to the coast, maybe to Seaside, but decided the Jansen River trail was just as nice and a heckuva lot easier to get to. Plus Seaside on a beautiful Sunday afternoon was almost always crowded. And P.J. had learned early in their relationship that in this she and Alex were alike—neither enjoyed crowds. The carnival yesterday was enough for one weekend.

"This is nice," Alex said once they were comfortably into their ride along the river. He smiled at her. "Thanks for not asking about the morning."

"Just because I didn't ask doesn't mean I'm not curious."

"I want to tell you. I just wasn't in the mood to talk about it until now." He grimaced. "I hope that's my last encounter with the criminal justice system."

He then proceeded to explain what had happened.

"She must have been awfully scared," P.J. said when he was finished.

"Yes. I only hope it lasts. Julie has a tendency to forget about consequences when she's out raising hell." He sighed. "The problem is, she's never had to take responsibility for anything. Someone always bails her out. Today I did the bailing."

P.J. knew he was as frustrated with himself as he was with his sister. "How old is Julie?"

"She just turned twenty-two."

"Has she been in any serious trouble before?" P.J. couldn't help but think about her own sister Jillian, who was a model citizen now, but who had been a wild child when she was young. Shoot, P.J. herself hadn't exactly been a model citizen. And she'd be extremely surprised if Alex had, either.

"Nothing too serious. She got into a few scrapes at her boarding school—the usual stuff—sneaking out at night, that kind of thing."

"Where did she go to boarding school?"

He seemed to hesitate, then said, "I doubt you'd know it—it's a private girls' school in the Bellingham area. St. Camille's."

P.J. gave a mental whistle. St. Camille's was pricey. Very pricey. "On scholarship?"

"No. Her father has money. Nothing but the best for his daughter. He's spoiled and indulged her all of her life."

"Sounds like she's her father's only child."

"Yes."

Realizing this was her opportunity to learn more about Alex, P.J. said, "So…your other brothers… they have a different mother than you do?"

He smiled cynically. "Yes."

"Are they younger than you are, too?"

"One of them is."

"One of them? How many brothers do you have?"

At first she thought he wasn't going to answer. But he finally said, "I have three brothers. My father's been married four times. My mother three. As you can see, I have an unorthodox family, and if you don't mind, I really don't want to talk about them anymore. It's not a pleasant subject for me."

He hadn't needed to tell her. P.J. could see her questions had bothered him. Why? she wondered. Was it just because his family didn't fit the all-American mold?

Or was it for a darker reason?

All her old uncertainty about him came rushing back. Was Alex hiding something? And if so, what?

Great, Alex thought. Just great. Now I've roused her suspicions again.

Well, it couldn't be helped. He could hardly refuse to answer her questions. If he had, she'd be even more suspicious than she was now. It was just bad luck that he'd been with P.J. when Julie had called. And he hoped nothing like this would happen again.

Anyway, it wouldn't be long before he could level with P.J. Then there would be no more need to hide anything from her. *In fact, I'll call Cornelia*

tomorrow. Tell her all about P.J. And if she approves,
there will be no more reason to wait at all.

"Alex, I would *love* to see you!" Cornelia said.
"Come for dinner."

Alex smiled. "What time?"

"How about six-thirty? We'll have cocktails first.
I'll call Georgie. Maybe she'll come, too."

After they hung up, Alex walked back through
the grounds to the outside entrance of the cafeteria.
Spying Rick sitting with a couple of the other guys,
he headed for his table. He also saw P.J. sitting and
eating with her buddy Anna, but all he did was nod
as he walked by. They were being very careful not
to let anyone from work know they were seeing
each other, and so far he didn't think anyone even
suspected. If anyone knew, it would be Anna, and
that would only be if P.J. had confided in her.

"I looked for you," Rick said when Alex reached
their table, "but you'd already taken off. Where'd
you go?"

"I had to make a phone call," Alex said, grabbing
a chair and joining the group, which consisted of
Rick, Wayne and Jim.

"Uh-oh," Jim said. "Gotta be some chick." He
poked Wayne in the arm. "Remember those days,
Crowder?"

"Barely," Wayne said. "I've been married too long."

"I had to call my aunt," Alex said.

"Aunt. Sure you did," Jim said.

They laughed and kept kidding him good-naturedly. Alex just let them talk. If they thought he had a girlfriend, great. Then they wouldn't be watching him and P.J.

After lunch was over, Rick and Alex walked back to their quad together.

"Hey, Alex, were you really calling your aunt?" Rick asked.

"Actually, yes. Although she's not really my aunt. She's an old family friend of my father's, but we've always called her our aunt."

"You sure?"

Alex frowned. "What's the problem, Rick?"

Rick hesitated, then blurted out, "I know you've been seein' P.J. and I guess I just wanted to make sure you aren't stringing her along or anything."

Alex barely managed to keep his mouth from dropping open. "How'd you know about me and P.J.?"

"I got ways. No, seriously, I've seen your truck parked outside her condo a coupla times. And I saw you together at the carnival Saturday."

"Really? I didn't see you."

"I know you didn't. I steered Maria and the kids in the other direction."

"I wouldn't have cared if you'd said hello. In fact, I'd have liked to meet Maria and the girls."

"I know, but I figured maybe P.J. would care. I mean, seein' as how she's your boss and all."

"Is that really a problem?"

"Not for me, it isn't. But I know how P.J. is. She wouldn't want anyone to get the wrong idea. And some of 'em would, Alex. Some might think she was playing favorites, like if you should happen to get a good raise and they should get wind of it."

Alex knew he wouldn't be playing this game of masquerade for much longer. Certainly not long enough to be eligible for a raise.

"Anyway," Rick continued, "I think a lot of P.J. I don't want to see her get hurt."

"I would never hurt P.J."

By now they'd reached the quad and Rick took a stack of orders out of the Fill box by P.J.'s desk.

"Glad to hear it," Rick said, "'cause she's pretty special, you know."

"I do know."

"So is it serious?"

With anyone else, Alex would have been irritated at the questioning, but just as Rick thought a lot of P.J., Alex thought a lot of Rick, and he knew Rick's questions weren't prompted by nosiness but by real concern for P.J.

So Alex answered truthfully. "It is on my part."

Rick nodded thoughtfully.

"I know you said she's not interested in marriage," Alex added. "I hope to change her mind."

A long moment went by before Rick answered. "If anyone can, it'll be you."

P.J. was exhausted and hoped Alex didn't suggest coming over that evening. All she really wanted to do was go home, take a long soak in the tub, maybe give herself a pedicure, have a glass of wine or two, and hunker down in front of the T.V.

Alone.

This was definitely a first in their relationship.

But they'd been together practically nonstop the last few weeks, and a girl needed some time to herself. She especially needed time to think. When P.J. was with Alex, too much of the time she wasn't thinking at all.

But when quitting time rolled around, she didn't even see Alex. And by the time she walked out to the parking lot, his truck was long gone.

Instead of feeling relieved to have her wish granted, she felt annoyed. More than annoyed. Hurt.

Honestly. What was he *doing* to her? She was a mess of contradictions who didn't know what she wanted.

She did know one thing, though.

She should never, *ever,* have started dating him. She'd known from the beginning it was a mistake, and her reaction just now proved it.

If she was disappointed and hurt now, just because he'd left work without saying goodbye or kiss my foot, how was she going to feel when he moved on?

Because he would. Of course he would.

Alex Noble would eventually want to get married. And when he did, he would want someone young and fertile.

And P.J. was neither.

If she had any sense at all, she'd break it off now, while she still had her pride.

"This is so nice," Cornelia said, raising her glass to Alex. "It's been too long since you visited me." She was seated in one of the two rose brocade chairs placed on either side of the fireplace in her living room.

Alex, seated in the other, smiled at her. "It *has* been too long."

Cornelia looked particularly lovely tonight, he thought, in a long black velvet skirt and cream satin blouse. A tall, slender woman, she carried her years lightly, looking a full ten years younger than she was. Her pale hair waved softly around her face, and diamond studs winked in her ears.

Alex had always suspected his father was in love with Cornelia, and he wondered now if she felt the same way.

"So tell me about this young woman you've met," Cornelia said. She sipped at her dry martini.

So Alex told her all about P.J. Everything except the fact she was Peter Prescott Kincaid's daughter. "I think she's perfect for me, and I hope you'll agree, because if you do, so will Harry."

"I see." Her shrewd blue eyes studied him. "You've fallen in love with her, haven't you?"

Alex blinked. "I—" He stopped. *Was* he in love with P.J.?

Cornelia watched him affectionately.

"Maybe I am," he said slowly. "I don't think I realized it until just this minute."

"Does she have any idea of who you really are?"

"No." Alex chuckled. "And she doesn't know that I know who *she* is."

Cornelia drank a little more of her martini and gave him a curious look.

"She's the daughter of Peter Prescott Kincaid."

Now it was Cornelia's turn to look stunned. "Whatever is she doing working at HuntCom's Distribution Center?"

"Good question. I'm not positive because I haven't revealed what I know about her, but just from our conversations about college, I know she didn't like the corporate world. I also know she shares my world view about excessive wealth and its evils." He finished off his vodka and tonic.

"I hope this doesn't turn out to be a problem."

Alex frowned. "How could it be? I would think Harry would be delighted by her background, since she obviously isn't a gold digger." Once again, he heard the bitterness in his voice.

Cornelia sighed. "Alex, dear, haven't you punished your mother long enough?"

"No offense, but I don't want to discuss my mother."

"No," she murmured. "I'm sure you don't. But surely you realize how your feelings toward her have affected everything in your life."

Alex reached for a cracker and spread it with brie. "Aunt Cornelia…"

"I know, I know. But I can't help trying to effect a reconciliation between you. Lucinda loves you, Alex. And you have no idea how tough it was for her once Harry put pressure on her. But I do."

Alex's jaw hardened. He would never be rude to Cornelia, but he wished she'd drop the subject. There was nothing she could say that would make him feel any different.

"Back to the subject of your P.J.," Cornelia said.

"When I said I hoped there wouldn't be a problem, I meant she might be upset when she finds out who *you* are. Especially if, as you say, she isn't seduced by the thought of money." She raised her eyebrows. "More to the point, though, is the fact you've lied to her."

"For a good reason."

"She might not see it that way."

"Do you really think so?"

"It's very possible. It sounds to me as if she has a great deal of integrity. And pride."

"But she's not exactly playing it straight, either," Alex pointed out.

"Perhaps she hasn't revealed exactly who her father is, but she didn't change her name." Unspoken was *like you did*.

"You know I had no choice."

"I know. It's the one part of your father's challenge that has bothered me from the beginning. I share his sentiment about young women who—" She broke off as Elizabeth, her long-time housekeeper, appeared in the doorway. "Yes, Elizabeth?"

"Dinner is ready, Mrs. Fairchild."

Cornelia rose gracefully. "Thank you, Elizabeth." She looked at Alex. "Shall we?"

He stood, giving her his arm, and together they walked into the softly lighted dining room. Over succulent rack of lamb, baby peas and tiny new potatoes, they continued to discuss Harry's challenge, then moved on to an update about each of Cornelia's daughters.

"I'm sorry Georgie couldn't make it tonight," Alex said. He grinned. "She doesn't think much of Harry's challenge."

"Oh, I know," Cornelia said with a wry smile. "She gave me an earful about my role in the whole thing. She said she couldn't believe I'd be a party to such shameful blackmail."

Alex laughed. "That's our Georgie. She always says exactly what she thinks."

"And I tried so hard to instill old-fashioned manners in my girls. To no avail, I'm afraid."

"You wouldn't change any of them if you could, and you know it," Alex teased.

Cornelia smiled. "You're right. I wouldn't. I just like to grouse a bit, that's all. It's a mother's prerogative."

Alex almost said, *I wouldn't know,* but thought better of it. The last thing he wanted was to get into another discussion about his own mother.

After a generous slice of Elizabeth's famed butterscotch pie for dessert, Alex leaned back and patted his stomach. "If I ate like this every day, I'd weigh a ton."

"As would I," Cornelia said. "But tonight was a special occasion."

Alex couldn't help feeling guilty that he didn't visit Cornelia more often. He knew she considered him and his brothers almost like her own sons.

Cornelia poured cream into her coffee. "I want you to bring your P.J. to meet me just as soon as you finalize things with her."

"Of course I will."

After they finished their coffee, Alex reluctantly said he'd better be going. "I have a long drive back."

Cornelia walked with him to the front door. When he bent down to kiss her cheek, he thought how much he loved her, and how great it would have been if she'd been his mother instead of Lucinda.

"Don't wait too long to tell P.J. the truth, Alex," was her final piece of advice as he walked out the door into the evening drizzle. "Lies have a way of magnifying the longer they're perpetuated."

Yes, Alex thought, he needed and wanted to tell P.J. the truth. But how could he do that and still fulfill the terms of Harry's conditions?

Chapter Eleven

Alex's cell phone rang Tuesday morning as he was on his way to work. Picking it up, he glanced at the caller ID and saw the number for his office.

"Marti?" he said, knowing it had to be his assistant.

"Oh, Alex, I'm so glad I caught you. We've got a crisis looming. Is there any way you can come into the office today?"

"What kind of crisis?"

"It's Richard Priest."

Alex swore. Richard Priest was an eccentric

multi-millionaire who had founded an electronics empire. He was one of the few donors from whom the Hunt Foundation accepted money unquestioningly. This was due to the fact that nothing his companies manufactured or sold conflicted with the purpose or goals of the foundation. But his money came at a price. He'd demanded a seat on the board, and periodically he managed to insult another board member, a donor, and once in a while even a head of state.

"What's he done now?" Alex asked wearily.

"He told Philippa Von Kohler it would be a cold day in hell before KeepKidsWell got another nickel from us."

For a moment, Alex was speechless. KeepKidsWell was the brainchild of Mrs. Von Kohler—widow of the founder of a popular chain of doughnut shops—and she not only ran the charity with an iron hand, she funded fifty percent of its costs herself. KKW, as Alex thought of it, was one his favorite projects. "What the hell brought *that* on?"

"Apparently she gave an interview to Will Crosby and she badmouthed Richard. Said he was an idiot. This is because he disapproves of giving condoms to kids, which she advocates as part of her safe-sex educational program. Anyway, he's called a board meeting for ten o'clock this morning. When I told him I didn't know if I could reach you or not, he said, quote, we don't need Alex as long as we have a majority, unquote."

Alex sighed.

"I think you'd better be here, Alex. You know how he can intimidate some of the board members. I'm afraid he'll get the vote he wants and block that big payment that's supposed to go to KeepKidsWell on the first of the month."

If Alex had had Richard Priest there, he would have throttled the man. "All right, I'll come. It's going to be tight, though. You know what morning traffic is like going into town. Just don't let the meeting start without me."

After disconnecting the call, Alex called P.J. Dammit, anyway. He had to go back to the apartment to call P.J. because he still hadn't done anything about buying a new cell phone. Mentally berating himself, plus crossing his fingers against getting a speeding ticket, he raced back to his complex.

He was relieved when she didn't answer her phone and it went to voice mail. Easier to lie to voice mail than to talk to her in person.

"P.J.," he said, "I'm sorry, but something urgent has come up and I need to take a day of personal leave. If I'm not eligible for leave, just dock my pay. Thanks. I'll call you tonight."

He'd figure out what that "urgent" matter was later. Right now he didn't have time.

It was almost ten o'clock before he reached downtown Seattle—the traffic had been horrendous and the trip that would normally take him ninety minutes had taken two and a half hours. Alex had hoped to make a stop at his apartment there so he could change into a suit, but he didn't have enough time, so his jeans, sweater, and work boots were going to have to suffice.

When he walked into the paneled conference room of the foundation's offices, he had to bite back a smile at the expressions on the faces of the eight board members sitting around the huge cherrywood table. Greeting them, he saw that Alicia Herman and Jonathan St. Clair were missing. Too bad. They were both realistic members with progressive views on health care and would have been unlikely to be swayed by anything Richard would have to say to the contrary.

Marti smiled at him. "Nice outfit," she murmured as he took his seat at the head of the table. "Want some coffee?"

Alex nodded gratefully. "Thanks."

When she left the room to get his coffee, Richard said, "I didn't know you were going to be here, Alex."

"Wouldn't have missed it," Alex said dryly.

"You're looking well," Lydia Cross, who was a partner in a prestigious Seattle law firm, said. "Have you been traveling?"

Alex kept his answer vague and pretended he hadn't seen the avid curiosity in her eyes.

Once Marti returned and was ready to take the minutes, Alex called the meeting to order. The only agenda item was Richard's request to cut off funding for KeepKidsWell. Alex listened courteously while Richard presented his case and made his recommendation.

Without stopping for questions, Richard said, "I move that—"

"Let's have some discussion before you make a formal motion," Alex said, interrupting before Richard could finish.

"According to Robert's Rules of Order, discussion comes *after* a motion is made," Richard said angrily.

"It can be done either way," Alex contradicted. "And this is the way I'd like to do it."

Richard's jaw clenched, and he glared at Alex.

Alex didn't care. In fact, right now he didn't care if Richard took his money and his weirdness and left the Hunt Foundation for good. Sometimes the price you had to pay to keep things moving smoothly was more than you were willing to pay. And this was one of those times.

"Now," Alex continued, "I agree that Philippa stepped over the line when she called you an idiot in public, Richard, but the fact is, you provoked her. I personally heard you telling Winston over there…" Alex inclined his head toward Winston Legrand, a retired bank president "…that Philippa didn't exhibit good sense and was running KeepKidsWell into the ground. And if you said that to him, I'm sure you've said it to others."

"Too bad if the truth hurts," Richard sputtered.

"Maybe she felt she was expressing the truth, too," Alex said.

There was an audible intake of breath from some of the board members.

"What does *that* mean?" Richard said.

"Just what I said."

"I don't have to sit here and listen to this!" Richard stood so abruptly, he knocked his chair over. "You, young man, think you're God here. You think you can do whatever you want, whenever you want, just because you're Harry's son. Well, let me tell you something. I carry some weight here, too. Let's just take a vote on this and see who's right and who's wrong."

"Sit down, Richard," Alex said calmly.

"I'll stand if I want to." Richard's face had turned a dark, mottled red.

Quietly, yet firmly, Alex said, "As long as I'm chairman of this board, we will conduct our business in a professional, courteous manner. You will either sit down and lower your voice or I will ask you to leave."

A person could have heard a pin drop. No one moved. No one said a word. And although Richard glared at Alex, he reached back, righted his chair, and sat back down. "I demand you let me make my motion."

"Fine," Alex said, "make it."

"I move that the Hunt Foundation stop giving any money to KeepKidsWell and that we permanently strike them from our list of recipients."

"Seconded," said Winston Legrand.

Alex wasn't surprised. He'd figured Winston would vote with Richard. "Any discussion?"

Lydia Cross spoke up. "I think Mrs. Von Kohler exhibited bad judgment by casting doubt about a board member's intelligence, but I don't think her lapse should be held against a charity we all know is doing a remarkable job in helping kids at risk."

"Helping kids have sex is more like it," Winston grumbled.

Richard snorted. "You can say that again."

"The condoms are only given to teens who are

already having sex," Lydia pointed out. "And that's to protect them against HIV."

The discussion continued in this vein for more than twenty minutes, with neither side yielding an inch. Finally Alex said, "If there are no new points to raise, I think it's time for a vote." He didn't know what would happen, but clearly, this discussion was a waste of time.

Alex breathed a sigh of relief when the vote was three in favor of the motion, five against. Alex only voted in the event of a tie, so his vote wasn't needed.

"I won't be a party to this any longer," Richard said. "I'm resigning from this board, and I will no longer lend my financial support to the foundation."

"We're sorry to see you go," Alex said, "but it's your prerogative."

Winston looked as if he was going to say something, but he didn't. Alex almost smiled. Winston liked being on the foundation's board. Since he'd retired, he had too much time on his hands and he no longer felt that people viewed him as important. Being on the board of the Hunt Foundation helped assuage those feelings and gave him opportunities to pretend he was still a mover and shaker.

After everyone had gone home, Marti said, "God, I miss you, Alex. When are you going to be done with whatever it is you're doing?"

"Soon, I hope." Alex looked at his watch. It was almost noon. It was too late to worry about going into work at the distribution center today. Besides, he wasn't sure he wanted to see P.J. until he had a good story for her. "What else do I need to catch up on here? I can give you a few more hours."

Marti smiled. "Well, since you asked…"

"P.J., you're not going to believe this!" Anna's voice fairly quivered with excitement.

P.J. wasn't in the mood for gossip. She'd been working for hours, and she couldn't make her inventory and her orders balance. No matter how many times she added her columns, she had more equipment in several categories than she was supposed to have. And in two other categories, she had less than she should. "What?" she said impatiently.

"I don't want to tell you over the phone. Come to the mail room and I'll show you."

"Anna, I'm up to my eyeballs in—"

"P.J., I'm telling you, you want to see this." She lowered her voice. "It's about Alex."

"Alex? You mean Alex who works here?"

"What other Alex is there?" Anna said dryly. "Now get your butt over here. Hurry. You're going to die when you see this."

Five minutes later, P.J. entered the busy mailing

center and headed straight for Anna's office, which was in the far corner. Anna sat behind her desk and when she spied P.J., she beckoned her in.

"Close the door," she said. Her dark eyes sparkled with excitement.

"This had better be good," P.J. said.

"C'mere." Anna had an open magazine on her desk.

P.J. walked around to stand next to Anna. The magazine was one of those celebrity rags Anna was so fond of. P.J. started to say something derogatory when she saw what Anna was pointing to. It was a photo in a section called VIPs. P.J. looked closer, then snatched up the magazine. She stared at the photo. It showed a beautiful, dark-haired young girl in a yellow dress seated across from a slightly older man who was a dead ringer for Alex. They were obviously in a restaurant, leaning toward each other intimately and talking.

P.J. swallowed. The caption under the photo read:

Julie Fitzpatrick, who is usually part of the Seattle club scene, shown on a recent Sunday enjoying a quiet brunch with her half-brother, Alex Hunt, son of Harrison Hunt, billionaire founder of HuntCom.

Alex *Hunt!*

P.J.'s heart pounded in her ears. She kept staring at the photo. She couldn't believe it. Alex. Her Alex was really Alex Hunt.

"P.J.?"

P.J. blinked. She'd almost forgotten Anna was there.

"Can you *believe* it?" Anna said. "You were right all the time. You thought he didn't belong here. What do you think he's doing here, anyway?"

"Can I have this magazine?" P.J. said. "Or at least this page?"

Anna frowned. "Um…sure."

P.J.'s hands trembled as she tore the page from the magazine. She was so angry and so upset, she wasn't sure she could talk to Anna. Thank God she'd never told Anna that she was seeing Alex. She almost had, one day, but had changed her mind at the last minute. It had been the only rational decision she'd ever made concerning Alex.

Oh, God. Hunt. He's a Hunt. Harrison Hunt's son. No wonder he didn't want to talk about his family. He's been lying to me the whole time I've known him. Everything about him is a lie. Everything he's said. Everything he's done.

She couldn't look at Anna, but she knew she had to say something. "Don't tell anyone about this, okay? Let me deal with it first."

"Okay. What are you going to do?"

"I don't know. I have to think about it."

Anna nodded. "I didn't think you'd be so upset."

P.J. knew she needed to get a grip. Anna was suspicious now, and that's the last thing P.J. wanted. "I just don't like being lied to. He was probably sent here to spy on us."

"You think?"

"Why else?"

"But we do a great job here. That just doesn't make sense."

"Look," P.J. said, "I've got to get back to my desk. Remember. Don't say anything about this."

"I won't."

P.J. knew Anna was probably frowning as she watched P.J. leave and head back to the floor. But right then, P.J. didn't care what Anna thought. All *she* could think about was what a fool she'd been. Oh, God, she thought, remembering the way she'd offered absolutely no resistance to Alex. She'd been like putty in his hands. And all the time, he'd just been toying with her. Amusing himself while putting in his time as some kind of spy for his father.

She thought about how concerned she'd been when she got his message this morning. How she'd even considered covering for him because he was right; he hadn't worked there long enough to have a personal day. Oh! How could she have been so stupid?

And to think she'd even been going to tell him about her medical problems, feeling it was unfair to keep seeing him without letting him know she was damaged goods. Tears stung her eyes, and that made her madder still. She *never* cried! Crying was weak, and she wasn't weak.

By the time she reached her desk, she had managed to get herself under some kind of control, because she needed to think. She was suddenly very glad Alex wasn't there today, because when she confronted him, she wanted to be calm and prepared.

"P.J."

She jumped. Chick, her assistant, stood there frowning down at her. "Yes, Chick?"

"Everything okay?"

"Why wouldn't it be?" she snapped.

"I don't know. I just thought—"

She almost said, *Don't think*. In the nick of time, she stopped herself and said instead, "I'm fine. Did you need something?"

He shook his head and backed away. "No, no. I just wanted to see—" This time he broke off. "Never mind. I'm going back to work."

"Good. See if you can have the weekly report on

my desk by…" She made a show of looking at her watch. "Two o'clock."

Chick saluted. "Your wish is my command."

P.J. was ashamed of herself. She hadn't been very nice to Chick, and aside from Rick, he was her most valuable employee. This, too, could be laid at Alex Noble/Hunt's door, she thought bitterly.

For the rest of the afternoon, she didn't even try to work. She knew it would be a lost cause. Instead, she looked up everything she could find about Alex Hunt on the Internet. The more she learned, the more confused she became. He was nothing like what she would have imagined a son of Harrison Hunt to be. He wasn't a playboy. He didn't do the party circuit. He didn't constantly have some gorgeous model or actress on his arm. And he didn't throw his money around. According to a profile the Seattle paper had done on him several years ago, Alex Hunt lived quietly and worked hard. He'd headed the Hunt Foundation for ten years, and according to all reports, it was his passion.

In an article about one of the charities supported by the Hunt Foundation, there was the text of a speech he'd given at the charity's annual fund-raiser. P.J. found herself nodding as she read what he'd said. She agreed with every word.

At the end of the day, she didn't know what to

think. Everything she'd learned about Alex indicated he held the same beliefs she held. That he was a man she could admire and respect.

But if that was true, why was he working at the distribution center? Why had he lied?

None of it made sense.

And none of it changed the fact that P.J. felt like the biggest fool who had ever lived.

While Alex was in Seattle, he had decided to take care of some things. He decided to stay in the city overnight and do the things he hadn't been able to do from Jansen, like visit his bank, touch base with a couple of his pet charities, and take Georgie to dinner.

He'd put off calling P.J. but once he was back in his Seattle apartment, he knew he couldn't stall any longer. So at ten o'clock, he placed the call.

The phone at the other end rang four times. Then it revolved to voice mail. "This is P.J.," the message began. "Can't take your call right now. At the tone, leave a message."

Alex frowned. Where was she? he wondered. "Hey, P.J., it's me, Alex. I'm on my way back to Jansen, but I probably won't get there until late. I'll see you in the morning."

Since he would have to leave the city by five-thirty to insure getting to the distribution center on time tomorrow, Alex decided to call it a night.

Thirty minutes later, he was sound asleep.

P.J. stared at the phone.

She didn't pick up.

She had no desire to talk to Alex tonight. Not on the phone. She wanted to face him when he lied to her. She wanted to see his face when she confronted him with what she knew about him.

Right now, that was about the only satisfaction she was likely to have in this whole sorry affair.

If only it didn't hurt so much.

If only she could just laugh this off.

After all, as Courtney had pointed out, *she* wasn't who she was pretending to be, either.

But the situations were entirely different. She had never lied to Alex. Any question he'd ever asked her, she had answered truthfully, whereas he'd lied to her from the get-go.

Well, never again.

Never, never, never again.

This time, P.J. had learned her lesson. She'd thought Alex was different. She'd even begun to imagine the possibility of a future with him. Even begun to think that maybe her medical problems wouldn't matter to him. Even begun to admit to herself that she was falling in love with him and had harbored a secret hope that he felt the same way.

Tears ran down her face as the truth sank in.

Alex didn't love her.

And now he never would.

Chapter Twelve

P.J. arrived at the distribution center before seven. She knew she looked terrible, with dark circles under her eyes that no amount of makeup could disguise. She'd had a bad night, had tossed and turned and slept fitfully. And what little sleep she'd been able to manage had been filled with dark dreams where she was lost in some kind of horrible maze, and no matter what she did or which way she turned, she couldn't find her way out.

You didn't have to be a psychiatrist or analyst to know the significance of *that* dream, she thought wryly.

"You're here early."

P.J. managed a smile for Terri Wayland, the night supervisor on the floor. "Yeah, I've got a few things hanging fire. Thought I'd get an early start."

"Anything I can help with?"

"Thanks, no. But I appreciate the offer."

"Okay. Just holler if you need me." Terri waved and walked away.

P.J. headed for the kitchen, got herself a cup of coffee, then walked across to her office. After closing the door firmly, she booted her computer. Once it was finished loading programs, she opened Word and began composing a letter.

At eight o'clock, as the day shift began coming in, she opened her office door and strode out onto the floor. A glance at the time cards showed that Alex had already clocked in. She was just about to look for him when she saw him walking toward her. As usual, he was dressed in jeans, work boots, and today—a chilly, late October day—a red plaid flannel shirt with a black T-shirt underneath. Unfortunately for her, he looked even more handsome and sexy than usual. He held a mug of coffee.

"'Morning," he said, giving her one of his dimpled smiles. "I wanted to apologize for yester—"

"Let's go into my office," she said, interrupting him. She didn't return his smile.

His smile slowly faded. She could see he was startled by her abrupt tone. Good. He obviously had no idea she was on to him. Not waiting to see if he was following her, she turned and marched off.

By the time she reached her office, her hard-won calm had disappeared and she was seething. God, he must think she was stupid. *Well, he's right, isn't he?* Once they were both inside the office, she shut the door and gave him a hard-eyed stare.

"P.J., what's wrong? I know I shouldn't have taken off without asking you first, but it couldn't be—"

Once more she interrupted him. "I'll tell you what's wrong, Alex. *This* is what's wrong." She grabbed the page she'd torn from the magazine, which was sitting on the edge of her desk, and thrust it at him.

He frowned. "What's this?"

"Just read it." She jabbed her finger at the offending photo. "That."

Her chest felt too tight and her head pounded from a killer headache that no amount of Advil had been able to banish. He finished reading and lowered the page. His dark eyes, eyes that she loved— *had* loved, she corrected, met her gaze. Although she was trembling inside, she told herself she could do this. *This isn't the first time you've had to face*

*something painful. Grit your teeth. Don't let him see
how much you're hurting.*

"P.J.," he said softly. "I can explain."

"Really?" she scoffed.

"It…I know it looks bad, but there's a reason
for—"

"For pretending to be someone you're not? For
lying to me?"

"The only thing I lied about is my name…and my
reason for being here. Everything else was the truth."

"Why the hell *are* you here, Alex? Was I right in
the beginning? Were you sent here to spy on us?"

"No." He walked over and put his coffee on the
desk. "Absolutely not. My reasons for being here
are personal. They have nothing to do with the
business or the job you're doing here or anything
remotely like that."

She glared at him. How could he continue to lie
to her? And with such sincerity, too? If she didn't
know better, she'd absolutely believe him. Fury and
heartbreak warred within as she fought to maintain
control of emotions that threatened to erupt. "I can't
believe you are *still* lying to me. What possible
personal reason could you have for leaving the Hunt
Foundation, which is supposedly so important to
you? Oh, yes," she added, seeing the surprise on his
face. "I read about you. I read all about you."

"I…" He seemed to be struggling with himself. Finally, with a heavy sigh, he said, "Look, P.J., can we sit down? I'll explain everything."

P.J. wanted to say no. She wanted to tell him to get out of her office. But he was Alex Hunt, wasn't he? He was the son of the owner of HuntCom and she was just an employee. She actually worked for *him*, not the other way around. "Fine," she said. She walked behind her desk and sat in her swivel chair.

Alex sat across from her.

Why did he have to look so damned gorgeous? Obviously, *he'd* had a great night's sleep. She certainly didn't see any bags under *his* eyes. "Well?" she said coldly. "I'm waiting."

"The reason I'm here is because of my father."

"I figured that."

"It's not what you think. Do you know much about my father? His personal life, that is?"

P.J. shrugged.

Seeing she wasn't going to help him out, he said, "He was married four times. None of his marriages lasted longer than two years. Each marriage produced a son. When I told you I was one of four brothers, that's the truth. Neither I nor my brothers have ever been married." He grimaced. "We didn't have a great example of marriage."

P.J. wished she had a fresh cup of coffee. Anything to occupy her hands. Anything to wrest her gaze from his.

"Last spring my father had a heart attack. It was a pretty serious one, and it scared him."

P.J. nodded. She remembered. At the time, Steve Mallery had been concerned about what would happen if Harrison Hunt died.

"Afterwards," Alex continued, "he seemed different. More reflective. I guess he finally realized he wasn't indestructible and wouldn't live forever." Alex smiled crookedly. "Anyway, he called a meeting of the four of us—me and my brothers—in July, and told us he was tired of waiting for us to get married and give him grandchildren. He said, quote, left to our devices, he never would have any, unquote. He said a few other things…then he gave us an ultimatum. Within a year, he wanted each of us married, and by the end of that time, he also wanted our wives to be pregnant or already to have given birth."

P.J. wasn't sure she'd heard him correctly. "You're kidding, right?"

"No, unfortunately, I'm not. That wasn't the end of the ultimatum, either. The women we married couldn't be gold diggers. My father isn't big on gold diggers," Alex added sarcastically, "because he married enough of them himself. To accomplish this, he said we couldn't tell our prospective brides who we were. That was the only way we could be sure they were marrying us for ourselves and not for his money."

As what Alex told her sank in, P.J. stared at him, appalled. "And this is why you *lied* to me? Because of some kind of stupid agreement you made with your father? You're here at HuntCom looking for a *bride?*"

"I'm sorry, P.J. I didn't want to lie to you. But I had no choice. If I'd told you who I really was, I would have been letting my brothers down. Hell, I'm letting them down *now*. See, that's the way Harry got us to agree to his scheme. He threatened to sell the entire corporation, everything that makes up HuntCom, including the foundation, which is my passion, and the special projects and places that are important to my brothers."

P.J. couldn't believe what she was hearing. This whole situation had been bad enough when she'd thought Alex was a corporate spy. *That*, at least, she could understand. She didn't have to like it, but she could understand it. "So this is about money."

"It's not about money."

"Oh, of course it is. You can dress it up any way you like but at the root of everything is money. Your father certainly understands that."

"I don't care about the money. I do care about the foundation and the work we're doing, but I would even have given that up if I'd had to. But my father put one other condition on his proposal to us—we all had to agree. If even one of us didn't, all of us would lose out. I couldn't do that to my brothers."

"So you went along with his nutty scheme that's like something out of the Dark Ages. You came here under false pretenses and you lied to me and everyone else. Tell me, Alex, just when *did* you plan to tell me the truth? Or didn't I figure into your plans at all? Was I just some kind of side diversion while you were looking for the perfect, gullible candidate to be Mrs. Alex Hunt?" She was trying not to think about the baby Alex had mentioned. The baby Harrison Hunt had ordered. The baby P.J. could never give him.

He stared at her. "How can you say that? You must know it's not true. I was attracted to you from the moment I met you." He heaved a sigh. "Look, this isn't the way I'd have chosen to say this. I'd rather be doing it over wine and candlelight. The truth is, I love you, P.J. I'd want you to be my wife even if my father'd had nothing to do with my meeting you."

"You expect me to *believe* that? How can I ever believe another word you say? By your own admission, you *have* to go along with your father's demands, so you'd say anything to keep from upsetting your little applecart."

"I've already upset it. You know who I am, so I've broken my father's rules."

P.J. gripped her hands below the desk to keep them from shaking. She wanted, more than anything, to believe him, but how could she? And what if she *did* believe him? What good would it do her? She couldn't give him a child. When he found out about that, he would no longer want her, anyway.

"You know, you haven't exactly been playing it straight either, P.J., or should I say…Paige."

She wasn't even surprised he knew about her family. "Don't try to make this about me, Alex. I repudiated my family's money. But *you!* You did what you did *for* the money. And nothing you can say will ever change my mind about that." Then she reached for the letter she'd typed that morning and handed it to him.

"What is this?" he said.

"It's my letter of resignation."

"Don't be ridiculous." Without even looking at it, he ripped the letter in two, then in four, then in eight, throwing the pieces in the wastebasket. "If you want to quit, go talk to Steve Mallery. He's your boss, not me. But I'll save you the trouble. I'll leave instead. In fact, I'll go right now. Unless you want two weeks notice?"

She swallowed. She wanted to say, *Please don't go*. But she didn't say anything.

Ten seconds later, he walked out the door. He didn't look back.

"Hey, Alex, what's going on?"

Alex was angry and frustrated, and the last thing he wanted to do was talk to anyone, but he could hardly ignore Rick. "Look, I can't talk right now. But if you want, we can meet for a beer after work."

"*Meet* for a beer? Where're you going?"

"I'll explain later, okay? Right now, I have to get out of here." Alex gestured toward P.J.'s office. "But if you can't wait till tonight, you could always go ask P.J. what's going on. She's got all the answers."

"Oh, Alex," Cornelia said. "I was afraid of this."

"Yeah," he said glumly. "I guess I should have been worried, but somehow I thought everything would work out."

"Did you tell her you love her?"

"Yes, but I handled it badly. She doesn't believe me."

Cornelia sighed. "Shall I try to talk to her?"

He shook his head. "This is something I have to

do. First I'm going to let her cool off. Then I'll try talking to her again." He looked up, and the sympathetic look on his aunt's face was nearly his undoing. "I don't want to lose her, Aunt Cornelia. Even if it means losing the foundation and J.T., Justin and Gray losing the ranch and the island and the company."

"She's that important to you?"

"Yes."

"Then do whatever it takes to get her back, Alex. Don't let anything, especially not pride, stand in your way. Because love like that doesn't come along very often. And it rarely comes twice."

P.J. didn't last the day. At two o'clock, she could no longer keep up the pretense that all was normal. She told Chick she wasn't feeling well and was going home.

"You're going *home?*" he said in disbelief.

"Yes." She knew what he was thinking. P.J. never took a sick day. In fact, in the nearly eight years she'd been with the company, she could count on one hand the amount of days she'd missed, and two of them were when she was called for jury duty.

She barely made it to her car before she burst into tears. She, Paige Jeffers Kincaid, tough girl, someone who never cried, bawled her eyes out.

She was still crying when she arrived at her condo.

She cried off and on all evening. She'd stop, decide to quit feeling sorry for herself, tell herself she wasn't the first woman to be taken in by brown eyes and dimples, then she'd start crying again.

The phone rang once. She looked at it, then jumped up to see who it was.

Alex.

She put the phone back in its base. She didn't want to talk to him. What was there left to say?

Maybe he does love you. Maybe it wouldn't matter to him that you can't have a baby. Maybe he'd want to marry you, anyway.

Oh, sure. And give up his foundation? Give up all that money? Give up the chance to have dozens of little Alex Hunts? Yeah, and pigs can now fly.

You could test him.

But if she did, and if he failed the test, she knew she would be so devastated, she might not be able to pretend otherwise. At least this way, she still did have her pride.

And not much else.

On and on her thoughts raged. But the outcome was always the same. Alex was history.

Get over it! It's not the end of the world. It's not the death of a child. It's just the end of a love affair you always knew was going to end anyway.

And then the tears started again.

Finally, at midnight, she fell into an exhausted sleep.

Alex's night wasn't much better than P.J.'s. He met Rick for a beer after work and told him the whole sorry tale. Rick just kept shaking his head.

"Geez, Alex. You sure have made a mess of things," he said when Alex finally wound down.

"Tell me about it."

"Are you *really* old Harry's son?"

"Afraid so," Alex said dejectedly.

"You know, if this wasn't so damned serious, and if it didn't involve P.J., who I think the world of, it would be funny."

"Really? You think it's funny?" Alex said. He finished off his beer and ordered another.

"Think about it. You're a millionaire pretending to be an ordinary Joe, and P.J., also no slouch in the money department, is pretending to be an ordinary Jane. I mean, it's like a comedy. It could be a movie."

Alex smiled. Rick had a point. "It's a comedy of errors."

"Look," Rick said, finishing off his own beer, "I know P.J. She's got a temper and she's stubborn. She would also hate thinking she'd been made to look like a fool. But she's also smart and I think she probably really cares for you, so if you keep after her, she'll probably come around."

"You think?"

"Worth a try. I mean, what have you got to lose?"

Alex thought about what Cornelia had said and what Rick had said and knew they were both right. He decided not to wait until morning, when he'd planned to try to talk to P.J. again. Instead, he called her as soon as he got to his apartment, but there was no answer. When her voice mail kicked in, he decided not to leave a message. He would call her tomorrow.

Better yet, he would go to see her tomorrow. He would sit in front of her condo until she came home and she wouldn't be able to avoid him. She would have to listen to him.

And this time, he would not take no for an answer.

Chapter Thirteen

Over the next two weeks, Alex tried everything. He called P.J. He cornered her at her condo. He sent e-mails. He sent flowers. He sent a singing telegram. He wrote her a long letter.

Nothing worked.

She kept saying no.

The week before Thanksgiving, he decided to play his trump card. He drove to Bellevue, went into Tiffany's, and bought the prettiest rose-cut diamond ring they had. He knew better than to get something ostentatious, so he settled for a one-carat stone set in platinum. Understated and elegant.

When he got back to Jansen, he called her and asked if he could come and see her that night for "one last time."

"Alex, it's over. Why can't you just accept that?"

"Thing is, I'm leaving Jansen. I just wanted to say goodbye. And I have something for you that I wanted to give you before I go," he added quickly, before she could point out that they could just as easily say goodbye by phone.

She sighed. "Okay. You can come. But make it early because I'm going out at seven-thirty."

"I'll be there by six."

Promptly at six, Alex rang her doorbell. The Tiffany's box was safely secured in the zippered pocket of his leather jacket. His heart turned over when she opened the door. She looked tired.

More than tired. Sad.

And he knew he was the cause of that sadness. He'd hurt her and now she'd erected a barrier around her heart, and so far, he hadn't been able to get past it. It was the first time in his adult life he hadn't been able to accomplish a goal he'd set for himself, and Alex didn't like the feeling. More than that, he hated that he was the reason for the wounded expression in her eyes.

"Come on in," she said.

She invited him to sit on the sofa in her living room, but he said he'd rather stand. "I'm not going to keep you long."

There was an awkward silence for a few seconds. Then they both spoke at once.

"So you're leaving," she said.

"I've really missed you," he said.

She didn't smile. "What is it you want, Alex?"

"You know what I want."

"Tonight, I meant."

"Tonight and every night," he said, looking into her eyes.

She swallowed and backed up, even though he hadn't come any closer.

Deciding it was make-or-break time, Alex unzipped the pocket containing the Tiffany's box, removed it and held it out.

"Wh-what is that?" she whispered, backing up even more.

This time, he stepped forward until she had nowhere else to go. Now only a foot separated them and he could smell the combination of the light fragrance she wore and the lemony shampoo she used on her hair.

"P.J., I love you. I never thought I could fall in love like this. More than anything, I want us to be together." He reached for her hand and put the box into it. "Please say you'll marry me. But if you're determined not to marry, then I'll be content for us to just live together. And if that doesn't prove to you that I don't care about my father's money, then I guess nothing ever will."

She stared at the box. And then, shocking him, her eyes filled with tears. She shook her head and held her hand out. "I—I can't take this, Alex. I can't marry you. Please stop asking me. Because the answer is always going to be the same."

"P.J...." He didn't take the box.

"I want you to go now." She pushed the box back into his pocket.

"This doesn't make sen—"

"Goodbye, Alex." She'd brushed the tears away.

He didn't know what else to say. He could see she wasn't going to be swayed. There was something here he didn't understand, something she wasn't telling him, but what it could be, he couldn't imagine.

She walked to the door and opened it.

Okay, he thought, *I'll go. But this isn't the end of this. Hunts don't quit. They just regroup for another time.*

He walked to the door, but before going out, he bent down and kissed her. Although she held herself stiffly, he felt her body's reaction.

She loves me. She can deny it as many times as she wants, but I know she loves me.

"Take care of yourself," he said softly.

"You, too."

The door shut firmly behind him.

P.J. was so sick of herself. So sick of crying. So sick of being the kind of woman she had always despised. Why? Why had she let Alex get under her skin this way?

Please, God, she prayed. *Please help me get over him. Because I can't live this way. And I don't know what to do to change things.*

Alex took care of everything that needed taking care of in Jansen. He paid his landlord the necessary amount to get out of his lease. He closed his Jansen bank account, settled with the utility companies and cancelled the phone and cable service.

He called Goodwill and gave them all his furniture and most of his distribution-center work clothes. He donated the television set to the local women's shelter. Then he packed up the few belongings he was keeping, tossed the bags in the bed of his truck, and drove back to Seattle.

* * *

"Hey, Rick, what's going on with P.J.? Jenny said she's taken a leave of absence." Jenny was the switchboard operator at the distribution center.

"Hi, Alex. Yeah, she left right before Thanksgiving and she won't be back till January second."

"Where'd she go?"

"I don't know. She just said she needed a vacation. I, uh, kind of figured it might have something to do with you."

"Damn," Alex muttered. "Do you think she's staying with her family?" Alex had tried her at home and been told by a recording that her number had been changed and the new number was unlisted. And when he'd tried her cell phone, he got a message saying that number was no longer in service. It was obvious she was deliberately cutting him out of her life.

"Like I said, she didn't say what her plans were."

"If you hear from her, would you let me know?"

Rick hesitated. "Thing is, Alex, I really don't want to be in the middle of this. P.J.'s been my friend a long time, and—"

"I understand," Alex said wearily. "You're right. I shouldn't have put you on the spot like that."

They talked awhile more, Alex asking about Maria and the kids, Rick asking about Alex's job at the foundation, then they promised they'd get to-gether before too long, and hung up.

Alex sat at his desk and thought a few minutes. Then he made a couple of phone calls and on the third try got what he wanted—the private number of the Kincaid family home. Two minutes later, he was listening to it ring.

"Kincaid residence," said a soft female voice.

"This is Alex Hunt. May I speak with Paige, please?"

"Miss Paige?"

"Yes."

"I'm sorry, sir, but Miss Paige isn't here."

"When do you expect her back?"

"No, you misunderstood. Miss Paige doesn't live here."

"I know," Alex said, "but I understood that she was staying there for the holidays."

"No, sir, I'm sorry, she's not."

"You wouldn't happen to have a number where I could reach her?"

"I'm sorry, Mr. Hunt. I cannot give out that kind of information. If you want to leave a message, I'll be happy to give it to her if she should call here."

Alex heaved a frustrated sigh after thanking the housekeeper or whoever it was who had answered the phone and disconnected the call. He wondered if P.J.'s e-mail address was still the same. He was sure her work e-mail was unchanged, but he didn't want to send her a message that way. No telling who might read her e-mail while she was gone. And e-mail was totally unsatisfactory, anyway.

He was back to square one.

With no idea how to advance.

P.J. loved Italy. It suited her perfectly. The weather, the people, the food, the wine, the attitude. She especially loved that nothing there reminded her of Alex. It had been worth borrowing against her 401(k) plan to come.

She spent a week in Venice, then moved on to Florence, then to the hills of Tuscany. In Tuscany, she rented a small villa. Even now, in December, the sun shone, the flowers bloomed and the sky was filled with a golden light she'd never seen anywhere else. It was glorious. If she'd been a painter, she'd have tried to capture the beauty of the place. If she'd been a musician, she'd have composed something glorious there, she was sure of it.

She was neither; all she could do was be thankful for the chance to experience the country's wonder.

She healed in Italy. Yes, she still felt melancholy at times, but the constant pain subsided and she grew—if not happy—then content.

But Italy wasn't reality.

And sooner or later, everyone had to face reality. So on her birthday—three days before Christmas—she packed up her things, locked the villa, drove her rental car back to Florence, and flew home.

It took Alex some time, but with persistent digging, he obtained the home phone number of P.J.'s sister Courtney.

"Hello, Alex," she said after he'd introduced himself. "I've heard a lot about you."

He quickly explained what he wanted.

"Where do you live?" she asked.

Taken aback, he said, "I have an apartment in downtown Seattle. Why?"

"Would you like to meet me for lunch tomorrow? I think it's better if we talk in person." She named a small restaurant that was fairly close to his office.

The next day, Alex arrived at the restaurant at twelve-forty-five. He'd made the reservation for one o'clock and had wanted to be early. Courtney was shown to the table a few minutes after one. Although her coloring was very different from P.J.'s, he could see the family resemblance, especially in the shape of her eyes and her smile.

She was very attractive and very pregnant, which—in his eyes—only added to her appeal.

After she was seated and they'd placed their orders, she said, "Paige would kill me if she knew I was here."

He nodded. Knowing P.J., he was sure Courtney was right. "Why *are* you here?"

"Because I know Paige loves you, and I want her to be happy."

"And I love *her*. But it doesn't seem to be doing me any good. Where *is* she, anyway?"

"Actually, she should be home today. Not in Jansen, though. She's going to spend the holidays with our parents."

"Where was she?"

"She went to Italy."

"What can I do to convince her to marry me?"

Courtney eyed him thoughtfully. "Tell me something, Alex. Does your wanting to marry her have anything to do with that crazy scheme of your father's?"

"No."

"You're sure?"

"Positive."

Still she studied him, as if trying to make up her mind about him. "I want to tell you something, but

I'll be betraying a confidence. Very few people know about this, and that's how Paige wanted to keep it."

Alarm bells went off in Alex's mind. Was P.J. sick? Did she have some kind of terrible disease? Is that what was behind her refusal to marry him? He was almost afraid to hear what Courtney had to say.

Just then their waiter came with their food, and they stopped talking until he was gone again.

"Please tell me," Alex said. He ignored his lunch.

Courtney sighed heavily. "Six years ago, Paige had to have one of her ovaries removed. She'd been having a lot of pain, and tests revealed that her right ovary was badly infected. They couldn't save it. The following year she developed endometriosis. Do you know anything about that?"

"No, I don't."

"I'm not going to try to explain it. If you want to know more about it, you can research it on the Internet. However, most women who get it have problems getting pregnant. Because Paige only has one ovary and because the endometriosis affected it, there's very little chance she can ever get pregnant. That's why she's been saying no to you, Alex. She knows she can never give you children."

Alex was stunned. At first, the knowledge dismayed him, but it wasn't long before he realized it made no difference to him. He still loved P.J. and he still wanted to marry her. Hell, they could adopt kids. Half a dozen of them, if she wanted.

Courtney smiled. "You don't care," she said softly.

Alex smiled back. "No, I don't."

She picked up her fork to begin eating her salad. "Now I know why P.J. loves you. Of course, the fact that you're gorgeous doesn't hurt."

Alex laughed, the first real laugh he'd had in weeks. Then he, too, began to eat his lunch.

P.J. would be glad when the day was over. She'd always loved Christmas, but this Christmas had been hard for her. Her composure had threatened to crack several times, especially during the family's traditional carol-singing around the piano, and the effort to keep a smile on her face had exhausted her.

If only …

But all the if onlys in the world wouldn't change a thing. Alex was no longer part of her life. The sooner she was able to accept that gracefully, the better off she'd be.

"So do you have any plans for tomorrow?" Courtney said, coming over to where P.J. stood.

P.J. shrugged. "I thought I might hit the sales."

"You? Shopping? Has hell frozen over?"

P.J. couldn't help laughing. "I need some new workout clothes and I know the shopping is better here than it is in Jansen."

"How about if I come with you?"

"You don't really want to do that, do you?"

"Sure. It'll be fun. We can have lunch out, then shop till we drop. Well, until I drop, anyway."

"Well…" P.J. didn't really want to make a day of it. Yet what else did she have to do?

"I'll come by about eleven-thirty," Courtney said. "Brad's on vacation. He can stay home with the kids." She grinned. "Do him good."

Later, as P.J. prepared for bed, she thought about how much she loved Courtney. And all her family. Her mother got under her skin sometimes, but she still loved her. Thinking about all the things she'd never have—a husband, children, grandchildren— she could feel herself getting weepy again. This made her mad. *Stop that. Moping around and feeling sorry for yourself does no one any good, especially not you. Suck it up. Act like an adult.*

But it was so hard.

Much harder than she would ever have believed.

P.J. decided to wear something dressier than her standard pants and casual blouse. So she unearthed a soft forest-green wool skirt and paired it with an ivory cashmere sweater and high-heeled boots. Now she wouldn't embarrass Courtney, who, even six months pregnant, always looked stylish.

P.J.'s parents had left the house about nine to attend a brunch and bridge party given by some friends, so P.J. and the housekeeper were the only ones home. P.J. went downstairs to wait for Courtney and settled herself in the living room where she could look at the tree—a giant Douglas fir trimmed in gold and white.

If I ever have a tree, it'll be traditional, with all colors of balls and tinsel and multicolored lights. A real family-type tree.

Oh, God, she was pathetic. She couldn't seem to make her mind go in a different direction. Every single thought she'd had since coming home from Italy had somehow been tied to husbands, kids, families.

I wish I could have stayed there forever.

Restless, she got up and stood at the big bay window. It was a pretty day outside—cold but sunny. She was glad now that Courtney had suggested their day together. As she watched, a silver SUV turned into the drive and slowly came up the hill toward the house.

P.J. frowned. Who was coming? She didn't recognize the truck.

A moment later, the SUV entered the circle in front of the house and came to a stop. And a moment after that, the driver's-side door opened and...*oh, my God*...it was Alex! Sudden panic filled her. And yet, as he got out of the SUV and walked to the door, she stood frozen at the window. She couldn't take her eyes off him. Dressed in dark gray slacks and a matching sweater worn under a black suede jacket, he looked sophisticated and handsome and...wonderful.

Heart pounding, P.J. finally moved, went into the front hallway and, taking a deep breath, opened the door. *Please, God, let me be strong.* For long seconds, they simply looked at each other.

Then Alex smiled. "Aren't you going to invite me in?"

P.J. licked her lips. She was fiercely glad she had taken pains with her appearance today. "What are you doing here, Alex?"

"I came because I have something to tell you, and afterwards—after we talk—I'm hoping you'll let me take you to lunch."

"I already have a lunch date."

"Courtney's not coming," he said softly.

P.J. tried not to let the shock she felt show on her face. "You've talked to Courtney?"

"Are you going to make me stand out here all day?" he countered.

Mind whirling with the implications of what he'd revealed, P.J. stepped back and gestured him in. "Let's go into the living room." She led the way, all the while telling herself not to lose her cool. *But when I get my hands on Courtney, I'll kill her.*

She deliberately chose one of the Queen Anne chairs on either side of the fireplace. Alex, though, didn't sit. Instead, absolutely shocking her, he dropped down on one knee in front of her.

"P.J.," he said, "I'm not going to waste time. We've already wasted enough time. I love you more than I thought I could ever love anyone, and I want you to be my wife. Courtney told me about your fertility problem and it doesn't make one iota of difference to me. I still want to marry you, and if we decide we want children, we'll adopt them. Now I'm not moving and I'm not leaving until you say yes."

And then he reached into his jacket pocket and pulled out a velvet box.

She looked into his eyes and saw the truth of what he'd said. And suddenly, the way she had too many times to count over the past week, she burst into tears.

Without a word, Alex stood and, taking P.J.'s hand, helped her to her feet. Then, setting the Tiffany's box on the table beside her, he put his arms around her and kissed her. And as P.J. responded, twining her arms around him and giving herself up to the kiss, she knew this was where she belonged, right here, with Alex, who really did love her after all.

Eventually P.J. repaired her makeup and Alex took her to lunch. He couldn't stop smiling, and it seemed, neither could she. In fact, they spent a lot of time just looking at each other and smiling like fools.

But after lunch, Alex knew it was time to get serious. "How would you feel about eloping?" he said.

"Eloping?"

"Yes."

"When?"

"Today."

"Today?"

He grinned. "Are you going to repeat everything I say?"

She laughed sheepishly. "I'm sorry."

God, she was adorable. He loved everything about her. Her wild red hair. Those incredible blue eyes. Her pale redhead skin with the smattering of freckles on her breastbone. Her strong body. Her stronger mind and convictions. Her honesty and courage. She was perfect.

"Here's what I thought we could do. Fly to Vegas, get married tonight or tomorrow, depending on when we get the license, spend two nights there—the Bellagio is beautiful and I've already booked a suite—"

"Wait a minute," she said. "You've *already* booked a suite? Pretty damned confident, aren't you?" She was trying to sound indignant, but her eyes and the laughter in them gave her away.

"I told you, I wasn't taking no for an answer. Not this time." He reached for her left hand. The ring looked beautiful there, just as though it had been made especially for her. "Anyway, there's no waiting period in Nevada." He smiled into her eyes. "So what do you say?"

"I do," P.J. said.

"I do," Alex said.

"I now pronounce you husband and wife," the Justice of the Peace said. He smiled at Alex. "You may kiss your bride."

P.J., thrilled beyond measure, kissed Alex with all her heart. The kiss lasted so long, the J.P. cleared his throat and said, "Ahem."

Laughing, Alex broke the kiss. Then, arms around each other, they thanked the J.P. and his wife, who had been their witness, and said goodbye.

Ten minutes later, tucked into the back of a limousine, they held hands and kissed over and over again and marveled over the fact they really were Mr. and Mrs. Alexander Hunt.

Forever.

P.J. sighed.

She was the luckiest woman in the world.

Epilogue

New Year's Eve Day...

"Nervous?" Alex asked.

"A little," P.J. admitted. "What do you think he'll say?"

"Don't know. Really don't care."

But P.J. knew Alex did care what his father thought. They were on their way to break the news that they were married. Alex wouldn't admit it for the world, because he would never want her to think he regretted marrying her, but she knew he hoped his father would back down on their agreement and accept her as Alex's wife without penalizing either him or his brothers.

They didn't have long to wait. They were almost to the Shack, as Alex wryly referred to his father's mansion overlooking Lake Washington.

P.J. had seen photos of the place, but even that didn't prepare her for the reality of its size. It was mammoth. "Holy cow," she said. "Your father really *lives* here?"

"Afraid so. It's disgustingly vulgar, isn't it?"

"Actually, it's beautiful, but who needs a place this big?"

"My sentiments exactly," Alex said. He pulled into the front turnaround and parked there.

P.J. knew his father was expecting Alex. He wasn't expecting her, because Alex had only said he was bringing someone with him and not who that someone was. Would Harrison Hunt have guessed it might be a woman? P.J. had no idea. She had butterflies in her stomach as they climbed the shallow stone steps leading to the enormous carved walnut double entrance doors.

A young maid dressed in black and wearing a white apron opened the doors at Alex's ring. She smiled tentatively. She looked as scared as P.J. felt and like P.J., was pretending she wasn't. P.J. gave her a sympathetic smile. She imagined it might not be easy to work for Alex's father.

"Mr. Hunt is expecting you," the maid said.

"Thank you," Alex said.

They were shown into a very formal living room. To P.J., the brocades and velvets and heavy dark furniture, the ornate paintings and many sculptures seemed cold. She almost shivered. She knew Alex was feeling the same way. Slipping her hand into his, she gave it a squeeze. When he looked down at her and smiled, she whispered, "I love you."

"I love you, too."

They sat close together on one of the dark-blue brocade sofas. Alex kept a tight hold on her hand.

A moment later, footsteps sounded in the hallway, and seconds later, a very tall man entered the room. P.J. would have recognized Harrison Hunt anywhere. First of all, she'd seen numerous pictures of him. Secondly, she'd always thought he bore an uncanny resemblance to the actor Jeff Goldblum. Older, of course, but strikingly similar.

Alex, still holding her hand, rose at his father's entrance.

"Well, well," Harrison Hunt said. "What have we here?" He directed his laser-like gaze to P.J.

P.J. held herself tall, with her chin up.

"Dad," Alex said, "This is P.J." He waited a beat. "My wife."

If Harrison Hunt was surprised, he hid it well. "Is that so?"

Extricating her hand from Alex's, P.J. stepped forward. "Hello, Mr. Hunt." She held out her right hand.

He took it, giving it a strong shake. P.J. returned it in kind. He examined her face carefully. "And how long have you been married to my son?"

She smiled proudly. "Three days."

"P.J.'s the daughter of Peter Prescott Kincaid," Alex said. "I met her at our distribution center. She manages the floor."

Finally Alex had managed to elicit a reaction from his father, for Harrison Hunt was visibly taken aback. "You're Peter's daughter?"

"Yes," she said.

"And you work for *me?*"

"Yes."

"Why?"

"Because I wanted to succeed on my own merits, and because I don't like the corporate world."

A huge smile broke over the older man's face. "I've known your father for many years. He's a good man."

"Yes, he is."

Clapping Alex on the back, Harrison said,

"This calls for champagne. Has Cornelia met your bride yet?"

"We're going over there when we leave here," Alex said, "but first, we have something else to tell you. You may not like this, but whether you do or not makes no difference to me...to us."

Alex's father frowned.

P.J. took a deep breath. This was something she needed to do. "I know about Alex's and his brothers' agreement with you, Mr. Hunt. Unfortunately, I probably cannot have children. I wish I could, but several specialists have said there's only a slim chance I can ever become pregnant."

Alex put his arm around her. "It doesn't matter to me. We intend to adopt."

Hearing the firm commitment in his voice, P.J. knew she had never loved him more than she did at this moment.

"How you build your family isn't important to me, either," Harrison said. "I'm just glad you want one." His smile was rueful. "And I hope you'll be a much better father to your children than I was to you."

Alex's smile was slow in coming, and P.J. heard the catch in his voice as he said, "You did your best."

"It wasn't good enough," Harrison said. He

turned his gaze to P.J. "You'll keep *him* on the straight and narrow, though, won't you?"

P.J. chuckled. "Absolutely."

"Come here, my dear," Harrison said. "Let me give you a proper hug. And welcome to our family."

After a warm hug and a kiss on the cheek, Harrison said, "Let's go into my study. We'll have our champagne there and you can tell me all about yourself, P.J. And Alex? Nothing you've told me today affects the foundation or your brothers. As far as I'm concerned, you've fulfilled your part of our bargain." He smiled at P.J. again. "And I'd say you've fulfilled it extremely well."

Later, as they drove away, P.J. said, "Alex, since you didn't buy me a Christmas present..." She held up her left hand so she could see her rings sparkle in the sunlight. "Engagement and wedding rings don't count...there's something I really want."

Smiling over at her, Alex said, "Anything. Just name it."

"I want you to take me to meet your mother. I think it's time you mended that fence, too, don't you?"

He didn't answer for a few seconds, and she thought he was going to say no.

"I won't take no for an answer," she teased. "I'll keep after you until you finally say yes."

"You won't have to," he finally said, tenderness

and love in his voice. "You know what? Today, listening to my father, seeing how he's trying to change, I thought the same thing. It's past time to forgive my mother. Way past time."

And that was the moment P.J. knew that no matter what life might throw at them in the future, they would be able to handle it.

They were a team.

For better, for worse, for richer, for poorer, in sickness and in health, till death do them part, they were a team.

* * * * *

THE BILLIONAIRE'S
SCANDALOUS
MARRIAGE

EMMA DARCY

CHAPTER ONE

HER wedding was only two weeks away.

Just two more weeks.

Charlotte Ramsey knew she should be happy about it.

But she wasn't.

All this past week spent trying to stay positive about marrying Mark…it hadn't worked. No matter how determinedly she argued against letting her father ruin how she should be feeling, he *was* ruining it. So the problem had to be dealt with.

Right now.

Before tonight.

Her stomach was knotted with nerves, her mind churning miserably over her dilemma as she set out on the hour-long drive from the inner city of Sydney to the family mansion at Palm Beach.

It was impossible to have a happy wedding if her father persisted in his unacceptable attitude towards the man she was marrying. The way he had treated Mark on Christmas day…and if he did the same tonight…her heart clenched at the thought. It hurt. It really hurt. She had to talk to him, make him understand.

Okay, he didn't approve of Mark as a husband for her.

It was no use hoping he ever would. Mark was not his kind of man. But he was right for her—as right as she was going to get—and surely she could persuade her father to respect that, if only for her sake.

The wedding was so close now.

He had to listen to her this time.

Her cheeks burned as she remembered the flaming row they'd had over her engagement when she had openly defied his disapproval, throwing down the threat of possible estrangement.

"Whether you like it or not, Dad, I'm going to marry him."

Which had caused an eruption of frustration over her decision.

"You're too damned headstrong for your own good, Charlotte. Marriage to Mark Freedman…what on earth do you see in the man? He's a playboy, not a…"

"Not a bull in the financial world," she'd sliced in, cutting off his point of view to push her own. "Which is precisely what I love about Mark. He's there for me, Dad, not constantly flying off to do another deal in another country." As her billionaire father had done all her life. "He *wants* my company. He *enjoys* my company. We have fun together."

"Fun!" her father had thundered. "You've got *my* blood in your veins, girl. Freedman's kind of fun will pall after a while. By all means have him as a novelty. Not too bad a toy for you to play with as long as he gives you pleasure. But marriage is serious business."

"It's not about *business* to me," she had fiercely retorted, incensed by his contemptuous colouring of her relationship with Mark. "It's about feeling loved. And I'm very, very serious about having that in my life."

"It won't last," her father had growled.

But Charlotte was determined it would. She was thirty years old. She wanted to have children. Mark did, too. They were happy together, happy about the future they were planning. He wasn't a playboy. He was an events organiser and very successful at it, too. She was looking forward to helping him with his business after they were married.

But she didn't want to be completely estranged from her father.

For the past few months he seemed to have accepted Mark into the family's social circle—albeit grudgingly—but on Christmas day…she had to get this sorted out before the wedding. Before tonight's New Year's Eve party on the yacht. If her father snubbed Mark again…

Charlotte took a deep breath to relieve the tightness in her chest. A glance at the clock on the dashboard told her it was past lunchtime, almost two o'clock. With any luck she should be able to get her father to herself for a private chat, just say hello to her mother in passing.

She'd told Mark she'd be spending the day at the beauty salon, getting ready for tonight. Best he didn't know about this meeting. It would have to be a quick one, though. He would expect her to be back at the apartment they shared at Double Bay by late afternoon.

For the remainder of the drive along Sydney's northern beaches Charlotte mentally rehearsed what she wanted to say, hoping to reach a workable understanding with her father. By the time she emerged from her Mercedes at the family mansion, her mind was all fired up to win what she needed to win. She charged into the foyer and was unpleasantly surprised to see the butler wheeling a traymobile of coffee things towards the main lounge room.

"Have my parents got visitors, Charles?"

"Good afternoon, Miss Charlotte," he rolled out, reminding her that good manners should not be overlooked. He was a tall, imposing man in his fifties, the absolute authority when it came to running this huge household and a stickler for appropriate behaviour at all times.

She grimaced an apology. "Sorry. I'm in a hurry. I need to talk to Dad."

He gestured to the lounge room doors. "Mr Ramsey is enjoying the company of your brother and his friend from London, Mr Damien Wynter. Mrs Ramsey is out, keeping an appointment with her hair stylist."

Charlotte frowned. It was good that her mother was out of the way, bad that she'd have to meet Peter's friend and have a bit of social chat before requesting a private talk with her father, who wouldn't want to leave this new connection with the son and heir of another billionaire. The big business networking would definitely be in action.

But she was here.

She had to try.

"Will you be joining the gentlemen for coffee, Miss Charlotte?" Charles prompted while she was still chewing over his information.

"No. Thank you. I'm not staying that long, Charles." She waved to the doors. "I'll just say hello to Peter and his friend."

Charles left the traymobile to usher her into the lounge room, announcing, "Miss Charlotte," as she sailed in, trying to put on a polite face and hide her anxiety over the situation.

The three men rose from their seats at her entrance, Peter and his friend from armchairs with their backs to her, her father from the sofa facing them. Her gaze automatically zeroed in on him as he smiled a surprised but pleased welcome.

"Charlotte…" He held out his arms for a greeting hug.

"My sister," she heard Peter mutter to his friend, but she didn't glance their way.

She walked straight up to her father to give him his hug, relieved that his disapproval of Mark did not impinge on his love for her. Despite all his shortcomings as a parent, she loved him, too. He was her father. And she hoped—fiercely hoped—she could win his understanding this afternoon.

Miss Charlotte…Peter's sister…Damien Wynter's interest was instantly aroused. She was a spectacular woman, not at all like Peter who obviously took after his father—blue eyes, sandy hair, fair-skinned with a sprinkle of freckles on their strongly boned faces, big physiques.

Her hair was the colour of caramel with streaks of butter, a long mane of it, shining and bouncy. Her skin was light honey, smooth, gleaming, and she had brown eyes like her mother, though not quite as dark, more Boston cream sherry. They glowed with bright intelligence, bringing a natural vibrancy to a face that had a very individual attraction—certainly not a plastic mould of beautiful, but strong with character, mixed with a sensual appeal in the soft curve of her jawline and the rather wide, full-lipped mouth.

Her figure was wonderfully female, the almost voluptuous curves accentuated by the bold dress she wore. Not that it was blatantly sexy. In fact it was quite modest—a sleeveless bodice, square neckline, not low enough to show cleavage, and the skirt skimmed her hips and flared slightly to knee-length. The design was simple but the colour combination was stunning.

The dress was mostly a vibrant purple. Dominating the lower left hand side of the skirt was a big white flower with a bright red centre and red splashed around the edge of the petals. A similar but much smaller flower featured over her right breast. A wide black belt circled an enticingly small waist, and very stylish black-and-white strappy sandals added a lot of sexy class to her bare feet.

Only a very confident woman would choose such a dress—a woman who knew what she liked and was not afraid to express her own individuality. And she obviously didn't bother about being model-thin, either. Bold, confident and very sexy, Damien decided, feeling a highly stimulated interest.

Peter Ramsey's sister…

The thought flashed into Damien's mind that the partner in life he'd been looking for could be right here. She shared the same background of immense wealth, so wouldn't have her eye on how much *he* was worth. He could trust a relationship with her. Though whether she was ready to settle down and have the family he wanted was another issue. For all he knew she could be a spoilt brat, like many of the other heiresses he'd met.

But right now, there was a buzz of excited anticipation running through his veins. If Charlotte Ramsey was anything like Peter in character, this visit to Sydney could be the start of building the kind of life he'd craved since he was a boy—something real and solid and lasting on a personal level.

Charlotte leaned up to whisper in her father's ear. "I need to talk to you privately. It's important, Dad," she pleaded.

He frowned down at her as she drew back, her eyes eloquently begging him to fall in with her request. "Come and meet Peter's friend first," he commanded, a chiding tone in his voice.

"Of course," she quickly agreed, swinging around to face their visitor, totally unprepared for the flesh and blood reality of Damien Wynter.

He didn't look English. He didn't look like anyone she'd ever met. The man was stunningly handsome— movie star handsome—like a smoothly dangerous Latin lover, an aristocratic Spaniard with his dark olive skin, black hair and eyes so dark, they looked black, too— black and brilliant with sparkling speculation as they bored straight into hers, giving her heart an almighty jolt.

Her toes started to curl. The man was sexual dynamite. He was as tall as Peter but there was more of a lean grace to his perfectly proportioned physique, which was casually displayed in a collarless white shirt and tailored black jeans. There was a supple, animal quality about his body that gave Charlotte the feeling he was all primed to pounce and right at this moment, she was his target.

Her spine tingled with a weird little frisson of excitement. Shock at her response to his sexual magnetism kicked her mind into savage common sense. Damien Wynter was the kind of man who would make *any* woman feel like this. It wasn't special to her. But for one treacherous moment, she wished Mark had the same power.

Her father's large hand on the pit of her back, pushing her forward to greet their guest, snapped her out of her stunned bunny state. She plastered a smile on her face, hoping it covered her embarrassment at being caught up in his initial physical impact. Looks weren't everything, not by a long shot.

"Damien, it's my very great pleasure to introduce you to my daughter, Charlotte," her father said with far more warmth than he'd ever shown to Mark.

Which raised her hackles.

"It's a very great pleasure to meet you, Charlotte," the man responded in kind, stepping forward and offering his hand.

She took it out of automatic politeness and was shocked anew by the electric contact of his strong fingers encasing hers. It rattled her into gushing speech. "Peter has spoken of you. I'm sure he'll see you enjoy your visit to Australia."

The dark eyes engaged hers with very personal intensity. Heart-squeezing intensity. "I'm glad I came."

For you.

He didn't say those words but she felt them. And the pressure of his hand reinforced the totally unwelcome connection he was pushing.

"I'm sorry I can't stay and chat but I'm really short of time and I've got some urgent business with Dad," she rushed out, forcibly releasing her hand as she turned to her father. "Could we go to the library?"

Her father waved to Charles who had brought in the traymobile. "Can't it wait until we've had coffee?"

"Please, Dad. I've come all the way out here and I've got to get back…"

"All right, all right," he grumbled. "I'll be back," he threw at Peter and Damien.

"Please excuse us," Charlotte added with a swift, apologetic glance at both men, not quite meeting the dark gaze, which she felt boring into her back as she made her escape.

Damien Wynter was undoubtedly a well-practised womaniser, she fiercely told herself.

Not worth a second thought.

Damien watched her go, his mind buzzing with exciting possibilities.

"She's taken," Peter said dryly.

It snapped Damien's attention back to him. "What do you mean…*taken*?"

"Getting married. The wedding is only two weeks away."

Shock was chased by a sense of disbelief. He hadn't imagined it. Charlotte Ramsey had connected with *him*. She shouldn't be taken by some other man. He shot a probing look at Peter. "Do you like her fiancé?"

The roll of eyes expressed contempt. "He's a smarmy fortune-hunter, but no one can make Charlotte see it."

Aggression pumped through Damien. One way or another he'd make her see it. "Will they be at the party on the yacht tonight?" he asked.

Peter gave him a speculative look, then shook his head. "They'll be there but you don't know Charlotte, Damien. She's got her mind set on marrying Mark Freedman and believe me, my sister is very, very strong-minded. Rocking the boat is not on, my friend."

Rock it he would if he could, was Damien's instant reaction, but he shrugged and turned the conversation to another topic, choosing not to pursue his interest in Peter's sister too openly at this point.

Tonight he intended to know much more of Charlotte Ramsey and if he liked what he learnt, nothing was going to stop him from acting on his interest.

"So what's this urgent business?" her father growled as he shut the library door behind them. "You were downright rude to Damien Wynter, giving him short shrift like that."

The criticism stung, especially when the approval he'd denied Mark had been so quickly given to Peter's friend. Her carefully rehearsed words flew out of her mind. She turned on him, hot accusation leaping off her tongue. "Not as rude as you were to Mark on Christmas day, snubbing him when he was only trying to…"

"He was sucking up to me," her father cut in angrily. "I hate people sucking up to me. Damn it, Charlotte! Couldn't you see that for yourself?" He threw up his hands in disgust. "When are you going to come to your senses? Damien Wynter is the kind of man you should be marrying and you don't even give him two cents of your time."

Resentment burned through her. Damien Wynter had used the two cents, coming onto her so fast she was still disturbed by it. "I'm marrying Mark, Dad," she grated out through her teeth. "And I don't want you snubbing him tonight."

"Then keep him out of my way," her father snapped, scything the air with his hand in dismissive contempt.

Her chin lifted in defiant challenge. "You want me out of your way, too, Dad? Is that the way it's going to be?"

His face went red with furious frustration. His hand lifted, stabbing a finger at her. "I've told you before and I'll tell again. Get Freedman to sign a prenuptial agreement. If you do that, I promise I'll tolerate the man for your sake, Charlotte. That's the best I can do. Don't try my patience with you any further."

He swung on his heel and marched out of the library, slamming the door behind him.

Charlotte found herself trembling from the force of his anger. She had believed her father would come around to being reasonably pleasant to Mark. It was only a matter of time, once she'd proved how happy she was in the relationship. But now she was frightened that wasn't going to happen. Not ever.

Even if she pushed Mark to sign a prenup—which she didn't want to do—would it make any real difference to her father's attitude towards him?

She hated this. Hated it. And she hated Damien Wynter for coming here and setting up a comparison for her father to throw at her. Of course he won automatic approval. He was one of them—born to wealth and his whole life driven by accumulating more of it. She didn't want to be the dutiful social wife to a man like that, which was why she'd chosen Mark.

But she didn't feel happy as she left the Palm Beach mansion.

She felt torn by a multitude of needs, which couldn't all be answered.

CHAPTER TWO

DAMIEN WYNTER...

Charlotte shot mental bolts of rejection at the man emerging from the limousine, straightening up beside her brother, actually topping Peter's formidable height by an inch or two. He looked even more striking in a formal black dinner suit and she had no doubt that every woman at this party would be eyeing him over tonight. Which was fine, as long as he focussed on them and not on her.

From her position on the top deck of her father's yacht she watched the two men stride down the dock, chatting amiably with one another. It was a further irritation that Peter liked *him* so much and hadn't made any effort to become friendly with Mark. Was she going to lose both her father and her brother by going ahead with this marriage?

But I have my own life to live, came the sharp, anguished cry in her mind. Being a daughter, a sister, wasn't enough. She wanted a partner who was happy to share his life with her and until she'd met Mark, she'd despaired of ever finding one. It wasn't easy for her. Only Mark had made it easy.

Except she didn't feel at ease about anything now.

"Ah! The last arrivals!" Mark commented with satisfaction, noting where her attention had strayed.

Charlotte turned her gaze back to her fiancé. They'd been on board for a while, watching other guests coming onto the yacht, which would very shortly cruise to the centre of Sydney Harbour and take up a prime position for viewing the New Year's Eve fireworks. This was the first time Mark had been invited to join the Ramsey family on the *Sea Lion*, and he was obviously eager to enjoy the experience.

"They're not late," she said, glancing at the new Cartier watch her parents had given her for Christmas. "Right on time, in fact. Eight o'clock. Peter knows Dad won't wait a minute longer."

"Fearsome man, your father," Mark wryly remarked.

She forced a smile, wanting to lessen any anxiety he might be nursing over her father's attitude towards him. "Don't worry about Dad. We're going to have a brilliant night and I love having you here to share it with me."

He smiled back, his face lighting up with the warm, impish charm that had first drawn her to him. Mark was not in the mould of traditional macho male, though he was certainly masculine enough when it came to making love, and he did match her well above average height, making them a perfect physical fit.

His thick, wavy brown hair invited touch, unlike the short back and sides style her father favoured. His twinkling hazel eyes invited fun, rather than pinning her to the spot in forceful challenge. His arched eyebrows were used to waggle with wicked mischief. She'd never seen them lowered in a disapproving or impatient frown. His nose was sharply ridged and his chin was narrow and chiselled, but his mouth was soft, his smile was soft, and usually its warmth made her feel safe with him.

Safe in a nice, cosy sense.

She would never feel safe with Damien Wynter.

"I'm the luckiest man here," Mark murmured. "I've got the most beautiful woman with me."

She laughed, happy that he thought so. The compliment made all the hours of effort worthwhile; having blonde and copper streaks put through her long, brown hair, finding and buying a stunning dress, taking the utmost care with her make-up. She wasn't beautiful. She simply worked hard at putting herself together as best she could, using all the tricks the modelling school had taught her, highlighting her good points and minimising the not so good.

"I'm surprised your brother doesn't have a woman in tow tonight," Mark said, raising one eyebrow quizzically. "No romance in the air for him on New Year's Eve?"

"More likely he didn't want to give the time to it," she said with dry irony. "Dad will have his usual poker game running in the bottom saloon in between the fireworks displays. No doubt Peter will be introducing his new friend from London to it. Nothing beats the adrenaline rush of a high-rolling game."

"You've played?" Mark asked curiously.

She shrugged. "Since I was a kid, but only at home. It was the one game our father played with us. He enjoyed teaching us the percentages."

Mark shook his head in bemusement. "Strange childhood you had, Charlotte."

"I want to make it different for our children, Mark," she said earnestly.

"And so we will, my love." He curved his arm around her shoulders, giving her a comforting hug of assurance as he softly blew the same words in her ear. "So we will."

She leaned into him, wanting her inner turmoil soothed by the loving way he treated her, the easy physical closeness he invited so naturally. The Ramseys were not openly demonstrative in their affection though the family had always been a tightly knit unit, made so from being set apart from the ordinary stream of people by great wealth.

Charlotte had tried to reach out across that barrier many times, only to be rebuffed by hurtful comments like, "It's all right for you. You're a Ramsey"—meaning she could have anything she wanted or get away with doing whatever she pleased. Which wasn't true, but it was how she was perceived by others and nothing she said had ever changed their minds.

Mark was the only man who had looked beyond the face value of her family and cared about the person she was inside, the needs she'd secretly nursed that all the money in the world could not fulfil. Perhaps it was because he wasn't of her world and was curious about it, interested into probing more deeply than the surface. Whatever the reason, so much personal interest had made him very attractive, excitingly different to the many smugly arrogant heirs to fortunes who usually peopled her social circle.

But to her intense discomfort, she found herself wishing he excited her more sexually. Until this afternoon she hadn't realised a man could affect her as Damien Wynter had. But that was probably an initial impact thing. She shouldn't let it worry her. Mark was a very caring lover who was always concerned about giving her pleasure.

The powerful engines of the yacht thrummed with purpose. "Now that everyone's on board, let's stroll around to the front deck," she suggested. "Set ourselves up for the best view of the fireworks."

They met and greeted other guests along the way, stopped to chat, had their glasses refilled with champagne, sampled some of the gourmet finger food being circulated by the waiters hired for the night. The party atmosphere lightened Charlotte's private angst. She enjoyed Mark's quick wit and easy manner. He was good company, always had been for her, always would be, she thought.

It shouldn't matter—*didn't* matter—that her father and brother would always prefer the company of men like Damien Wynter. She didn't want her life to be like her mother's, filling in her time with charity functions while her husband wheeled and dealed in his own arena. She felt sorry for the woman Peter married, whomever she might be, doomed to always stand in second place to his business life.

Mark wanted her to be his professional assistant, helping to organise the events he arranged. They would share *everything*. This coming new year should be marvellous, she thought, the best ever.

Even the fireworks tonight had been advertised as something extra special. The harbour foreshores were crowded with people, waiting to see them. The *Sea Lion* was surrounded by all sorts of pleasure crafts, loaded with New Year's Eve revellers. As nine o'clock approached—the time for the first fireworks display for families—Mark shepherded her through the melee of guests to the railing, intent on ensuring a clear view of the spectacular show.

"There you are!"

Her brother's voice claimed her attention. She turned to find herself confronted by both Peter and the man whose company she definitely didn't want. His dark eyes instantly engaged hers with a riveting intensity that stirred a determined rebellion. No way would she be sucked in by his alpha animal attraction a second time, not for a minute. He was *one of them*, so arrogantly confident in his natural domination, undoubtedly expecting a woman to be his possession, not a real partner.

"Damien, you've met my sister, Charlotte, in passing, so to speak. This is her fiancé, Mark Freedman."

The introduction was completed by the man himself. "Damien Wynter." He barely flicked a glance of acknowledgement to Mark, concentrating his sexy charisma on her as he offered his hand again. "I hope we can further our acquaintance tonight, Charlotte," he rolled out, pouring on the charm, flashing a smile designed to dazzle.

It raised her hackles to such a bristling height, it took every skerrick of her will-power to keep them sheathed and present a civil demeanour. She forced out her hand to take the one he'd offered, constructed a coolly polite smile, and said, "Well, Sydney is about to put on its best face for you, but I doubt you'll get much out of me, Damien."

"I beg your pardon?" He frowned over the rebuff as though he'd never had the experience of being knocked back by a woman.

She raised her eyebrows. "Isn't that your aim in

making a connection? How much you can get out of the person? Peter did tell me…"

Her brother laughed. "Charlotte is referring to how you replied to that stupid toast Tom Benedict made to me at the London club last year, declaring I was amongst friends, when in fact, most of them were strangers to me, and the only common ground we had was wealthy fathers."

Damien shook his head over the reminder. "Tom Benedict doesn't have a brain in his head."

"Perhaps he only meant to be kind," Charlotte suggested. "And being kind does not necessarily rule out a brain." She paused a moment to punctuate her point. "Quite possibly it's simply one that works differently to yours."

As Mark's did.

Which was one of the reasons why she preferred him to Damien Wynter, despite the obvious assets of the man who thought he could just muscle in and capture her interest.

Damien's mind instantly registered a hit. His gaze narrowed on the brown eyes that remained flat, denying him any entry into what she was thinking. Why was he suddenly getting this flow of antagonism from Charlotte Ramsey? There'd been no trace of it in their brief meeting this afternoon. But that had been a surprise encounter. She'd had time to think about him since then—possibly as a threat she was intent on dispelling?

"Did Peter paint me as cruel?" he asked, cutting straight to the point she seemed to be making.

"Not at all." She gave a tinkling laugh to remove any offence he might have taken. "He liked your honesty."

"But you don't?" he queried, putting her on the spot.

She didn't miss a beat. "On the contrary, it's always infinitely preferable to know what one is dealing with."

"And what do you imagine you're dealing with, Charlotte?"

Her eyebrows lifted in mock chiding. "I don't imagine anything, Damien. As it was quoted to me, in reply to Tom Benedict's toast, you said Peter was not your friend because you'd never met him before, and you were only interested in meeting him because of who he was, what he had and how much you might be able to get out of him."

Damien smiled at the recollection. "In short, I cut through Tom's hypocritical bullshit."

"Winning my trust and my friendship," Peter tossed in.

"Which is happily mutual," Damien good-humouredly affirmed.

"Like minds finding each other is always good," Charlotte said with a suspiciously silky thread of approval. "I know how lucky I am to have met Mark."

She hooked her arm around her fiancé's, subtly but emphatically placing herself at *his* side, having cleverly established that Damien and Peter formed a completely separate unit on a different planet to the one she wanted to inhabit with Mark Freedman.

Damien obligingly turned his attention to the man Peter had described as a smarmy fortune-hunter who had his sister sand-bagged from seeing any sense at all. But she was no fool. Far from it. She had a mind as sharp as knives. So Damien concentrated on taking his own measure of Charlotte Ramsey's choice of partner.

"I'm sorry, Mark." He smiled apologetically as he offered his hand. "I didn't mean to ignore you."

"No problem," came the easy assurance. "I was interested in hearing the background to your friendship with Peter."

His handshake had a touch of deference, aiming to please, not make it a contest of male egos. His eyes sparkled with appreciative interest, wanting to engage, *wanting to be part of the world Charlotte seemed intent on turning her back on,* Damien thought.

"In fact, it made me reflect on whether all our close associations with people are linked to how much we get out of them," Mark commented whimsically. "We don't tend to hang around those who give us nothing, do we?"

It was a disarming little speech, opening up what could have been used as an attack on his integrity where his relationship with an heiress was concerned, then turning the picture around by making the principle a general one.

"We avoid boring people," he went on, "and naturally gravitate to those who make our lives more interesting and pleasurable."

He smiled at Charlotte, giving her the sense that she was at the centre of these last sentiments, and Damien felt a surprisingly strong urge to kick him. The man was a master of manipulation, a first-rate charmer, and the smile now lighting up the face that had refused him any positive personal response twisted something in Damien's gut.

He stared at her—this woman who was stirring feelings in him that demanded action to change the status quo. Was it because she was Peter's sister and he empathised with his friend's dislike of her being taken in by a user? Was it because she wouldn't give him what she was readily giving to her fiancé?

He had met many more beautiful women, yet her smile for Mark Freedman illumined her own unique attraction, making it immeasurably stronger. The graceful turn of her long bare neck struck his eye. Her throat was bare of jewellery and its nakedness somehow evoked a vulnerability that stirred some very primitive instincts. The aggressive hunter and the protector leapt to battle readiness inside him and Damien knew he wouldn't step back from involving himself with Charlotte Ramsey.

His gaze skated down the dress she had chosen for tonight. It was bright orange—a colour not many women could wear successfully, a colour that reinforced his initial impression that she was confident about herself.

Challengingly confident.

The style was a simple sheath attached to a beaded yoke. Very elegant. Again not overtly sexy yet all the more alluring because it subtly skimmed her curves instead of flaunting them in his face. Damien decided she was a woman who cared more about being seen as a person rather than a sexual object.

Had Mark Freedman played that card to win her?

"Countdown to the fireworks is starting," Peter said, waving Damien to join him at the deck railing as other guests automatically moved to make space for them.

Millions of voices around the harbour rose in the chant, "Ten, nine, eight…"

Charlotte broke apart from her fiancé to swing around and face the famous coat-hanger bridge that would obviously form the centrepiece of the display. Mark Freedman turned, as well, sliding his arm around her waist to hold her close. Damien stepped up between

Peter and Charlotte, determined on making her aware of him whether she liked it or not.

"...three, two, one..."

The great arch of the bridge was brilliantly outlined as white fireworks sprayed up from the entire span.

The start of something big, Damien thought, the excitement of this first explosive burst fuelling anticipation for what was to come. It reflected precisely how he was feeling about Charlotte Ramsey. One way or another he would take her from Mark Freedman, free her of a bad mistake.

Free her for himself.

CHAPTER THREE

THE night sky bloomed with magnificent bursts of colour, erupting over the spectacular white sails that roofed the opera house and above the great sandstone pylons of the bridge. The massive cascades of light were beautiful, awesome, yet the joy Charlotte had expected to feel in them was somehow sucked away by the presence of Damien Wynter.

Which was totally, totally wrong.

And upsetting.

Mark was holding her. Mark was talking to her, sharing his delight in the fantastic display, pointing out the marvellous special effects that particularly impressed him. Mark should have her undivided attention. And she tried to give it, tried to respond as she should be responding quite naturally.

Yet she was still bridling over how Damien Wynter had been looking at her just before the countdown started, taking in every detail of her appearance as though measuring it against some standard in his mind. She told herself he probably did the same to any woman who came into his firing line and it was totally irrelevant how he scored her in his estimation of female attraction. What he thought simply didn't matter. Which made it all the more intensely irritating that he'd set her nerves so much on edge.

Even his voice distracted her from what Mark was saying, her ears suddenly super-sensitive to the deep timbre of it as he made comments to Peter, comments that told her *he* was enjoying the show.

And why not?

No other city in the world had a more fabulous setting for such a night as this and the *Sea Lion* gave them a dress-circle view of everything. She was probably the only spectator wishing for the end of the fireworks. Only then would her brother lead Damien Wynter away and she'd be rid of this horribly acute awareness of him.

A crescendo of rockets built up to the fifteen-minute finale. A golden rain fell from the bridge and just below the centre of the arch, a huge red heart appeared, pulsing with graduations of light.

"The heart of Sydney," she murmured appreciatively.

"The heart of love," Mark breathed into her ear.

Which should have made her own heart beat with happiness, but her mind was too busy being sceptical about how much heart Damien Wynter had. No doubt he gave a sizeable slice of his wealth to charities, as a tax deduction, which didn't actually mean caring. Did he care about anything beyond staking out his territory and increasing it at every opportunity—all he could *get*?

"That's it for now," Peter told him. "There'll be a bigger show at midnight."

"Hard to top that," Damien commented. "Leaving the heart glowing is a nice touch."

"Yes, it really stands out in the darkness," Peter replied.

"A reminder to give," Charlotte couldn't resist tossing at them.

A mistake.

Damien Wynter's dark eyes instantly locked onto hers, glittering with speculative interest. He smiled, slowly and sensually, his teeth so white, the old saying, *all the better to bite you with,* slid straight into Charlotte's mind.

"Instead of to *get?*" he asked, provocatively raising *her* issue with him.

She tried to shrug it off, inwardly cursing herself for opening another conversation with him. "The two should go hand in hand, don't you think?" she answered blandly.

"Yes, I do." The quick agreement was instantly followed by a challenge. "Does that surprise you, Charlotte?"

Peter saved her from answering, chiming in with, "Damien gives an enormous amount to self-help development programs for Africa."

It surprised her enough to ask, "Why Africa?"

"Have you been there?" Damien queried.

"No. I've always thought of Africa as a scary, violent place, best avoided."

"Then let me take you. You'd be safe under my protection and you could see for yourself how I do my giving."

A part of her actually wanted to. Dangerous curiosity, she told herself, and retreated to safe ground. "Thank you for the invitation but Mark and I are getting married in a couple of weeks…"

"And I understand you're busy right now, but when it's convenient…" He smiled at Mark. "Would touring Africa as my guest appeal?"

"Absolutely," Mark rushed in, without discussing the choice with her.

They didn't *know* the man. Why would Mark want to be his guest on a tour through Africa? It wasn't on. Not with Damien Wynter. It felt wrong. Apart from anything else, no way could she feel comfortable in his company.

"You'd better take Damien down to the saloon if you're playing poker with Dad, Peter," she reminded her brother, wanting this encounter ended.

"Are you playing, Mark?" Damien asked, apparently happy to have her fiancé included in the poker party.

Charlotte resented the gambit to separate them as though *she* didn't count. Mark wouldn't desert her for some all male *fun*. Certainly not on the first New Year's Eve they were spending together.

"Not my game, I'm afraid," he said, which wasn't as positive about remaining with her as she would have liked. In fact, Mark had sounded downright rueful over missing out.

Damien's compelling dark eyes targeted her again. "What about you, Charlotte?"

The impertinence of the question left her momentarily speechless. As if she would when Mark couldn't!

Peter laughed, clapping his friend on the back. "Believe me, Damien, you don't want to play with Charlotte."

"Oh? Why not?"

"Because she'll take you. My sister is a killer player."

His mouth formed a very sexy moue. His eyes, which hadn't left hers for a second, simmered a sexy challenge. "I think I'd like the experience of being taken by your sister, Peter."

Charlotte burned.

Damien Wynter wasn't talking poker. He'd looked her over, decided he found her desirable, liked the spice that she was engaged to another man and supposedly unattainable, and was now laying out his line, dangling the bait of beating him at a game based on taking chances.

The outrageous arrogance of the man was insufferable. Her mind sizzled with ways to puncture his ego. Before she could come up with the perfect putdown, Mark intervened.

"You know, I'd like to watch that," he said musingly. "Are spectators allowed at this game?"

Annoyance sharpened her tongue. "Mark, I don't want to play. I want to be with you."

"Mark can come and watch, Charlotte," Peter put in, suddenly eager to oblige his friend's whim. "He can sit right at your shoulder."

"That's not the same," she shot at her brother.

"Truly, I would enjoy it, darling," Mark pushed, smiling persuasively as he added, "It's a part of your life that's still a mystery to me. I'd like the chance to watch and understand what you were talking about…the percentages."

"I thought we were going to dance," she protested, hating his unwitting collusion with a man who would take her if the opportunity presented itself.

"We can dance any night," he soothed.

"Course you can," Peter said dismissively. "Come on, Charlotte. You know you love to play. It's in your blood."

The sense of being railroaded increased the angry tension Damien Wynter had evoked, and Peter sounded so like their father with his *blood* comment, she almost stamped her foot in exasperation. "It's just a game, Peter. I can choose to play or not. I don't *need* it in my life!"

"Sorry, darling," Mark back-pedalled in concern. "Of course, it's your choice."

"But it would please all of us if you played," Damien slid in silkily.

Painting her as a selfish spoilt brat if she refused.

Charlotte grimly took stock. Mark could watch a poker match on television if he was so keen to understand percentages. That seemed like a very specious argument to her. More likely, the drawcard for him was being with Peter and Damien Wynter—part of the privileged circle at her father's poker game.

A nasty suspicion crawled around her mind. Was Mark using her as a stepping stone to where he wanted to be?

She didn't want to think that. She didn't want to but…why leap at the chance of being Damien's guest in Africa?

Damn Damien Wynter! He'd already spoilt her night with Mark.

"All right! I'm in!" she decided, a reckless streak of belligerence prompting her to take on a straight out fight with the man who had stirred so much unwelcome turmoil inside her.

"Splendid!" Damien approved, grinning like a wolf seeing the jugular of his victim bared.

If luck is with me, it's your blood that will be spilled, Charlotte thought viciously, turning a smile to Mark. "Let me know when you find it boring and I'll surrender my chips," she said, deliberately making it known she was indulging her fiancé, no one else.

Mark touched her cheek in a gentle salute of admiration, his eyes beaming warm pleasure at her. "My brave girl," he murmured. "I suspect you'll be swimming amongst sharks at this poker table but I'll rescue you whenever you say the word."

The tightness in Charlotte's chest eased a little. Mark did love her. It was stupid to get worked up over a few little things that could be put down to natural curiosity. Damien Wynter somehow emanated a magnetism that was skewing her thoughts.

As she turned to her brother and said, "Lead on, Peter. We'll follow you down to the saloon," she caught Damien staring at Mark as though measuring him for deep, dark annihilation.

So much for wanting him as his guest in Africa! He'd probably feed Mark to the lions so he could have her to himself! That was what he was angling for. Was his pride wounded because she hadn't instantly been smitten by him, worshipping at his feet for who and what he was, not to mention how much he was worth? Men like him always thought they could get any woman.

Not this one, she silently vowed, aiming the message straight at his back as Peter steered him away from the railing, heading for the lower saloon. Moreover, she wouldn't engage in any contest with him at the poker table. He'd like nothing better than for her to take him on.

Thwarting him should be the plan, not trying to beat him. If he was betting on his cards, she'd withdraw from betting on her own, regardless of how promising they were. No blood spilled...no grounds for any future comeback.

Satisfied that she had worked out a sensible course—one that Damien Wynter wouldn't like one bit—

Charlotte felt calmer and considerably more confident of handling the situation without any heartburn.

Music started in the upper saloon just as they reached the top of the stairs. The DJ had put on a great upbeat track to get the guests into a dancing mood. Charlotte smiled ironically to herself as she recognised Nancy Sinatra's voice belting out "I'll Be Your Good-Time Girl".

She might have lived up to that for Mark tonight, if he'd wanted to dance instead of watching a poker game.

But she was never going to live that role for Damien Wynter!

CHAPTER FOUR

DAMIEN had lost all trace of the jetlag he'd been suffering earlier. His whole body was buzzing with exhilaration. Pitting himself against someone else always gave him an adrenaline rush. That it was a woman this time made it more exciting, especially a woman as hard to get as Charlotte Ramsey.

Peter gave him an arch look as they descended the stairs together, asking in a low voice, "Do I detect a very determined personal interest in my sister?"

"Would you have a problem with my pursuing it?"

Brothers could be sticky about their younger sisters. Damien didn't want to mess with the Ramsey family in any negative way. Peter was a good friend to have, both personally and professionally, and his father would make a very bad enemy. Nevertheless, he didn't want to exercise any caution where getting Charlotte for himself was concerned.

A carefree grin answered him. "Won't affect me in any way whatsoever. But be warned, my friend. Charlotte is one hell of a fighter."

Damien grinned back. "That fires me up to win, Peter."

"If you're intent on winning, take nothing for

granted," came the swift advice. "I helped get her to the poker game for you but don't think for a minute she'll be easy pickings. She'd stand up to Dad any day of the week. Very strong-willed, my sister."

Definitely no pushover. That was already evident to him. Which meant Mark Freedman must have worked hard at discovering the cracks in her armour, sliding through them to reach her heart and turn it his way. No doubt the prize was worth some intense work to a man who was greedy for *the good life,* and the pay-off wedding was only two weeks away.

"She shouldn't be with Freedman," Damien muttered.

"Not my cup of tea, either," Peter ruefully agreed. "But he sweetens her life, Damien. And you're not sugar."

No, he wasn't. And he wasn't about to sugar-coat anything, either. There was no time for that. He had to act fast, change the parameters of Charlotte's thinking, strike at the heart, not seduce his way in. Sweetness could cloy after a while and his instincts were telling him that tart was more to her natural taste.

"I'm banking on pepper and salt," he said purposefully.

Peter chuckled. "Well, I'm a meat man, myself. Can't do without pepper and salt. And come to think of it, Charlotte never was a *sweet* young thing, not even when she was sixteen."

"How old is she now, Peter?"

"Thirty." The twinkling blue eyes sobered as he went on in a more serious vein. "Two years younger than me and wanting to start a family of her own. I doubt she'll swap a marriage she's set on for a fling with you."

"That marriage could turn sour very quickly once Freedman shows his true colours. He's already slipped up twice tonight. Better she doesn't enter into it, Peter."

"I'm right with you on that, but…" He shrugged. "Not even Dad could talk her out of it."

"She has to *want* out."

"If you can make her *want* out, I'll take my hat off to you, my friend."

They reached the lower deck and Peter ushered him towards the saloon. Damien was glad they were in agreement over Charlotte's future with Mark Freedman. Having children with the wrong man was a disaster, in his opinion, as was having children with the wrong woman. His instincts were telling him Charlotte Ramsey could be the right one for him. She wanted to start a family…no problem with that issue.

Marriage had not been on his immediate agenda. It was not something he could program since it depended on meeting a woman he *wanted* to marry. He was thirty-four years old and so far that feeling had been elusive. The relationships he had entered into had never lasted long, passion burning out when incompatibility made time together more irritating than exciting. He needed someone who could relate to his life…live it with him.

He was not about to turn aside from the possibility that Charlotte Ramsey was *the one*.

The *poker* saloon was all set ready for the game to begin; eight chairs spaced out around the large oval table, a spare place for the professional dealer to control the cards, betting chips distributed, her father's special guests milling around, finishing off finger food and drinks before play started, though there were side tables placed behind the chairs to hold refreshments within easy reach.

As Charlotte entered with Mark, she saw Peter having a word with her father, whose sharp gaze instantly zeroed in on her. She was the only woman in the room and could very well be an unwelcome addition to the poker party. Damien Wynter could not tell her father to let her stay. No one told Lloyd Ramsey what to do. Nevertheless, having come, Charlotte didn't want to be asked to leave. That would be slighting Mark.

Her arm tightened around Mark's as her father cocked his head in consideration, listening to Peter who was undoubtedly explaining the situation he and his friend had engineered. Her nervous tension kicked into anger as she saw her father's mouth twitch in amusement. This challenge by Damien Wynter was no joke. She wanted done with it as soon as possible. She kept her gaze trained on her father and brother, refusing to give the man from London the satisfaction of a glance his way.

"Charlotte, what an unexpected pleasure!" her father rolled out in welcome, his wide mouth breaking into the smile that invariably reminded people of a shark. The top of his head had gone bald some years ago and his high broad forehead, large nose and big white teeth, on top of his formidable physique, contributed to the impression of a fearsome predator. He turned to his aide-de-camp. "Two more chairs at the table."

"I won't be playing, sir," Mark quickly put in.

The deferential "sir" grated on Charlotte. She didn't want her husband-to-be kowtowing to her father, particularly not tonight in front of Damien Wynter.

"If you don't mind, I'd like to watch Charlotte play,"

Mark went on, his ingratiating tone annoying her further. It did sound like sucking up.

"Fine!" her father approved, flashing his shark smile. "Though you might get an unwelcome insight into the woman you're marrying."

He was putting in the bite, not snubbing Mark but virtually accusing him of having a superficial view of his fiancée. Which wasn't true. She was not just a lump of money to Mark. Though it did seem he was attracted to the life-style perks that marriage to her could bring.

"Oh, I think I know her fairly well," he said with a warm assurance that should have removed her irritation. Except he didn't know what was going on inside her right now—the absolutely perverse resentment that he wasn't more like Damien Wynter, just taking everything in his stride as though it was his right to be wherever he wanted and have whatever he wanted.

She savagely reminded herself that Damien had been born into a world of wealth, which cultivated that frame of mind. Mark hadn't. And she had liked the difference. It was crazy to start doubting her judgement on that. Before realising she was breaking her previous resolution, she turned a proudly defiant face to the man who was unsettling what she had settled on, her eyes mocking any influence he thought he might exert on her.

The sense that he'd been watching for her to look at him, waiting for it, willing it to happen, sizzled along her tense nerves. Satisfaction glinted in the dark eyes. She felt him thinking, *You can't escape me, Charlotte,* and her heart instantly skipped into a faster beat. *Yes, I can,* her own eyes telegraphed back to him.

His gaze flicked to the chairs being placed for her and

Mark, then very deliberately he stepped over to claim the chair directly across the table from where she was being accommodated.

"Seats, gentlemen," her father called, shooting an amused little smile at her. "My daughter is about to test her mettle against yours."

Good-humoured laughter rippled around the room. It was obvious to Charlotte that these high-powered guests didn't see her as a threat at the table. They were indulging her because of who she was. Their host had allowed her into the game so any protest was unthinkable.

"I caution you not to underestimate her as a player," her father tossed at them. "Charlotte has cleaned me out more times than I care to remember."

"Me, too," Peter said. "Nerves of steel. She didn't get to be one of the top guns on the trading floor without 'em."

"Top gun on the trading floor?" Damien queried, clearly surprised by this information and looking to Peter, who'd taken the chair next to his, for more enlightenment.

"Charlotte worked for an international bank. A star player on their scale for dealers."

"I didn't realise…"

Charlotte smiled her own triumphant bit of amusement as Damien Wynter's gaze turned back to her in swift re-assessment. He'd probably had her pegged as a socialite, with nothing better to do than attend fashionable functions—a woman groomed to hang off his arm and satisfy any social role he wanted her to play.

Peter grinned at her as he topped off his spiel with, "She was called *The Ram* at the bank, and I don't think that was entirely related to the family name."

"Fascinating," Damien murmured, his dark eyes

suddenly burning like hot coals, his interest in her fired, not dampened by this new knowledge.

To Charlotte's horrified consternation, her stomach contracted as though it had been punched and her breasts tightened, her nipples tingling into hard peaks. She didn't *want* to have this physical—a sexual—reaction to Damien Wynter. And why on earth did he like the fact she had a brain that most men shied clear of as too competitive for them?

"I have better things to do with my life now," she stated quickly, half-turning in her chair to reach out to Mark who was seated just behind her right shoulder. She took his hand and squeezed it in a show of solidarity with him. "I was happy to resign from my job to take on a far more fulfilling career as Mark's partner in everything."

So take that on board, Damien Wynter, she thought, furious over the strong response of her body to him and barely noticing Mark's delight in her little speech.

"Enough talk!" her father commanded tersely, shooting a look of distinct *displeasure* at Charlotte—a reminder that he had only grudgingly accepted her forthcoming marriage to Mark and he didn't enjoy a public expression of her devotion to a man he barely tolerated. He gestured to the dealer to get the game under way and was instantly obeyed.

As the cards were distributed around the table, Charlotte brooded over her father's disapproval. She understood he'd prefer to see her married to a man like Damien Wynter—connecting wealth to wealth—but where marriage was concerned, she had different priorities, and she was not going to be talked out of them or distracted from them by a blast of sexual chemistry.

She picked up the two cards dealt to her and focussed her mind on them, determined to keep to her game-plan, avoiding any direct contest with the man who wanted her to battle with him.

One hour later, Damien knew with certainty that Charlotte Ramsey had chosen the tactic of guerrilla warfare. She hit only when he wasn't betting on his cards. More times than not, she won the pot, so her foray into the gambling ring was not injudicious. She didn't always move in when he withdrew, but she always stayed out when he put himself in the running to win, even when the cards she held were highly pro-mising. At least that was definitely the case in one instance, because Damien caught Mark frowning over her decision to throw them in.

The man hadn't learnt to keep a poker face. Charlotte, on the other hand, revealed no expression whatsoever when she looked at her cards. It was impos-sible to tell if she was bluffing or not when she placed her bets, though she did bet aggressively, making the other players doubt the worth of what they held. If they hadn't respected her skill before play started, they very quickly learnt respect as her pile of chips grew while others' diminished.

Damien was winning, too, but he derived little satis-faction from it. He wanted Charlotte to engage with him, not evade him. Finally frustration drove him to challenge her.

"Are you afraid of losing to me, Charlotte?" he drawled sardonically, aiming to get under her armour-plated skin.

Her eyes mocked his purpose. "Have I deprived you of the pleasure of winning against me, Damien?" she replied as though she hadn't meant to. "Let's see what the next hand brings. If I get cards which give me a high percentage chance and you think the same about yours…who's to know until we see them?"

Her smile got under his skin. It wasn't a shrug-off smile. It was a smile of secret intent. Her actions did not depend on the luck of the draw. She knew precisely what she was doing and thwarting him was giving her pleasure.

The cards were once more dealt around the table. Damien picked up the ace of hearts and the ace of diamonds—an unbeatable pair at this point. He pushed chips forward, declaring himself *in* on this hand and waited to see what Charlotte would do, his gaze fastened on her lowered lashes as she pondered her play.

When her turn came she casually pushed chips forward, which instantly drew everyone's attention. Damien's direct challenge to her had titillated interest. The other players wanted to see them go head to head— the two biggest winners finally facing off.

Was it simply a ploy to satisfy them that she wasn't evading him? Would she pull out once the three flop cards were tabled? Damien's heart pumped into a faster beat as his mind buzzed with possibilities. Never had a woman engaged him so totally.

He glanced at Mark Freedman, hoping for some kind of signal from him as to what Charlotte's hand was worth. A slight crease between his eyebrows indicated puzzlement. Was she bluffing or didn't Mark understand the value of what she held?

A couple of other players were up for contesting the

hand. The rest folded. The dealer proceeded to lay out the three *flop* cards; the five of spades, the queen of hearts, the ace of spades. Excitement zinged through Damien. He now held three aces, which made him a very strong contender to win. Even if Charlotte now held three queens or three fives, she could not beat him.

Yet without any hesitation she declared, "I'm all in," and pushed every pile of chips she had into the pot.

She lifted her gaze to his, shooting him a hot bolt of challenge, deliberately inciting his active participation in her gamble. Excitement coursed through his entire body, stirring more than his blood. He wanted her. He wanted her so badly he was getting an erection right here at the poker table where it was impossible to have any physical engagement with her. But the mind-game was on. Win or lose, he was going with her on this hand.

The amount of chips she was wagering was an intimidating move. The other contenders immediately dropped out of the betting. To stay in, he had to match her bet and risk losing all he'd won and more.

He studied the cards. There were two spades on the table. If she held another two and if the *turn* card or the *river* card, both of them still to be played, turned out to be another spade, she could beat him with a five spade flush. But the odds were against that. She could be gambling on getting a straight—ace through to the five if she held two of the intermediate cards and the third was turned up, but that was a low percentage play, too. Four queens or four fives were remote possibilities, as well.

He looked at her.

Her mouth curved into a taunting little smile.

Loser, was the message she was telegraphing.

He didn't believe her—wouldn't believe her—not on any count.

"I'll call," he said, pushing in his chips, making it by far the biggest pot of the night and generating an air of electric tension around the table, everyone leaning forward to watch the outcome.

Charlotte leaned back as though she didn't have a care in the world. The smile was still tilting her mouth and her eyes glittered with some deep private satisfaction.

Certainty flashed into Damien's mind—*I've made the wrong move, the move she wanted me to make.* He was going to lose but it was too late to pull back. The dealer was already laying down the *turn* card.

It was the eight of diamonds.

No help to his hand.

He couldn't see how it could be to hers, either.

Finally the *river* card was revealed—the six of hearts.

Charlotte shrugged and threw down her cards—the two and four of spades. If the *river* card had been a spade, giving her a flush of five spades, or if it had been a three of any suit, making up a straight, she would have won. As it was, she had nothing.

"Bombed out on that one, I'm afraid," she said blithely. "What do you have, Damien?"

"Three aces." He laid them down.

"Your pot," she said, rising from her chair and reaching out to shake his hand across the table. "Congratulations!"

Understanding came in a flash. She'd deliberately played a high-risk hand—one that was plausible enough for others to marvel at, but with little chance of success. In effect, she let him have the win as an out for herself.

With all her chips gone, she could not play any more—the perfect escape—while he was trapped in the game by the mountain of chips she'd just ceded to him.

He rose from his own chair, admiration and frustration warring inside him. "Till we meet again, Charlotte," he said, his eyes burning the message that this escape was only temporary as he took the hand she'd offered, wrapping his fingers around it in a possessive squeeze before releasing it.

He noted she tried rubbing his touch away as she addressed the other players. "Thank you for the game, gentlemen. Enjoy the rest of it."

Appreciative comments were tossed at her as she and Mark Freedman made their departure from the saloon. Damien resumed his seat, whereupon Peter leaned over and whispered, "You've been had, my friend."

"I know it," he wryly acknowledged. "Your sister is one hell of a clever witch."

"I gave up playing chess with her in my teens," Peter slung at him.

"I'm not giving up," Damien muttered on a fierce wave of resolution.

Charlotte Ramsey was everything he wanted in a woman.

He'd kidnap her from her wedding to Freedman if he had to.

Over the next hour he stage-managed losing all his chips in a reasonable enough manner to leave the rest of the players happily satisfied with their winnings. "The night is still young," he murmured to Peter as he retired from the game.

"Good luck," was the amused reply.

It was eleven-thirty.

Damien made his way up to the top deck of the *Sea Lion* in search of the woman he now wanted more than ever. The New Year's Eve party was rocking, most of the guests singing and dancing, kicking up their heels to Nancy Sinatra's most popular track—"These Boots Are Made For Walking."

He caught sight of Charlotte stamping the floor with glee as she sang along with Nancy.

She wasn't going to walk away from him, Damien silently determined, carving his way through the crowd of dancers to cut in on Mark Freedman who was loosely partnering her. He wanted time alone with Charlotte Ramsey and nothing was going to stop him from getting it.

CHAPTER FIVE

'MIND if I have a dance with Peter's sister?"

Damien Wynter…again!

Shock turned Charlotte's happy feet into blocks of lead, anchored to the floor. She stared in disbelief at the man who would not go away, despite having been out-witted and outmanoeuvred at the poker table. In her experience, men never wanted a woman who outplayed them. Dented egos did not go hand in hand with desire.

He had to be angry.

Wanting to get back at her in some way.

Tread on her feet if nothing else.

Her heart thumped a painful protest as Mark stepped back to let him in as her dance partner. "As long as you don't mind my claiming her back before midnight," he replied, smiling at Charlotte, his warm, hazel eyes twinkling in anticipation of sharing that magic moment with her.

"Understood," Damien answered, nodding a dismissal of any further conversation with her fiancé.

"I'll be at the bar," Mark said to Charlotte in parting, possibly picking up the vibrations that his laissez-faire attitude towards Damien Wynter did not please her.

He was giving her an out if she chose to take it but

Charlotte didn't want to be given an out. She would have much preferred it if Mark had denied Damien Wynter any more time with her. He shouldn't be walking away from her.

"Let him go."

Her head jerked back from watching Mark's progress to the bar at the far end of the top saloon, her face turning up to the man who was determined on confronting her again. Her eyes blazed a fierce resentment at his contemptuous tone but there was no apologetic response in his.

"He's not worthy of you, Charlotte," he said with arrogant confidence.

"Who are you to judge?" The words flew out of her mouth on a violent surge of fury at his presumptuous criticism.

"If you were mine…"

"I'm not yours!" she snapped.

"…I would not have surrendered my place at your side to any other man. I would fight for you—" he paused to drive home the very personal point of his action "—as I fight now."

His eyes burnt with relentless purpose, causing Charlotte's heart to catch a beat before racing into a wild gallop. "Why are you doing this?" she blurted out, hating how he was tapping into her emotions and screwing them around. "Why aren't you downstairs playing poker?"

"Winning a poker game doesn't interest me as much as you do."

"But I left you with enough chips to…"

"To play in a cavalier fashion, risking too much on low percentage hands. As you did with me. Deliberately."

He smiled, appreciation of her ploy to get away from the game—from him—glinting in his eyes. It messed with her judgement of his ego. He hadn't minded her turning the tables on him down in the poker saloon. It had actually spurred him on to repeat her tactic, freeing himself to pursue her.

She shook her head, trying to clear the confusion of still being an object of desire to him. "I'm not in the mould of *trophy woman*," she muttered in exasperation. "Why try to win me?"

"There is an abundance of trophy women," he said in mocking dismissal.

Probably throwing themselves at him wherever he went, worshipping at the feet of the gorgeous money god. Was it her resistance that was making him want to *get* her?

His eyes bored into hers as he quietly and calmly stated, "I have the feeling you are my soulmate, Charlotte Ramsey."

It was so unexpected, so stunning, it took Charlotte's breath away. And he instantly moved in on her, stepping forward and wrapping his hands around her hips, the warmth of them sending a flood of heat through her entire body.

"Dance with me," he commanded, his voice a rumble deep in his throat, making the words sound like a primitive call to mate with him.

"Get your hands off me!" she commanded straight back. They were too hot, too possessive and he had no right to make any claim on her. Fighting a wild wave of panic at his closeness, at the threat of him imposing control over her, she fiercely held onto her independence, saying, "We can dance apart."

"Fine. Then let's do it," he agreed, his eyes simmering a challenge as he withdrew his hold on her. "Move to the music, Charlotte. I'll match you."

Another contest!

She should deny him. She should walk off the dance floor, join Mark at the bar. But wouldn't that mean she was afraid of the challenge in his eyes, afraid of his effect on her? Besides, she was angry with Mark for leaving her with this man. She used the anger to pump the beat of the music back into her body so she could move to it, telling herself she would dance Damien Wynter's feet off.

But he was good. She threw in everything she'd ever learnt at dance school and he didn't miss a trick, not only matching her but subtly pushing his own expertise, forcing her to match him. He was a dynamic dancer, and despite her fierce resentment of his arrogance, Charlotte found the contest exciting, exhilarating.

Damien Wynter brought an edge of danger to it. She had the sense he was stalking her, refraining from pouncing yet exuding the power to take her whenever he wanted. There was a wicked tease in his eyes, driving her to flaunt what he couldn't have without her permission. And she'd never give it. Never!

Her eyes told him so.

Her eyes said—*Look all you like. Want all you like. You won't get it, Damien Wynter!*

Though she had to admit he brought a sexual charge to dancing that she didn't feel with Mark. Dancing with Mark was fun. This was something darker, more primal, and it grabbed her in places she didn't want to think about. Nevertheless she was acutely aware of her physical response to him; the arrows of excitement shooting down her thighs whenever he moved close, the flutters in her stomach, the hard pounding of her heart, the tingling in her breasts.

"Break it off with Freedman," he said as they performed a sexy sashay around each other.

"For you?" she mocked.

"He's not your soulmate. He's your lapdog."

Charlotte was momentarily taken aback by the horribly demeaning description.

"You feel affection for him because he trots wherever you want him to go," the taunting voice continued. "And no doubt he'll lick you anywhere, making you feel loved."

She couldn't stop that image flooding through her mind and making her feel repelled by it. Then Damien Wynter was facing her again, his dark eyes burning with conviction. "He's no match for you, Charlotte."

"Better a lapdog than a wolf," she threw at him.

His teeth flashed very white against his dark olive skin. "Don't you know you're a wolverine, Charlotte? My match in every way."

Her cheeks flamed at his reading of her character, linking it to his. "I'm not like that," she cried.

"Yes, you are. You protect your territory with Mark better than he does. And you don't just bite, Charlotte. You go for the jugular when cornered."

"I don't see you bleeding," she argued vehemently. "And if I'm so vicious, why don't you back off?"

"Because you're already in my blood, vampire lady, and there's no going back."

The urge to really bite him zinged through her mind. She whirled away from him instead, working off the surge of violent energy in a frenetic set of dance steps. He followed, a magnetic presence she couldn't ignore, his energy whirling around her, demanding she face him again. Pride insisted she did.

"What I have with Mark is very serious," she declared, her eyes defying the raw desire in his even though it ripped through her body, firing treacherously primitive responses she had no control over.

"You've built a fantasy around him," he mocked. "It's not real, Charlotte. It can't be real, because there's passion pulsing between us."

"You're wrong."

"No, I'm not. You just don't want to admit it because it would spoil the plans you've made. But it will spoil them anyway, Charlotte."

"I won't let it," she said with teeth-gritting determination. "In case you don't know, there's a huge difference between animal attraction and love."

"Has Freedman signed a prenuptial agreement?"

Her chin jerked up in scornful rejection of his values. "I haven't asked him to."

The dark eyes glittered with derisive certainty. "In case you don't know it, there's a huge difference between love and money. Test him out, Charlotte."

"That would imply a lack of trust. Love and trust go hand in hand," she argued heatedly.

"If he truly loves you, he'll do it without blinking an eyelid."

"I'm not going to ask him."

"Coward."

That stung. Worse than anything else he'd said. She glared at him in mute frustration, hating the way he was digging past her defences, undermining her confidence in what she had with Mark. Her feet had stopped dancing. Her arms had dropped to her sides, hands clenching into fists. She didn't care if he thought her a coward for ending this encounter. End it she would.

"That's enough! Your dance is done, Damien Wynter, and I'd appreciate it if you kept away from me for the rest of the night."

She swung on her heel, ready to march off to Mark who was waiting for her at the bar. Before she could take a step, strong arms coiled around her waist, pulling her back into full body contact with the man she had just scorned.

"Take the feel of me with you, Charlotte," he murmured in her ear, then dropped a blistering kiss on the bare curve of her shoulder.

For a moment she was too stunned to react. Her chest felt as though iron bands were squeezing it. She was acutely aware of her bottom being pressed against his groin. Her skin was burning. She felt trapped.

"You'll never get from him what you could get from me," came the insidious whisper.

It goaded her into a savage reply. "I'd never get from you what I get from him. Now let me go or you'll get a stiletto heel stamped on your foot."

He loosened his hold on her as he mockingly answered, "Go and collect your lapdog. He won't be any protection from the truths I've put in your mind."

She wrenched herself away from the lingering touch of his hands and kept her back rigidly straight as she headed towards the bar, fuming over the outrageous presumption of the man she left behind her.

Damien Wynter was the devil incarnate, revelling in

stirring doubts and feeding temptations, but her resolution was not going to crumble under them. Mark Freedman was the man she'd chosen to marry for many good reasons, and marry him she would. Damien Wynter was just a dark ship passing in the night.

All these wildly unwelcome feelings he had aroused would pass.

What she had with Mark was not a fantasy.

It was solid.

It would last.

She would make it last.

CHAPTER SIX

ALMOST midnight.

Charlotte had downed a glass of champagne at the bar before she and Mark had left it to secure a good viewing position at the top deck railing again. The quick intake of alcohol, needed to dilute the physical impression Damien Wynter had stamped on her body, did not mix well with the fresh air outside the saloon.

Feeling unpleasantly giddy, she hung onto Mark until they reached the railing, then transferred her grip to it while she sucked in deep breaths, hoping to reduce the dizzy whirl inside her head. It didn't help to ease her discomfort when Mark moved behind her, sliding his arms around her waist and dropping a kiss on the same shoulder *he* had kissed. The instant recoil she felt was sickening. And deeply upsetting.

"Are you cold, darling?" Mark asked, concerned by the convulsive shiver that had frozen off any further casual intimacy.

"It is a bit fresh out here," Charlotte swiftly excused, hating herself for reacting so negatively to the man she loved. She did love him. She did. And to prove it she swung around and wound her arms around his neck, smiling invitingly as the countdown for the midnight fireworks began. "I think a ten-second kiss would warm me up."

He grinned happily at the saucy suggestion—not the slightest shadow on their love in his mind—and kissed her with a fervour that should have melted her bones. She worked hard at generating the heat of passion, her tongue tangling erotically with his, her thighs pressing hard, her breasts plastered to the heat of his chest, her hands curled possessively around his head, forcing the connection of their mouths to go on and on. But her mind did not co-operate.

It wondered if Damien Wynter was watching them. It sizzled with telepathic messages to him. *This is my man. Not you. See my passion for him. You haven't spoilt anything between us. I won't let you.*

The problem was, a very different truth had seized her body, robbing her of its usual natural response to Mark. She didn't feel excited. Despite her desperate need for reassurance in her choice of lover, she felt weirdly empty when Mark broke off their kiss and turned her attention to the cascades of colour flooding the night sky. He kept her snuggled close to him, his arm hugging her shoulders, yet she felt chillingly alone and suddenly frightened of going through with the future course she'd planned with him.

She stared at the red heart, still pulsing dramatically at the centre of the harbour bridge. Why isn't my heart still engaged with Mark? she silently cried. Everything was so good with him before Damien Wynter had stepped into her life. She didn't even like the man, let alone love him.

And she didn't *match* him, either. She wasn't beautiful and he was as handsome as sin. Though he had dismissed *trophy* women as of no interest to him. Words, she told herself, just words. She couldn't really believe she represented anything special to him. More likely it was the idea of conquering forbidden territory that had spurred his pursuit of her—much more fun than getting things easily.

The fireworks heralding in the new year sparked no sense of pleasure, despite the brilliant display that marked the end of them. The promise of what the new year would bring—her wedding, a happy marriage with Mark, getting pregnant, having a baby—felt as though it was slipping away, becoming less real. She wanted to hold onto it. Yet even her will-power was shaken by the kiss that hadn't sealed a solid togetherness for her.

"How long before the yacht cruises back to the dock?" Mark murmured, his mouth brushing her hair away from her cheek.

"We stay here until one o'clock," she answered.

"So long." He sighed, blowing his breath into her ear, then licking the outer rim of it as he whispered, "I want to make love to you."

Licking…like a lapdog.

Charlotte shut her eyes tight but it didn't shut the beastly image out of her mind. Her hands clenched, the need to fight it out of existence making every muscle in her body tense with desperate urgency. Mark *wasn't* like that. She cursed Damien Wynter for having hung that tag on him. It wasn't fair. Even if it was, there was more love to be had from a lapdog than a marauding wolf of a man who was more into taking than giving.

Though she inwardly shuddered at the thought of Mark making love to her tonight. She was frightened of it not feeling right, of not being able to make it feel right ever again. And pretending would be dreadful. She needed time to get over this, time to forget what could only be animal chemistry fermenting in her blood, injected there by a man intent on meddling with her life. If *he* kept out of her way and she kept out of his…

"Two more weeks and we'll be married, Mark. I was thinking…" A rush of shame at the deceit she'd been about to play halted her tongue.

"Yes?" he prompted.

Was it deceit or was it the best safeguard she could come up to protect what she believed she had with Mark? She took a deep breath and turned to face him, her hands spreading lightly over his chest as her eyes appealed for his understanding. "Would you mind if we didn't make love again until our wedding night?"

His mouth tilted ruefully. "A bit difficult when we're sharing the same apartment, sweetheart."

He'd given up his apartment and moved into hers months ago, putting his own furniture in storage until they bought a house together. The move had given rise to her father's scoffing remark that Mark was her toyboy, capitalising on the fact that her place was bigger and better than his, but she knew he'd only been considering what suited her best.

"I could go home with my parents tonight," she suggested, desperately hoping he would agree. "My mother will want me with her anyhow, checking off all the arrangements leading up to our wedding day. It will be easier if I'm right on the spot and…"

"And you want to feel like a bride on our wedding night," Mark interpreted, lifting his hand to her cheek and stroking it as he smiled indulgently. "If celibacy for the next fortnight will help make it special for you, Charlotte, then celibate I'll be."

The relief surging through her was so strong, it shook Charlotte into more uncertainty about her future with Mark. This will pass, she fiercely told herself. It has to.

"But it's a shame to waste the romance of tonight, my love," he pressed, making her heart jiggle nervously as her mind frantically sought a graceful way out of conceding to his desire to spend *this* night with her.

It was only natural—New Year's Eve. Denying him was mean.

"Hmmm…" she said as though playing with the idea, trying her utmost to quell the emotional havoc it stirred. "Let's go and dance while I think about it."

He laughed, probably thinking she was teasing him with a postponement and happy to go along with it for the duration of the cruise. Charlotte hoped that dancing with him would loosen her up, banish the tension that was making the idea of intimacy with him so gut-wrenching.

The DJ had moved on to playing more contemporary music now that it was after midnight and the older guests were content to relax around the deck. Gwen Stefani was singing "Hollaback Girl" as they re-entered the top saloon and the foot-tapping beat instantly drew them into moving with it. The lyrics struck a wry chord with Charlotte. She wanted to scream at what was happening to her.

Mark was in high spirits and she worked hard at lifting her own, throwing herself into every wild dance movement she could think of. It surprised her when the yacht's powerful engines started up. Had time passed so quickly? A glance at her watch told her no. It was still twenty minutes short of one o'clock. Frustration speared through her. Why of all nights did her father have to change the schedule when she needed every minute available to drive away the demons Damien Wynter had left her with?

"We're leaving early," Mark commented, looking happy with the cut in time.

"Looks that way," she answered non-committally, her instincts still shying from sharing the intimacy of a bed with him.

And the wretched reason for that—in person—had the arrogance to break into their dancing, when she had specifically told him to stay away from her for the rest of the night. He even had the temerity to clamp his hand around her arm, forcing her attention onto him. Outrage billowed up and almost spat off her tongue. But he spoke first, with a serious urgency that forestalled an angry barrage from her.

"Charlotte, you're wanted downstairs."

"What's up?" Mark asked, catching on that this was no light interruption.

Damien Wynter ignored him, his eyes boring past the antagonism in hers, alerting her to trouble that went beyond another personal challenge. "Your father's had a bad turn," he said quietly. "Peter's with him. I've already fetched your mother."

Shock clutched her heart. There was no disbelief in her mind. It instantly connected the yacht's early start back to the dock to what she should have realised had to be an emergency. "How bad?" she choked out, fear for her father's life surging over the shock.

Sympathy in the dark eyes made her stomach contract at the possibility of worse news. She stopped breathing until he answered, "I don't know. A doctor, one of the guests, is working on him. An ambulance has been called to take him to hospital as soon as we dock. I think you should come, Charlotte."

"Yes." She was too worried about her father to think of anything else. It didn't occur to her to protest when Damien Wynter gathered her protectively to his side and virtually scooped her along with him, carving a path through the crowd of dancers, leaving Mark to trail after them. She felt shaky and was grateful for the strength that emanated from him, guiding her with steady purpose down to the lower deck.

Her father's aide-de-camp was guarding the door to the saloon. He nodded in respect to her. "Miss Ramsey, your brother has asked me to make an announcement to the guests and request that they stay on the upper deck until your father is taken off. The family limousines have been alerted to the situation. They'll be standing ready to follow the ambulance to the hospital."

"Thank you, Giles."

He ushered them into the saloon. The poker players were gone. Her father lay on the floor, his usually ruddy face drained of all colour, his skin a frightening shade of grey. His eyes were closed. Charlotte recognised the doctor crouched at his side—the famous heart surgeon, Eric Lee. He was holding her father's wrist, checking his pulse, and Charlotte felt a flood of gratitude for her mother's charity work for the Heart Foundation, that such a man was her guest and on hand tonight.

Her mother was kneeling on her father's other side, his left hand clutched in both of hers, anxious concern written all over her face. She wrenched her gaze from her husband to dart a glance at Charlotte. Her big brown eyes looked as though they were drowning in anguish, and her coppery cap of hair, usually perfectly smooth, had been raked into disarray. It struck Charlotte hard that her mother was very deeply attached to her father, despite their different life-styles. If she lost him…

No, don't go there, Charlotte berated herself, feeling her own heart quiver at the thought. She wanted to rush over and hug her mother, but that brief sharing glance was followed by a return of intense concentration on her father, and Charlotte felt wrong about intruding on that silent communion, sensing that her mother was willing him to survive and come back to her.

Peter was sitting on a chair behind the doctor, his upper body hunched over, elbows on his knees, hands fretting at each other. They were the only people in the room which was deathly quiet, shut off from the noise above.

Damien drew up a chair beside Peter's to sit Charlotte in it. Her brother dragged his gaze up to acknowledge his friend's help. "Thanks." Then he grimaced at Charlotte, reaching out and gripping her hand as she sat down. "Looks like a heart attack. Don't know if it's minor or major. They'll check the damage once we get him to hospital."

She nodded, squeezing his hand in sisterly comfort. They waited in grim silence for the yacht to dock. She was aware of Damien moving behind the chairs to stand at Peter's side, ready to be of any further help he could, and despite all the angst he had given her tonight, she couldn't disapprove of his presence here.

Mark had set a chair next to hers and was sitting beside her, and she knew it was because he was attached to her, yet she didn't feel attached to him. Somehow he wasn't a part of what she and her family were going through here. He didn't know how it was for them. He hadn't lived the Ramsey life.

Her father was a giant of a man, in every sense, and while she had tried to slide away from the world he'd built, wanting to forge a different kind of life with Mark, she knew she would be shattered if he wasn't there, indomitable as always, challenging her to come to terms with who and what she was, being proud of his daughter.

Was he right about her toying with something that was wrong for her with Mark? Had she been bull-headed in her refusal to listen to him? He'd been so angry with her this afternoon—red-faced, high blood pressure. Was she to blame for this heart attack?

Just live, Daddy, please. Let us talk again.

The yacht slowed, stopped. The saloon door was thrust open. She heard Giles calling out instructions. It only seemed seconds before paramedics were rushing in with a mobile stretcher. Peter leapt to his feet and moved swiftly to help their mother to hers and draw her out of the way. Charlotte stood and began pushing the chairs back to the poker table, anxious to make more space for action. Mark helped, grabbing the opportunity to speak to her.

"Do you want me to come to the hospital with you, Charlotte?"

Guilt ripped through her at the uncertainty in his voice. Had she made him feel like an outsider? Yet he was in this instance. Her father didn't like him, wouldn't have him in the family if he had his way.

"I'll be with Mum, Mark. I think…only immediate family. Go on home. I'll call you when…when there's some positive news."

He nodded, looking relieved at being let off the hook of hanging around the hospital in an atmosphere of grim waiting, the odd one out of a tight family clique. Charlotte also had the uneasy feeling that he wouldn't care if her father died—a thorn removed from their relationship, a tie severed. She could hardly blame him for that, given her father's grudging acceptance of him, but she preferred not to have him at her side tonight. Any comforting from him would feel false.

As it turned out, her mother clung to Peter, wanting him beside her on the ride to the hospital—her son, made in the same mould as his father, not the rebellious daughter who had defied her father's judgement of Mark. Charlotte had thought her mother understood why she'd wanted a different kind of marriage, yet when it came to this critical time, it was Peter her mother turned to for understanding and solace, leaving her feeling painfully rejected.

It was her brother who empathised with how apart this made her feel, shooting a look of sharp appeal to his friend. "Will you stand in for me with Charlotte, Damien?"

"Of course," was the instant response. "Go, Peter. We'll follow."

Again she was taken under Damien Wynter's strong, protective wing. He steered her to the next limousine in line and saw her settled in the back seat before quickly skirting the vehicle to take his place beside her. She couldn't bring herself to resent his company. He was of Peter's world, her father's world, familiar with how it worked—its privileges and its penalties. Being *one of them* was not such a bad thing right now.

The limousine moved off, tailing her mother's. Charlotte held her hands tightly in her lap, needing to take a firm grip on the emotions churning through her, fight back the tears gathering behind her eyes.

"If it were your mother being rushed to hospital, your father would have chosen you to accompany him, Charlotte," Damien said quietly. "It's an instinctive thing, seeking comfort from the opposite sex. Nothing personal."

Was that true? Maybe it was. The sense that both her parents were deserting her eased, though the ache in her chest didn't go away. It occurred to her that Damien might be serving his own interest here.

She threw him a bleakly ironic look. "If that's an invitation to seek sexual comfort from you, I'm not about to take it up. But thank you for filling in a very empty space."

His dark eyes caught hers with searing intensity. "Why did you send Freedman home, Charlotte?"

She wrenched her gaze from his, staring blindly out the tinted side window. "Not because I wanted to be with you, so don't imagine that for one moment," she muttered fiercely.

"I don't imagine it," he dryly retorted. "I simply put to you a very pertinent question about your relationship with the man you're intent on marrying."

"It has nothing to do with how I feel about Mark,"

Charlotte answered tersely. "I was thinking of my father, not wanting him upset by anything while he's in a fragile state."

"So your father doesn't approve of this marriage."

The satisfaction in his voice goaded her into glaring at him. "Time will prove he's mistaken about Mark." Though she wasn't so sure about that any more. Was it right to go ahead with this marriage with doubts and fears bombarding her at every turn?

"Time may prove he's not mistaken," was shot straight back at her. "Time may prove Freedman *is* a fortune-hunter, manipulating you into giving him an easy ride through life."

Her chin lifted in belligerent scorn. "I'm not easily manipulated."

"No?" One black eyebrow rose mockingly. "Then get him to sign a prenuptial agreement, Charlotte. That will ease your father's mind. It might very well remove some of the stress that's brought on this heart attack."

She sucked in air, trying to ward off the wretched wave of guilt that had instantly attacked her own heart. "You can't make that judgement. It might have been caused by high cholesterol, thickening arteries, something physically wrong," she said wildly.

"True," he readily conceded. "I was just remembering the expression on your father's face when you left the poker saloon with Freedman tonight."

The guilt stabbed even more painfully. Her mind clutched at the possibility that Damien Wynter was painting a scene that suited his own purpose—wanting to push Mark out of her life. "No doubt you read into it what you wanted to read," she shot at him.

His mouth curled into a sardonic smile. "You either know the truth or don't want to know it."

"You're playing your own game, Damien Wynter, and this isn't the time to do it."

His eyes burned into hers. "I have to seize whatever time is available to make you realise I'm the man you want, not Freedman. I'm here beside you, Charlotte. Think about that."

"I didn't ask for you," she replied heatedly.

"You accepted me."

"In a moment of crisis."

"Precisely. You should trust your instincts. They'll steer you more truly than your head."

Her heart was galloping. She hated his power to do that to her.

"You're holding onto Freedman through pride," he went on in relentless attack. "And pride is a cold bed-fellow. I can promise you, any bed *we* shared would not be cold."

His gaze dropped to her breasts, making her acutely aware they were heaving in emotional agitation; to her hands still linked in her lap, forming a tight guard over the vulnerable sexuality he would storm, given the slightest encouragement; to her knees, which were shaking out of sheer fear that he would pounce anyway. And if he kissed her, *what would she feel?*

Tonight she could not have gone to bed with Mark.

It was a terrible thing to think her father's heart attack had been a godsend, delivering her from any pressure to do what should have been a natural act, a desired act, an *instinctive* act.

"Please stop," she begged, barely knowing what she

was begging for, feeling besieged by a man who wasn't even touching her.

"I can't stop what you make me feel, Charlotte," he answered quietly, his eyes challenging her brittle defences to the sexual magnetism he was exerting.

"It's the wrong time," she cried, her mind chaotically whirling over the fragile state of her father's health, over the fact that her wedding was only two weeks away. Though maybe she should call it off. How could she feel happy about it in these circumstances? And if her father died…

"Over some things we can't choose the timing," Damien said, homing straight in on the dilemma she had to resolve. "They just happen and we have to recognise that reality and deal with it."

"Well, right now I'm dealing with what's happened to my father and I'd appreciate it if you'd respect that," she burst out defensively.

"As you wish, but don't think I'll go away, Charlotte. I might not be in your heart yet, but I'm in your mind," he said with blazing certainty. "I'll let that be enough for now."

He said no more, for which she was intensely grateful.

But he was right. The damage was already done. He *was* in her mind.

And it was wrecking what she'd had with Mark.

CHAPTER SEVEN

'How's your father?' Mark asked, sounding more alert and caring than he had when she'd called him at eight o'clock this morning. She'd found it irritating, even offensive, that he had gone home and fallen into such a deep sleep, then just mumbled grumpily to her news that the heart attack had been more a warning than a death sentence and her father was resting comfortably. The less than sympathetic response had actually provoked her into wondering if he'd have preferred to hear that a funeral had to be arranged.

"I'm going home with Mum now," she'd stated tersely. "I'll call you again after I've visited Dad tonight."

"Sure," he'd slurred, as though he had a hangover from a heavy hit of alcohol—celebrating the possible demise of her father? She'd be worth a lot more with her father dead.

Bad thoughts.

And no real cause for them.

Her mind had been diseased by Damien Wynter.

It was now nine o'clock in the evening and she had secluded herself in her own private suite at her parents' Palm Beach mansion, away from Peter and his guest whom she'd discovered—too late—was also staying here instead of at a hotel. She couldn't wipe Damien Wynter out of her mind but she was determined to be completely fair to Mark during this call, listening to him without any tainted concerns about their future together.

"There's only one word to describe my father tonight and that's irascible," she said, trying to lighten up this exchange between herself and her fiancé. "He hates being ill. He hates being in hospital. He wants to come home and he's cranky because Mum insists he stay at least another day under medical observation."

"Sounds as though he's fighting fit again," Mark said dryly.

"I don't think he wants to believe anything else. I asked him if he wanted us to postpone the wedding and he informed me he was not an invalid and he'd be standing up for his daughter on the day if he had to, though he'd be much happier about it if I followed his advice first."

"What did he mean by that?" Mark quickly sliced in, his voice much sharper over this point.

She sighed, knowing she now had to put Mark to this test, and not only for her father's peace of mind. Her own growing doubts about their relationship needed to be settled. "Dad said if I really cared about him I'd do what he wants me to do before we get married. I know it's emotional blackmail, Mark, but…it won't make any difference to us, will it?"

"What won't?" he asked edgily.

"Signing a prenuptial agreement."

Silence.

Charlotte counted to ten, trying to drive away the tension building inside her.

"I thought you trusted our love, Charlotte," he finally said, his wounded tone squeezing her heart. "To enter into a marriage, anticipating divorce down the track… where's the commitment to each other?" he pressed plaintively.

"Please don't look at it that way, Mark," she started to appeal.

"How else can I look at it?" he cut in, acutely reminding her that these were same arguments she herself had used against signing a prenup, wanting to believe in a lasting love.

Charlotte steeled herself to push her point. "I want to relieve my father's mind. If we sign the agreement he'll feel much better about our marriage."

"It's an insult to me," Mark growled. "An insult to my feelings for you, Charlotte."

"Mark, if *I* know what your feelings are, and *you* know what your feelings are, it doesn't change anything. I'm sorry you feel insulted, but we can always prove Dad wrong in the long run. This is simply a form to sign. If we consider it meaningless to us, that's what it will be."

Another silence.

Charlotte began to think it wasn't meaningless to Mark.

And it should be.

It definitely should be, unless he had been counting on a hefty divorce settlement down the track.

And it wasn't Damien Wynter putting that in her mind. It was Mark himself, making storm waves out of what should be dismissed as an insignificant ripple on the way to the future they'd planned together.

She grew impatient with his silence, impatient with the sense he was thinking his way to some other negative position. "I put my father's peace of mind before my pride, Mark, particularly in these circumstances," she said strongly.

"You're putting your father ahead of me," he retorted, anger pulsing through every word.

What was behind the anger? Ego? Or the potential loss of millions of dollars if he signed the prenuptial agreement?

Either way, Charlotte didn't like it. Her voice hardened. "Yes, I am, in this instance. You haven't just suffered a heart attack, Mark. My father is not standing in the way of our marriage…"

"He's putting limitations on it," was flashed back at her.

"Only *financial* limitations," she pointed out coldly. "Do you have a problem with that, Mark?"

She heard a hiss of breath, then in a quick rush, "Only in so far as it implies he thinks I'm a skunk."

"Well, he won't after you sign the agreement, will he?"

"I guess not," came the reluctant reply.

"Look, I told Dad when I saw him tonight that we would sign it, Mark. I saw no reason not to. I'm sorry you're upset by the idea…"

"That's okay. I'll get over it," he said quickly. "It was just a bit of a shock, being hit with it so close to the wedding."

Hit?

Charlotte frowned at the word. In all fairness, she had to concede that being asked to sign the agreement was a strike at Mark's integrity, but it shouldn't really hurt him if his integrity was unassailable.

"Dad did want it all along, Mark," she explained. "Apparently he was stressing over my stubbornness in refusing to follow his advice. Anyhow, I promised him we'd sign the agreement he'd had prepared in his lawyer's office tomorrow morning. So what time would suit you?"

After considerable humming from Mark, they settled on ten o'clock. Charlotte felt so out of sorts with him, she ended the call with an abrupt, "See you there," not wanting to hear or participate in any *love* talk.

It's all spoilt, she thought, hating Damien Wynter for his part in undermining her happiness with Mark, hating herself for being so disturbed by the man. Why couldn't she recapture what she'd had with Mark before *he* had stepped onto the scene? Had she woven a fantasy around the marriage she wanted—a fantasy Mark had worked hard at fitting because she could supply him with the kind of wealth he craved—wealth that was legally limited if he signed the agreement.

Would she feel right about their relationship again if he signed with a good will tomorrow morning?

Charlotte tossed and turned over that question long into the night, her bed more like a torture chamber than a place of rest. It was a relief when morning came. She had a long shower, hoping to wash away the fatigue of too much worrying, telling herself everything would feel better when she met Mark.

There was a bowl of fresh fruit in her sitting room. A banana and a peach served her well enough for breakfast. She didn't want any contact with Damien Wynter this morning, messing with her head. And body. The man oozed sex appeal, but that meant any woman at all—not just her—would feel a hormonal buzz around him. It was wrong to let it distract her from working through what was really important.

It was already hot, and since the weather forecast warned it would be a sizzling January day of up to forty degrees Celsius—high fire hazard—Charlotte dressed accordingly: a sleeveless black top with a scooped neckline, a white and black skirt with a striking geometric pattern and minimal black sandals.

Her own car was still at the Double Bay apartment, but the taxi she'd called was waiting for her in the driveway at nine o'clock, and she succeeded in making a quick getaway without running into anyone to whom she had to explain anything. The hour-long ride from Palm Beach to the inner-city in air-conditioned comfort gave her time to compose her mind along positive channels.

She'd called Giles to set up the ten o'clock meeting with her father's lawyer. Mark would join her at the King Street office. They would sign the agreement, then go and have a nice lunch together. Everything should then be fine, just as it was before.

Except it didn't work out like that.

Her heart did not fill with happy warmth when Mark greeted her with a smile and told her she looked gorgeous. His eyes didn't smile and she sensed he was still angry about being forced into signing the agreement. They walked into the lawyer's office, hand in hand, but she didn't feel joined to Mark in spirit. They sat in separate leather chairs, facing the legal expert behind his desk as he explained the terms of the prenuptial agreement—which seemed reasonable to her—and her nerves got tighter and tighter at all the questions Mark asked.

Why did it matter so much to him?

He wasn't required to pay out anything if they got

divorced. Any quibbling over the terms felt terribly wrong to her.

However, when he was finally requested to sign, he did rise to his feet, stepped briskly over to the lawyer's desk, took the pen offered to him and wrote on the legal document, fulfilling what she'd insisted upon for their wedding to go ahead—the wedding they'd planned, the wedding that no longer looked so bright and beautiful on her horizon.

"I'm afraid that won't do, sir," the lawyer said, lifting his gaze from what had been written to eye Mark sternly.

"It's the truth," Mark growled.

"The words—*under duress*—renders the document useless in a court of law. It doesn't serve the purpose of the agreement."

"You wrote *under duress?*" Charlotte queried, rising from her chair to see for herself, appalled disbelief pounding through her head.

"It's how I feel," Mark shot at her, possibly expecting her to lick his wounds and make peace between them by setting the agreement aside.

She stared down at the black and white evidence that the wealth a marriage to her promised was a driving factor in his *love* for her. It curdled her stomach. The fantasy crumbled. No way could she put it together again. Very slowly and deliberately she drew off the diamond engagement ring he'd given her and held it out to him.

"What are you doing?" he asked, shocked by her action.

"It's over," she stated flatly. "I won't marry you."

He looked incredulously at her. "You'll let your father come between us?"

Her mouth tilted with black irony. "He didn't. Money did."

Still he couldn't believe she would make such a decision. "But the wedding…"

"The wedding is off." He hadn't taken the ring. She set it down on the document he'd rendered useless. "Goodbye, Mark."

"All right. I'll sign it properly." He gabbled in panic, reaching out to the lawyer. "You must have another copy."

"It's pointless." She directed at the lawyer, turned her back on Mark and held it rigid as she walked to the door.

He pleaded.

She didn't soften. Her heart was closed to him.

The last words he hurled at her were, "I'll sue you for ownership of the apartment. We had a de facto relationship, Charlotte…"

The Ramsey wealth was a curse, she thought. And there was no fairy godmother to wave her wand and lift it. She'd been a fool to believe in living happily ever after with Mark. Reality had just bitten hard and now she had to deal with it.

The worst part was—reality wore the face of Damien Wynter.

And the future felt as dark as the eyes that had challenged her to re-appraise everything she'd built around Mark.

CHAPTER EIGHT

FORTUNATELY a vacant taxi was coming down King Street as Charlotte emerged from the lawyer's office. She quickly hailed it and in a matter of seconds, was whisked away from any possible threat of a physical follow-up by Mark Freedman. Her stomach was churning in revolt against having any further contact with him. He could have the apartment, she thought savagely. Living there again would only bring her bitter memories.

Having directed the cab driver to the family home at Palm Beach, she settled back in her seat with a sense of deep relief that breaking up with Mark was now behind her. The sick feeling eased as the taxi put more distance between them, but a black fog of depression started rolling through her mind.

She'd given up her job at the bank in anticipation of her marriage to Mark—marriage *and children*—and right now she had big fat nothing in her life. Thirty years old and going nowhere. Apart from which, she had a huge chunk of humiliation to swallow.

Everyone was going to wonder why the wedding had been called off. No doubt, gossip would run rife. Maybe taking the planned honeymoon trip overseas would

serve as an escape, though it would probably accentu-
ate the wretched hollowness of being alone—the honeymoon that was not a honeymoon.

Several times tears threatened and she fought them
back with anger; anger at having been fooled, at having
fooled herself that Mark was everything she'd wanted
him to be. Blind, blind, blind. And bull-headed. She
should have listened to her father, respected his judgement. Listened to her mother, too. "Don't you think
he's a bit too charming, dear?"

Not like her father, Charlotte had interpreted at the
time. Her mother judged all men by her husband and
Lloyd Ramsey had never been charming. But you did
know exactly where you were with him. No being
fooled. Charlotte didn't want to be fooled, ever again.

Facing her parents with the truth was going to be the
hardest part—acknowledging they'd been right and she'd
been wrong. On the other hand, maybe they'd be so
relieved at not having Mark as a son-in-law, they'd simply
say they were glad she'd realised her mistake before the
marriage took place. But that didn't alleviate her misery
over having made the mistake. It made it worse.

She blinked hard to hold back another rush of tears
as the taxi entered the family compound at Palm Beach.
There was so much to be cancelled and time was short—
less than two weeks now. It would be totally irrespon-
sible—cowardly—to give into the urge to run away and
hide, lick her wounds in private. She had to find her
mother, tell her what had happened.

Having paid off the taxi driver, Charlotte stuck
grimly to her purpose, eventually finding her mother in
the conservatory, showing off her prized exotic plants.

To Damien Wynter, of all people.

Her stomach instantly cramped. Her chest hurt. The constriction in her throat made it impossible to speak. Both of them had heard her enter, her sandals clacking on the tiled floor, and they had turned enquiringly, expecting her to say something. Charlotte's aching eyes could not bear the sharp intensity in Damien Wynter's. She fixed her gaze on her mother, desperately trying to exclude him from her mind.

"Yes, dear?" her mother asked as Charlotte worked hard at swallowing the block in her throat.

"Is something wrong, Charlotte?" *he* asked, the concern in his voice causing an emotional surge that shattered the control she'd barely been hanging onto.

"The wedding is off," she blurted out.

The bald announcement was like a bomb blast in her head. The damn of tears broke, spilling in a shaming rush. Regaining any composure was utterly impossible. She fled, the blind need to escape the gut-wrenching humiliation driving her feet along the fastest way to her private suite.

I don't want him back!

Charlotte woke to those emphatic words ringing in her mind. They were the last words she'd spoken to her mother, arguing for immediate action on cancelling the wedding. The flood of tears had passed soon after Kate Ramsey had come to sit on her bed, stroking her hair and murmuring soothing words. Charlotte had managed to spill out everything about the meeting in the lawyer's office, how Mark had reacted to the prenuptial agreement, why she wasn't going to marry him. Her mother had sympathised with her feelings but still insisted they wait until tomorrow before doing anything.

"Have a nap, dear," she'd said before leaving for the hospital. "You're emotionally exhausted right now."

Which was true enough, but it didn't change the situation. Maybe her mother thought Mark would recant his stance and she would forgive him. No way!

The time on the bedside clock read 15:23. Mid-afternoon. She was hot and sweaty. Why wasn't the air-conditioning working? She rolled over and saw the sliding glass door to her balcony wide-open, letting in the sizzling forty degree heat outside. She'd done that herself, pacing around in agitation after her mother had left, forgetting to close the door before finally crawling onto the bed and dropping into oblivion.

I'll have a swim, she thought. It would cool her down and lighten up the heaviness in her head. She swung herself off the bed, closed the balcony door so the air-conditioning would come into effect again, washed her face, brushed her hair up into a pony-tail, pulled on a sleek black maillot for serious swimming and headed down to the indoor lap pool which was mostly used by her father for his favourite form of exercise.

It was a relaxing place with lounges placed near the glass wall which gave a view of one of the marinas in Pittwater. One could sit and watch the yachts sailing by. A bar in the corner provided any desired drink. Charlotte expected to be alone there. Her mother and Peter would be at the hospital and Damien Wynter would surely be about his business in Australia, whatever that entailed.

Except he wasn't.

Charlotte's heart sank like a stone at the sight of him

casually stretched out on one of the lounges, a pen in one hand and a folded section of newspaper in the other. He was naked, apart from a brief black swimming costume—formidably naked, with a lot of very male muscles powering his arms, thighs, calves.

Her feet stopped dead.

His head turned. Dark riveting eyes swiftly catalogued everything about her appearance, making her feel raw and unprotected. Her teeth gritted with steely determination. She would not turn tail and run. Pride insisted she face him down and go right ahead, doing what she'd come to do—swim!

"How are you at cryptic crosswords?" he asked. "I need a four-letter word for a cad whose complexion turns red."

"Crud!" burst off her tongue, applying it instantly to Mark.

"Perfect!" Damien Wynter acclaimed with a wolfish grin that set her pulse racing.

"You're welcome," she snapped, and forced herself to ignore him, stepping forward and diving into the pool.

Ten laps without a pause worked off the frenetic energy *his* presence had fired up, coincidentally demonstrating she was not wilting under the trauma of calling off the wedding, despite the weeping fit he'd partially witnessed. What had to be faced would be faced. Including *him*. And if he offered her one grain of sympathy for her mistake, she'd probably do him some violence for being an out an out hypocrite.

"Feeling better?" he asked, when she'd stopped thrashing the water and was hanging onto the ladder for a breather. His disembodied voice floated over her head, and the fact that he wasn't visible made it easier to attack the issues between them.

"Feeling smug about being right?" she retorted, deliberately loading the bait for him to make some offensive remark about her break-up with Mark.

"What was I right about?" he countered, putting the ball back in her court.

"My ex-fiancé wanted the Ramsey wealth more than he wanted me."

"As well as you, more probably," came the considered reply. "Don't knock yourself, Charlotte. Amongst the women I've known you shine like a diamond, every facet of you fascinating. I'd take you without a penny to your name."

Despite the coolness of the water, her blood ran hot. The man was a devil, adept at turning anything to his advantage. And getting under her skin.

"Is that supposed to make me feel good?" she mocked, wanting to deny his effect on her.

"Yes. Why not? It's a waste of time, mourning a dream," he mocked right back, arrogantly adding, "especially when you can fill up the emptiness with me."

She gave a derisive laugh. "That would be another dream."

"Oh, I don't think so," he drawled. "I imagine everything we'd have together would be very, very real. One certainty particularly leaps to mind. We'd both know the fortune factor is irrelevant to our relationship."

"We haven't got a relationship," she tersely reminded him.

"That's not true. We've already started one, Charlotte. And the barrier of Mark Freedman is now down."

The satisfaction in his voice rankled. "That doesn't mean the gate is open for you, Damien Wynter."

To prove the point, she kicked off the wall and started swimming again, away from him and his insidious attraction. He was just amusing himself with her, playing word-games. Which, she had to admit, sharpened up her mind considerably, not to mention revitalising the rest of her.

She reached the other end of the pool, turned and saw that he'd risen from the lounge and was standing behind the ladder where she'd rested before, holding a towel ready for her to emerge from the water. In this upright position, his physique was even more formidable.

He was built like a champion swimmer; broad-shouldered, powerful chest, lean hips, no soft flesh anywhere. A magnificent man, Charlotte couldn't help thinking, and felt a very female ripple of sexual interest. Which irritated her into swimming hard again—three more laps, ignoring his waiting for her to finish, at least until he realised that she was not about to let her will be dominated by his.

All the same, she couldn't stop thinking about him— a completely different kettle of fish to the man who'd deceived her so badly—maybe the antidote she needed right now to counter the poisonous debacle of her relationship with Mark. If nothing else, Damien Wynter served to make her feel fighting fit again. Adrenaline was still pumping through her when she hauled herself out of the water and took the towel he offered.

"Thank you," she said, determined on being coolly polite.

He waved to the bar. "Can I fix you a drink?"

She nodded. "A Bloody Mary might go down well."

He laughed. "A substitute for sinking your fangs into me, Charlotte?"

"You could have removed yourself from my line of fire," she tossed at him as she proceeded to mop up the drips of water, steeling herself not to react to his watching her.

His dark eyes twinkled wickedly. "Being with you is so invigorating, I wouldn't miss a moment of your company."

She raised a mocking eyebrow. "Were you lying in wait for me here?"

"A hot afternoon. A need to work off negative energy. I thought you might come down for a swim. Happily I was right," he rolled out, startling her with the logic he'd applied to pursue his interest in her.

Her eyes defied the interest, which was far too fast for her to feel comfortable with. "I'm not particularly *happy* about it."

"Nonsense! Hitting off me is a much more satisfying alternative to lonely hours of beating up on yourself for not realising Freedman wanted everything."

His confidence definitely needed pricking. "I'm glad you didn't say hitting *on* you, because you'll be waiting a long time for that to happen, Damien Wynter."

"Good!" he approved with another wolfish grin. "There wouldn't be any fun in the game if you made it too easy."

She gave him a blistering look. "This is *the get Charlotte Ramsey game,* is it?"

The grin grew wider. "For better or for worse."

That was a hit below the belt—a direct reference to the marriage vow Mark hadn't been prepared to take

without a gilt-edged lining. *Worse* hadn't been acceptable to her ex-fiancé. Charlotte sucked in air. Savage
replies ripped through her mind. But the glittering satisfaction in the dark eyes told her he was waiting for
such a response, planning on turning it to his advantage.

She forced her mouth to smile. "Are you as good as
your word, Damien?" she asked silkily.

"Always," he stated without so much as a blink.

She nodded to the bar. "I like a generous splash of
Tabasco in the Bloody Mary you said you'd fix for me."

"As spicy as your side-step," he remarked appreciatively, then headed for the bar to follow through on his
word.

Charlotte stared at his cheeky butt, as tautly muscled
as the rest of him. She felt an almost overwhelming
urge to run after him and smack it. Which surprised her.
And gave her an understanding of why people did resort
to physical violence when they were deeply frustrated
by a situation.

The sense that Damien Wynter would never accept
defeat in any shape or form made it all the more perverse
that she should want to stay and fight him. Maybe it was
the wounded animal effect, an instinctive need to lash
out at someone, especially the someone who'd seeded
the painful doubts that had led to today's devastating
revelation. Or maybe she wanted to find out if his
supposed attraction to her was genuine, or just an entertaining power play.

Having wrapped the towel around her waist,
Charlotte walked over to the lounge adjacent to the one
he'd occupied and stretched out on it, pretending to be
completely relaxed. He'd set the folded newspaper page

and pen on the low table between the two lounges and she picked them up, curious to see if he really had been working on a cryptic crossword.

"Want to help me finish it?" he asked.

There were five clues still to be worked through. "I can't see where you've written 'crud.'"

"I made that one up for you."

She flicked him a challenging glance. "A test?"

He was coming towards her, a long red drink in each hand, his eyes twinkling devilment as he answered, "You didn't disappoint me."

"Don't count on that continuing," she warned, her nerves tightening as he came closer and closer, his strong masculinity making her feel distinctly threatened.

But he didn't touch her, didn't try to hand her the drink. He set the long glasses down on the table. He'd even put a twist of lemon on their rims, ensuring there was nothing to criticise. However, instead of lying back on the lounge, he sat on the edge of it, facing her, a whimsical little smile playing over his perfectly sculpted lips.

"Thank you," she said, setting down the pen and crossword page as she picked up her drink. "I'll pass on doing the puzzle with you. I'm really not in the mood for mind-games today."

"Then let me put a proposition to you, Charlotte," he tossed at her very casually.

She eyed him warily over the rim of her glass, sipping the Bloody Mary which had been mixed to her taste. Assume nothing, she told herself. Let him spell out what he had in mind. No doubt it would reveal where his interest in her lay.

"My guess is you've organised the kind of wedding you've dreamed of since you were a little girl," he mused, the dark eyes gently probing hers, not aiming to stir up hurt, just trying to see how it was for her. "Everything meticulously co-ordinated to create it, right down to the last little detail," he went on. "The perfect day…"

"Hardly perfect without a groom," she sliced at him, forgetting to guard her tongue.

"True. Which is where I come in."

"You?" She frowned over the weird leap he'd just made.

"Let's have that perfect day, Charlotte. With me waiting at the end of the aisle instead of Freedman."

It completely blew her brain. She stared at him in stunned disbelief, finally finding her tongue enough to splutter, "You've got to be joking!"

"No, I'm not. Think about it." His eyes glinted with deadly serious intent. "There won't be a guest at the wedding—I promise you—who won't think it's a perfect match. They'll forget all about Freedman. There won't be any questions over why you dumped him. You won't suffer the slightest dint to your pride. Tongues will only wag over the amazing romance of it all."

"Romance!" She almost choked on the word.

"Big-time romance. Prince of wealth sweeps in and nabs princess of wealth in whirlwind strike. Couldn't be a better story. It will zip around the world."

She shook her head, feeling as though she'd been caught up in a whirlwind. "This is madness."

He smiled, dazzling her with a blast of magnetic delight. "A beautiful madness, Charlotte."

"Stop it!" she demanded, anger beginning to break

through shock. "You're concocting a story of a fairy-tale wedding. And this—" her eyes flashed scorn "—after you claimed anything between us would be real. A wedding marks the start of a marriage. It's not just a…a showday for its own sake."

"But it will be a brilliant showday," he came back without missing a beat. "It will show everyone I *want* to marry you. Show that I want *you* as my wife, as my partner in everything."

He'd rocked her again.

She was breathless, speechless.

This was so totally unexpected…surreal.

His eyes gathered an intensity that bored straight through the wild floundering in her mind and struck at her heart. "Don't think for a second this isn't real. It's as real as the two of us being here together right now. And I have no doubt in my mind that you and I can make ourselves a very real marriage."

He wasn't joking.

He meant it.

And he proceeded to punch home how it could actually happen.

"All it needs from you is the will to carry it through." Conviction poured from him with an almost mesmerising power as he unequivocally stated, "You have that strength of will, Charlotte…I know you have."

CHAPTER NINE

THE will to do it...

Charlotte's mind spun around those words. And everything else he'd said. No cancellation of the wedding. No humiliating gossip. No hiding her head in shame at having been taken in by Mark. With Damien Wynter starring as her bridegroom, everyone would see her as a triumphant bride, certainly not an object of pity.

And her father would positively beam approval at her new choice of husband. It would undoubtedly do his heart a power of good. Everything in the Ramsey garden would be rosy again. No thorn bleeding the family fortune, showing her up as a patsy who'd had the wool pulled over her eyes. Damien Wynter would be a blinding blast of sunshine, obliterating her mistake.

But it meant *marrying* him!

Marrying a man she barely knew, throwing in her lot with him, not even knowing what that would entail!

"I can't do it," she blurted out, appalled that she'd let her pride and the need to make peace with her father tempt her into actually considering his proposition.

"Why not?" he fired at her.

"I don't love you," tripped straight off her tongue.

"Irrelevant." His eyes mocked the concept as he argued, "Half the people of the world marry without being in love. They join their lives for the mutual purpose of sharing property and having children."

"You want children?"

"With you, I do, Charlotte." He smiled, inviting her to imagine how it could be. "I think we'd make marvellous children together."

Maybe they would. But still…she did want her husband to love her. And she wanted to love him. Without that emotional bond…

"You do want children," Damien pressed.

"Yes." One more dream she'd been mourning.

"You're thirty years old," he harshly reminded her. "Peter told me. If you want to have a family, it's time to start on it."

She *knew* that. He didn't have to rub salt into that particular wound. Mark had seemed to be the answer to that very special need, but she couldn't marry Mark now. Would she ever find another man to love? Could she ever again trust any *professed* love for her? Her faith in human nature had just taken a lethal battering.

At least unconditional love flowed between a mother and her children. She would always know that wasn't tainted by other factors. And if she had to choose a sperm donor, Damien Wynter's genes had a lot going for them. He had a superb body and an extremely clever mind. Which he was undoubtedly using to plant these thoughts in hers.

For what purpose?

He wasn't professing love for her. Which was just as well, because no way would she believe in it. So something else was behind his proposition, and he knew better than to soft-soap it with any talk of *love*. Cold, hard facts for her to weigh—bitter facts—were the tools he was using to tip her his way. But she wasn't stupid. Jumping out of one bad scene into another wouldn't bring her any happiness.

She stared hard at the man, needing to acquire some firm handle on where he was coming from and what he meant to get out of marrying her. A tumble in bed was one thing. He'd been pushing the sexual angle from the start. But marriage was something else—a huge commitment, tying their lives together.

Would it seal some business merger with Peter? Obviously he had asked her brother for some personal information about her—how old she was…and what else? Had they spoken about sharing property?

"Where does Peter come into this?" she asked point-blank, hoping to jolt some truth from him.

"He doesn't."

The answer was completely straight-faced. But the poker game had taught her he was good at bluffing. "Oh, come on!" she scoffed. "Lying is not a good idea. When I find out…and I will…"

"Peter only knows I have a personal interest in you," he assured her. "He tuned in on it when we met up on the yacht. In fact, he gave me a friendly warning it was highly unlikely you'd change your mind about marrying Freedman." The dark eyes glittered with triumphant satisfaction. "But you have, Charlotte. Which gives me this opportunity to suggest an alternative path for you to take—a better path—forging a future with me."

"Because I'm my father's daughter?" she swiftly probed.

"Your father is a very challenging man, and you are, indeed, his daughter," he answered, his smile carrying a dash of relish.

"That's what gets to you, is it? The challenge?"

"It certainly adds spice to one's life."

"But having got me, I wouldn't be a challenge any more, so how do you see this proposed marriage after the wedding?" she tossed at him, then sipped her drink as though it was a foregone conclusion that he couldn't give a satisfactory answer.

"I can't imagine that life with you would ever be dull." He grinned. "You'd be coming at me every which way, just as you're doing now, keeping me on my toes. One false step and I'm dead. Have I got that right, Charlotte?"

It tugged a wry smile out of her. "Absolutely. You're playing with a dangerous woman, Damien Wynter."

He laughed, not the least bit perturbed by the prospect, and the laughter seemed to tingle over her skin, making her acutely aware of the attraction she had tried to push aside. He was an exciting man, both physically and mentally. It would not be a dull wedding night, she thought, temptation sliding through her again.

"You like living on the edge?" she asked, pushing for more knowledge of him.

"You do, too, Charlotte. You wouldn't have been a trader on the floor, otherwise. Nor play poker as you do. The mental balancing of percentages, the adrenaline flow of the risk, the thrill of pulling off the gamble…" He smiled knowingly. "It's in your blood as much as it's in mine."

She frowned over the repetition of her father's words. She didn't want a life with a man like her father, did she? Or was it the kind of marriage her mother had had with him she didn't want?

"I was looking for security," she slung at him. "The reverse of what you're saying, Damien. Knowing I could count on my husband being there for me when I need him, not the other way around, like it's been for my mother."

His eyes narrowed thoughtfully. "Maybe your mother chose a subservient role, happy to remain in the wake of your father's drive with the flow on of all its benefits. Different generation, Charlotte. I wouldn't expect that of you, nor want it from you."

She flashed him a sceptical look. "Easy to say."

"Try me," he countered. "What have you got to lose? If our marriage isn't to your liking, I can't hold you to it. And I'll sign a legal guarantee that I won't be demanding a divorce settlement, screwing you for money if you walk out."

She grimaced at the reminder of Mark's parting shot to her. At least the Ramsey wealth appeared to be irrelevant to Damien Wynter, *if* she could take him at his word. Not that she would. A financial agreement would certainly be signed before any wedding took place. Acting on faith was clearly a fool's game.

"You can't give me back the time spent on finding out whether I like being your wife," she muttered through a bleak cloud of disillusionment. "That's what I'd lose. Time, and probably a bit more pride."

"The same for me, Charlotte," he answered quietly. "But I'm betting we can make it together."

He exuded confidence, which, for some perverse reason, spurred her into arguing, "The time factor isn't the same for you. What are you? Mid-thirties?"

"Thirty-four."

"You could still have children decades from now. You don't need me. Why are you pushing this?"

"Because my instincts tell me it's right. Start listening to your own, Charlotte." He hitched himself forward on the lounge, leaning towards her with an air of intense purpose. "Forget Freedman. That was a side-track with the lure of having your needs answered. But the real connection is with me. You feel it, just as I do. It flows between us whether you like it or not, and there's no longer any reason for you to deny it."

The real connection...those words thumped into her mind and heart. Charlotte knew she had been fighting it, pushing up the barrier of loyalty to her relationship with Mark, labelling it a sexual hormone thing of no solid importance, hating the feeling of vulnerability to it. He was too arrogant, too dominating, too *everything*, which meant he would expect to get his own way in everything. *One of them.* Like her father. Yet he had struck chords in her that wanted what he could give.

As frightening as his strength was, hadn't she wanted to lean on it? And the protection thing. She liked that. He would certainly protect her from any sense of humiliation if she went through with the wedding. But she didn't feel safe with him. Not on any emotional level. Her instincts were telling her to be wary.

"You want something out of this, Damien," she threw at him suspiciously.

His gaze locked onto hers, and there was no mistaking the simmering desire reaching out and encompassing her, even before he put it into words. "I want *you*. I want you, Charlotte Ramsey, as I've never wanted any other woman."

A flood of heat burned her brain. She watched in mesmerised helplessness as he rose to his feet; a predatory male with all the attributes to make him overpowering. Her heart fluttered wildly. He stepped over and took the glass from her hand, her fingers weakly releasing it to him. Her body started buzzing with sexual anticipation. She wanted him to take her, to lift her up from the lounge, envelop her with his strong masculinity, make her feel how right it was to be with him.

Yet even as he reached for her, a sudden spurt of fear bucked her off the lounge on the other side and drove her to take a defensive stance, the realisation jerking through her mind that if she surrendered control to him, she'd be left with no cards to play and that was a losing situation.

"If you want me so much you can wait till our wedding night," she hurled out defiantly, facing him with a burst of steely resolve. "Let me see you live up to your words, Damien Wynter. You can ask my father for my hand in marriage tonight. And then you'll have to get a special marriage licence to make the wedding day legal. Not to mention signing an agreement that you will never make any claim on my personal fortune."

His mouth quirked into an amused little smile. "You think I won't meet that challenge, Charlotte?"

It hit her like a pulverising sledgehammer that she had just committed herself to marrying him if he did. Her stomach quaked. Convulsive little quivers ran down her thighs. Yet somehow she couldn't bring herself to take back the gauntlet she had just thrown down.

"Pay the price, Damien," she shot at him mockingly. "There'll be no freebies before you do."

It didn't worry him one bit. His eyes danced with devilment. "I quite like the idea of a bride I haven't slept with. A perfect piece of sexual anticipation built into our perfect wedding. And, of course, you will make it worth the price, won't you, Charlotte?"

Despite the mounting assault on her nerves, she stood her ground, proudly independent of him. "Since you want me more than you've wanted any other woman, I'd say that was built-in satisfaction for you, Damien. Just don't expect me to suddenly become your sexual slave."

"Slave, no. Bed partner, yes."

She shrugged. "As you so kindly pointed out, I want children so being bed partners is a given."

Her mind seized on that end goal to block out the madness of what she had just done. They *would* have marvellous children together, making this marriage worthwhile. As for the rest…well, she would simply let it happen. Planning out a life with Mark hadn't worked. Maybe taking this wild gamble with Damien Wynter was the best course to take. They were two of a kind—both of them born to great wealth—so, at least, they would always have that background understanding between them.

She was acutely conscious of his gaze slowly travelling down to the towel, still tied around her waist. His mouth was curved in a sensual little smile, as though he was imagining her naked, ready, willing and waiting to join with him in every intimacy. Her toes started curling. It was a relief that he couldn't see them.

"Then let's get this show on the road," he said, his gaze flicking up to put her to the test. "We get dressed and go visit your father. Agreed?"

Her heart skittered nervously at the speed he was using to cement her decision. "You mean…right now?"

"Right now," he confirmed. "Nothing like action to prove I'm a man of my word."

Which she had demanded.

Yet she was suddenly assailed with the sense that a trap had been set and she had been lured into it. Nevertheless, her pride wouldn't allow any backward steps at this point. He was watching her. She refused to let him see any sign of weakness on her part. If he was committed to going forward with this plan of action, so was she.

"Give me half an hour to get ready," she said, keeping her voice very steady.

He nodded. "I'll have a car waiting at the front door."

Her mouth twisted with irony. "It should be an interesting meeting with my father." Who would certainly favour Damien as a son-in-law, but how would he view her headlong plunge from one choice of bridegroom to another? Would he respect *this* decision?

"Don't think for a second that I'm not up for it, Charlotte," Damien warned, relentless purpose underlining every word.

"But will you win?" she tossed at him over her shoulder, having already turned to walk out of the pool room.

He laughed.

She kept walking as his laughter echoed around high walls, seeming to say it was what he lived for…*to win.*

Charlotte told herself she didn't care what he wanted

to win because she would win, too, taking from him the children he'd promised.

She'd give them all the love she had to give.

Apart from that, if the sex between her and Damien Wynter was something beyond what she'd ever experienced…that was a bonus.

CHAPTER TEN

DAMIEN had been concerned that his announcement might aggravate Lloyd Ramsey's heart condition, but there was no catching of his breath, no change in the normal florid complexion, which he had regained in the past two days. The bright blue eyes were very sharp as he assessed the situation.

"You want to marry Charlotte," he said as though tasting the words for his liking.

"Yes, I do," Damien affirmed.

The beetling grey eyebrows lifted quizzically. "Does she know?"

Damien nodded. "Charlotte accompanied me here. She's waiting for me to come out with your approval."

That startled him. "Damned quick work! She only tossed Freedman this morning."

"Freedman was a distraction from the main event."

Lloyd's mouth quirked in amusement. "Namely you?"

"That's my belief and I'm acting on it."

"Sure of yourself?"

Damien met the laser eyes with unflinching conviction. "Very sure."

The emphatic reply evoked a more thoughtful mood.

"I was with Kate, too. First night we met," Lloyd said slowly, then cut to the problem in his mind. "But she wasn't committed to marrying someone else."

Damien was determined to ignore what was already over and focus on the immediate future. "There's no need to cancel the wedding. The plans have been made. We'll use them."

Lloyd chewed that arrangement over for several seconds while Damien's nerves tightened into fighting mode. Charlotte's father might very well baulk at how fast this marriage was being driven to the altar, yet speed was of the essence. Charlotte was on a roller-coaster with him right now and he didn't want to risk a long pause for second thoughts.

An ironic little smile tilted Lloyd's mouth and an appreciative twinkle warmed his eyes. "Well, I don't mind a son-in-law who's prepared to save me money," he drawled.

"Speaking of which," Damien swiftly slid in. "If you'd instruct your lawyer to draw up a prenuptial agreement, detailing that I waive any claim to Charlotte's personal fortune, I'll sign it as soon as it's ready."

"What about your own fortune, Damien?" was the equally swift counter.

"I'll gamble the marriage will last."

"*That* sure of it?"

"Faith is a powerful tool. I'm not about to undermine it. Not when Charlotte needs to trust."

"Smart man." Lloyd nodded approval. "Though you are taking one hell of a risk. If you don't perform as Charlotte thinks a husband should, she might very well take you to the cleaners."

"Then I'll pay the price for being a poor judge of character."

Again there was another nerve-chewing pause while Lloyd weighed Damien's stated position. Finally he said, "Before I start formulating a Press Release to cover this extraordinary turn of events, send my daughter in. I want to hear what Charlotte has to say about this marriage."

"Of course," Damien agreed, maintaining an air of unshakeable confidence. "Thank you."

He left Lloyd Ramsey's VIP hospital suite, knowing this was the sticking point if he was to win the wife he wanted. If Charlotte wavered on their agreement in front of her father, the house of cards he'd built could come crashing down. The wedding machine had to be driven forward to its natural end—a legally binding marriage, and everything it entailed respected by both of them.

No freebies before the wedding night, she'd said.

But that didn't mean he couldn't use sex to bind her to him—at least a taste of what they would share. She was vulnerable to the powerful chemistry between them. Her vehement refusal of any physical contact when they'd been dancing; her defensive rigidity when he had held her back from rushing off to Freedman; the skittish refusal of any sexual surrender to him in the pool room...all strong indications that highly active pheromones were in battle with her will to hold control over them.

He couldn't count on pride keeping her on track.

Didn't want to.

He needed to hold her, kiss her, make her feel the desire for her burning through him. Because it was. Had been from the moment she'd mockingly challenged him on New Year's Eve. He *would* have her—lock, stock and barrel—but he'd only push it enough now to ensure she was with him and *wanting* to be with him. So much so it would be stamped on her mind when she went in to face her father.

Taking risks was in his blood.

But any gamble he took was always loaded his way.

This wedding was not going to be cancelled.

Charlotte paced the visitors' waiting lounge. Since it was the dinner hour, she had the room to herself—no one observing or wondering at her restless agitation. It was impossible to sit down and relax. Her mind was buzzing, imagining a dozen variations of the conversation going on between Damien and her father.

She had no doubt Damien Wynter could talk his way through any contretemps, swinging her father's vote for *this* wedding. Nevertheless, her change of heart would surely come under fire. Though it wasn't Damien in the hot seat. She was the one who would have to answer the really tricky questions. Could she simply stonewall— say this was what she wanted and leave it at that? How much did her father care about her life?

He'd fought her decision to marry Mark.

But that had been a fortune-hunter, social climber thing—irrelevant in this case.

Did her feelings matter to him, or would he be only too happy to rubber-stamp Damien's proposal and her acceptance of it, regardless of the circumstances? Perhaps the match up of wealth would look so good on the surface, the only person who would question her sanity was herself.

She could still back out of the agreement.

Nothing had been made public yet.

A moment of madness could be easily dismissed if it remained private.

She paused in her pacing at one of the fifth floor windows, staring down at the traffic in the street below—busy people going about their lives. Should she stand still, take a long, hard look at what else could be done with her own before rushing into a life she hadn't planned for?

"Charlotte…"

The deep timbre of Damien Wynter's voice seemed to vibrate right through her, breaking up her train of thought, making her nerves twang, her heart flutter, stirring a host of butterflies in her stomach. She scooped in a deep breath, trying to calm herself, needing her brain in reasonable working order to deal with him again.

Her skin started prickling from the magnetic field that seemed to flow from him—a warning that he was coming close. Dangerously close. She had to face him, keep him at bay so she could think straight. A hand fell on her shoulder just as she was in the act of turning. His other hand slid around her waist, and only her own hands flying up to press defensively against his chest stopped him from drawing her into full frontal contact.

"Are you okay?" he asked, concern throbbing through his voice, forcing her eyes to meet the heart-tugging probe of his.

"Did you convince my father of your good intentions?" she threw out flippantly, fighting the sense of feeling trapped, of drowning in a relentless force that would sweep her along with Damien Wynter, denying her any choice.

His mouth moved into a slow, sensual smile as he answered, "I believe so. But he wants to hear it's right for you from your own lips."

As she had expected, but still felt horribly uncertain about defending her decision. Or, indeed, whether or not to go ahead with it.

"And you know what, Charlotte?"

"What?" she echoed in distracted disarray. The heat of his body was seeping through his shirt, making her acutely aware of the muscled strength of his broad chest.

"I want to hear it, too." His tone deepened to a sexy huskiness as he added, "Or more importantly...*feel* it."

His eyelids lowered, his gaze focussing on her mouth, but not before she glimpsed a flash of raw desire. Her heart catapulted around her chest as she realised he intended to kiss her.

Stop him! a wild, panicky voice shrieked in her head.

Her lips parted to gulp in air enough to speak. No sound came from her throat. Her tongue remained still, poised to feel, not to act. Her hands did nothing, remaining glued where they were. Her stomach contracted in excited anticipation. A wave of rebellious belligerence rolled through her mind, carrying other wild words—*I don't care. I want him to kiss me. I want him to make it right.*

The first contact seemed to fizz with electricity. She would have jerked back from it, but the hand on her shoulder had slid under her hair, around her neck, fingers thrust up to hold her head steady, and the startling burst of tingling eased as his mouth moved over hers with a mesmerising sensuality, not so much taking as tasting.

With her mind focussed on how he was kissing her,

she didn't even realise her own hands were creeping up from their defensive position on his chest. It came as another shock when the arm around her waist scooped her lower body hard against his. Awareness of his erection furrowing her stomach exploded through her, just as his tongue invaded her mouth, hard and deep, instantly driving a sexual possessiveness that fired her blood with a totally wanton excitement.

Her fingers wrapped around his head, grasping fiercely as her tongue duelled with his, forcing an invasion of her own. He pressed for domination and she sucked him in, turning his possession of her mouth into possession of him, exulting in the wildly passionate intimacy, revelling in the hard heat of his body, the tense power of his muscular thighs, the strength of his embrace pushing her breasts against the pulsing wall of his chest as he breathed hard, intent on winning her surrender to him.

Never!

The word powered through her like a drumbeat of defiance. She was on fire, her heart booming in her ears, red-hot desire making bullets of her nipples, convulsing her stomach muscles and shooting quivers of melting heat down her thighs. But she would not give him the satisfaction of wilting under his marauding mouth. She kissed him back with as much violence of feeling as he poured into his passionate onslaught, and there was no sigh of submission from her when he finally pulled away.

The harsh rasp of their breathing was mutual. She met his glittering gaze unflinchingly, wilfully denying him any power over her. The hand tangled in her hair slowly eased out of it and moved to touch her cheek. It wasn't so much a caress as a tap of recognition.

"You would have eaten Freedman alive, but not me, Charlotte. Not me," he said, and she realised he was elated, not frustrated by her fighting response. "We *are* well matched. Remember that when you speak to your father."

Her father! It had completely slipped her mind that he was waiting for her, wanting her take on this marriage to Damien Wynter.

"You think a kiss proves your point?" she retaliated, not prepared to meekly fall in with his flow.

He smiled, desire still simmering in his eyes. "Let's say the wedding night can't come soon enough for me."

Her body agreed with him, but her eyes flashed home the more vital point to her. "There's more to marriage than sex, Damien. Don't you forget I want a father for my children. A hands-on father, not the occasional drop-in-Dad."

It didn't faze him one bit. "I know where you're coming from, Charlotte. I've been there, too. We both want it different for our children."

"We'll see," she muttered, unconvinced by mere words, though it struck her she needed to know a lot more about Damien Wynter's personal life. Maybe they were well matched in more ways than she had counted.

"Yes, we will," he said confidently, removing his arm from her waist to gesture towards the corridor that led to her father's hospital room. "In the meantime..."

"I'm on my way," she tossed at him, forcing her shaky legs to turn and take the steps they had to take towards the meeting with her father. Her body felt as though it had been hit by an earthquake and it was difficult to assert control over its aftermath. Nevertheless, by the time she entered the VIP hospital suite, Charlotte had managed to regain a reasonable amount of composure.

"You're looking better, Dad," she opened up, trying to deflect the acute targeting of his sharp intelligence on her.

"Feeling all the more so for hearing you gave the flick to Freedman," came the pertinent retort.

"Yes. Well…" She shrugged, trying to reduce the tension twisting her insides. As always with her father, it was better to face any issue head-on. Forcing a wry smile, she said, "I'm not here to talk about him, am I?"

"Apparently not. Don't hover at the end of the bed." He pointed to the chair her mother had sat in beside him. "Come and sit down."

Feeling like a prisoner entering the dock to face a stern judge, Charlotte did as she was told, conscious of her father studying her demeanour, looking for cracks in it. She tried to appear as relaxed as possible, settling on the chair, crossing her legs, returning his gaze with intrepid steadiness.

"Is this new marriage rebound stuff, Charlotte?" he demanded gruffly.

"No," she answered firmly. If she married Damien it was a move to something positive.

"I threw Damien Wynter at you as a suitable man to marry and I think he's a good match for you. In every sense. But if you're only taking him to save face…"

"No. He does suit me, Dad," she insisted.

"I'm not about to die, Charlotte," her father stated belligerently. "I don't want you marrying him just to please me."

She smiled, glad to hear he really did care about her

personal happiness. That meant a lot to her. She cared about him, too. Before Mark they'd always shared a good rapport. She wanted that back.

"You were right about Mark." The acknowledgement didn't even hurt now. "Why shouldn't I trust that you're right about Damien?"

He brooded over that point for a few moments then nodded. "I don't think you'll do better than Damien Wynter. In fact, it was good to hear he wanted you to be his wife. My daughter…" Pride and pleasure threaded those last words and spread into a wide smile. "He's up to your mettle, my girl. You won't be marrying beneath yourself. Got yourself a man you can respect."

The heartburn over her decision eased. She certainly wouldn't be losing her father over it. The rift caused by her relationship with Mark was closed.

A flash of caution suddenly stopped the flow of positive comments from her father. "I'll look a fool if I issue a press statement on this marriage and you change your mind before the wedding," he barked at her.

"I won't change my mind," she assured him.

Strangely enough, there was no longer any sense of vacillation over her decision. Her father's strong approval was probably the push she'd needed to settle the mental turmoil.

"There's no need to rush into it," he ran on. "I can well afford to pay for another wedding."

No. No waiting, her mind screamed. *Move straight into this marriage and get out of it what you can.*

"I don't want to plan another wedding," she replied decisively. "I've poured everything I like into this one."

Damien was right about that—the perfect production, down to the last minute detail. She couldn't go through it again, and she didn't want anything different.

"You're bent on having Damien Wynter as your husband, come hell or high water?" her father probed, searching for any doubts.

"Yes, I am," she answered, speaking what had now become the absolute truth.

"Tell me why, Charlotte," he shot at her.

The reasons were too private to explain. She smiled as she found an answer her father would empathise with. "Because he's *the man*, isn't he, Dad?"

The man with the money, the man with the drive, the man with the right genes for Lloyd Ramsey's grandchildren—*one of them!*

"Yes, I have to agree." He nodded happily. "I'm delighted you see it, too."

Her father was right in many respects. Damien fitted into their lives. Whether he would fit into the right husband mould for her could only be answered by time. She was prepared to risk that time on this marriage gamble. The promise of children made it worthwhile.

"So it's full steam ahead," her father said, his eyes twinkling satisfaction. "I won't argue with you over this one, Charlotte. He's even willing to lay his fortune on the line for you to grab if the marriage fails."

"I'll have no interest in grabbing it, should I have made a mistake in marrying him," she stated, red flags of pride scorching her cheeks. No way would she act as Mark Freedman had. She'd walk away with dignity, claiming nothing but the children she hoped to have.

"That's my girl!" Her father said with warm affection. "Hold your head high and I'll parade you proudly to the altar without a queasy stomach, which I would have had if you'd stuck to marrying Freedman." He waved an airy dismissal. "Let tongues wag as much as they like. I feel good about this wedding."

His burst of exuberance lightened the weight holding on to her resolve. "I'm glad it's not worrying you into another heart attack."

He laughed. "I'm going to enjoy releasing this news to the press. Don't you be worrying over the situation, either. I'll cover every angle. No one—believe me—no one…is going to cast Mark Freedman as the jilted groom when I'm finished with him. I'll roll out the colours of both men in no uncertain terms, making your choice the brilliant one it is."

Brilliant?

It could be made to look that way, Charlotte thought. She hoped it would end up being so but she was far from confident about it. Nevertheless, she projected happy confidence as she rose from her chair and leaned over to drop a kiss on her father's forehead.

"Thank you, Daddy. I'll leave you to the fun of concocting a cover story. Damien and I should be getting back home now to break the news to Mum and Peter."

"No, no, go out on the town and celebrate." He shooed her off benevolently. "I'll let your mother and brother know. It'll give me pleasure, spreading the news."

The last bit of tightness around her heart eased as a sense of inevitability took over.

The line had been crossed and there was no going back.

In less than two weeks, she would be Damien Wynter's wife.

CHAPTER ELEVEN

Tycoon Wedding Takeover
Wynter Wealth Wins
Tycoon Hijacks Bride
Changing Grooms—Ramsey Style
It's a Rich Man's World
Rollover Ramsey Romance

IT WAS a media frenzy—one sensational story after another—right up to the wedding day. Her father came home from hospital after the initial press release and instantly tightened security around the Palm Beach mansion to keep out the paparazzi. Rather than subject Charlotte to an onslaught of reporters and camera-men, Damien arranged for a selection of engagement and wedding rings to be brought to them by the top jewellers in Sydney. Everything else had been pre-planned.

There was no need for Charlotte to go anywhere and she didn't, though she was very busy on the telephone, answering the buzz of curiosity from invited guests. Mark's closest friends and associates uninvited themselves—his best man, groomsmen, the people on his staff. Charlotte wrote politely apologetic letters to his family, though apology wasn't really required, given the published "under duress" response to the prenuptial agreement.

As Damien had predicted, no one was critical of her decision. They were simply agog at Mark's replacement and the speed with which *he* was sweeping her into marriage. For the most part, Charlotte let all the buzz float past her, keeping her mind focussed on the future and what Damien had promised she would get out of it with him.

He asked Peter to be his best man. He flew other friends out from London to make up the rest of the wedding group. His father, Richard Wynter, insisted on coming, arriving by private jet and bringing Damien's current stepmother—his third—and a party of VIPs, all of whom Lloyd Ramsey had met before on his overseas business trips. There was a lot of entertaining to be done, all of it very celebratory.

It was, everyone declared, the perfect match.

Charlotte did not argue about any of it.

She simply let it happen.

In a way, she was grateful that the days were so hectically busy—less time to think and at night she dropped into bed exhausted, falling asleep almost instantly. With so many people coming and going she was rarely alone with Damien and their conversation was mainly about arrangements.

He was always obliging, considerate of her feelings, protective when any sticky questions were thrown at her—the perfect gentleman—though she invariably felt his dark wolf eyes taking in everything about her and the sense of his waiting for the wedding night to pounce and take was very strong.

He didn't kiss her again. Not intimately. He'd hold

her hand in company, put his arm around her waist, keep her close to him, make her physically aware of him, give her light greeting kisses, but he didn't push her sexually, respecting her dictate of *no freebies* before the wedding.

Perversely enough, instead of soothing her nerves, his restraint put them on edge, and she suspected he knew it, which made her determined to maintain a serene composure in his presence. But day by day, he *was* getting to her, more and more deeply, and she began to feel very vulnerable about being married to him. What if she ended up wanting this man more than she wanted their children? How could she control the feelings he stirred in her?

They were questions that couldn't be answered so she kept pushing them aside as the juggernaut of the wedding preparations rolled on. Marquees were erected in the grounds. Wedding planners supervised the setting up of the decor. Truckloads of pink roses were brought in by the florists. The gowns for the bride and brides-maids were delivered and tried on to check that no last-minute alteration was needed.

The day arrived.

It was fine and sunny.

Perfect.

The hours flew by; brunch with her bridesmaids, sessions with hairdresser and beautician, calming down her mother who was suddenly weepy at losing her daughter to a man who would take her away from Australia.

"I won't see my grandchildren," she cried.

"You can take time off your charities to travel, Mum,"

Charlotte reasoned. "You could accompany Dad on his overseas trips, drop in and visit us. And we'll come back here. I'm not gone forever."

"It's just…" She sighed and shook her head. "No, Damien is the better husband for you. Your father's right. I do hope you will be happy with him, dear."

Happy… Charlotte wasn't even thinking in terms of happiness, though she kept that to herself, smiling serenely at her mother, projecting a confidence she wasn't feeling at all. She had surrounded her inner turmoil with a cloak of surreal calm as she went through the motions of getting ready for the wedding. The commitment was already made. Today was the day she got to be the bride. She'd think about afterwards…afterwards.

"You make a beautiful bride," her mother declared, eyeing Charlotte over when she was fully dressed for the ceremony.

Her reflection in the full-length mirror told her she had never looked better. Her hair was drawn back in soft waves and pinned up on the crown of her head, apart from a few curled tendrils softly framing her face. A tiered, three-quarter length veil was attached to an exquisitely delicate diamond tiara, which belonged to her mother—something borrowed.

A fine gold anklet chain held a small turquoise pendant for something blue. The only other jewellery she wore was the magnificent square-cut diamond Damien had put on her engagement finger—very different in style to the one she had given back to Mark. With Damien, of course, cost had not been a factor. He had pressed her into choosing whatever she liked and she'd done so without a quibble.

The make-up, which had been applied gave her skin

a fresh, glowing, almost dewy look. Her lips were a glossy pink, her eyes subtly shadowed to highlight them. The beautician had performed a work of art. She actually did look beautiful—or as beautiful as she could be made to look.

The dress was a dream. An oval cut out of satin fell from the edge of a low V-neckline to her waist and was filled in by chiffon, intricately beaded with tiny crystals, as was the rest of the bodice radiating out from the curved satin band and gathered up to her shoulders, which were lightly covered by softly flowing cap sleeves.

The satin skirt was fitted to the lower section of the oval, form-fitting to mid-thigh, then gored with wonderfully draped insets of chiffon, frothing out at the front and forming a beautifully elegant train at the back. It made Charlotte feel both sexy and bridal and the feminine heart of her hoped Damien Wynter would be completely knocked out by it.

The fact that she had bought it for her wedding to Mark was irrelevant. This was her big moment dress as a woman, about to link her life to a man who would be her husband, for better or for worse. She had loved it on sight and still did.

"Damien said to give you this." Her mother passed her a small packet wrapped in silver paper. "He hoped you might like to wear them."

Diamond earrings, dangling with drops of pink diamonds surrounded by white diamond chips. They were stunningly beautiful and must have cost him a fortune. The colour also matched the pink roses in her bridal bouquet. Charlotte had no hesitation in putting the earrings on, pleased with such a thoughtful, caring gift—at least she hoped it was and not just a show-off statement on how wealthy he was. She would find out afterwards. Right now she did feel happy to be his bride…or maybe all the romantic trappings of being a bride had momentarily lifted the weight of doubts over what she was doing.

It was time to go downstairs.

Her father was waiting to give her away.

All the guests assembled in the big marquee were waiting to witness this spectacular merger.

Damien Wynter was waiting for the right to have her in his bed.

And Charlotte didn't know if it was trepidation quivering in her legs…or excitement.

Damien, Peter, and the two groomsmen lined up on the right of the rose-covered arbour where the marriage celebrant stood, waiting to perform the wedding ceremony. Behind them were some four hundred guests, squirming around in their seats, eager not to miss anything. The music being played by a chamber orchestra came to an end.

"This is it," Peter murmured, cocking a quizzical eyebrow at Damien. "Are you okay?"

He was tense. It had been one hell of a long day to this point—the point of no return for Charlotte. He had done everything he could to lock her into this marriage, but she could still back out until the fateful words— *husband and wife*—were spoken.

He slanted a wry smile at her brother. "Wish me luck, my friend."

Peter frowned. "Getting cold feet?"

Damien shook his head. "I just need Charlotte to come down that aisle."

"Don't worry. She will."

"I've pushed her into this, Peter."

"You can't push my sister into doing anything she doesn't want to do. Always had a mind of her own. I did warn you about that."

But Peter didn't know how ruthlessly he had manipulated the situation to his advantage. Not that Damien regretted his actions, not for a moment. He wanted Charlotte Ramsey and would have used any tactic to pull her his way. Nevertheless he was acutely aware of the tightrope he was treading with her. Any slip…but he hadn't slipped, had he?

Apparently sensing that he hadn't lessened Damien's tension, Peter tried some ironic humour, leaning over to whisper confidentially, "I feel a bit sorry for you actually. Not sure you know what you're taking on."

"You can forget that concern," Damien slung back at him. "Charlotte is everything I've been looking for in a woman."

"Well, you're about to get her." Peter nodded over his shoulder. "Here comes Mum down the aisle and the bridesmaids are in position to lead the bridal procession."

Both men turned to look as the harpist on the other side of the rose arbour started a virtuoso performance. As soon as Kate Ramsey was seated the chief bridesmaid began walking. To Damien she was a blur of dusky pink. She wasn't important. Neither were the next two bridesmaids.

His chest felt like a tight cage, his heart racing as though it was trapped on a treadmill. His gaze was fixed on the filmy white curtain at the far end of the marquee. He channelled every atom of mental concentration into willing Charlotte to come to him, not to falter at the last minute.

The bridesmaids lined up on the left side of the arbour.

Still no bride.

Damien's hands clenched. Aggression wired his whole body. If Charlotte didn't appear soon…

The harpist stopped playing. The sudden silence was gut-wrenching. Then the orchestra began playing—Mendelssohn's "Wedding March."

Damien breathed again as two footmen drew the curtain apart…and there she was! A triumphant pride soared through him. *His* bride…radiantly beautiful, absolutely regal in her bearing as she walked down the aisle, her arm lightly linked to her father's, not leaning on him for any support, sensually elegant in a dress that lusciously caressed her curves, its sexual appeal so strong, Damien's stomach contracted as desire hit him hard.

Tonight she'd be his, he fiercely told himself. The wait was almost over. He fastened his gaze on her face, determined on quelling the rampant urges gripping his body. What was she thinking, feeling? A slight smile tilted her mouth. Had she seen the impact she'd had on him? Was that a smile of satisfaction, of sweet pleasure, or a cover for a nervousness she refused to show?

Charlotte could stand up to anything.

His woman.

She was wearing the earrings—his wedding gift. Intense pleasure in her broke out in a smile of his own as she came closer and closer, each step bringing her more firmly into his life. Her gaze was locked on him, no glance at the guests on either side of the aisle. He sensed she was blocking them out, keeping her mind focussed on doing what she'd determined on doing. Her eyelashes lowered, veiling her expression as she took the last few steps to his side.

He held out his hand. She slipped her arm from her father's, transferred the bouquet to her left hand, and placed trembling fingers on his palm. Damien swiftly closed his own around them, gripping hard…the words, *to have and to hold,* burning through his mind.

"I give you my daughter," Lloyd Ramsey murmured, then stepped back to sit beside his wife.

Charlotte's lashes slowly lifted, her eyes looking directly into his—eyes swimming with vulnerable uncertainties that evoked a weird mixture of emotions in him…a surge of tenderness, a strong instinct to protect, a fierce desire to fulfil all her needs.

He *was* her man.

He'd prove it to her.

But first, he had to get her married to him.

He nodded to the celebrant to start the ceremony and held tightly to Charlotte's hand. No way was she going to escape being his wife now. Ahead of them was the challenge of making the marriage good. Damien silently vowed to meet that challenge, whatever it took.

CHAPTER TWELVE

THE wedding reception passed in a reasonably pleasant blur for Charlotte. It was obvious that all the guests thought she'd scooped the pool by getting Damien Wynter as her husband—a positive triumph for her. He, of course, charmed everyone—master of the situation. For which, she was grateful. He made it very easy for her to be his bride in public. While he was clearly considered a prize husband, Damien himself projected how very fortunate he felt to have met and won her as his wife.

Not once was Mark Freedman mentioned. It would have been in bad taste to do so, but Charlotte couldn't help thinking how quickly he had been obliterated from her life. Damien was such a dominant force, it was difficult not to be completely swept away by him. Nevertheless, this whirlwind marriage would undoubtedly come down to earth soon, and then she would learn what she really had to deal with.

The calmness she had maintained all evening began to disintegrate when they boarded the helicopter, which was to fly them from Palm Beach to the inner city hotel where Damien had booked the bridal suite, and where their luggage had already been taken. They no longer had masses of people around them. Apart from the pilot she was alone with the man she would be sharing a bed with tonight…for the first time!

He held her hand, as he had for most of the wedding reception. The helicopter was too noisy for conversation so they sat together in silence for the duration of the short trip. Charlotte looked out at the lights of Sydney, wondering when she would see them again, trying to keep her mind off Damien's acutely distracting touch— a touch that would not be restricted to her hand after they had arrived at the hotel.

Tomorrow they were flying to Mexico for their honeymoon. She and Mark had planned to go to Thailand. A different place, a different man. Why was she thinking of Mark again? Probably because they'd had the familiarity of being lovers and she was panicking over how it was going to be with a virtual stranger. One passionately challenging kiss was hardly enough preparation for total intimacy.

Maybe insisting he wait had not been a smart move. All her nerve-ends were twitching, sensing his tightly compressed energy—sexual energy, which had not been blunted by drinking too much alcohol at the reception, only a sip of champagne now and then. He certainly wasn't about to fall into an inebriated sleep.

They landed on the roof of the hotel and management staff escorted them to their suite with discreet efficiency. The decor was bridal luxury to the nth degree—all white and romantic except for the baskets of red rose petals for the massive spa bath and the chocolate coated strawberries on a silver platter beside the complimentary bottle of champagne on the coffee table. Charlotte noted it was midnight as Damien ushered out the man who'd insisted on showing them everything and how it worked.

The witching hour.

Was her new husband about to turn into a marauding wolf?

She walked over to the picture window view of Sydney Harbour, keeping her back rigidly straight so that Damien would not be aware of the shivery feelings inside her. The big red heart, which had been lit up on New Year's Eve, was still glowing on the arch of the bridge and her own heart suddenly craved what it signified—love.

Real love.

The curse of being Lloyd Ramsey's daughter was never to know if she ever could be loved for the person she was. Mark had left a very empty ache where emotional security should have been. Whether being Damien's wife—having his children—would fill that void, she didn't know, but she'd put herself in that place now and panicking over it was not doing her any good.

She could hear him undressing, ready for *action*. She should probably do the same, adopting a fearless attitude, but her bones had turned to water and fumbling tremulously would not be a good look. He would come to her. That was inevitable. In the meantime it was easier to hold still and wait for him to initiate the sexual connection.

"You don't stand alone any more, Charlotte," Damien said quietly, his deep voice coming closer as he added, "You're with me."

"For better or for worse," she muttered wryly, her gaze lingering on the red heart as her own heart pounded erratically over the commitment she had made. She didn't have to turn and face him. He'd won what he wanted. Let him do the running. Make her feel like a winner, too.

"It will be better, I promise you," he purred in her ear, then dropped a soft kiss on her shoulder—a small island of warmth which, perversely enough, sent another shivery wave through her.

She didn't reply. Only time would prove that promise true or false. She felt his hands in her hair, taking out the pins that had held the upswept style in place. The bridal veil had been discarded earlier on in the evening, left in her mother's keeping. Gentle fingers were loosening the long tresses now, raking them down, massaging her scalp where the pins had been.

It was nice...caring for her comfort...or was he simply getting her ready for bed?

Didn't matter.

It was still nice.

Not pouncing.

She sucked in a deep breath and slowly exhaled, telling herself to relax. "I don't have a headache," she said dryly, not wanting him to think she'd use that excuse to wimp out of having sex with him.

He laughed, pleasure and amusement rippling in his voice as he said, "That's my Charlotte."

I'm not yours, she thought fiercely, reacting against the possessive statement. But then she realised he had every right to think like that. She'd given him that right in becoming his wife. On the other hand, he was hers, too.

"My Damien," she said sardonically, trying it out for his reaction.

"Your servant...letting your hair down after a long day," he responded, his voice still vibrant with good humour. Obviously he didn't mind being called hers one bit.

Get over it, Charlotte, she told herself. You're not an independent woman any more. You're one of a married couple. "It has been a long day," she agreed on a sigh. "I just wanted a quiet moment."

"Having finally escaped the milling crowd and the watching eyes."

"Yes."

"You were a fabulous bride."

The warm words caressed her cold heart, melting some of the protective ice around it. Nevertheless, her mind rebuffed any sense of romance in their wedding and supplied an ironic reply. "I had to live up to my fairy-tale groom."

"Was the wedding all you wanted it to be?"

No.

The pain of that truth ripped through her.

The wedding had been planned as a wonderful celebration of love and that dream had been irrevocably smashed in the lawyer's office when Mark had put money first. Today had been like fitting all the pieces of a jigsaw together so the picture of the dream was in place but there had been no real substance to it.

No joy bubbling over.

No blissful faith in a *happy ever after.*

Just going through the motions with love drained out of them.

A hollow sham.

Nevertheless, the commitment to marriage had been made and her new husband certainly wouldn't appreciate her mourning a dream on their wedding night.

He was still fiddling with her hair, running his fingers through it as though enjoying its silky texture, or revelling in the freedom to do it. Freedom she'd chosen to give him and she now had to live with that choice. No point in tarnishing it with private miseries over what had been a deceit by Mark anyway.

"Everything went perfectly," she said out loud. It was true on a superficial level.

"I thought so, too," he murmured, and she could feel his pleasure and satisfaction in her reply.

Better to pretend everything was fine.

At least she wasn't dealing with any deceit from Damien.

He wanted her.

And that desire was very definitely being expressed as the pads of his fingers grazed down the bare curve of her spine to the head of the long zipper, which fastened her dress.

"Was it a man who designed this dress?" he asked as he released the hook and eye above the zipper.

Her whole body was gripped by nervous anticipation. Damien's question rattled around her brain, seeming totally out of order. Somehow she found wits enough to answer a simple, "Yes."

"He knew what he was doing." The warm approval flowing from him momentarily soothed her jagged nerves. "It's a masterpiece of sensuality. Not blatantly sexy, yet all the more provocative because it's delectably feminine as well. I like your style, Charlotte. It has dignity with a wicked touch of female devilment."

She hadn't thought of it like that. She simply chose to wear what she felt good in. "I'm glad you like it because I'm not about to change it any time soon," she said, feeling she had to hold onto her own individuality and not become something she wasn't by taking on the role of his wife. Damien Wynter was very much an alpha male, used to getting his own way, but she would not allow herself to be swamped by his dominant personality.

"I don't want you to change anything about yourself. To me you're perfect as you are."

The reassuring remark lessened some of her self-consciousness about being undressed, but her spine automatically stiffened as the zipper was slowly pulled down, loosening the back of her bodice, baring more of her body to the intimate view of a man she didn't love.

It was easier not facing him, just feeling his hands sliding up her back to her shoulders, gently drawing the flimsy cap sleeves down her arms. She wasn't wearing a bra and her nipples tightened into hard prominence as the fabric dropped from her breasts, leaving them exposed for him to take in his hands whenever he wanted to.

Breasts for babies, she told herself, clinging to that thought as the satin skirt fell to her feet and much more of her was exposed since her only underclothing was a white satin G-string. If she was *perfect* for him, being naked shouldn't be worrying her. It was okay. And having sex with him was a necessary prerequisite to getting pregnant. That was the aim here. She didn't need *love* to accomplish that.

The G-string was pulled down, joining the frothy mass of her bridal gown at her feet. "Step out of it, Charlotte," Damien instructed. It took an act of will to make her legs move. They felt like jelly. Somehow she lifted one foot and then the other as the last piece of her wedding was whipped away from them. No, not the last piece. She still wore his pink diamond earrings. No doubt he'd leave them on—marks of his possession.

The touching began…featherlight caresses over her calves, circling the sensitive area behind her knees, a teasing glide up her inner thighs, the spread of his hands cupping the rounded voluptuousness of her bottom, then the heat of his body making contact with hers, the hard, thick shaft of his erection pressing along the cleft between the soft cheeks, his hands moving to the erotic zones underneath her stomach, fingers parting the moist folds of her sex, stroking with tantalising gentleness, knowing how to build excitement.

All the muscles in her body clenched. Charlotte forgot to breathe until the tightness in her chest forced her to remember. She sucked in air. He stopped the almost unbearable caress, his arms winding around her waist, hugging her tightly, his head bending close to hers, his cheek brushing her hair away from her ear.

"What are you looking at?" he asked in a throaty murmur.

Her mouth was dry. She worked some moisture into it. Although she'd stopped seeing anything once he'd started touching her, she didn't want him to know how completely he'd turned her focus inwards, dominating her consciousness with *feeling*. "The heart on the bridge," she answered.

They were simply throwaway words yet they lit an explosive charge. Violence literally crackled from him as he spun her around. His hands grasped her face, no longer gentle, demanding she look him straight in the eye. "You will not think of him!" he seethed, his teeth bared in anger.

Him?

Did he mean Mark?

Bewilderment clouded her brain. She couldn't think why he was so angry? She was never going back to Mark. Didn't he know that?

"You're mine, Charlotte Wynter," he fiercely asserted. "You *belong* with me. And I'm going to make you know it!"

The wolf in him came raging out. He picked her up, swinging her through the air as he strode to the bed, hurling her onto it, pinning her there with his own body, aggression pumping through him, his eyes blazing jealous fury. Weirdly enough, Charlotte didn't feel frightened. A wild exhilaration was coursing through her.

Gone was the masterful control Damien had exerted over every situation since she'd met him. This was the raw man running rampant, and it was strangely exciting to have all his sophisticated expertise as a lover ripped away, to have his real nature in play, forced into the open by the intensity of his desire to tie her irrevocably to him—an intensity that somehow transferred power to her.

She didn't feel so shaky and vulnerable any more. It was as if his need had injected her with the strength to meet it head-on and not be swallowed up by it. When his mouth crashed down on hers—any idea of seduction totally dismissed—Charlotte instinctively denied him the male supremacy he was aiming for, counter-attacking his assault, sucking in his energy, driving her own tongue into his mouth in a fierce duel of deeply invasive kissing.

She bucked against his physical dominance, twisting, rolling, her limbs tangling with his, their bodies slamming against each other, nakedness no longer an issue of concern, more a highly volatile sensual excitement generated from the friction of flesh against flesh, every contact whipping up a lust to try something else, win the unspoken, gut-deep contest between them.

She kicked off her shoes, her bare feet finding better purchase on the strong muscularity of his legs, raking them, making him know she was no pushover to be taken as he liked. His hands clamped on her upper arms, holding them down as he tore his mouth from hers and went for the jugular, sucking on the pulse at the base of her throat as though feeding on her heartbeat, heating her bloodstream with the fierce passion of primal urges, unleashed from any control.

She liked that—liked him needing to do it, the intense wanting burning into her, through her, but his life-force was not going to reduce her to being his slave. Right now she was the taker not the taken.

Except that changed when he swooped on her breasts, making them ache with bursts of excitement, tongue-lashing her highly sensitised nipples and grazing his teeth over the soft swell of her flesh as he drew it into his mouth, the pleasure so intense she almost wanted him to bite. Her hands scrabbled in his hair, tugging, pulling his head from one breast to the other in a frenzy of lustful greed for more and more sensation.

He released her arms and heaved himself down between her legs and she writhed as he kissed and licked her into the sweetest torment, building a fire of need, stoking it until she could bear it no longer, her hands plucking at his shoulders, clawing at them, her hips arching, her thighs clenching with tension, her inner muscles convulsing, the moist heat of urgent sexual desire craving deeper satisfaction.

"Enough!" The cry tore from her throat.

"Not until you say you want me," he growled, running his tongue around the pulsing edge of her vagina in tantalising provocation.

Her feet dug into the bed as she bucked a violent protest, driven to the edge of madness, yelling at him, "Damn you, Damien Wynter! I want you now!"

"Right!" he snapped with satisfaction, surging up and driving himself into her, the hard, hot fullness of him spearing deep, filling the aching need, and her legs wound fiercely around his hips, holding him in, squeezing him tight in a wild rush of exultation.

"You've got me and I've got you," he said, his voice a harsh rasp, his eyes blazing sheer animal triumph. "That's the way it is and that's the way it's going to be, Charlotte Wynter."

And he kissed her hard to enforce the mutual possession, stamp it on her mind, make her body acutely aware of being intimately connected to his, every cell humming a deeply primitive pleasure in it. Yes, she thought, yes, yes, yes…caught up in the passion of the moment, the sweet elation of feeling him where she'd needed him fuelling a wildly fervent agreement to how it had to be for them.

She rocked to his rhythm, loving the stroke of him inside her, urging him into a faster pounding, revelling in his strength, in the dynamic stamina that took her to one pinnacle of ecstasy after another, to a continual roll of glorious climaxes. Never had she experienced anything like this. Her body wallowed in a sea of pleasure. Her mind floated on it.

There was no fight left in her, nothing to fight any more. She loved having him like this, loved stroking his magnificently muscled body, loved feeling its heightened tension as his rhythm escalated to the explosive spill of his own climax, loved how tightly he hugged her afterwards, as though he wanted to keep her joined to him forever.

Her head was tucked under his chin, her mouth close to the pulse at the base of *his* throat. She kissed it, wanting him to feel her in his bloodstream. One of his hands slid into her hair, fingers fanning out around her scalp, holding her to the kiss and the deep throb of his heartbeat.

She no longer minded the strong possessiveness flowing from him. It was an affirmation of what she was feeling herself. The sense of intense togetherness shut out everything else, pulsing through the silent stillness of all energy having been spent. It was a time of peace, of comfort, of not being alone, and Charlotte was content to lie at rest with him, her mind lulled by the continued physical closeness.

"You are my soulmate, Charlotte," Damien murmured, deep satisfaction rolling through his voice. "And whether you want to acknowledge it or not, I'm yours."

No, she thought, reluctant to think at all, yet the denial of his claim had come automatically, and her mind couldn't leave it alone. Perhaps sexual mates, she acknowledged, having been made acutely aware that his emotional and physical ferocity had tapped into a very similar primitive vein in her make-up, releasing any inhibition about expressing it. Maybe the gateway to total freedom in love-making was in not being worried over what the other thought, not caring, just doing what instinct dictated.

Though what they'd just done together wasn't really making love, was it? It had been more a wild animal thing and she wasn't at all sure where that was going to take them in this marriage. A wave of sadness washed through her as pleasure in the purely physical ebbed away. Love had played no part in this. It was just...

"*Mating*," she said, the word spilling from her lips as she wryly realised that was what animals did to create new life. It was what she had set out to do with Damien so it was foolish to feel bad about it now.

"A perfect match it is, too," he replied.

The smug pleasure in that statement made her want to challenge it, but a heavy wave of fatigue blunted her mind and brought a sudden pricking of tears to her eyes.

It had been a long day. A long night. Love would have made it perfect. As it was, she'd made this bed with Damien Wynter and she'd lie in it with him, but he did not fill the emptiness in her soul. She didn't believe he was the kind of man who could.

The tears suddenly welled and trickled through her lashes. It was difficult to speak over the lump in her throat and the plea for an end to this night came out as a husky little whisper. "I need to sleep now."

There was a long pause before he replied—a pause that stirred an anxious yearning to be released from meeting any more demands from him tonight. He was satisfied, wasn't he?

"How do you like to sleep, Charlotte? On your side?"

The soft question brought an enormous wave of relief. "Yes," she answered, desperately hoping this meant no more talking, no more doing, no more anything tonight.

He gently rolled her onto her side and fitted himself around her spoon-fashion, his arm around her waist, still holding her possessively, but she didn't mind the physical closeness. It was warm and comforting as though she was curled into a safe cocoon, covered and protected, and it occurred to her that this was how it could be as Damien Wynter's wife if she simply let it be.

It was an instinctive part of his alpha male nature to look after his woman, and despite the survivor independence Charlotte was trying to cling onto, a deeply female part of her liked the sense of being looked after by her husband, liked letting him be the strong one, liked feeling safe in his keeping.

"Have a good sleep," he murmured, as though he really cared that she should. Then pressing a soft kiss near her temple, he added, "Everything will be much easier tomorrow. Just you and me, Charlotte. We'll leave all the rest behind. Okay?"

"Okay."

She sighed away the last little bits of tension, closed her eyes tight to block another gush of silly tears, and told herself Damien was right—everything would be much easier tomorrow.

It had to be so.

They were married.

CHAPTER THIRTEEN

CHARLOTTE slanted him a doubtful look. "Do you think the driver knows where he's going?"

Damien would have wondered the same thing if he hadn't read the review on Ikal Del Mar, mentioning that the access road was bumpy, and the Mayan jungle through which it ran gave no visible sign of any civilisation being at the end of it, let alone a luxury resort. He checked his watch. They'd left Cancún airport forty minutes ago and the transfer to their destination was only supposed to take forty-five.

"We should be there within another ten minutes," he said, giving her hand a reassuring squeeze. "It's a very private place."

Which was precisely what he'd wanted, having Charlotte to himself, no chance of running into people whom either of them knew, nothing to break up the intimacy that a week-long stay should forge. It had been a fortnight of intense pressure leading up to their wedding. The aim of this honeymoon was to get Charlotte feeling relaxed with him, and hopefully ending up happy to have him as her husband.

Her tears on their wedding night had been gut-tearing. He'd completely lost his cool over her memories of Freedman and pushed far too hard to obliterate the man from her mind, acting like a raging bull instead of a caring lover intent on giving her pleasure. It was little consolation that she had responded physically to the rough sex. He knew he'd driven her to climax after climax, but afterwards…

Damien grimaced over his short-lived satisfaction in having his instincts proved right. To his mind, they'd been great together, and it had come as a shock that Charlotte had not felt good with him. The silent tears, the plea for sleep…he had to change tack, not try to force anything. Her love for Freedman might have been a fantasy of her own making but it had been real to her for a lot longer than any feelings she had for him.

He had time on his side now—time to prove the decision to marry him had been right. They did belong together. Somehow he had to get Charlotte to see that—believe it as firmly as he did. Right now she was playing the dutiful wife, going along with what he'd planned, putting a reasonably cheerful face on it, but he sensed her heart was withdrawn to a very heavily guarded place, and getting it to open up to him was not going to be easy.

"Oh!"

They had arrived, and the exclamation of delighted surprise from Charlotte gave Damien's heart a kick of pleasure. He'd got this right for her. Ikal Del Mar was Mayan for "Poetry of the Sea" and he was counting on the romance of this place to be so seductive, the emotional barriers she'd put up would be impossible to maintain.

* * *

Charlotte was amazed by Damien's choice for their honeymoon. A resort on the Mexican Caribbean had suggested a very flashy environment crowded with tourists, like the Gold Coast in Queensland—casinos and beaches, nightclubs and open-air restaurants with a constant parade of people adding their colour to the scene.

This was a very private tropical paradise, shielded from the rest of the world, and the accommodation was limited to twenty-nine separate villas, nestled into the jungle and overlooking a beautiful turquoise sea. There was only one restaurant on the property plus a full service spa, which was a beautiful facility offering a wonderful range of pampering treatments.

Damien immediately booked a massage for them to soothe the aches from travelling. Though this was in keeping with the thoughtful consideration he'd shown her during their trip here, there was a look in his eyes that suggested the massage would more likely serve as foreplay for what he really had in mind.

He had not pressed her for sex the morning after their wedding, nor had he taken any physical liberties with her on the long flight. Given they'd made the journey to Mexico in a private jet, she'd expected to be a member of the Mile High Club by the end of it, yet he had surprised her by not claiming his rights as a husband, especially since he'd been so ruthlessly possessive the night before.

They had played chess on the plane. He was very good at the game and it had been a challenging pastime, keeping her mind occupied so it wasn't prey to fears and doubts about the decision she had made. He'd also explained his main business interests, which revolved around property and technology development.

She'd known his father owned a string of casinos, but apparently Damien preferred to use his wealth in more constructive ways, more like her own father, and she could see herself fitting quite easily into his world. The irony was she'd tried to escape from it with her ill-fated relationship with Mark, but maybe there had never really been an escape. It was the world she had been born to, so she might as well accept it with good grace now that she had married into it.

She was Damien Wynter's wife and she now realised he had simply been biding his time, waiting for the optimum situation before pursuing more physical pleasures with her. As they were shown through the presidential villa, which was exclusively theirs for a whole week, Charlotte was acutely aware of how very intimate the setting was.

None of the other villas could even be seen from it. Built of indigenous natural wood, with a thatched roof, and surrounded by jungle gardens, even this two-storey structure was hidden away from other guests. While the villa looked primitive on the outside, the interior was stunning. Decorated by a Mexican artist who had obviously taken a minimalist approach, it had a classy elegance that had five-star quality written all over it.

On the ground floor was a dining room, living room, a spacious terrace with chaise lounges and a crochet hammock for handy lazing beside the private swimming pool. A huge four-poster bed dominated the bedroom on the second floor from which there was a spectacular view out over the sea to the island of Cozumel. The marble and wood bathroom featured his and hers sinks and walk-in closets. The high ceiling palapa roof gave a marvellous sense of luxurious space and the whole villa was air-conditioned for cool comfort.

It was the perfect place for honeymooners.

If they were in love with each other.

Charlotte was conscious of a heavy tightness in her chest as the hotel staffer left the villa—left her and Damien alone together. Forget love, she fiercely told herself. This marriage was workable. And certainly worthwhile for having the children she wanted.

Damien gestured towards the pool and asked, "Feel like a swim before we head off for the spa?"

"Yes." Any activity was better than thinking about what she didn't have. She flashed him a smile as she turned to leave the terrace where they'd watched the staffer take the meandering path back to hotel reception. "I'll go and unpack my swimming costume." Their luggage had been delivered to the bedroom and as she crossed the terrace to go inside, Charlotte was thinking she might as well unpack everything.

"No need for a costume. There's no one here but us, Charlotte," came the pointed reminder.

Which stopped her in her tracks. There was no reason not to skinny-dip, he meant. Except she'd never done it. And it would plunge her straight into nakedness with Damien, right out here in the open.

Why he made her feel so wretchedly vulnerable she didn't know. Being nude with Mark had not worried her. Maybe it was because she'd felt in charge of that relationship. The thought ran through her mind there was a huge difference between a lapdog and a wolf.

She'd wimped out of facing Damien on their wedding night. The sense that he was challenging her on that now swept in hard and strong, stiffening her backbone. She'd chosen to marry this man. No way would she let him think she was some weak, fearful creature who couldn't cope with what she'd taken on. She swung around, constructing a whimsical little smile to help excuse her hesitation.

"Well, this will be a first," she tossed at him.

He was already unbuttoning his shirt, a darkly brooding expression on his face which had undoubtedly been directed at her back. Charlotte's heart skipped a beat. What would he have done if she'd kept walking? As it was, her comment seemed to lift the cloud on his thoughts. He raised a quizzical eyebrow.

"A first?"

She shrugged, trying to lessen the tension that had gripped her at the realisation she might have stirred the beast in him again with her lack of ready compliance to what was a reasonable expectation. "I'm not in the habit of swimming nude, but you're right," she rattled out. "Why not when we have this pool to ourselves?"

His face relaxed into a grin, his dark eyes twinkling pleasure in her acquiescence. "You'll like it," he assured her.

Charlotte couldn't help staring at his very male muscular torso as he removed his shirt. His olive skin gleamed in the sunshine. Very un-English skin, she thought, but then he was only half English. He'd told her his mother had been Spanish, a professional flamenco dancer who had died of an embolism just after giving birth to him. He'd been raised by nannies until he was packed off to boarding school at seven years of age, not ever having experienced any real family life at all.

Maybe he wanted her as his wife because she would provide that for him. He was so physically handsome, there could have been no lack of women willing to share his bed, but perhaps actively wanting to have children was something else. The weird part was in being both drawn to his magnetic sex appeal and intimidated by it, feeling she probably compared badly to the more beautiful women he'd surely been with over the years. It was impossible for her not to be inhibited about being naked with this man, yet she couldn't allow that to show.

It would imply she didn't feel good enough for him.

And she was.

What did how she looked matter?

He'd chosen her to be his wife and it had nothing to do with her personal fortune since he'd waived all rights to it. That had to mean she was better than all the rest in his view, so it was stupid not to feel confident in his presence.

He dropped his shirt onto a chaise lounge and sat down to remove his shoes and socks. Charlotte forced herself to walk over to the next chaise lounge and sit down to do the same. When he stood up to unzip his jeans and strip them off, she stood up and started removing her clothes, determined not to be undressed by him this time.

Being nervous about it only made the situation difficult. Better to be blasé, or at least pretend to be blasé. Just because he was naturally gorgeous and she was… more ordinary…shouldn't mean a thing. She was happy with the person she was inside and that was what really counted.

Nevertheless, her heart was pumping hard, her stomach was knotted with tension, her nipples froze into hard nubs despite the heat of the day, and her hands fumbled over the zip of her own jeans, unable to execute a smooth action. To her enormous relief, Damien didn't stop and watch her, moving straight over to the pool and diving in while she was still pulling off her pants. "Feels like warm silk," he called out encouragingly.

Having laid her last bit of clothing on the chaise lounge, Charlotte took a deep breath, squared her shoulders and walked with all the defiant dignity she could muster to the edge of the pool, facing Damien who was now at the other end of it, waiting for her to dive in and join him.

Her chin automatically lifted as she saw his gaze flick over her from head to foot. This is what you went after. This is what you got, she silently flung at him, determined not to flinch under his appraisal of her unadorned physique.

He looked up and grinned at the hot challenge in her eyes. "Come on in, Charlotte," he invited.

The head of steam she'd built up dissipated as she hit the water and felt it slide over her bare body. It was like a caress of warm silk and there was a delicious freedom—a very sexy freedom—in having absolutely nothing between her and the water streaming all around her. It was so sensually pleasurable, when she surfaced at the other end of the pool, she was perfectly happy about being naked, regardless of what Damien thought of her.

In fact, he was still grinning, his eyes twinkling knowingly. "Nice?"

A natural smile burst across her own face. "Yes. Lovely."

"I bet you'll never want to wear a swimming costume again."

"That would depend on where I was and who I was with."

"It's okay with me. Very okay."

The emphatic assurance held a wealth of appreciation, causing Charlotte to wonder whether he liked the fact that nudity made her more sexually accessible or actually liked the shape of her figure which was certainly not model-thin by any stretch of the imagination.

"Have you always gone for fleshy women?" she asked curiously.

"Fleshy?" He frowned at the word.

She rolled her eyes in droll self-mockery. "Well, I can't call myself skinny and I refuse to call myself fat."

He laughed. "You're perfect, Charlotte. What I'd call woman incarnate—beautifully rounded shoulders and arms, lovely lush breasts, no ribs sticking out, very sexy hips curving out from your waist, spanning a wonderfully soft stomach, not to mention one hell of a provocative bottom, and good strong legs to hold a man where he wants to be held."

"Good strong legs for swimming, too," she flipped at him, kicking off the pool wall to surge through the water again, feeling ridiculously churned up by his catalogue of her femininity—the admiring relish of her physical attributes in his voice, the wicked sparkle in his eyes that clearly anticipated enjoying them actively very soon now.

In an instant he was swimming beside her, matching her stroke for stroke. They did a few quick laps together, with Charlotte becoming more and more conscious of his body scything through the water, not touching hers but very, very close.

It was not a big pool. It was not built for serious swimming. It was built for wallowing in sensual delight, midnight dips, cooling down after sex, enjoying each other's bodies in a different medium, floating under the stars. And that was okay, she told herself. There was absolutely no reason why she shouldn't simply relax and enjoy carnal pleasures with Damien.

He was certainly expecting to get them from her from the way he'd spoken about her body. And she did want to touch him, feel him. If she just did it instead of getting herself in a twist about losing out on love, losing to him, she would definitely be getting a win out of this marriage, even if it was only on a physical level.

That was what her head told her.

And following its dictate, she stopped swimming, let her feet sink to the bottom of the pool, raked her long wet hair away from her face, and summoned up a confident smile for the husband she now had. Damien had come to a halt about a metre away from her and he returned her smile.

"Enough?" he asked, not moving any closer.

"I'm definitely going to enjoy this pool while we're here," she said, determined on not feeling inhibited with him.

"Good!"

His smile widened to a grin of satisfaction that instantly raised the suspicion he was playing a game with her and had just scored a goal. But so what? She was winning, too, wasn't she?

"I'll go get us some towels," he said, turning and wading to the steps that led out of the pool.

Charlotte was stunned that he hadn't tried anything with her. No touching at all! She watched him emerge from the water, staring at the glistening ripple of muscles in his back, the taut cheekiness of his bottom, the long, powerful legs—so different to Mark. Better than Mark. And he was hers to have and to hold. Except she couldn't bring herself to make the first move, to actively invite or incite a sexual connection. Somehow that smacked of a surrender she wasn't willing to give. Not to Damien Wynter.

He picked up one towel from the end of a chaise lounge and tucked it around his waist, which surely had to mean he wasn't about to push for any physical intimacy at this point. Charlotte wondered what he was waiting for. He brought another towel to the edge of the pool, holding it out for her, a quirky little smile tilting his mouth, suggesting he knew what she was thinking and was enjoying an anticipation that would only be fulfilled when he chose.

Charlotte inwardly bridled at the arrogant confidence of this teasing game. If he thought she would crack and fall upon him, he could think again. She waded out of the pool, thanked him for the towel, wrapped it around herself and smiled expectantly as she said, "Are we off to our massages now?"

"Mmm…" It was a happy hum of agreement. "No need to get dressed again. Robes and sandals will take us to the spa and back. "

Within a few minutes they were on their way, Charlotte determined to match Damien's casual manner, despite the highly charged consciousness of her own sexuality and his. At the spa they were led into a couples massage room and virtually lay side by side as their bodies were treated to aromatic oils and a rub-down that was sheer sensual bliss. It was also incredibly sexy, having a massage together, sharing the pleasure of it, feeling totally relaxed, skin tingling with well-being.

They weren't actually touching, but Charlotte couldn't imagine more erotic foreplay than this, and she knew Damien knew it, knew this was all part of a plan designed to excite her into wanting him. It was working, too. The memory of her response to him on their wedding night was very sharp and kept running through her mind. By the time they left the spa to return to their villa, her body was buzzing with the need for a much deeper, more intense pleasure.

"Ready for lunch now?" Damien tossed at her as they headed upstairs to the bedroom.

Her rapidly pounding heart instantly dropped a beat. Her mind screamed that he couldn't prolong this waiting. In a burst of frustration, she turned to him, her eyes sizzling with a mocking challenge. "Is that what you want, Damien?"

"I want to please you, Charlotte," he answered, maintaining a carefree aplomb that needled her into completely losing her cool.

"You can please me by getting me pregnant," she snapped. "That's what I married you for."

The teasing sparkle in his eyes winked out and a dark ruthlessness glinted in its place. "Then perhaps you'd like to show an eager willingness to join me in that enterprise."

The realisation speared through her that she'd turned her back on him on their wedding night, and kept it turned until… "I thought you were into taking, Damien," she slung at him, fighting a rush of guilt for not meeting him halfway in the bargain they had struck for this marriage.

He stroked her cheek as his eyes derided her claim. "I'm just as good at giving. In fact, I'll give you as much time as you need to get past Freedman and start wanting me. Having a passive partner doesn't really appeal."

The passive accusation really stung, making her squirm over the wimpish negativity she had wallowed in since agreeing to marry Damien. So did the implication she was maundering over Mark who'd comprehensively lost all desirability in the lawyer's office. For her own self-esteem, it was imperative that both impressions be immediately overturned.

"Forget passive!" she bit out through gritted teeth. "I want you right now!" She grabbed a handful of his robe. "Let's get to it!"

She stamped up the rest of the stairs, still hanging onto his robe though not exactly dragging him after her since he kept pace with her onward rush. As soon as they reached the bedroom, she swung on him, tearing the loose garment off his shoulders and arms. "Is this eager enough for you?" she demanded.

"Encouraging," he drawled. "Taking off your own robe would be more enticing."

"Done!" She whipped it off, stepped up to him, flung her arms around his neck and pressed the length of her body to his. "How's that?"

"Definitely willing," he conceded, his eyes gleaming provocative satisfaction.

"But are you able?" she taunted, deliberately rolling her hips so that her stomach brushed against his erection, which was exhilarating proof that she had excited him.

"Close. Very close," he murmured, a smile twitching his lips as his mouth descended on hers, tantalisingly gentle, playing at a kiss instead of taking one.

It goaded her into poking her tongue out, sliding it into his mouth and sweeping it around his palate in erotic provocation. That got action aplenty. Suddenly his hands were clutching her bottom, hauling her into a more intimate fit with him and the playful kiss exploded into hungry passion.

He walked her backwards to the bed, rock-hard thighs steering hers. They fell on it together, rolling away from the edge, their bodies sleek from the lingering traces of aromatic oils, sliding sensually over each other, driving the desire to feel everything there was to feel; hands stroking, legs entwining, mouths fuelling the heat of compelling need.

There was no lack of eagerness in opening up to him. Charlotte wanted him inside her and felt a wild rush of elation when he plunged deep. She wrapped her legs around his hips and rocked to his rhythm, abandoning herself so completely to it, nothing else existed for her. Her inner muscles sucked in the powerful length of him, revelling in it, wanting the glorious sensation of being filled by him to be endlessly repeated. The thought of love didn't enter her mind. She was consumed by sensation—wonderful sensation, incredibly satisfying sensation, escalating into extremely exciting sensation.

He was gorgeous.

She adored what he was doing to her.

Sheer ecstasy.

And when she finally floated down from utter satiation, she could not deny the pleasure of still being held by him. It might only be sexual intimacy but it felt good. Really really good. Skin against skin, softness pressed against hard strength, hearts beating to a languorous contentment. She could take a lot of this with Damien Wynter.

She smiled to herself as she feather-fingered the erotic zones below his hip-bones and said, "You can assume I'm eager from now on. Okay?"

After all, the more they did it, the more chance of her getting pregnant.

A chuckle rumbled up from his chest. "I might test you on that, Charlotte."

"I've always done well at tests," she blithely answered.

"Let's see."

He swivelled around on the bed, picked up one of her legs and started sucking her big toe, his eyes dancing sheer devilment at her. To her intense surprise a bolt of exquisite sensation shot straight to the apex of her thighs, spread a fan of excitement through her stomach, caused her nipples to spring erect, and punched the air out of her lungs.

"Oh!" she cried, jack-knifing into a sitting position.

"Is that a positive response?" he asked, cocking a confident eyebrow.

She waved airily. "Suck away." And lay back to enjoy it, deciding she might as well enjoy every bit of Damien's expertise as a lover. Even if he ended up being a rotten husband, at least she should have a marvellous honeymoon to remember.

Which was definitely a plus tick in the box for marrying him.

Especially if she got pregnant.

CHAPTER FOURTEEN

POETRY By The Sea...

If poetry was supposed to appeal to all the senses, Ikal Del Mar certainly delivered on its promise. Charlotte happily mused over their time here as she lay in the four-poster bed, looking out at the brilliant Caribbean Sea on their last morning, waiting for Damien to wake beside her. She could not remember ever having spent a more pleasurable week.

Sex with Damien had very quickly become addictive. Not only was his stamina amazing, but he made her feel so desired and desirable, for the first time in her life she was absolutely loving being a woman. And it was impossible to deny the lust he stirred, nor the wild passion he invariably triggered in the heat of making love.

Physical love.

She refused to think it was anything more than that, though she had to admit she did enjoy Damien's company; the matching of wits and the sharing of so many pleasures in this place. The food had been fabulous, every meal a delicious adventure into Mediterranean cuisine with a Mexican influence. She was looking forward to the fresh croissants and apricot rolls the pastry chef made for breakfast. The last one, she thought with a twinge of regret about their imminent departure.

She felt so gloriously relaxed, spoilt, pampered. The Temazcal bath by the sea-side yesterday afternoon had been a fantastic prelude to last night. The cleansing sweat bath with herbs, flowers, music and a soothing massage had left her skin tingling and beautifully scented. She'd been acutely aware of her body all through dinner—wonderful tempura prawns, accompanied by a heady Spanish wine—then afterwards…no doubt about it, Damien was a marvellous lover.

His arm slid around her waist and a soft kiss brushed her shoulder. "Are you awake?"

She rolled over and smiled. "Another beautiful morning. I'll miss waking up to our view of the sea."

He propped himself on his side, smiling down at her, a caressing warmth in his eyes. "I'm glad you've enjoyed it."

"I was just thinking what a great week it's been."

"With me," he prompted, clearly wanting the admission.

"Mmm…you did contribute quite a lot to my pleasure." She wasn't about to feed his arrogant ego too much.

He laughed, happy enough with that concession. "Speaking of pleasure, I'm taking you to Las Vegas for a few days."

"Las Vegas!" She frowned over his choice. "Are you a mad gambler, Damien?" She didn't care for that idea at all.

"No more than you are, Charlotte."

"But I'm not! I've never been to a casino."

"Then it will be a new experience for you."

Charlotte wasn't at all sure she'd like it, but she held her tongue, remembering that casinos were his father's business, and Damien would have to be well acquainted with them. If a propensity for gambling was going to be a problem in this marriage, she might as well learn about it now, know what she would be facing in the future.

He traced her lips with a lightly teasing finger. "Our marriage was a gamble," he reminded her. "How do you feel about it now?"

She nipped his finger with her teeth to show she still had some, despite his skill as a lover. "Not a total gamble," she corrected. "I went with the percentages. You have an admirable set of genes and some of them should get passed on to our children."

"Admirable, huh?" His eyes danced devilment. "And that's the only reason you've been drawing from my sperm bank all week?"

"It's called power planning." She curled an arm around his neck to draw his head down. "Got to make the most of it while I can."

"Mmm…" He played with a kiss. "I don't see it easing up any time soon."

"Thank you for being so obliging," she said, moving her body wantonly against his.

"Pleasure," he murmured.

And they didn't speak again for quite a while.

They arrived in Las Vegas late in the afternoon. A limousine picked them up from the airport. Damien had told her he'd booked them in at the Bellagio Hotel, which meant nothing to Charlotte. She knew her father stayed at the Mirage when he wanted to enjoy a high stakes poker game, but apart from that, she only had television knowledge of the glitzy city and its many theme-park casinos: Treasure Island, New York, New York, MGM, Egypt, Paris, Venice…

Damien pointed them out as they were driven along the main drag—amazing architectural fantasies. Charlotte decided she would enjoy walking around and simply sight-seeing while she was here. Everything looked so zany and colourful. Her gaze was drawn to a packed crowd filling the sidewalk just as Damien said, "We're coming up to the Bellagio now."

"Where the people are?"

"Yes."

"What are they looking at?" They were all turned away from the street, necks craning to see something.

"You'll see in a minute."

Charlotte's first sight of the hotel was stunning. It was so beautifully elegant in its majestically curved symmetry, and all white with a wonderful colonnade of Roman columns sweeping around the driveway up to it and away from it. The actual entrance to the hotel over-looked a huge lake, and just as the limousine turned up the driveway, a long row of fountains shot plumes of water high into the air. Then another row of fountains started interweaving with them in perfect time to the musical track of "Big Spender." It was such an enthralling sight Charlotte instantly appreciated what the crowd had been waiting for.

"The dancing fountains at the Bellagio are quite famous," Damien said, smiling at her delight.

"How often do they put on this show?" she asked.

"Every hour I think. Maybe two. I can't remember but

often enough to easily catch it again. It's more spectacular at night with a light show to accompany it. We can dine at the restaurant that overlooks the lake if you like."

"Yes, please," she said so enthusiastically he laughed and squeezed her hand, which instantly reminded her how much she had come to love his touch. It would be dangerous to become too dependent on it, Charlotte thought, wanting him always beside her. She hadn't anticipated feeling so...*connected*...with Damien.

Honeymoon stuff, she told herself. It would be different when they settled into real life. Damien would be off about his business and she would occupy herself setting up a family home. This sense of closeness would not last and she should not expect it to. It had been a pragmatic decision to marry Damien Wynter for the purpose of having the children she wanted and her wisest course was to stay pragmatic, not get herself into an emotional twist about anything.

"How many times have you been here?" she asked, wondering how much tripping around the world he did and whether or not he would want her to accompany him.

"I've stayed at the Bellagio only once before. Though I have also visited most of the casinos in Vegas, and most of the high-end casinos in Europe and Asia. My father expected me to be in the business with him, but it's not a world I feel drawn to. I'd rather help make things happen. See something grow, develop."

"Like a family," popped out of her mouth before she could stop it—words smacking of hope that he would really share a life with her and their children. A stab of fear struck her heart. She *was* beginning to want too much from Damien.

The smile left his eyes. His grip on her hand tightened. "I won't let you down, Charlotte."

Hard resolution in his voice, making her heart gallop with more hope. Maybe she could trust him to be all she wanted in a husband. He'd kept his word on everything so far.

The limousine had come to a halt and the chauffeur was opening her door. Embarrassed by a need she hadn't counted on, let alone meant to show, Charlotte quickly disengaged her hand, turned and almost leapt out of the passenger seat, instinctively using action as a diversion. Damien followed her out and they were immediately given a red carpet greeting by the hotel manager.

"A pleasure to have you with us again, Mr Wynter. And Mrs Wynter, welcome to the Bellagio."

They were ushered inside and given so much attention, any onlooker would have thought they were a royal couple. The world of the very, very rich, Charlotte thought, realising life with Damien was always going to be like this. They might have been relatively anonymous at Ikal Del Mar, but multi-billionaires were well-known currency in most places. And despite the sense that any kind of normal relationship with other people was impossible to them—it was invariably tainted by money—almost anything else was possible.

"The concierge has put aside the tickets to the shows you were interested in and I have secured front row seats for you in the Fontana Room tonight," the manager informed them—no trouble at all.

"What shows?" Charlotte asked, once they were left to themselves in their elegantly luxurious suite.

"Celine Dion, Cirque du Soleil's 'O' innovative

water-acrobatics show…" Damien shrugged. "Whatever else you might like to see. We'll go talk to the concierge tomorrow morning." He smiled. "One thing about Vegas—it offers all sorts of top-line entertainment."

Not just gambling then.

Charlotte's smile held a tinge of relief. "So tell me what's in the Fontana Room."

Damien wasn't about to risk a knock-back on this particular arrangement. "Let it be a surprise," he tossed at her teasingly, then cocked his eyebrow in deliberate challenge. "This is a test for how much you're going to nag me."

She planted a hand on her hip in a provocative stance. "Oh, I think I'll let you get away with keeping me waiting this time."

He pretended to look worried. "Do I hear a threat in there somewhere?"

"Test me too far and you'll find out," she flipped back at him.

He laughed, moving forward to draw her into his embrace. "It's only a few hours away. I think I can provide a few distractions to while away the time."

She didn't nag.

In fact, there was absolutely nothing he'd change about Charlotte's personality. He'd never enjoyed any other woman's company so much. She enjoyed his, too, now that she was more relaxed with him. Damien had no doubt about that. The occasional flash of reservation in her eyes was directly related to her being afraid to dream of actually sharing a happy future with him. Which was perfectly understandable, given the recent shattering of her faith in the marriage she'd planned with Freedman.

Damien understood it, but he hated the lack of trust that flowed over onto him. He wanted to drum it into her mind how much they shared. On every level. Real sharing. Nothing pseudo about any of it. He'd instinctively recognised the possibility of it right from the beginning. She'd tried to deny it at their first meeting on New Year's Eve, but tonight...*tonight she had to feel it, had to admit it to herself.*

Charlotte contained her curiosity until they were riding the elevator to the Fontana Room. "I hope this is a good surprise," she said, looking askance at him.

"I hope so, too," he answered, his eyes teasing the crack in her patience.

She heaved a much-put-upon sigh and he relented. They were so close now, he was sure she wouldn't back off the idea at this point, despite her reservations about the gambling that went on in casinos.

"The World Tour Poker Final is being held here tonight," he rolled out casually. "Being a killer player yourself, I thought you might enjoy watching the professionals pit their poker skills against each other at the table."

Her eyes instantly widened in excited anticipation. "A world final?"

He smiled. "The best of the best."

"And we're going to see them play it out?"

"Front row seats."

"Oh!" She clapped her hands in delight. "I'm going to love this!"

Yes!

Triumph zinged through Damien. This was something she could never have shared with Freedman. That artful manipulator hadn't really known her. Would never have known her. Would never have appreciated the mathematical clicks in her sharp brain, the same clicks that guided Damien's—weighing, assessing, pointing the direction to take, following through with decisive action.

It was a brilliant night in the Fontana Room; the posturing of the players, their highly unique characters—each with their own idiosyncrasies, which added colour to the game—the gambles taken, incredible rides of luck, bluffs that required nerves of steel, the tension when all a player's chips were laid on the line, the eruption of excitement from the spectators when huge jackpots were won and lost, the groans when a favoured player was knocked out of the game.

Charlotte was enthralled by the drama of it all, caught up in the emotional highs and lows of the play, awed by the unbelievable daring of some of the players. No flat brown eyes tonight. They openly expressed everything she was feeling, sharing the experience with him, knowing he appreciated the way the percentages were being played as much as she did.

She was still bubbling over the final gamble as they rode the elevator back to their suite. "I can't believe he took it out with a pair of deuces!"

"A brave stand!" Damien said, shaking his own head over the end result.

"Brave? It was positively perverse! This was the guy who'd folded on two aces earlier in the night."

"He was playing his opponent not the cards. The psychology was right. The pattern of play indicated the other guy frequently bet with high cards, hoping to pick up a winning pair or better with the five cards still to come from the dealer. Actually holding a pair was the better chance to take it out."

She thumped his arm. "I know that, Damien! But a pair of deuces! That's the bottom of the bottom!"

He grinned at her. "Sheer arse! And speaking of arse…"

The elevator doors opened on their floor, and he curved his hand around her sexy bottom to steer her out.

"You're being very cheeky," she admonished him, though clearly not offended by the action.

"You have a highly provocative rear end," he retaliated, swiftly using the key card to open the door to their suite.

"Huh! You'd have to be the most provocative man I've ever met. In every department!"

Her eyelashes were flirting with him, the high excitement of the evening rippling through her voice…no guard on her tongue, no guard on anything. Elated at having made this breakthrough, Damien was on fire for her as he swept Charlotte into their suite, closed the door and whirled her over to the bed, tipping her onto it and falling beside her, grinning joyfully as he said, "No more belittling a pair of deuces. Two is definitely a powerful number. You and me, Charlotte."

She raised her eyebrows in mock challenge. "You don't want to ace me?"

"A single ace doesn't beat a great pair. And we are a great pair."

Which he proceeded to prove in a long physical celebration of what he felt with Charlotte. He'd been single so long—as an only child put in the care of nannies, as an adolescent surviving the rigours of boarding school, as a man seeking a place in life that felt right to him.

But it never would have been *right* if he hadn't met

Charlotte. He knew that in his mind, in his heart, in his soul. Above everything else, he wanted what she wanted—a family unit of their own, the sense of deeply rooted belonging that would make the rest of their lives far more meaningful than walking alone, partners in all they did, sharing with a more intimate understanding than could ever be achieved with anyone else.

Damien was sure he was closer to that tonight.

A big step closer.

CHAPTER FIFTEEN

CHARLOTTE'S first month in London was a whirlwind of activity; settling into Damien's townhouse, which was very handily situated at Knightsbridge, especially with Harrods nearby, shopping for clothes suitable for a biting winter cold she had not been prepared for, meeting Damien's friends and being drawn into their social circle, going to the theatre, dining out.

It was all new and apart from the bleak weather, she enjoyed every minute of it. Damien did not sideline her from his work life. He shared what he was doing with her, inviting her participation in his projects, wanting input from her, discussing his plans, listening to her viewpoint with serious interest.

She hadn't expected to be happy in this marriage but she was. No denying it. More so than she'd been in her relationship with Mark. Looking back now, it seemed only like a comfortable cosiness with Mark who had probably worked hard at ensuring that nothing jolted her out of it. Every moment with Damien carried an exhilarating vibrancy.

He'd said they made a great pair and she was beginning to believe that really might be so, both in bed and out of it. Though it was early days yet. Damien could well be into proving he was right about them as a couple, but that didn't cover how he would handle being a father. A baby in the household would disrupt what they shared now.

For one thing, spontaneous sex would not be so easy when there were baby's needs to be considered. Damien might not like playing second fiddle to an infant. The generous amount of time he spent with her now might be cut down with excuses to be away, concentrating more on his projects where he would always be at the centre of what was happening, just like her father.

Charlotte couldn't bring herself to trust in any lasting happiness with Damien. Nevertheless, when the pregnancy test she'd bought confirmed her suspicion that she had indeed conceived a child, it was impossible to contain her joy. She raced out of the bathroom and dived onto the bed, giving Damien's shoulder a shake to wake him up and hear her news.

"Guess what?" she demanded gleefully.

It was still early morning. She'd barely slept all night, hoping she was right. Aroused so abruptly from his slumber, Damien opened only one eye and squinted at her.

"What?" he asked, her question having finally penetrated his foggy brain.

She grinned. "I'm pregnant!"

That galvanised his attention. Both eyes opened sharply but only to half-mast, his brows lowering into a frown. "So soon?"

It was not the reaction Charlotte had wanted. Her heart, which had been bursting with happiness, felt like a pricked balloon. Before she could sensibly monitor the response that leapt off her tongue, the words were out, a terse reminder of their initial bargain.

"It *is* what I married you for."

It sounded mean, even to her own ears. That time was past. They'd moved on in their relationship, building a togetherness that deserved respect and recognition. She felt horribly guilty as she saw Damien's face tighten as though hit by a particularly nasty blow. A black resentment flared into his eyes.

"Well, I'm glad I delivered satisfaction, Charlotte," he said, a mocking twist to his mouth.

This was all wrong.

A weird panic cramped her stomach.

She didn't want to lose the wonderful sense of intimacy that had been growing between them—the quick understanding, the pleasure in all they shared.

"I'm sorry," she blurted out. "You're not just a sperm bank to me, Damien. I like being your wife... your partner..."

"But not as much as you want a child," he said with an ironic resignation that somehow increased her guilt, making her feel she'd been unfair to him.

She hovered over him, at a loss for how to fix things, her eyes begging his patience while her troubled mind tried to come to grips with how much the situation had changed for her.

"It's okay," he said, heaving himself up and rolling her onto her back. "More than okay," he assured her, smiling as he gently stroked the anxious lines from her forehead. "We're going to have a great baby."

"Yes," she choked out, a huge roll of emotion clogging up her throat.

"Guess I'm more potent than I thought. I just didn't anticipate this happening so quickly. It's only been two months."

It wasn't okay to him. He was covering up. Maybe he didn't really want a baby at all. Or, at least, not yet.

"Though we have given it lots of chances," he said, wanting to tease a smile from her.

"Yes, we have," spilled from her lips as a wave of relief washed over her inner turmoil. It stood to reason that a quick pregnancy was on the cards, given all the sex they'd had. Damien had to have known that. If she'd led up to the news instead of just hitting him with it, his reaction would have been...*more prepared.*

Her heart wilted again.

He didn't share her happiness over being pregnant. He was simply accepting the inevitable, hiding his true feelings about it. There was no going back from a done deed.

"So—" his smile grew into a grin "—I'm going to be a father."

He was moving on, being good about it. Charlotte tried to relax. She had to move on herself. Needing to reach into him, she lifted a hand and stroked his cheek, saying, "I hope you'll like being a dad, Damien."

"The biggest challenge of all—parenthood," he replied cheerfully. "Don't worry. I intend to be a brilliant dad."

She smiled, thinking if there was a challenge to be met, Damien was certainly the man to meet it.

"And you'll be a great mum," he said, leaning down to kiss her.

She kissed him back. His hand slid down her body, softly caressing her newly tight breasts, then lower, gliding possessively over her stomach—her womb where the life of their child had already started. It triggered a huge welling of emotion. Charlotte didn't know if it rose from a need for the comfort of feeling one with him, or the desire to shut her mind to doubts and lose herself in what they did share—brilliantly. She didn't want to think about it. She just wanted him.

They made love.

It wasn't like the sex before.

It was different.

The love Charlotte instinctively felt for the baby growing within flowed over onto Damien, and whether she imagined it or not, it seemed to be returned in full measure.

It *was* okay, she thought afterwards.

They would *make* it okay.

The next few weeks flew past on wings of excitement. Her pregnancy was confirmed by a doctor and she listened eagerly to his advice on how best to look after herself, bought what was virtually a pregnancy bible and devoured its pages. She called her mother to share the wonderful news. Damien arranged a dinner with his father who seemed pleased with the idea of becoming a grandfather. Her own father telephoned to congratulate them, delighted with the prospect of a new generation for the family line. Peter landed in London, bringing gifts for the nursery to be.

She was happy.

Until she woke up one night with a dragging feeling in her stomach. Her initial thought that she must have eaten something that had disagreed with her, was shockingly dispelled once she reached the bathroom.

She was bleeding.

A red haze of terror seized her mind, paralysing her from taking any action. What could she do—should do—to stop what was happening?

No answer came to her.

All her life she'd prided herself on being able to cope, stand up to anything, but not this…not this. It was too shattering.

She screamed out for Damien. He was the fighter, the protector. He wouldn't let this happen to her.

He came, he saw, he took charge, calling the doctor, carrying her to the car, driving her to the hospital.

Charlotte was gripped in a nightmare of fear. Her arms were folded protectively over her stomach, desperate to hang onto the child inside. Damien kept talking to her, but she didn't really hear what he was saying. Her mind was endlessly repeating, *I can't lose the baby, I won't lose the baby, I must not lose the baby.*

But all the will-power she so fiercely concentrated on getting past this crisis failed to bring about the desperately needed outcome.

Her baby was lost.

And Charlotte lost her grip on everything that had made her life meaningful.

It was the blackest moment of all, being told by the doctor that nature had taken its own course and there was nothing he could do to change it. Something had gone wrong. This child was not meant to be.

Out of the maelstrom of her grief came the thought, *it's a punishment. It's because I married for this instead of all the right reasons.*

She shut her eyes tight and lay absolutely still, consumed by the tortured feelings erupting from her empty womb. The doctor left after a few more words to Damien who remained seated beside the hospital bed, holding her hand as though that could make things better for her.

"I'm sorry, Charlotte," he murmured sympathetically.

She hated his sympathy. Hated it. The hand he was holding instinctively curled into a fist, fighting against any soothing from him as she bit out, "Don't! It didn't matter as much to you."

She heard him suck in a quick breath. "It was my child as well as yours."

Her eyes opened to narrow slits, stabbing a bleak accusation. "You didn't want it. Not this soon. You're probably relieved this has happened."

"Relieved!" He looked appalled. "What do you take me for, Charlotte?"

"A man who wants everything his own way," she shot back at him, lashing out because she couldn't bear the guilt in her own heart for wanting a child too much, putting that first, regardless of anything else. "Having a baby straight up didn't suit you, Damien, so don't pretend it did."

The tears that had been frozen inside her, trapped in the shock of utter devastation, made a sudden powerful surge, pouring into her eyes, rendering her speechless. It wasn't grief he shared. It wasn't. So she snatched her hand from his hold, turned her back to him, curled up to nurse her loss and wept, her whole body wracked by sobs that were impossible to contain.

Damien was out of the chair and on his feet, the need *to do something* paramount, his heart pounding a painful protest at what was going down here. He wanted to gather Charlotte up in his arms and hug her tight until the storm of weeping passed but she would fight that and force wasn't right, certainly not in these circumstances. It might even cement her rejection of him.

The hell of it was he was hamstrung by the truth. He hadn't welcomed the news that she was pregnant, but not because he didn't want a child. This miscarriage had torn him up, too. He'd wanted more time with Charlotte—just the two of them. It had been so good since their honeymoon, the best time of his life. And she had liked being with him, too. He'd been winning. He couldn't—wouldn't—let it all fall apart now.

Too wrought up to remain still, Damien paced around the private hospital room, his mind set on taking action. But what? Charlotte had married him to have children. That had been her primary motivation, clearly stated, and it had come up again and again since their wedding day. No deviation from it, despite sharing so much else with him.

She'd been so luminously happy since her pregnancy was confirmed. To have it ripped away from her…what could he do to move her past this gut-wrenching grief? He couldn't bear listening to it. If she'd only turn to him…but she wasn't going to. She'd shut him out, closed in on herself.

He had to find a door to open—a door into her head, her heart.

She wanted to be a mother.

Becoming his wife had been the most practical route to that end.

If he wanted to keep her as his wife, keep everything

he'd established with her in place, he had to answer her need to be a mother. Right now! Before the loss of this child became too destructive to their marriage.

An idea burst through the frenzied turmoil in his mind. He grasped it as fiercely as a drowning sailor would a lifebuoy. Without giving it so much as a second thought, he acted, striding to the chair he had vacated, carrying it around to the other side of the bed, placing it where Charlotte would face him if she opened her eyes.

The dreadful weeping had finally abated. She looked totally spent, as though her own life had been ripped away. For a bleak second, Damien wondered if he meant anything at all to her. But he refused to believe he'd made no impact on her. She *was* his soulmate. Given enough time, Charlotte would know that, too. He just had to hang in and give her something positive to hang onto.

"Charlotte…please listen to me."

Her mind felt drained. Her body felt drained. She didn't have enough energy to speak or to move. She lay in a listless heap, unable to do anything but listen, though she wearily wished Damien would go away and leave her alone.

"I can't give you back what you lost—what *we* lost—today," he said sadly. "It's gone."

Yes, gone.

Gone for him, too.

The sadness in his voice pricked her conscience. She shouldn't have used him as a whipping boy for her own pain. It wasn't Damien's fault that she had lost the baby. He'd done everything he could to save it. And he had been looking forward to having their child. No denying that, even though it might have come too soon for him.

"Sorry," she mumbled, ungluing her eyelids enough to shoot him a look pleading forgiveness.

He shook his head, his face clearly pained by the apology. "Charlotte, you took every care. Don't blame yourself. The doctor said miscarriages aren't uncommon with a first pregnancy for women over thirty, but usually second pregnancies carry through okay."

She hadn't heard that.

It wasn't a punishment for wanting a baby too much. It was a punishment for being over thirty, starting late. She heaved a sigh to relieve the ache in her chest and tried again to mitigate her meanness in denying him any sense of loss.

"I know you wanted this child, too, Damien. I shouldn't have said…what I did."

"Don't worry about it," he said in quick dismissal. "But I do want us to have children together, Charlotte. I've just been thinking…"

He reached out and took her hand again, pressing his plea for togetherness. She let him have it, vaguely registering that his touch seemed to have lost its power, not generating any sense of intimacy with him. Or maybe she was simply drained of all feeling.

"We don't have to wait," he went on earnestly. "We could fly to Africa and adopt an orphan. I actually fund an orphanage there. There are so many children—babies, too—left without parents because of the many problems on that continent…"

Words poured from him, explaining the situation, assuring her that it would be a good thing to do, he'd be with her all the way, being a father to however many children she wanted to mother.

Charlotte was totally stunned by the suggestion. She stared at him, struggling to believe that he cared so much about giving her what she wanted. "Why?" The question burst from her lips, needing to be answered.

He frowned. "Why what?"

"You didn't want us to have a child so soon. I wasn't wrong about that, Damien," she insisted.

"No," he readily admitted. His fingers interlaced with hers, gripping hard as his eyes burnt with a need she'd never seen before. "I wanted you to trust our marriage first, Charlotte, to feel confident in it, knowing I would always be here for you and our children. You didn't marry me with that emotional security in place and I haven't had enough time with you to build it up. But if you need a child to come first…if that is the proving ground…"

The heart she'd thought was broken started swelling with different feelings, vibrating with life again. "I thought you just wanted me, Damien, and were determined to have me."

"I do. I am." His mouth tilted in ironic appeal. "But driving that is another truth, Charlotte, though I can't make you feel it if you don't."

She did feel it. She was feeling it now. Had felt it in hundreds of ways before this, though she hadn't allowed it to be too real to her, instinctively shying away from believing it because believing it made her too vulnerable to hurt. But how could she not believe it when he was offering to adopt a child for her sake? What kind of alpha man did that unless…

Despite having cried herself dry of tears, Charlotte

felt them welling again, spilling into her eyes in a great gush of emotion. She'd given up on any man ever loving her, counting only on her own children returning the love she wanted to give. She'd been so blindly wrong, hopelessly prejudiced from the start, resisting the man who'd done all he could to make her see, make her realise…

"Hold me…please," she begged huskily.

He gathered her into his embrace and held her tight.

"I'm sorry I went into my shell and closed you out," she sobbed onto his shoulder.

"It's okay," he soothed, rubbing his cheek over her hair. "I know you saw the baby as a kind of anchor for your life, Charlotte."

"I do like our marriage. I was just so set on…"

"I promise you we can adopt."

"No. You're right. More time for us would be good. I want to learn to trust. Thank you for…for being so…so determined, Damien. I was…lost…"

"All your anchors were adrift, Charlotte. You needed to be rescued."

"Yes. Yes, I did."

"You rescued me, too."

"I did? What from?"

"A lifetime of loneliness. I'm never going to let you go, you know."

She sighed in fuzzy contentment. "I'm never going to want you to."

"We'll make a real home together, Charlotte," he murmured into her ear, making it tingle with warmth.

"Yes, we will."

A real home began with love.

She felt it flowing from him, encompassing her,

melting away the last of her protective barriers, filling the cold, empty places with a shining hope that dispelled the black despair of loss. She loved him for being the man he was…strong enough, big enough, to take on rescuing her even from herself.

And there would be other children, naturally born to them or adopted.

It didn't really matter which.

As long as there was love.

CHAPTER SIXTEEN

Fifteen months later...

RICHARD WYNTER had insisted on hosting the christening at his country estate near Oxford. After all, Charlotte's father had done the wedding. It was only fair that the next big event in the family went to him. Besides, Damien had been christened in the local village church and it was entirely appropriate that Damien's son have his name written in the same church register as his father.

And so it was—Matthew James Wynter—on a beautiful June Sunday, in front of a large gathering of family and friends, all come to celebrate the occasion. They moved on to Richard's massive English mansion afterwards, filling the huge reception room with happy chatter and laughter. Everywhere Charlotte looked there were smiling faces. The power of a baby, she thought, her own joy in Matthew brimming over as she watched the response he evoked in so many others.

"Dad looks well," she remarked to her mother. "No more heart scares?"

An arch look accompanied her reply. "One warning

was enough. I watch his diet like a hawk and he's in better health now than he has been for years." She smiled at her husband who had just claimed Matthew from Damien and was rocking the baby in his arms. "Look at him, crowing like a rooster over his grandson."

Charlotte couldn't help crowing a bit herself. "Well, he is beautiful, Mum."

And perfectly healthy.

Her second pregnancy had been problem-free, every step of it carefully checked, and Damien had been with her all through the birthing process, as eager as she to welcome their child into the world.

"Utterly adorable," her mother agreed, her eyes sparkling her own delight in him. "I'm so happy for you, Charlotte. I was worried about you rushing into marriage with Damien but your father was right about it. He is the man for you, isn't he?"

"In every way." No doubt about it. She couldn't even begin to measure the depth of love she now had for her husband.

"You were well rid of Mark Freedman. Showed his true colours, claiming your apartment. A man should house himself."

"Yes, Mum." And provide a home for his family, she thought, smiling over the bigger residence Damien had just bought for them.

"Here comes Lloyd, beaming from ear to ear. You've certainly done his heart good, producing a family heir. Peter is dragging the chain with not even a marriage prospect in sight yet."

It's not easy, being a Ramsey, Charlotte thought. She was the lucky one. Not only did her fortune have no relevance to Damien but he loved her for the person she was. She hoped her brother would find a woman who loved the man behind the money.

"Charlotte…" Her father fronted up, his big barrel chest puffed out with pride, Matthew looking tiny, cradled in his bear-like arms. "Got to say this baby is a winner, so don't take this as a criticism, but I would like to put in an order for blue eyes next time around."

"The odds are against you, Dad," she warned. "Mine are brown and Damien's are almost black."

"Yes, but even a one per cent chance can take the jackpot."

"True. Damien and I watched a world poker final where a pair of deuces won the last hand."

"There you go. I can scoop the gene pool with the power of blue. You've got a lot of me in you, my girl," he declared with satisfaction.

Charlotte laughed. "You never give up on anything, do you, Dad?"

He grinned back at her. "Not when I want it. And might I say your husband is of the same mind. Good man. You made a brilliant choice, marrying him, Charlotte."

"Yes, I did." Her gaze flicked to where Damien was now chatting with Peter. "I'm very happy with him."

As though he heard the words, Damien turned his head, caught her gaze and smiled at her.

She smiled back.

"You're positively besotted with her, aren't you?" Peter commented in a tone of amused exasperation.

Damien pulled his attention back from Charlotte to grin at him. "Your sister is the best thing that ever happened to me. And for that I thank you, my friend. I would never have met her without you."

Peter rolled his eyes. "And there I was, actually feeling sorry for you at your wedding." He made a dismissive grimace, then looked seriously earnest. "So tell me…how did you know Charlotte was the one to marry? Damned if I can find a woman I feel confident about spending the rest of my life with."

"You'll know when you do, Peter. It's not just the sexual chemistry. There's a buzz in your brain that tells you not to miss out on what you could have with *this* woman. She fits what you've been waiting for."

"As easy as that, huh?"

"Not so easy when she's about to marry someone else," Damien dryly remarked. "Then you do whatever you have to do to win her."

"Put you on the spot a bit, did she?" His blue eyes twinkled. "Wouldn't be my sister if she didn't. Very challenging woman."

"Nothing like a challenge to stir the blood."

Peter laughed. "Well, you've sure got Charlotte won now. I've never seen a couple so happy to be with each other. And it's good for me, too. No way could I have been friends with Freedman."

Damien smiled. The fantasy Freedman had woven for Charlotte was long gone. What she shared with him was a very solid reality—deeply solid—untouchable by anything or anyone else. He looked at her, his heart filling with the warm pleasure of knowing their relationship was all he believed it could be.

"Excuse me, Peter. Charlotte's just taking Matthew from your father. It's past his feed time so…"

"You couldn't bear to miss being with them," Peter drawled, shaking his head over the degree of besottedness.

"Wait till you have your first child," Damien tossed at him. "Everything's magic."

Especially when you've had the experience of losing one, Damien thought, making his way through the crowd of guests to Charlotte's side. The joy of having Matthew was all the more precious.

Charlotte felt him coming before she looked up from Matthew and saw him carving a path towards her, people automatically stepping aside for him to pass, aware of him as a natural force that commanded its own space. Except for her, she thought, intensely grateful that his space was always open to her, inviting her in, wanting her sharing it.

He did have all the attributes of *one of them*, but there was so much more to Damien—so much that linked directly to how she thought and what she felt. He'd said they were soulmates right from the beginning, and Charlotte no longer had any argument against that description of their relationship. Their connection was so deep and strong, she knew it could never be broken.

"Want to take Matthew upstairs now?" he asked as he reached her side.

"Yes. He's been happily distracted by all the attention but…"

"He's bound to start yelling if you don't feed him," Damien finished for her. "Let's go."

His arm curled around her shoulders as he started leading her out of the reception room, and the warm security he imparted flowed through her, triggering a flood of pleasure. She snuggled her head close to his neck and murmured, "Do you know how much I love you, Damien Wynter?"

"Since my love for you is beyond measure, I'll take that as mutual," he said with arrogant confidence.

She laughed.

He was right.

They were right for each other.

And with their darling little son, life could not be sweeter.

Best of all, Charlotte knew this wonderful sense of togetherness would last for the rest of their lives. They wanted to share everything. They did share everything.

She smiled over her father's comment, thinking, *Yes, Daddy, I did make a brilliant choice to marry Damien. He is the man for me, now and always.*

Dear Readers,

A few months ago I read a newspaper report on a wedding that didn't happen. The bride was the daughter of a billionaire and the groom was asked to sign a pre-nuptial agreement the day before the big event. He wrote "under duress" on the document, which meant it wouldn't stand up in a court of law. The wedding was called off.

It set me wondering how that bride felt when she realised the man she had fallen in love with was marrying her for her money. Most of us don't have this problem. Most of us can feel secure about being loved for ourselves, and I truly believe every person in the world wants that, regardless of their circumstances. However, it stands to reason that the richer people are, the more difficult it is to know if the love they are being shown is genuine.

I started weaving a story about the conflicts which mega-wealthy people must invariably face in their love lives. Because it was the bride in this newspaper report which captured my interest, I created Charlotte Ramsey and proceeded to plunge her into situations that finally did lead her to a love that encompassed everything a woman wants in her heart. I hope you will feel for her every inch of the way. I know I did.

As I was writing her story, it struck me that Charlotte's brother, Peter, needed a woman who would love him. He hadn't found one. So, dear readers, I am now writing his story, which has as many exciting twists and turns as Charlotte's. Look for my next book. Peter Ramsey is a hero you will love.

Read on now. Enter the mega-wealthy Ramsey world with me and experience how it is. Enjoy…

With love always—Emma Darcy.

THE UNEXPECTED
HOLIDAY GIFT

SOPHIE PEMBROKE

For Auntie Barbara and Uncle Viv,
for so many perfect Christmas days!

CHAPTER ONE

CLARA TUGGED THE candy-striped ribbon just a millimetre farther out, then leaned back to admire the neatly wrapped present with beautifully tied bow. Really, it was a shame to give it away.

'Are we done?' Her business partner, Merry, added one last gift to the pile and looked hopefully at Clara. 'That was definitely the last one, right?'

'For this client, yes.' Clara grinned. 'But I'm fairly sure we've got another three Christmas lists to work through before the big day. Not to mention the five decorating projects, three last-minute requests for tickets as presents and two Christmas dinners we need to arrange.'

'And a partridge in a pear tree,' Merry grumbled. 'Whose stupid idea was this business anyway?'

'Yours,' Clara reminded her cheerfully. 'And I know you love it, really.'

Clara hadn't been sure there was a market for this sort of thing when Merry had first suggested it. Did Londoners really need another concierge and events service? Would people really pay them to organise their lives, buy their gifts, arrange special access and perks, plan their parties and family gatherings, their holidays and so on? Merry had been adamant that they would.

With your magic at making things perfect and my business knowledge, we can't fail, she'd insisted over a bottle of wine at Clara's tiny rented flat one evening.

So Perfect London had been born and, four years later, business was booming. Especially at Christmas.

'I suppose it's all right,' Merry said, the smirk she threw Clara's way showing her real feelings. 'Pays the bills, anyway.'

And then some. Clara was still amazed at just how successful they'd been. Successful enough that she'd been able to move out of that tiny flat into her own house two years ago. Successful enough that she no longer lay awake at night, panicking about how she would provide for her daughter, Ivy, alone.

Clara stared at the mountain of presents again, then turned her attention to the Christmas tree standing in their shop front office window. Gazing at the star on top, she made a wish. The same wish she'd made every year since Perfect London had taken the city by storm that first Christmas, when media mentions and word of mouth had seen them triple their income in a month and the numbers had held at that level for the following year.

Please, let things stay this good for another year?

The fact that they had so far went a long way to wiping out some of the less than wonderful Christmas memories from her childhood. Clara would even go so far as to say that, these days, Christmas was a magical time of year for her—especially with Ivy around to share it with.

'What have you and Ivy got planned for Christmas?' Merry asked.

Clara shrugged. 'Nothing much. She wants a bike, so I imagine we'll be taking that out for a ride.' She frowned just for a moment, remembering that a bike wasn't the only thing her daughter had asked Father Christmas for that year. Ivy didn't know that she'd overheard, but Clara couldn't shake the memory of her whispering to the man in the red suit at the shopping centre that what she wanted most in the world was 'to have a dad'.

At least the bike was more achievable, even if keeping it hidden was proving tricky. She could walk out and buy a bike at any number of shops in the city.

A father was rather more difficult to procure. Especially Ivy's real dad.

She shook the thought away. There were only a couple of weeks until the big day, and Clara was going to focus on the wonderful Christmas she *could* give her daughter.

'Other than that,' she went on, 'pancakes for breakfast, the usual turkey for lunch and a good Christmas movie in the afternoon.' Quiet, cosy and just the way Clara liked it.

Worlds away from the Christmases she had once expected to have, before Ivy had come along, before Perfect London. Before she had walked out on her marriage.

It was strange to think about it now. Most of the time, she could barely imagine herself still married to Jacob. But every now and then, something would happen to remind her and she'd find herself picturing the way her life might have gone. Like a parallel universe she kept getting glimpses of, all the might-have-beens she'd walked away from.

They would probably be spending Christmas in one of his many modern, bright white, soulless properties. They were barely houses, let alone homes, and they were certainly not cosy. Maybe his family would be with them this year, maybe not. There'd be expensive, generic presents, designer decorations. Maybe she'd have thrown a party, the sort she loved organising for clients these days—but it would have felt just as much like business, when all the guests would have been Jacob's business associates rather than friends.

But there was the other side of it too. They'd only managed two Christmases together, but they had both been packed with happy moments—as well as the awful ones. She had memories of waking up in Jacob's arms, the times when it had been just the two of them and a bunch of mistletoe. A walk in the snow with his arm around her waist. The heat in his eyes as he watched her get ready for another party. The way he smiled, just sometimes, as if she was everything he'd ever imagined having in the world and so much more.

Except she wasn't, and she knew that now. More than that, she knew that she was worth more than he was willing to give her—only bestowing his attention on her when it suited him, or when he could drag himself away from work. When you truly loved someone, it wasn't a chore to spend time with them and they should never have to beg you for scraps of attention. Ivy had taught her that—and so much more. She had taught her things Clara couldn't imagine she'd spent twenty-seven years not understanding but that Ivy had been born knowing.

So Clara seldom thought twice about her decision to leave—she knew it had been the right one. But still, from time to time those parallel universes would sneak up and catch her unguarded, reminding her of the good things about her marriage as well as the bad.

'What are you thinking about?' Merry asked. 'You've been staring at that tree for five solid minutes and you haven't even asked me to start on the next job. I'm beginning to worry.'

Clara shook her head and turned away from the tree. It didn't matter, anyway. Because in all those visions of that other life, there was always one person missing.

Ivy.

And Clara refused to imagine her life without her daughter.

'Nothing,' she lied. 'Just Christmas Past, I suppose.'

'I prefer Christmas Presents,' Merry joked. 'Or even Christmas Future if it means we're done working for the year.'

'Done for the year?' Clara asked incredulously. 'Have you forgotten the Harrisons' New Year's Eve Charity Gala?'

Merry rolled her eyes. 'As if I could. Who really needs that much caviar anyway?'

'Two hundred of London's richest, most famous and most influential people.' Twenty tables of ten, at ten thousand pounds a plate, with all proceeds going to the children's charity the Harrison family had set up in memory of their youngest child, who'd died ten years ago from a rare type of blood cancer.

No one else would have dared to hold such an important—and expensive—fundraiser on New Year's Eve. The one night of the year when everyone had plans and people they wanted to be with. But the Harrisons had the money, the influence, the charm and the celebrity to pull it off. Especially with Perfect London organising everything for them.

Clara had been nervous when Melody Harrison—activist, author and all-round beautiful woman—had approached her. The Harrisons were possibly the most recognisable family in London: the epitome of a perfect family. And Melody wanted *Clara* to organise the most important charity event in their calendar.

'You did such a beautiful job with the True Blue launch event,' she'd said. 'I just know Perfect London is the right fit for our little charity gala.'

'Little', Clara had found out soon enough, had been the biggest understatement of the year. Possibly of the last decade.

But they'd managed it—with plenty of outsourcing, hiring in extra staff for the event and more than a few late nights. Everything was in place as much as it could be while they finished dealing with their more usual Christmas bookings. Clara planned to take Christmas Eve, Christmas Day and Boxing Day off entirely to spend the time with Ivy. Her own perfect little family.

It was natural for Ivy to be curious about her dad, Clara knew. But she also knew, deep in her heart, that they were better off with just the two of them. They were a team. A duo. They didn't need anyone else, people who could walk out at any moment or decide they'd found something better or more important to focus on.

Right now, Ivy knew she was the most important thing in her mother's world, and Clara would never do a thing to risk ruining that.

'You're staring at the tree again,' Merry said. 'It's getting creepy. What's got you all pensive? Christmas Past… Are you thinking about your ex?'

'Sort of, I suppose.' Clara busied herself, tidying up the wrapping paper and ribbons. As much as she loved Merry, she really didn't want to talk about Jacob.

Merry, apparently, didn't get that memo. 'Do you ever regret leaving him?'

'No,' Clara said firmly. Did she feel guilty about it? Yes. Did she wonder what might have happened if she'd stayed? Sure. But regret… How could she regret the life she had now, with her daughter? 'But…I guess I'm still missing some closure, you know?'

'You know what would help with that?' Merry said. 'An actual divorce. Honestly, it's been, what, five years?'

'It's not like I haven't asked for one. Repeatedly.' But Jacob had money and, more important, better lawyers. If he wanted to stall, they knew all the possible ways to make it happen. And, for some reason, he didn't seem to want their divorce to go through.

'Yeah, but it's not like you're even asking for anything from him. Not that it wouldn't have been a help at the start.' Merry still hadn't quite got over the fact that Clara had walked out with nothing but the clothes on her back and a small bag of personal belongings. But she had wanted to leave that whole part of her life behind, and taking money from Jacob would have tied her to him.

Although, as it turned out, she'd walked away with something much more binding than money. Even if she hadn't known it then.

That was where the closure came in. It wasn't just about them—it was about Ivy too. Had she done the right thing, not going back when she'd discovered she was pregnant? At the time, she'd been so sure. Jacob had made it very, very clear that they would *not* be having a family together. And she'd wanted her baby so desperately, in a way she'd never realised she would until the moment she'd seen the word *pregnant* appear on the test.

But, every now and then, she couldn't help but wonder what might have happened if she'd told him.

'I don't know what goes on in my ex-husband's brain,' Clara said. 'I never did. If I had known, maybe we'd still be married.'

'And then you wouldn't be here with me,' Merry replied. 'And that would suck. So, let's just forget all about him.'

'Good plan,' Clara agreed, relieved. 'Besides, I need to talk to you about the decorations for the Colemans' house…'

The Christmas lights twinkled along the length of the trendy London street, illuminating coffee shops and gift boutiques with flashes of glittering brightness. Jacob Foster moved slowly through the crowds of shoppers, feeling conspicuous in his lack of shopping bags, lists and most of all haste, even in the cold winter drizzle.

It wasn't that his errand wasn't urgent. He just wasn't all that keen to jump into it. Especially since he had no idea how it was likely to go. He'd been trying to think his way through it for the whole journey there; which approach had the best chance of success, what he could say to get her to say yes. He'd still not come to a final decision.

He still wasn't completely sure he should be there at all. This might be the worst idea he'd had since he was sixteen. He'd spent five years putting distance between them, moving on and forgetting her. The last thing he needed was to let Clara in again.

But he was doing it anyway. For family. Because, despite everything that had happened between them, Clara was still family—and this job couldn't be given to anybody but family.

He turned down a small side street lined with offices and within moments he found himself standing outside a neat apple-green office with the words 'Perfect London' emblazoned above the door, and knew his thinking time was up.

He paused, his hand on the door ready to push it open, and stared for a moment through the large window. There she was. Clara.

Her dark hair hung down over her face as she leant across a colleague's desk to point at something on a computer screen. It obscured her eyes but, since that meant she couldn't see him, Jacob supposed that was for the best.

She looked well, he supposed. The cranberry-coloured wrap dress she wore clung to curves he remembered too well, and his gaze followed the length of her left arm from the shoulder down to where her hand rested on the desk. He looked closer. No ring.

Jacob took a breath, trying to quieten the large part of his brain that was screaming at him that this was a stupid idea and that he should just turn and leave now. It had been five long years; what was five more? Or ten? Or forever? He'd already been stung by failure with Clara before. Why risk that again?

But no. His plan mattered, far more than any history he and Clara shared, no matter how miserable. He'd decided he would make this thing happen, and he would. Jacob Foster kept his word and he didn't let people down. Especially not his family.

And they were all counting on him. Even if they didn't actually know about his plan just yet.

But he needed help. Clara's help, to be specific. So he couldn't turn and walk away.

He just had to make it clear that this was business, not

pleasure. He wasn't there to win her back, or remind her how good they'd been together. He was there to ask for her professional help, that was all.

He took another deep breath and steeled himself to open the door.

She'd listen, at least, he hoped. Hear him out. She had to. She was still his wife, after all.

Clara brushed the hair back from her face and peered at the screen again. 'I'm still not sure it's going to be big enough.'

Sitting at the desk beside her, Merry sighed. 'It's the biggest I've been able to find, so it might just have to do.'

'*Have to do* doesn't sound very Perfect London,' Clara admonished. 'If it's not right—'

'We keep looking,' Merry finished for her. 'I know. But can I keep looking tomorrow? Only I've got that thing to-night.'

'Thing?' Clara searched her memory for the details. Best friends and business partners were supposed to know this stuff, she was sure. 'Oh! The thing at the art gallery! Yes! Get out of here now!'

Merry pushed her chair back from the desk, obviously wasting no time. 'Thanks. Don't you need to pick Ivy up?'

Clara checked her watch. 'I've got another twenty minutes or so. She's having dinner round at Francesca's tonight, so I might as well use the time to finish things up here.'

'Okay.' Grabbing her bag and coat, Merry started lay-ering up to face the winter chill outside. 'But don't work too late tonight, right?'

'I told you; I've got to leave in twenty minutes. I'll be out of here in no time.'

'I meant once you get home, and Ivy's in bed.' Merry leant over and gave Clara a swift kiss on the cheek. 'I mean it. Take a night off for once.'

Clara blushed, just a little. She hadn't thought her friend

knew about all the extra hours she put in during the long, dark evenings. It was just that, once Ivy was asleep, what else was there to do, really, but work? She didn't have dates or any real desire to go out and meet people, even if her childminder was available to babysit for Ivy. It made more sense to get on top of the work, so that when she did have time with her daughter at weekends she didn't have to be tied to her computer. That was all.

'I was just going to finish up the accounts,' she admitted.

'Leave it,' Merry instructed. 'I'll do it tomorrow. You can take over finding the biggest Christmas tree in existence!'

'Somehow, I think I've been played,' Clara said drily.

'Go on, get gone. You don't want to be late.'

Merry flashed her a grin and reached for the door but before she could grab the handle it opened, revealing a dark shadow of a man in the doorway. Clara stared at the shape. It was too dark to make out any particulars, certainly not a face or any recognisable features. And yet, somehow, that shadow was very, very familiar…

'I'm very sorry,' Merry said politely. 'We're just closing up, actually.'

'I only need to talk to Clara,' the man in the doorway said, and Clara's heart dropped like a stone through her body.

'Jacob.' The word was barely a whisper but Merry's head swung round to look at her anyway, her eyes wide.

'Maybe you could come back—' Merry began, already pushing the door closed, but Clara stopped her.

'No. No, it's okay.' She swallowed, wishing the lump that had taken up residence in her throat would lessen. 'Come in, Jacob. What can I do for you?'

Maybe he'd met somebody else at last and was here to

finalise the divorce. That would make sense. For a brief moment, relief lapped against the edges of her panic—until a far worse idea filled her mind.

Maybe he's found out about Ivy.

But no. That was impossible. She'd covered her tracks too well for that; even Merry believed that Ivy was the result of a one-night stand shortly after her marriage broke down. There was no one in the world except Clara herself who knew the truth about Ivy's conception.

And she had no plans to share that information.

'Want me to stay?' Merry asked as Jacob brushed past her. When he stepped into the light, it was hard to imagine that she hadn't known who he was, even for a second. He was exactly the same man she'd walked out on five Christmases ago. Same dark hair, with maybe just a hint of grey now at the temples. Same broad shoulders and even the same style of classic dark wool coat stretched across them. Same suit underneath, she was sure. Still all business, all the time.

Which made her wonder again what he was doing there, wasting time on her. Clara had no illusions about how her still-not-officially-ex-husband felt about her. He'd made it crystal-clear every single time he'd refused to sign the divorce papers, purely out of spite it seemed, sending his decision via his lawyers rather than talking to her in person. He'd made it clear how unimportant she, and what she wanted, was to him long before she'd ever left. He had never needed her before. What on earth could have made him start now?

Merry was still waiting for an answer, she realised. 'I'll be fine,' she said, shaking her head. Her friend looked unconvinced but resigned.

'I'll call you later,' she promised, and Clara nodded. 'And don't forget—you need to leave in twenty minutes.'

The seconds stretched out as the door swung slowly shut behind Merry. And then, with the noise of the street blocked out, it was just them again. Just Clara, Jacob and the sense of impending dread that filled Clara's veins.

CHAPTER TWO

SHE *DID* LOOK DIFFERENT.

Jacob hadn't been able to clock all the changes through the window, it dawned on him now. He'd thought she looked the same, but she didn't, not really. And it wasn't just that her hair was longer, or that slight extra curve to her body, or even that her wedding ring was missing.

It was just *her*.

Her shoulders straightened, just an inch, and he realised that was part of it. An air of confidence he hadn't seen in her before. When they'd been married—properly married, living together and in love, not this strange limbo he'd been perpetuating—she'd been…what, exactly? Attentive, loving…undemanding, he supposed. She had just always been there, at home, happy to organise his business dinners or fly with him across the world at a moment's notice. She'd been the perfect hostess, the perfect businessman's wife, just like his mother had been for his father for so many years.

His father, he remembered, had been delighted in Jacob's choice of wife. *'She won't let you down, that one,'* he'd said.

Until she'd walked out and left him, of course.

Perhaps he'd been underestimating Clara all along. So much for a five-minute job convincing her to help him. This was going to take work. This new Clara, he feared, would ask questions. Lots of them.

'Jacob,' she said again, impatiently. 'What can I do for you?'

'You need to leave soon, your friend said?'

Clara gave a sharp nod. 'I do. So if we could make this quick…'

Unlikely. 'Perhaps it would be better if we met up later.

For dinner, perhaps?' Somewhere he could ply her with wine, good food and charm and convince her that this was a good idea.

'Sorry, I can't do that.' There was no debate, no maybe and no other offer. Even the apology at the start didn't sound much like one. This Clara knew her own mind and she was sticking to it.

It was kind of hot, actually. Or it would have been if he didn't sense it was going to make his life considerably more difficult.

Clara sighed and perched on the edge of the desk. 'You might as well start talking, Jacob,' she said, glancing down at her watch. 'I'm leaving in…fifteen minutes, now. Whether you've said what you came here to say or not.'

What was so important, he wondered, that she still had to run out of here, even after the arrival of a husband she hadn't seen in five years? Another man? Probably.

Not that he cared, of course. All that mattered to him was her professional availability. Not her personal life.

'I want to hire you. Your firm, I mean. But specifically you.' There, he'd said it. And, judging by the look on his wife's face, he'd managed to surprise her in the process. The shock in her expression gave him a measure of control back, which he appreciated.

'Whatever for?' she asked eventually.

'My father.' The words came out tight, the way they always did when he spoke about it. The unfairness of it all. 'He's dying.'

And that was the only reason he was there. The only thing that could make him seek out his ex-in-all-but-paperwork-wife and ask for her help.

'I'm so sorry, Jacob.' Clara's eyes softened instantly, but he didn't want to see that. He looked down at his hands and kept talking instead.

'Cancer,' he said harshly, hating the very word. 'The

doctors haven't given him more than a couple of months. If he'd gone to them sooner...' He swallowed. 'Anyway. This is going to be his last Christmas. I want to make it memorable.'

'Of course you do,' Clara said, and he felt something inside him relax, just a little. He'd known that she would understand. And what he needed would require more than the sort of competence he could buy. He needed someone who would give *everything* to his project. Who would do what he needed, just like she always had before.

And, for some reason, Clara had always been very fond of his father.

'I'm planning a family Christmas up in the Highlands,' Jacob explained. 'Just like one we had one year when I was a boy.'

'I remember you all talking about it once. It sounds perfect,' Clara agreed. 'And like you've got it all in hand, so I don't really see why—'

'That's it,' Jacob interrupted her. 'That idea. That's all I have.'

'Oh.' Clara winced. 'So you want to hire Perfect London to...?'

'Do everything else. Organise it. Make it perfect.' That, she'd always been good at. She'd been the perfect businessman's wife, the perfect housewife, the perfect beauty on his arm at functions, even the perfect daughter-in-law. Up until the day she wasn't his perfect anything at all.

'But...' Clara started, and he jumped in to stop whatever objection she was conjuring up.

'I'll pay, of course. Double your normal rate.' He'd pay triple to make this happen but he'd keep that information in reserve in case he needed it later.

'Why?' Bafflement covered Clara's expression.

'Who else?' Jacob asked. 'It's what you do, isn't it? It's right there in the name of your company.' The company she'd left him to build—and which, by the looks of things, seemed to be doing well enough. He'd never even imagined, when they were married, that she'd wanted this—her own business, her own life apart from him. How could he? She'd never told him.

Well. If she was determined to go off and be happy and successful without him, the least she could do was help him out now, when he needed it.

'Perfect *London*,' Clara said, emphasising the second word. 'We mostly work locally. Very locally.'

'I imagine that most of the arrangements can be made from here,' Jacob conceded. 'Although I would need you in Scotland for the final set-up.'

'No.' Clara shook her head. 'I can't do that. I have… obligations here. I can't just leave.'

Obligations. A whole new life, he imagined. A new man…but not her husband, though. That, at least, she couldn't have. Not unless he let her.

Jacob took a breath and prepared to use his final bargaining chip.

The only thing he had left to give her.

This made no sense. None at all. Why on earth would Jacob come to her, of all people, to organise this? There must be a hundred other party planners or concierge services he could have gone to. Unless this was a punishment of some sort, Clara could not imagine why her ex-husband would want to hire her for this task.

Except…she knew his family. She knew his father, and could already picture exactly the sort of Christmas he'd want.

Maybe Jacob wasn't so crazy after all. But that didn't mean she had to say yes.

She had her own family to think about this Christmas— her and Ivy, celebrating together in gingerbread-man pyjamas and drinking hot chocolate with Merry on Christmas Eve. That was how it had been for the last four years, and the way it would be this Christmas too, thank you very much. She wasn't going to abandon her daughter to go and arrange Christmas deep in the Highlands, however much Jacob was willing to pay. Especially not with the Harrisons' gala coming up so soon afterwards.

'No,' she said again, just to make it doubly clear. 'I'm sorry. It's impossible.'

Except…a small whisper in the back of her mind told her that this could be her chance. Her one opportunity to see if he'd really changed. If Jacob Foster was ready to be a father at last. If she could risk telling him about Ivy, introduce them even, without the fear that Jacob would treat his daughter the way Clara's own father had treated her.

Even twenty years later, the memory of her father walking out of the front door, without looking back to see Clara waving him goodbye, still made her heart contract. And Jacob had been a champion at forgetting all about his wife whenever work got too absorbing, walking out and forgetting to look back until a deal was signed or a project tied up.

She wouldn't put Ivy through that, not for anything. She wanted so much more than that for her daughter. Clara might work hard but she always, *always* had time for her child and always put her first. Ivy would never be an afterthought, never slip through the cracks when something more interesting came up. Even if that meant she only ever had one parent.

But Jacob had come here to organise a family Christmas. The Jacob she'd been married to wouldn't have even *thought* of that. Could he really have changed? And could she risk finding out?

'This Christmas I'd like to have a dad, please.' Ivy's whispered words floated through her mind.

She shook her head again, uncertain.

'What if I promise you a divorce?' Jacob asked.

For a moment, it was as if the rain had stopped falling outside, as if the world had paused in its turning.

A divorce. She'd be completely free at last. No more imagining a life she no longer possessed. Her new life would truly be hers, clear and free.

It was tempting.

But then reality set in. That divorce would cut the final tie between them—the last link between Ivy and her father. How could she do that before she even told Jacob he had a daughter?

Clara bit the inside of her cheek as she acknowledged a truth she'd long held at bay. It hadn't just been Jacob holding up their divorce for five long years. If she'd wanted to push for it she could have, at any time. But she'd always known that she'd have to come clean about Ivy first...and she was terrified.

The risk was always, always there. Jacob might reject them both instantly and walk away, but she could cope with that, she hoped, as long as Ivy didn't know, didn't hurt. But what if he wanted to be involved? What if he wanted to meet her, to be a part of her life—and then ignored Ivy the same way he'd kept himself apart from Clara after they were married? What if he hurt Ivy with his distracted, even unintentional, neglect? Nothing had ever meant more to Jacob than his work—not even her. Why would Ivy be any different?

So even if he thought he wanted to be a father...could she really risk Ivy's heart that way?

No. She had to be sure. And the only way to be certain was to spend time with him, to learn who he was all over again. Then she could decide, either to divorce him freely, or to let him into Ivy's life, whichever was best for her daughter. That was all that mattered.

But to spend time with him she'd have to organise his

perfect family Christmas. Could she really do that? With all her other clients, the Harrisons' Charity Gala—and her own Christmas with Ivy? It was too much. And she was still too scared.

'I'm sorry, Jacob. Really I am.' She was; part of her heart hurt at the thought of James Foster suffering and her not being there to ease it. An even larger part, although she hated to admit it, stung at the idea of Jacob going through this without her too.

That's not my place any more. It's not my life.

She had to focus on the life she had, the one she'd built. Her new life for her and Ivy.

'I can't help you,' she said, the words final and heavy.

Jacob gave her a slow, stiff nod. 'Right. Of course.' He turned away but as he reached the door he looked back, his eyes so full of sorrow and pain that Clara could have wept. 'Please. Just think about it.'

I can't. I can't. I won't. I... She nodded. 'I'll think about it,' she promised and instantly hated herself.

This was why she'd had to leave. She could never say no to him.

I'll think about it.

One year of marriage, five years of estrangement and now she was thinking. He supposed that was something.

Jacob paused briefly on the corner of the street, rain dripping down his collar, and watched from a distance as Clara locked up the offices of Perfect London and hurried off in the opposite direction. She was a woman on a mission; she clearly had somewhere far more important to be. Things that mattered much more in her life than her ex-husband.

Well. So did he, of course.

The office was deserted by the time he'd walked back across the river to it, but the security guard on duty didn't look surprised to see him. Given how rarely Jacob made it to the London office, he wondered what that said about the legend of his work ethic.

But once he had sat at his desk he found he couldn't settle. His eyes slid away from emails, and spreadsheets seemed to merge into one on the screen. Eventually, he closed the lid of his laptop, sat back in his chair and swung it around to take in the London skyline outside the window.

Was it just seeing Clara again that was distracting him? No. She didn't have that kind of power over him any more. It was everything else in his life right now, most likely. His father's illness more than anything.

His mobile phone vibrated on the glass desk, buzzing its way across the smooth surface. Jacob grabbed it and, seeing his younger sister's name on the screen, smiled.

'Heather. Why aren't you out at some all-night rave or something? Isn't that what you students do?'

He could practically hear her rolling her eyes on the other end of the phone.

'We're having a Christmas movie night at the flat,' Heather said. 'Mulled wine, mince pies, soppy movies and lots of wrapping paper. I was halfway through wrapping my stack of presents when it occurred to me that there was still one person who hadn't got back to me about what they wanted…'

'You don't have to buy me anything,' Jacob said automatically. It wasn't as if he couldn't buy whatever he wanted when he wanted it, anyway. And, besides, Heather, more than anyone, never owed him a gift. Her continued existence was plenty for him.

'It's Christmas, Jacob.' She spoke slowly, as if to a slightly stupid dog. 'Everyone gets a present. You know the rules. So tell me what you want or I'll buy you a surprise.'

Only his sister could make a surprise gift sound like a

threat. Although, given the tie she'd bought him last year, maybe it was.

'A surprise will be lovely,' he said, anyway. 'Anything you think I'd like.'

'You're impossible.' Heather sighed. 'While I have you, when are you heading home for Christmas?'

'Actually…'

'Oh, no! Don't say you're not coming!' She groaned dramatically. 'Come on, Jacob! The office can cope for one day without you, you know. Especially since *no one else will be working*!'

Jacob blinked as an almost exact echo of Heather's words flooded his memory—except this time it was Clara speaking them, over and over. He shook his head to disperse the memory.

'That's not what I was going to say,' he said. 'In fact…I went to see Clara today.'

'Clara?' Heather asked, the surprise clear in her voice. 'Why? What on earth for?'

'I wanted to ask for her help.' He took a breath. Time to share the plan, he supposed. If Clara wouldn't help, it would all fall on him and Heather anyway. 'I was thinking about Dad. This is going to be his last Christmas, Heather, and I want it to be special.'

His sister went quiet. Jacob waited. He knew Heather was still struggling to come to terms with their father's diagnosis. He wouldn't rush her.

'So, what have you got planned?' she asked eventually.

'Do you remember that year we hired that cottage in Scotland? You can only have been about five at the time, but we had a roaring log fire, stockings hung next to it, the biggest Christmas tree you've ever seen… It was everything Christmas is meant to be.' It had also been the last Christmas before the accident. Before everything had changed in his relationship with his family.

'You mean a movie-set Christmas,' Heather joked. 'But, yeah, I remember, I think. Bits of it, anyway. You want to do that again?'

'That's the plan.'

'And what? You're going to rope Clara into coming along to pretend that you've made up and everything is just rosy, just to keep Dad happy? Because, Jacob, that's exactly the sort of stupid plan that *will* backfire when Dad defies all the doctors' expectations.'

'That's not… No.' That wasn't the plan. He had no intention of pretending anything. Except, now that Heather had said it, he was already imagining what it would be like. Clara beside him on Christmas morning, opening presents together, his dad happy and smiling, seeing his family back together again…

But no. That was *not* the plan. The last thing he needed was to get embroiled with his almost-ex-wife again. And, once Christmas was out of the way, he'd give her the divorce she wanted so desperately and make a clean break altogether.

'She runs a concierge and events company here in London now,' he explained. 'They can source anything you need, put together any party, any plan. I wanted to hire her to organise our Christmas.'

Heather sounded pitying as she said, 'Jacob. Don't you think that's just a little bit desperate? If you wanted to see your ex-wife, you could have just called her up.'

'Wife,' he corrected automatically, then wished he hadn't. 'We're still married. Technically.'

His sister sighed. 'It's been five years, Jacob. When are you going to get over her?'

'I'm over her,' he assured her. 'Very over her. Trust me. But she knows Dad and she knows the family. She could make this Christmas everything it needs to be, far better than I ever could. You probably don't remember the parties she used to throw...'

'I remember them,' Heather said. 'They were spectacular.'

'Look, she hasn't even said yes yet. And if she doesn't I'll find someone else to do it. It won't be the end of the world.' But it wouldn't be the perfect Christmas he wanted either. Somehow, he knew in his bones that only Clara could give them that. She had a talent for seeing right to the heart of people, knowing exactly what made them light up inside—and what didn't.

He wondered sometimes, late at night, what she'd seen inside him that had made her leave. And then he realised he probably already knew.

'Okay,' Heather said, still sounding dubious. 'I guess I'm in, in principle. But Jacob...be careful, yeah?'

'I'm always careful,' he joked, even though it wasn't funny. Just true.

'I'm serious. I don't want to spend my Christmas holiday watching you nurse a broken heart. Again.'

Jacob shook his head. 'It's not like that. Trust me.'

Not this time. Even if he was harbouring any residual feelings for Clara, he would bury them deep, far deeper than even she could dig out.

He wasn't going to risk his heart that way a second time. Marriage might be the one thing he'd failed at—but he would only ever fail once.

CHAPTER THREE

'WHAT DID HE WANT?' Merry asked the moment Clara picked up the phone.

Clara sighed. 'Hang on.'

Peeking around Ivy's door one last time, she assured herself that her daughter was firmly asleep and pulled the door to. Then, phone in hand, she padded down the stairs to the kitchen, poured herself a glass of wine and headed for the sofa.

'Right,' she said, once she was settled. 'Let's start with your thing at the art gallery. How was it?'

Merry laughed. 'Not a chance. Come on, your ex-husband walks into our offices right before Christmas, after five years of nothing except letters from his lawyers finding reasons to put off the divorce, and you think I'm not going to want details? Talk, woman.'

So much for diversion tactics. 'He wanted to hire Perfect London.'

There was a brief moment of shocked silence on the other end of the phone. Clara took the opportunity to snag a chocolate off the potted Christmas tree in her front window and pop it in her mouth.

'Seriously?' Merry said at last. 'Why?'

'God only knows,' Clara replied, then sighed again. 'No, I know, I suppose. He wants us to arrange a perfect last Christmas for his dad. He's sick. Very sick.'

'And he thought his ex-wife would be the best person to organise it because…?'

It wasn't as if Clara hadn't had the same thought. 'I guess because I know him. All of them, really. I know what he means when he says "a perfect Christmas for Dad". With anyone else he'd have to spell it out.'

'So nothing to do with wanting to win you back, then,' Merry said, the scepticism clear in her voice.

'No. Definitely not.' That, at least, was one thing Clara was very sure of. 'He offered me a divorce if I do it.'

'Finally!' Merry gave a little whoop of joy, which made Clara smile. Sometimes, having a good friend on side made everything so much easier. Even seeing Jacob Foster again for the first time in five years. 'Well, in that case, we have to do it.'

'You haven't heard the fine print.' Clara filled her in on the details, including the whole 'have to travel to Scotland on Christmas Eve' part. 'It's just not doable. Especially not with the Charity Gala at New Year to finalise.' Which was a shame, in a way. A project like this would be a great selling point for future clients. And a good testimonial from Foster Medical—especially alongside delivering a great event for the Harrisons—could go a long way to convincing people that Perfect London was a big-time player. It could make the next year of their business.

Merry was obviously thinking the same thing. 'There's got to be some way we can pull it off.'

'Not without disrupting Ivy's Christmas,' Clara said. 'And I won't do that. She's four, Merry. This might be the first proper Christmas she's able to remember in years to come. I want it to be perfect for her too.' Of course, it could also be an ideal opportunity to discover if Jacob was ready to hear about the existence of his daughter. The guilt had been eating her up ever since he'd left her office that evening. Watching Ivy splash about in her bath, tucking her in after her story... She couldn't help but think how Jacob had already missed four years of those things. And even if he didn't want to be part of them, she knew she owed him the chance to choose for himself.

Except that he'd already made his decision painfully
clear five years ago. She had no reason to imagine that decision had changed—apart from him wanting to organise
Christmas for his family. Was that enough proof? How
could she be sure? Only by spending time with him. And
there was the rub.

'You always want everything to be perfect,' Merry
moaned. 'But I take your point. Does…does he know?
About Ivy?'

A chill slithered down Clara's spine. 'I don't think so.
Not that it would be any of his business, anyway. I didn't
fall pregnant with her until after I left.' She hated lying.
But she'd been telling this one for so long she didn't know
how to stop.

If she told Jacob the truth, she'd have to tell Merry too.
And Ivy, of course. And Jacob's family. She'd be turning
everybody's lives upside down. Did she have the right to
do that? But then, how could she not? Didn't Jacob's father deserve the chance to know his granddaughter before
he died? Or would that only make it worse, having so little
time with her?

What on earth was she supposed to do? When she'd left,
it had all seemed so clear. But now…

'I know, I know. Your one and only one-night stand,'
Merry said, still blissfully ignorant of the truth, and Clara's
internal battle. 'Still, it might make a difference if you explained why you can't go to Scotland for Christmas. Maybe
he'd be satisfied with me going instead, once you've done
the set-up.'

'Maybe,' Clara allowed, but even as she said it she knew
it wasn't true. Jacob wouldn't take second best. Not that
Merry was, of course—she was every bit as brilliant at
her job as Clara was at hers. That was why Perfect London worked so well. But Jacob's plan involved Clara being
there, and she suspected he wouldn't give that up for any-

thing. Even if it meant letting down a little girl at Christmas. 'I'd rather not tell him,' she said finally. 'The dates are close, I'll admit, and I don't want him using Ivy as an excuse to hold up the divorce while we get paternity tests done and so on. Not when I'm finally on the verge of getting my freedom back.' And not when the results wouldn't be in her favour.

'Only if you take on the project,' Merry pointed out. 'That was the deal, right? Organise Christmas, get divorce. Turn him down…'

'And he'll drag this out with the lawyers for another five years,' Clara finished. 'You're right. Damn him.'

She tried to sound upset at the prospect, for Merry's sake. But another five years of limbo meant another five years of not having to pluck up the courage to tell Jacob the truth. And part of her, the weakest part, couldn't deny that the idea had its appeal.

But no. If his arriving unannounced had taught her anything it was that it was time for the truth to come out, or be buried forever. No more *maybe one day.* She needed to move on properly. If Jacob still felt the same way about kids as he had when they were married, then her decision was easy. Get the divorce, move on with her life and let him live his own without worrying about a daughter that he'd never wanted.

If he'd changed his mind, however…

Clara sighed. If she'd known she was pregnant before she'd left, she would have had to tell him. But finding out afterwards… She hadn't even known how to try.

Jacob had always made it painfully clear that he didn't want a family. At least he had once they were married. During their frantic whirlwind courtship and their impulsive elopement, the future had rarely come up in conversation. And, if it had, all Clara could imagine then was them, together, just the two of them.

It wasn't until the next summer, when she'd realised she was late one month and Jacob had come home to a still-boxed pregnancy test on the kitchen table, that she'd discovered how strongly he felt about not having kids.

What the hell is that? Clara? Tell me this is a joke...

The horror on his face, the panic in his eyes... She could still see it when she closed her eyes. The way he'd suddenly decided that her oral contraceptive wasn't reliable enough and had started investigating other options. The tension in the house, so taut she'd thought she might snap, and then the pure relief, three days later, when her period finally arrived. The way he'd held her, as if they'd avoided the Apocalypse.

And the growing emptiness she'd felt inside her as it had first dawned on her that she *wanted* to be a mother.

So she'd known, staring at a positive pregnancy test alone in a hotel bathroom six months later, that it was the end for them, even if he didn't realise it. She could never go back.

He wouldn't want her if she did and she wanted the baby growing inside her more than anything. She hadn't changed her mind about that in the years since. Had he changed his?

'There's got to be a way,' Merry said thoughtfully. 'A way we can take the job, still give Ivy a wonderful Christmas—*and* pull off the New Year's gala.'

Clara sat on the other end of the phone and waited. She knew that tone. It meant Merry was on the verge of something brilliant. Something that would solve all of Clara's problems.

She'd sounded exactly like that the night they'd dreamt up Perfect London. Clara had been clutching a wine glass, staring helplessly at the baby monitor, wondering what on earth she would do next—and Merry had found the perfect solution.

Clara reached for another chocolate while she waited,

and had just shoved it into her mouth whole when Merry cried out, 'I've got it!'

Chewing and swallowing quickly, Clara said, 'Tell me.'

'We do Christmas together in Scotland too!'

For a second Clara imagined her, Ivy and Merry all joining the Fosters in their Highland castle and worried that she might be on the verge of a heart attack. That, whatever Merry might think, was possibly the worst idea that anyone had ever had. In the history of the world.

'Not with them, of course,' Merry clarified, and Clara let herself breathe again. 'We find a really luscious hotel, somewhere nearby, and book in for the duration, right? You'll be on hand to manage Project Perfect Christmas, I'll be there if you need me and to watch Ivy, and then, once things are set up at the castle, we can have our own Christmas, just the three of us.'

Clara had to admit, that did sound pretty good. It would give her the chance to get to know this new Jacob—and see if he was ready to be Ivy's father. Then, in January, once the crazily busy season was over, she could find the best moment to tell him.

It gave her palpitations just thinking about it, but in lots of ways it was the perfect plan.

'Do you think Ivy will mind having Christmas at a hotel instead of at home?'

'I don't see why,' Merry said. 'I mean, we'll have roaring log fires, mince pies by the dozen and probably even snow, that far up in the country. What more could a little girl want?'

'She has been asking about building snowmen,' Clara admitted. *And about having a father.* Maybe this could just work after all. 'But what about you? Are you sure you don't mind spending Christmas with us?'

'Are you kidding? My parents are heading down to Devon to stay with my sister and her four kids for the holidays. I was looking at either a four-hour trek followed by three days minding the brats or a microwave turkey dinner for one.'

'Why didn't you say?' Clara asked. 'We could have done something here. You know you're always welcome.'

'Ah, that was my secret plan,' Merry admitted. 'I was going to let on at the last minute and gatecrash your day. Ivy's much better company than any of my nephews and nieces anyway.'

'So Scotland could work, then.' Just saying it aloud felt weird. 'I mean, I'll need to talk to Ivy about it…' She might only be four, but Ivy had very definite 'opinions' on things like Christmas.

'But if Ivy says yes, I'm in.' Merry sounded positively cheerful at the idea. In fact, the whole plan was starting to appeal to Clara too.

As long as she could keep Jacob away from Ivy until she was ready. If he didn't want anything to do with his daughter then it was better if Ivy never knew he existed. She wouldn't let Jacob Foster abandon them.

Clara reached for one last chocolate. 'Then all I need to do is call Jacob and tell him yes.' It was funny how that was the most terrifying part of all.

Jacob awoke the next morning to his desk phone ringing right next to his head. Rubbing his itching eyes, he sat up in his chair, cursed himself for falling asleep at work *again* and answered the phone.

'Mr Foster, there's a woman here to see you.' The receptionist paused, sounding uncertain. 'She says she's your wife.'

Ah. That would explain the uncertainty. But not why Clara was visiting his offices at—he checked his watch—eight-thirty in the morning.

'Send her up,' he said. The time it would take her to

reach his office on the top floor, via two elevators and a long corridor, should give him time to make himself presentable.

'Um…she's already on her way?' Jacob wondered why she phrased it as a question as Clara barrelled through his door with a perfunctory knock.

He put down the phone and made a mental note to send all the company's receptionists for refresher training on *how to do their job*.

'Clara. This is a surprise.' He made an effort to sound professional, and not as if he'd just woken up two minutes earlier.

Except Clara knew exactly what he looked like when he'd just woken up. 'Your hair's sticking up at the back,' she said helpfully.

Smoothing it down, Jacob took in the sight of his ex-wife. Clara stood just inside the doorway, a dark red coat wrapped around her, her gloved hands tucked under her arms for added warmth. She had a grey felt hat perched on top of her glossy brown hair and her make-up was immaculate.

He knew that look. She was wearing her 'impressing people' make-up—lots of dark lipstick and she'd managed some trick or another that made her eyes look even larger than normal. He blamed the receptionist a little less for letting her through. This new confident Clara, combined with her old charm, was hard to say no to.

'You've come to a decision?' he asked, motioning her towards the comfortable sitting area at the side of the office. It was too early for guessing games. And visitors, come to that.

'Yes.' She took her hat from her head and placed it on the table by the sofas, then removed her coat to reveal another flattering form-fitting wrap dress, this one in a dark forest green. Settling onto the chocolate-brown leather sofa, she looked utterly at home. As if she belonged not just in his office but in the corporate world. He supposed she did, now.

Jacob turned away, moving towards the high-end coffee machine behind the sitting area. This conversation definitely needed coffee.

'I've spoken with my partner,' Clara said. 'We think we've found a way to work around our other commitments so we can take on your project.' She didn't sound entirely happy about the conclusion, but that wasn't his problem. Neither was this partner, whoever the unlucky man was. Jacob felt something loosen inside him, something he hadn't even realised was wound up too tight.

She was going to help him. That was all that mattered.

'That's good news,' he said, trying not to let his relief show too much. Instead, he busied himself making them both a cup of strong black coffee. 'I assume you have a standard contract with payment schedules and so on?'

'Of course,' Clara replied. 'Although, given the timescales, I rather think we're going to require full payment up front, don't you?'

'Understandable.' Paying wasn't a problem. And once she had his money, she'd have to follow through. It was far harder to pay back money than walk out on the potential of it. And heaven knew Jacob would do everything in his power to stop Clara walking out on him again.

He placed the coffee on the table in front of her, and her nose wrinkled up. 'Actually, I don't drink coffee any more.'

'Really?' She used to drink it by the bucketload, he remembered. Her favourite wedding present, in amongst far more expensive and luxury items, had been a simple filter coffee maker from Heather. 'I can offer you tea. Probably.' He frowned at the machine. Did it even make tea? 'Or ask someone else to bring some up.' Maybe he'd ask the receptionist—a small, perhaps petty act of revenge.

Especially if he insisted that she bring it via the stairs instead of the lift…

'It's fine. I don't need anything.' Jacob bit back a sharp smile at her words. Clara had made that clear five years ago when she'd refused any support after she'd left.

'So, just business then.' Jacob lifted his own coffee cup to his lips and breathed in the dark scent of it. *This* was what he needed. Not his ex-wife in his office at eight-thirty in the morning.

'Yes. Except…the usual contracts don't cover the more… personal side of this arrangement,' Clara went on delicately.

Jacob would have laughed if it weren't so miserable a topic. 'You mean the divorce.' The idea that she wanted one still rankled. What was it about him that made him want to just keep flogging this dead horse? Why couldn't he just cut her loose and get on with his life? Even his lawyer had started rolling his eyes whenever the subject came up. Jacob knew it was time to move on—past time, really. But, until the paperwork was signed, he hadn't failed at marriage. Not completely.

He rather imagined that Clara would say differently, though.

'Yes,' she said. 'The divorce. I think…I'd like to get that sorted in the New Year, if we could. I think it would be good for us both. We could move on properly.'

'Are you planning to get married again?' He regretted asking the moment the words were out of his mouth, but it was too late.

'No! I mean maybe, one day, I suppose. But not right now. Why do you ask?'

Yes, Jacob, why did you ask that? He didn't care what she did now. So why let her think he did?

He shrugged, trying to play nonchalant. 'You mentioned a partner.'

'Business partner. Merry. You met her yesterday, actually.'

The redhead at the office. Well, in that case, unless Clara had changed far more than he'd realised, there wasn't a marriage in the making. 'You're not seeing anyone then?' He wished it didn't sound as if he cared, but he couldn't not ask. He needed all the facts. He always had done.

'No. Not right now. It's hard when…' She cut herself off. 'Well, you know.'

'When your husband won't give you a divorce,' he guessed. Although why that should make a difference he wasn't sure. They'd been apart five years as it was; if she'd really wanted to move on with another guy, he couldn't imagine a lousy piece of paper would stop her. Her wedding vows hadn't kept her married to him, after all.

If she'd really, truly wanted the divorce, he doubted he could have stopped her. His lawyers were good, but some things were inevitable. He'd known all along he was only stalling, and somewhere on the way he'd even forgotten why. But Clara hadn't wanted to take anything from him, hadn't wanted to make anything difficult. Really, it should have been straightforward.

But she'd never pushed, never insisted, never kicked up a real fuss. Surely, if she'd really wanted this divorce she'd have done all that and more.

Unless she *didn't* really want it. Unless she'd been waiting for him to come after her.

Which he was doing, right now, in a way.

It didn't feel like Clara, that kind of complicated long game. And to drag it out over five years seemed a little excessive. But still, logic dictated that *something* had to be stopping her from forcing through the divorce. And he couldn't for the life of him think of anything else it might be.

But working with her on his Perfect Christmas project would give him the ideal opportunity to find out.

CHAPTER FOUR

CLARA TRIED TO BREATHE through her mouth to avoid taking in the smell of the coffee. It was ridiculous, really. She'd *loved* coffee, almost as much as she'd loved Jacob. But then she'd fallen pregnant and suddenly she couldn't stand the smell of it, let alone the taste. She'd always assumed that once the baby was born she'd get her love of coffee back again, but no. Even now, four years later, the very smell made her want to gag.

So unfair.

As if this morning wasn't bad enough already, the universe had to throw in coffee.

Ivy had woken up bright and early at six and Clara hadn't seen much point in dragging things out so, over their traditional weekday morning breakfast of toast and cereal, she'd broached the subject of Christmas.

'How would you like the idea of going somewhere snowy for Christmas? With Merry?' Merry was a definite favourite with Ivy, so that was bound to be more of a draw than most other things, Clara had decided.

'Where?' Ivy had asked in between mouthfuls.

'Scotland.' Clara had held her breath, waiting for an answer.

'What about Norman?'

'Norman?' Clara had been briefly concerned that her daughter had suddenly gained a seventy-year-old imaginary friend until Ivy clarified.

'Our Christmas tree,' she'd said. 'You said he was called Norman.'

Clara had blinked, ran back through a mental movie of

the day they'd bought the tree and finally figured it out.
'Nordmann. He's a Nordmann Fir.'

Ivy had nodded. 'Norman the Nordmann. What will
happen to him while we're away?'

'We'll ask Mr Jenkins next door to come and water him,
shall we? Then Norman will still be here when we get back.'
Good grief, she had a Christmas tree with a name. How had
this happened? 'Is that all you're worried about? Do you
think Scotland might be okay for Christmas?'

Ivy's little face had scrunched up as she considered.
'Will they have pancakes there for Christmas morning?'
she'd asked.

Clara had added pancakes to their list of hotel requirements, dropped Ivy at the childminder's house and headed
off to talk to Jacob. There was no point putting it off, especially since she knew exactly where to find him—Foster
Medical head office. He might more usually work from one
of the American offices these days, but if he was in London, Clara knew he'd be at work.

But his work was going to have to wait. They only had
a week and a half to put together a perfect Christmas. Two
Christmases, if you counted Ivy's, and Clara did. So she'd
rushed across London to the imposing skyscraper of an
office, only pausing long enough to explain to the receptionist exactly who she was, and then bustled along to Jacob's office.

But now, with the scent of coffee making her queasy, and
Jacob's sleep-ruffled hair looking all too familiar, Clara really wished she'd waited. Or even called instead.

'Anyway. If that's all settled…' She picked up her hat
from the table.

'I wouldn't call it settled,' Jacob said and she lowered the
hat again. No, of course not. That would be too easy. 'We
still need to discuss the particulars.' Putting his coffee cup
down, Jacob came around from the counter to sit beside her.

The leather sofa was vast—ridiculously so, for an office—and there was a more than reasonable gap between them. But, suddenly, it wasn't coffee she could smell any more. It was *him*. That familiar combination of aftershave, soap and *Jacob* that tugged at her memory and made her want to relive every moment. To imagine that this was that other life she could have been living, where they were together in London, still married, still happy.

'Particulars?' she asked, shaking her head a little to try and stop herself being so distracted by his nearness.

'Like where we want it to take place, how many people, what the menu should be, timings… Little things like that.' He was laughing at her, but Clara couldn't find it amusing. It just reminded her how much there was to do.

'I'm assuming the timings are fairly self-explanatory,' she said drily. 'Christmas Eve to Boxing Day would be my best guess—I can't imagine you wanting to take any more time off work than that, regardless of the circumstances.' Even that was two days more than he'd managed for their last Christmas together. Two and a half if she counted him sloping off to the study for an hour or two after Christmas lunch. 'Guests. I'm assuming just your parents and Heather, unless she has a partner she'd like to bring? Or you do,' she added, belatedly realising that just because her love life was a desert didn't mean his was.

'No, you're right, just the four of us.' He still looked amused, but there was less mockery in his expression. 'Go on.'

'Location. you said the Highlands, and I happen to know of a very festive, exclusive castle that would be brilliant for your celebrations.' And particularly helpful to her, since the client she'd originally booked it for had pulled out and she'd promised the owner she'd do her best to find some-one else to take over the booking. If she didn't find someone, thanks to a contract mishap Perfect London would be losing the rather hefty deposit.

'Sounds ideal.'

'As for the menu—traditional Christmas turkey dinner plus appetizers, puddings, wine and liquors, cold cuts and chutneys in the fridge, then smoked salmon and scrambled eggs with croissant for breakfast. Sound about right?'

'Yes.' He blinked, looking slightly bemused. 'How did you know all that?'

'It's my job, Jacob,' Clara said, irritation rising. He might not have appreciated everything she'd done to keep his nice little business gatherings and parties ticking over, but even he had to respect that she'd built up a successful business with her skills. 'And it's not like you're asking for anything out of the ordinary.' If she was lucky and used every contact she had, she could pull this off for Jacob and manage her own wonderful Christmas with Ivy too.

'No, I suppose not. Of course, snow is obviously essential,' Jacob added.

Clara stared at him. Was the man insane? 'Snow. You want me to arrange snow?'

Jacob lifted one shoulder. Was he teasing? She never *could* tell when he was teasing her. 'Well, it is Christmas, after all. I think we can all agree that the perfect Christmas would have to be a white one.'

Clara's mouth tightened. 'I'll check the weather forecast then.' Jacob looked as if he might be trying to dream up some more outlandish requests, just to throw her off her game, so Clara hurried on.

'Which just leaves us with the presents.' This, she knew, was the real test. If Jacob truly had changed—if this perfect Christmas idea was a sign that he was ready to embrace a family and, just possibly, the daughter he didn't know he had—the presents would be the giveaway.

'Presents?' Jacob frowned, and Clara's heart fell. 'Aren't

you going to buy those? I'd have thought it would be part of the contract.'

'Usually, Perfect London would be delighted to source the perfect gift for every member of your family,' she said sweetly. 'But, under the circumstances—with less than a fortnight to go, not to mention this being your father's last Christmas—I am sure that you will want to select them yourself.' She stared at him until he seemed to get the idea that this was not a suggestion.

'But what would I buy them?' He looked so adorably flustered at the very idea that for a moment Clara forgot that she was testing him.

Then she realised this could be an even better opportunity.

'I'll tell you what,' she said, making it clear that this was a favour, just for him. 'Why don't we go shopping together and choose them?'

'That would be great.' The relief was evident in his voice.

'Right now,' Clara finished, and his eyebrows shot up.

'Now? But I'm working.'

'So am I,' she pointed out. 'By taking a client shopping.'

'Yes, but I can't just leave! There are meetings. Emails. Important decisions to be made.'

'Like whether your sister would prefer a handbag or a scarf.'

'Like the future of the company!'

Now it was Clara's turn to raise her eyebrows. 'Do you really expect that to come up in the three hours you'll be gone?'

'Three hours!' Clara waited and finally he sighed. 'No, I suppose not.'

'Then I think that your father's last Christmas might matter rather more than emails and meetings. Don't you?'

He looked torn and Clara held her breath until, finally, he said, 'Yes. It does.'

She grinned. The old Jacob would never have left work at 9:00 a.m. on a weekday to go Christmas shopping. *Ha!* He'd never left work *or* done Christmas shopping.

Maybe he really had changed after all. She could hope so. After all, Christmas *was* the season of hope and goodwill. Even towards ex-husbands.

'What about this?' Clara held up a gossamer-thin scarf in various shades of purple that Jacob suspected cost more than his entire suit. Everything else Clara had suggested had and, since his suit had been handmade especially for him, that was quite an achievement.

'For Mum?' he asked with a frown.

'No. For Heather.' Clara sighed. Jacob had a feeling she was starting to regret her insistence on taking him shopping.

'She's a student,' he pointed out. 'She wouldn't wear something like that.'

'She graduating this summer, right? So she'll have interviews, internships, all sorts of professional opportunities coming her way. A statement accessory like this can make any outfit look polished.' As always, Clara had a point. He'd almost forgotten how irritating that was.

'Maybe,' he allowed. But Clara was already walking on, probably in search of an even more expensive gift for his sister. He didn't begrudge spending the money but he was beginning to think this was some sort of game for Clara. She'd certainly never encouraged him to buy such luxurious gifts for her.

The high-end shopping district Clara had directed the taxi to was filled with tiny boutiques, all stocking a minimum of products at maximum cost. Even the Christmas decorations strung between the shops on either side of the street, high above the heads of the passing shoppers, were discreet, refined and—Jacob was willing to bet—costly.

'Is this where you usually shop for your clients?' he asked, lengthening his stride to catch up with her as she swung into another shop.

Clara shrugged. 'Sometimes. It depends on the client.'

Which told him nothing. Jacob wasn't entirely sure why he was so interested in the day-to-day details of her job, but he suspected it had something to do with never realising she wanted one. He'd thought he'd known Clara better than anyone in the world, and that she'd known him just as well. It had been a jolt to discover there were some parts of her he'd never known at all. What if this entrepreneurial side of her was just the start?

Of course, for all that he'd shared with Clara, there were some things *he'd* kept back too. He couldn't entirely blame her for that.

'This would be just right for your father.' Jacob turned to find her holding up a beautifully wrought dark leather briefcase, with silver detailing and exquisite stitching. She was right; his father would love it. Except...

'He won't be coming in to the office much longer.' It still caught him by surprise, almost daily. In some ways, he suspected he was in denial as much as Heather; he wanted to believe that if he could just make Christmas perfect then the rest would fall into place.

But he couldn't save his father's life. Even if a part of him felt he should be able to, if he just worked long enough, tried hard enough. If he was good enough.

Jacob knew he'd never been good enough, had known it long before his father fell sick.

Clara dropped the briefcase back onto the shelf. 'You're right. Come on.'

Even Jacob had to agree the next shop was spot on.

'You want something your dad can enjoy.' Clara opened her arms and gestured to the bottles of vintage wine lining the shelves. 'From what I remember, this should suit him.'

Jacob smiled, turning slowly to take in the selection. 'Yes, I think this will do nicely.'

One in-depth conversation with the proprietor later, and Jacob felt sure that he had the perfect gift for at least one member of his family, ready to be delivered directly to Clara's offices in time to be shipped up to Scotland.

'How are they all?' Clara asked as she led him into a tiny arcade off the main street. The shops inside looked even more sparse and expensive. 'Your family, I mean. The news about your dad… It must have been terrible for you all. I can't imagine.'

'It was,' Jacob said simply. 'It still is. Mum… She takes everything in her stride—you know her. But Heather's still hoping for a miracle, I think.'

Clara looked sideways at him. 'And you're not?'

'Perhaps,' he admitted. 'It's just too hard to imagine a world without him.'

Watching as she paused by a display of necklaces, Jacob remembered the first time he'd brought Clara home to meet his family—just days after their elopement. He remembered his mother's shock and forced cheer as she realised she'd been done out of the big wedding she'd always imagined for him.

But, more than anything, he remembered his father's reaction. How he'd taken him into his study and poured him a brandy in one of the last two crystal glasses handed down from James's own great-grandfather. A sign of trust that had shocked Jacob's hands into trembling, even as he'd reminded himself that he was grown up now. A married man.

'You've taken on a big responsibility, son,' James had said. 'A wife is more than a lover, more than a friend. More even than family. She is your whole world—and you are responsible for making that world perfect.'

He'd known instantly what his father was really saying. *Don't screw it up this time. Remember what happened last time we gave you any responsibility. You can't take that kind of chance again.*

And he hadn't. He'd thought that Clara—easy-going, eager to please Clara—would be safe. She was an adult, her own person, after all. Far less responsibility than a child, far harder to hurt. He'd tried to make things just right for her—with the right house, the right people, the right levels of success. But, in the end, he'd done just as his father had so obviously expected him to, that day in the study drinking brandy.

Why else would she have left?

'They must all be looking forward to this Christmas together, though?' Clara had moved on from the necklaces, Jacob realised belatedly, and he hurried to join her on the other side of the shop.

'I haven't told them yet,' he admitted, admiring the silver-and-gold charm bracelet draped across her fingers.

Clara paused, her eyebrows raised ever so slightly, in that way she always had when she was giving him a chance to realise he was making a mistake. Except he was giving his family a dream Christmas. What was the mistake in that? How had he screwed up this time?

'Don't you think you'd better check with them before we go too much further?' Clara went on, her eyebrows just a little higher.

'I want it to be a surprise,' Jacob said mulishly.

'Right. Well, if that's how you want to play it.'

'It is.'

'Fine.' Somehow, just that one word made him utterly sure that she thought he was making a mistake. Now she had him second-guessing himself. How did she do that?

She was almost as good at it as his father was.

'So, beyond the wine we've already ordered, what would James's perfect Christmas look like?' Clara asked, and suddenly Jacob felt on surer ground again.

'That's easy,' he said with a shrug. 'He always says the best Christmas we ever had was the one we spent in Scotland, just the family, spending time together.'

'How old were you?' Clara asked.

'Fifteen, I think.'

'Okay, so what did you do that Christmas?'

'Do?' Jacob frowned, trying to remember. 'I mean, there were presents and turkey and so on.'

'Yes, but beyond that,' Clara said with exaggerated patience. 'Did you play games? Charades or Monopoly or something? Did you sing carols around a piano? Did you open presents on Christmas Eve or Christmas morning? Were there cracker hats? Did you go to church? Were there stockings? Did you stay up until midnight on Christmas Eve or get an early night? Think, Jacob.'

'Cluedo,' Jacob said finally. 'That Christmas was the year we taught Heather to play Cluedo. Sort of.'

Suddenly, the memory was unbearably clear. Sitting around the wooden cottage kitchen table, Heather watching from her dad's lap, him explaining the rules as they went along. Jacob wanted to take that brief, shining moment in time and hold it close. That was what he wanted his father's last Christmas to be—a return to the way things used to be. Before the accident. Before everything had changed for ever.

Clara beamed at him. 'Wonderful! There's a shop down here somewhere that sells high-end board games—you know, gemstone chess sets and Monopoly with gold playing pieces. I think they had a Cluedo set last time I was in... Come with me!'

Jacob followed, wondering if the board would be made of solid gold, and whether his perfect Christmas might actually exhaust even his bank accounts.

Maybe then it would be good enough for his father.

CHAPTER FIVE

'I KNEW THIS WAS a bad idea,' Clara grumbled, tagging yet another email from Jacob with a 'deal with this urgently' flag. If five hours of Christmas shopping hadn't convinced her that his demands were going to require going far above and beyond the usual levels of customer service, his half hourly emails since certainly had. 'Why on earth was he sending me emails at four a.m.?'

'Because he couldn't sleep, thinking about you?' Merry suggested.

Clara pulled a face. Merry's new enthusiasm for her ex-husband wasn't encouraging either. Just because he'd sent flowers and chocolates the day after they had signed the contract. Her friend was cheaply bought, it seemed.

'More likely he was still at the office and counts email-ing me about Christmas as taking a break.' She was al-most certain he'd slept at his desk the night before she'd taken him shopping. It had happened often enough towards the end of their marriage that she'd begun to suspect an affair—until she'd realised he wouldn't have time in be-tween meetings. 'Trust me, he's only thinking about what we—as a company—can do for him.' All business; that was Jacob. It always had been.

'Then why send the flowers?' Merry asked, rummag-ing through what was left of the box of chocolates for one she liked. 'I mean, flowers are personal.'

'Not when he had his assistant send them.' Clara dived into the chocolates too. There was no point in letting Merry have all the soft centres just because she was still mad with the man who'd sent them.

'How do you know that?' Merry asked around a mouthful of caramel.

Clara shrugged and picked out a strawberry and champagne truffle. *Divine.* 'That's just what he does,' she explained. 'Our last Christmas together, he gave me this really over-the-top diamond bracelet.'

'Damn him,' Merry said, straight-faced. 'What kind of guy gives a girl diamonds for Christmas?'

Clara glared at her. Merry knew better than most that she wasn't a diamonds sort of girl. She liked her jewellery small, discreet and preferably featuring her birthstone. And, since Merry had given her a pair of tiny garnet earrings for her birthday last year, she clearly understood that better than Jacob ever had.

'The diamonds weren't the worst part.' She could remember it so clearly, even so many years later. The weight of the heavy gold clasp and setting on her wrist, the sparkle of the stones, the awkward smile she'd tried to give. And then the moment when she'd looked back into the jewellery box it had come in. 'I found a note, sitting next to the bracelet. It was from his assistant, saying she hoped this would do for his wife's Christmas gift.'

'He had his assistant choose your Christmas present?' Merry asked, incredulous.

'Why not?' Clara asked. 'That's how he does things, after all. He's a businessman. It's all about delegating the unimportant tasks so he can get on with the ones that matter.' That bracelet had been her number one reason for forcing him to go Christmas shopping with her. His father deserved that much.

'So diamonds, in this instance, were a sign that you didn't matter.'

'I clearly didn't even matter all that much to his assistant,' Clara replied. 'If her note was anything to go by.'

Merry pushed the box of chocolates towards her and

Clara dug out another strawberry truffle. It was strange, but the image that next came to mind wasn't of that Christmas, no matter how dreadful she'd felt in that moment. It was of another Christmas, a few years after her mother's remarriage, after the twins were born. Her half-siblings would have been maybe eighteen months old to Clara's thirteen. As she'd unwrapped the one present under the tree with her name on it to find a pair of pyjamas—pink, with roses on, and two sizes too small—she'd watched as the toddlers dived into a mountain of wrapping paper, brightly coloured plastic and all-singing, all-dancing toys and tried not to feel jealous.

Of course, even that year had been better than the following one—when her father had called to say she couldn't come and stay for Christmas after all because his new girlfriend wanted it to be just the two of them. And both of those memories were trumped by the first Christmas after she'd left for university, when her mum and stepdad had taken the twins to Lapland for the festivities, leaving Clara behind.

'You're eighteen now! You don't want to come on holiday with us. You should be with your boyfriend, or your friends!'

Never mind that she hadn't had either.

Christmas, Clara mused, had always been a complete let-down—until the year she'd met Jacob on Christmas Eve, when she was twenty-one. They'd been married by Valentine's Day.

She'd thought she'd never feel unwanted again. How wrong she'd been.

Merry's voice broke through her thoughts and she realised she'd just eaten four chocolates in quick succession. 'What did he say when you asked him about the bracelet?'

'I didn't,' Clara admitted. 'I know, I know, I should have confronted him. But it was Christmas Day, his family were all there…and besides, by the time I could have got him alone to ask, he'd already gone back to work.'

'Suddenly I have a better understanding of why you left this man.' Not just once, but many times—although Clara didn't really want to go into that sort of detail with Merry. Besides, every other time she'd left, she'd gone back, so they didn't really count.

'I left the bracelet too.' Clara could still see it sitting there on the dressing table, a symbol of everything she didn't want from her marriage. 'I walked out the next day.' And almost had a breakdown when she discovered she was pregnant two weeks later.

'Is that why you left?' Merry asked. 'I mean, you've never really spoken about it. All you said was that you couldn't be married to him any more.'

'It was part of it, I suppose,' Clara said. It was hard to put into words the loneliness, the isolation and the feeling of insignificance she'd felt pressing down on her. Jacob had so many things in his life; she was just one more. But she only had him, and the big, empty white houses he owned across the world. And when she'd thought of having more… he'd shut her down completely.

It had reached the point where she couldn't even bring herself to *ask* for what she wanted because she didn't want to risk driving him further away. But that didn't stop her wanting. She remembered watching mothers with their babies in prams during the long seven days that summer when she'd thought she might be pregnant. She remembered the glow that had started to fill her, slowly lighting her up from the inside with the knowledge of what her future should be.

Until Jacob had snuffed out that light with the revulsion on his face as she'd told him she might be expecting his child. Then the realisation had come that she wasn't— and that if Jacob had his way she never would be. *'I have no space in my life for children, Clara. And no desire for them either.'*

And no space for her either, she'd realised as the months had trickled on. Desire... They'd still had that, right to the end. Even if it turned out that was *all* that they'd had.

She hadn't set out to become pregnant. She'd never trick someone into parenthood and wouldn't wish being unwanted on any child. Her own experience—a mother who'd fallen pregnant at sixteen, been forced to marry the father, then had resented both her child and her husband ever since—had ensured that she understood those consequences better than most. But when she'd realised that she *was*... That glow had returned, brighter than ever before. And she'd known that this was her chance—maybe her only chance—to have a family of her own. One where she mattered, where she belonged—and where her child could have all the love and attention that she'd missed out on.

Would Merry understand any of that? She'd try to, Clara knew. She was her best friend, after all. But if you hadn't lived it, the pain and weight that grew every day from simply not mattering... It was hard to imagine.

'Mostly, we wanted different things,' she said, gathering up her paperwork. Time to move on. 'I wanted a family—he didn't.' *Didn't* was a bit of an understatement. *Vehemently refused to even consider the idea* was closer to the truth.

'And now you have Ivy,' Merry said. 'So everything worked out in the end.'

'Yes, it did.' She wouldn't give Ivy up for all the diamond bracelets in the world. She'd hate for Ivy to suffer the sort of rejection she had suffered—the feeling of knowing you were unwanted by your own family, the very people who were supposed to love you more than anyone in the world. She knew how that burned. She never wanted Ivy to experience that.

But now she had to make a choice. Let Jacob into his

daughter's life—or cut him out forever. And the worst part was, it wasn't entirely her choice to make.

Clara sighed and picked up a stack of email printouts. It was far easier to focus on organising the perfect Christmas than to figure out how to tell her ex-husband he was a father.

'Right. These are all the latest things Jacob has requested for his Christmas retreat. Think you can start working your way through them?'

Merry looked resigned as she took the pile of paper from Clara. 'Any chance you think he might give you another diamond bracelet this year?'

Clara laughed in spite of herself. 'I doubt it. Why?'

'If he does, don't leave it this time, yeah? Some of us like a bit of sparkle in our lives.'

Jacob pressed the code into the number pad and waited for the gate to swing open before driving through and parking behind his father's big black car on the gravel driveway. Heather's pink Mini was missing but his mum's little red convertible was still there. That was okay. Heather already knew what he was planning and it was probably best to tell his parents together anyway.

It hadn't occurred to him until Clara asked what his parents thought about their Scottish Christmas that they might be anything other than thrilled. He was giving them the perfect retreat—what more could they want? But the look in Clara's eye on their shopping trip had told him he was missing something. Hence the drive to Surrey to fill them in on the plan.

He let himself in the front door without knocking, and the scent of evergreen pine and cinnamon hit him instantly. The hallway as a whole was dominated by an oversized Christmas tree, tastefully decorated in gold and red, with touches of tartan. The wide, curving staircase had garlands of greenery and red berries twirling around the banister all the way to the first floor, and bowls of dried fruits and spices sat on the console table next to the front door.

Christmas, as he remembered it at home, had always been a very traditional affair. Apart from that year when everyone had come out to California to his beach house, to celebrate with him and Clara. Clara had cooked a full English roast and they'd eaten it in the sunshine. The stockings had hung by the artisan steel-and-glass fire display, looking out of place in their red velvet glory.

It hadn't been traditional, maybe, but he'd been happy. Happy—and terrified, he realised now. Scared that it could all go wrong. That he'd screw it up.

They'd gone from meeting to marriage so fast, and never even thought to talk about what their lives together would look like. And it had never felt real, somehow. As if, from the moment he'd said 'I do' in that clichéd Vegas chapel, he'd been waiting for it to end. For Clara to realise that he wasn't enough, that she couldn't rely on him. That he was bound to hurt her, eventually.

Even his family knew better than to trust him with anything more than business. Work was easy. People were breakable.

He'd woken up the next morning to find Clara gone, a note propped up against the bracelet he'd given her the day before.

Jacob shook away the memories and called out. 'Any chance of a mince pie?'

His mum appeared from the kitchen instantly, a tartan apron wrapped over her skirt and blouse. 'Jacob! What a surprise. Why didn't you call and let us know you were coming?'

'Spur-of-the-moment decision.' He pressed a kiss to her cheek. 'Is Dad here?'

'Upstairs. Working, of course.' She rolled her eyes. 'I

thought he might slow down a bit once…well, never mind. He seems happy enough.'

'Think we can risk interrupting him? I've got something to talk to you both about.' He knew as soon as he said it that it was a mistake, but it was too late. His mother's eyes took on the sort of gleam that meant she was picturing grandchildren, and the smile she gave him made him fear for his life once he'd explained what was actually happening.

'By all means,' she said, grabbing his arm and leading him towards the stairs. 'It'll do him good to take a break, anyway. Now, let me see if I can guess…'

'It's nothing to do with a woman,' Jacob said quickly, then realised that wasn't strictly true. 'Well, not in the way you're thinking, anyway.'

'So you're saying I shouldn't buy a hat but I might want to start thinking about nursery curtains?'

'No! Definitely not that.' The very thought of it made him shudder. If people were breakable, children were a million times more so. He'd learnt that early enough. Fatherhood was one responsibility he'd proved himself incapable of, and sworn never to have. And, given how badly he'd screwed up his marriage, it just proved that was the right decision.

His mother might be disappointed now, but even she had to accept that. There was, after all, a reason why she'd never asked him to babysit Heather again. Not after the accident.

Jacob sighed as they reached the top of the stairs. There was no way out of this that wasn't going to make things worse. 'Just…wait. Let's go and find Dad. Then you'll both know soon enough.'

James Foster's office was at the far end of the hallway, its window looking out over the apple orchard behind the house. Jacob knocked on the door and waited, feeling like a sixteen-year-old boy again, in trouble because his science marks weren't quite as high as they needed to be.

In the end, of course, it had been his flair for business that had taken the family company to new heights, not his scientific talents. For him, science had become something to work around rather than to experiment in. It was safer that way.

'Come in.'

Even his dad's voice sounded tired, Jacob realised. Whatever Heather wanted to believe, there was no denying that he wasn't as healthy as he'd been even one month ago. But maybe his Christmas surprise would help. Remind his father of everything he had to live for.

Jacob pushed open the door and stepped into the study, his mother close behind him.

'Jacob!' James said, struggling to his feet. His arms felt brittle around him, Jacob thought. 'To what do we owe the pleasure?'

'Jacob has something to tell us.' His mum had already settled herself into the armchair by the window, ready to listen. 'And it has absolutely nothing to do with a woman, except that it might.'

'Sounds interesting,' his father said, sitting back down in his desk chair. 'So, do tell.'

Jacob perched on the edge of a table, pushed up against the old fireplace. 'Well, it's about Christmas, actually.'

'You're bringing someone new?' His mother clapped her hands in enthusiasm. 'Except you said not a woman.' Her eyes grew wide. 'Is it a man? Because, darling, really, we just want you to be happy. And you can adopt these days, you know—'

'I'm not bringing anyone,' Jacob said firmly. 'But I am taking you somewhere.'

'Somewhere…not here?' she asked. 'But it's Christmas.'

For a horrible moment it struck Jacob that Clara might actually have read his parents better than he had this time.

'Do you remember that year we spent Christmas in Scotland?' he asked, changing tack.

'In the cottage?' James said. 'Of course. It was possibly the best Christmas we ever had.'

Of course it had been. The last Christmas before the accident. The last time his family had been able to look at Jacob without that shadow in their eyes. The one that told him that they *loved* him, of course—they just couldn't trust him. Couldn't believe in him. Couldn't move past what had happened.

And neither could he.

This Christmas might not fix his mistakes but it was at least one more step in a long line of atonements. Maybe the last one he'd get to make to his father. He had to make it count.

Jacob forced a smile. 'Well, good. Because I wanted to give you another Christmas like that.'

'So you hired the cottage for Christmas?' James frowned. 'I thought that cottage was sold on, a few years later. Do you remember, Sheila? We tried to book again, didn't we? Let me check my files…'

'Not the same cottage.' The last thing he needed was his dad disappearing into his filing cabinet for the afternoon. 'Actually, I've found a castle, up in the Highlands. It has huge old fireplaces, four-poster beds… It'll be perfect.' Or so Clara promised him.

'A castle? Jacob, where on earth do you find a castle for Christmas?' His mother asked, astonished.

'On the Internet, I imagine,' his father said. 'Was it on eBay, Jacob? Because I've heard some stories…'

'I haven't bought the castle,' Jacob explained. 'We're just hiring it. Clara said—'

'Clara?' Mum might be woolly on some things, but she homed right in on the mention of her ex-daughter-in-law. Jacob winced. He'd half hoped to get through this without having to explain the exact logistics. 'What has Clara got to do with this plan? Are you two back together? What happened?'

'No, it's nothing like that.' How to explain? 'She runs a concierge and events company in London now, you see. I've hired her to organise us the perfect Christmas. I figured that since she already knew us...'

'And left you,' his mum pointed out. 'Jacob, really. Are you sure this isn't just an excuse to see her again? We all remember how mad you were over her. And how heartbroken you were when she left. We just don't want to see that happen to you again.'

Jacob had a horrible feeling that they were going to believe this was all a cunning ploy to win his wife back, whatever he said. Unless...unless he told them about the divorce. He took one glance at his father and dismissed the idea. He couldn't bear to lay that last disappointment, that last failure, on the old man.

'I'm sure,' he said instead. 'My heart is fine.'

'Well, I suppose it will be good for you to have some closure at last,' his mum said dubiously. 'But are you sure—'

'Apparently it's done,' his father interrupted. Jacob's mother looked at James in surprise.

'Well, I only meant—'

'And I meant it's decided. We're all having Christmas in Scotland.' Jacob couldn't quite tell if his father was pleased or disappointed by this news until he smiled, a broad grin that spread slowly across his whole face.

The tension in Jacob's shoulders relaxed slightly. This *was* a good idea after all.

'It'll be good to see Clara again too,' James said, casting a meaningful look in Jacob's direction.

Jacob wasn't at all sure that Clara planned to hang around long enough to be seen, but the moment his dad spoke the words he knew he'd try to make it so. His dad had always adored Clara; they'd had a strange connection she'd never quite managed with his mum or sister. Suddenly, Clara was just one more thing Jacob wanted to give his father for his perfect Christmas.

Even if it was only temporary. After all, Clara had never stayed past Boxing Day.

CHAPTER SIX

'HAVE WE GOT the decorations?' Clara asked, checking the list on her clipboard for the fiftieth time. They'd started their final checks at 6:00 a.m., and now it was almost seven. The early start was a pain, but necessary. Nothing could go wrong with this project.

'Ours or theirs?' Merry's head popped out from deep inside a box emblazoned with courier logos. 'I mean we have both, but which list are you ticking off right now?'

'Theirs first.' Organising two perfect Christmases at once had turned out to be rather more work than Clara had anticipated. What with Jacob's ever-increasing wish list and Ivy's last-minute announcement that, actually, she needed to send another letter to Father Christmas because she'd changed her mind about the colour of her bike, the last week had been rather more tense than Clara had hoped for.

Still, it was only two days until Christmas Day and the courier boxes were almost ready to go. Most would be sent to the Highland castle for the Fosters' Christmas, and one or two would go to the hotel down the hill from the castle where Clara, Merry and Ivy would be spending their Christmas.

Ivy was still snoozing at home with her usual childminder, who'd come over super early as a favour. Clara had them all booked on the mid-morning train, first class, and planned to be at the hotel in time for tea.

She had an hour-by-hour plan for the next seventy two hours, much to Merry's amusement. But there was plenty of setting up still to be done, and Clara wasn't taking a single chance with the project. Everything had to be sorted, seamless and—most important—all in place before Jacob and his family arrived on Christmas Eve. That way she could be back at the hotel with Ivy and Merry in time for mince pies and mulled wine by the fire, and she wouldn't have to see her ex-in-laws at all. She couldn't run the risk of any of them meeting Ivy before Clara wanted them to.

It was all going to be perfect, as long as they stuck to the plan.

The plan also had an extra secret page that Merry would never see. A page planning exactly how and where to tell Jacob about Ivy. At the moment, she was opting for January. She'd set up a meeting with him early in the New Year, ostensibly to review the Perfect Christmas Project and discuss terms for the divorce. There was no sense in doing it sooner—she was pretty sure that discovering he was a father would *not* give Jacob his ideal Christmas. And by January surely she'd know for sure how best to do it.

Merry taped closed the box of decorations and added it to the stack waiting for the courier. 'Okay. What's next?'

'Presents.' It might have taken five hours, but Clara was pretty sure they'd found just the right gifts for Jacob's family. Of course, if they had any sense they'd know instantly that Jacob hadn't chosen them by himself. But then, Clara had found in the past with clients that they believed what they wanted to believe. So the chances were that James, Sheila and Heather would all open their gifts on Christmas morning and gush at how wonderful they were to Jacob.

Quite honestly, as long as Clara wasn't there to see it, she didn't care if the whole family spontaneously began believing in Santa again when they opened them.

'Right. I've got all the gifts from Jacob to his family here, wrapped and labelled. I've got the presents that he dropped round from his mum and dad to ship up there too. And I've got Ivy's bike, plus her stocking, and a suspiciously shiny gold parcel with no tag on it…' Merry looked at Clara expectantly, gold parcel in hand. She gave it a little shake and listened carefully.

Clara rolled her eyes. 'Yes, that's yours. And no, you can't open it until Christmas Day.'

'Spoilsport.' Merry pouted.

'What about our suitcases?' Clara asked as Merry put the gold parcel back in the courier box.

'All packed and ready to go too.' Merry gave her a patient smile. 'Honestly, Clara, I know you want everything to be just perfect, but we're on top of it. In fact we've gone one better than Santa already.'

Clara frowned. 'One better than Santa?'

'We've already made our list and checked it at least *three* times! We're ready. It's time to start looking forward to Christmas instead of fretting about it.'

Clara didn't think she was going to be looking forward to anything until at least January the first—especially with the Harrisons' Charity Gala still to pull off when they got back from Scotland. She'd been working double time after Ivy was in bed all week to try and get everything organised, and to make sure she could still take Boxing Day off to spend with her girl.

'I just don't want anything to go wrong. We just need to stick to the plan...'

As she said the words, the door from the street opened and she felt her heart drop. There, standing in the doorway in his coat and bright red wool scarf, was the one person guaranteed to make her life more difficult.

'Jacob,' she said, trying to muster up a smile. It would all be so much easier if the very sight of him didn't send her mind spiralling into thoughts of what might have been, all over again. 'You're up bright and early. What can we do for you? We're pretty much ready to go here, so if you've got anything you need to add to the courier boxes, speak now.'

'No, I think you're right.' He flashed her a smile but his eyes were still serious. 'We're all ready to go.'

'Great!' Merry clapped her hands together. 'In that case, I'll get these picked up and we can go and catch our train!' Clara allowed herself just a smidgen of hope. Maybe her plan could stay intact after all.

'Actually, I came here to suggest some alternative arrangements,' Jacob said.

No. No alternative arrangements. No deviating from the plan.

Clara swallowed, her mouth suddenly dry and uncomfortable. 'Alternative arrangements?'

'Yes. It seems silly for you to go by train when I'm driving up myself. We'd get up there with much more time to spare. Why don't you come with me?'

Clara glanced across at Merry, wondering how exactly to explain without words that driving to Scotland with her ex-husband sounded like the worst idea anyone had ever had in the history of the world. From the wideness of Merry's eyes, she suspected her friend already knew that.

And she didn't even know about Ivy being Jacob's daughter.

Oh, this was just a nightmare.

Jacob watched as Clara and Merry appeared to undertake some sort of lengthy conversation without actually saying anything. He wished he was adept at translating the facial expressions and eye movements they employed but, as it was, he couldn't follow at all.

Still, he could probably guess the gist of it. Clara would be begging her friend to help her get out of driving to Scotland with him, and Merry would be asking how, exactly, she wanted her to do that.

He was still the client, after all. And the client was always satisfied when it came to Perfect London.

The idea of asking Clara to drive up with him hadn't occurred to him until he was halfway home from his parents' house the day before. Once it had, it had all seemed astonishingly simple.

His father wanted Clara there for Christmas. And, if he was honest, so did Jacob. This was a last-chance family Christmas and, whether she liked it or not, Clara was still family. She was still his wife.

But not for much longer. He was ready to let her go. But if keeping her by his side one last time made his dad feel like all was right with the world, then Jacob would make it happen.

He'd spent the last fifteen years trying to win back his father's pride and love through the family business. It was time to try something new—and marrying Clara had been one of the few decisions Jacob had made outside business that his dad had ever approved of.

Besides, Clara *owed* him. She'd walked out, left him alone on the day after Christmas with barely a word of explanation. Well, there'd been a letter, but it hadn't made any sense to him.

All he'd understood was that he'd failed. Failed as a husband, as a partner. Failed at the whole institution of marriage.

And Fosters did not fail. That one universal truth had been drilled into him from birth and even now it rang through his bones, chastising him every time he thought of Clara.

Jacob had failed once in his life—just the once that mattered—before he'd met Clara. And after that he'd vowed that it would never happen again.

This Christmas, fate had given him a chance to keep that vow. To prove to his father that he was still a success.

He just needed to convince Clara to go along with it.

Eight hours trapped in a car with him should do it, he reckoned.

'So?' he asked, breaking up the silent discussion going on before him. 'What do you think? Drive up with me? You can choose the music.' Which, given what he knew of Clara's musical taste, was quite the concession indeed.

'I can't,' she said, sounding apologetic even though he knew she wasn't. 'I've already got a seat booked on the train up with Merry, and we'll have a few last-minute items to bring up with us...'

'I'm sure she can manage that alone, can't you, Merry?' Jacob turned his best smile onto the petite redhead. Merry, flustered, turned to Clara, her hands outspread.

'I don't know,' she said. 'Can I?'

'Well, there's that...um...extra special thing that needs... transporting,' Clara said, the words coming out halting and strange.

Interesting. Given that he was paying for and had ordered everything that needed to go up to Scotland, what exactly was she trying to hide from him?

Merry knew, it seemed, and caught on instantly. 'Exactly. I mean, if you're happy for me to transport...it, then of course I will. I mean, I'm sure we'll... I'll... I'm sure it will be fine,' she finished, obviously unable to say whatever it was she actually wanted to.

Something else for Jacob to uncover during that eight-hour drive.

'Are you sure? I mean it's a big...responsibility,' Clara said, and the concern in her eyes told him that this had nothing to do with his Christmas. Which just made the whole thing even more interesting.

Merry shook her head. 'It'll be fine,' she said, belying the movement. 'Honestly. I'll just meet you up there with...it.'

'Okay. Well.' Clara turned to Jacob. 'I guess, if you insist.'

'I do,' Jacob confirmed. 'You and I have an awful lot to talk about.'

Clara actually winced at that. He almost wasn't sure he blamed her.

He was going to have a lot of fun on this drive.

'Are you ready to go now?' he asked, more to fluster her than anything else.

'Now?' Her eyes grew extra wide and she looked to Merry in panic. 'No! I mean, I have to do a few things first. And pop home. Um, can we leave a little later?'

By which point they wouldn't arrive any earlier than the train. Since his reasoning for insisting she travel with him was sketchy enough to start with, he really didn't want to put the journey off any longer than necessary.

'I'll pick you up at nine,' Jacob said. 'That gives you over an hour and a half to get everything squared away here. I'm sure, for someone with your efficiency and work ethic, that will be plenty of time.'

'I'm sure it will,' Clara said. But he was pretty sure she was talking through gritted teeth.

He'd take it, anyway.

'I'll see you then,' Jacob said, turning and leaving the office.

It was a rush but Clara managed to get home, explain to her daughter and childminder that Ivy was going to have a brilliant train adventure with Merry and meet Mummy in Scotland, apologise to Merry again for putting her in this position, explain all of Ivy's routines and travel quirks, load her friend up with games, colouring books, snacks and other entertainment for the journey, grab her case and get back to Perfect London by nine o'clock.

Which was why she was still reapplying lipstick and trying to do something with her weather-stricken hair when Jacob arrived again, looking every bit as calm and collected as he had been when he'd demanded that she travel with him.

She'd loathed him when he'd insisted. Even though she knew the problem was half hers. If she'd been able to explain about Ivy, he'd have understood and probably relented. But she couldn't—and even Merry was starting to get suspicious.

At first a one-night stand had seemed like the ideal explanation, when she had realised she was pregnant just weeks after walking out on her husband. The dates were close enough to be believable—even likely, given that Ivy had been born a full two weeks late. But still, it was a little too close for Clara's comfort.

She'd been telling the 'ill-advised one-night stand who didn't want to know when she told him she was pregnant' story for so long now, sometimes she almost believed it herself. But then Ivy would do something—look at her a certain way, tilt her head the same way Jacob did, or just open those all too familiar blue eyes wide—and she'd know without a doubt that Ivy was Jacob's daughter.

Of course, barring a miracle, she'd have to be. There hadn't been anyone else for Clara since she'd left. Or before, for that matter.

'Are you ready?' Jacob asked, eyebrows raised.

Clara pushed the lid back onto her lipstick, checked her reflection one last time, then nodded.

'Ready.'

Part of her wasn't even sure why she was bothering with make-up, just to sit in a car with Jacob for hours. But another part knew the truth. This was warpaint, a mask, camouflage. All of the above.

She needed something between her and her ex-husband. Something to stop him seeing through her and discovering the truth she'd been hiding all these years.

Truths, really. But one of those she wouldn't admit even to herself. 'Let's go,' she said, striding past him.

It was just too depressing. Who wanted to admit they were probably still in love with their husband, five years after they'd walked out on him?

CHAPTER SEVEN

OUTSIDE, PARKED ON the street in a miraculously free parking spot, was the car Clara knew instantly had to be Jacob's. Top of the range, brand-new, flashy and silver—and only two seats. 'Why would I need more?' he'd always said when she'd questioned his penchant for two-seater cars. 'There's room for me and you, isn't there?'

Jacob, she knew, would never understand the need for space; a boot to fit the shopping in, or even a pram. The joy of a tiny face beaming at you from the back seat the minute you opened the door. The space for toys and spare clothes, cloths and nappies and board books and, well, life. Everything she'd lived since she left her marriage.

And everything she'd felt was missing while she'd stayed.

Jacob opened the door for her and she slid in, trying to keep her feet together in their tall black boots, even though her skirt came down to touch her knees. It was all about appearances. Decorum and manners could mask even the most unpleasant of situations.

Wasn't that the British way, after all?

Except Jacob had clearly been living in America too long. The moment he shut the door behind him and started the engine, he dived straight into a conversation she'd been hoping to avoid.

'So, what little extra is Merry bringing to Scotland that you don't want me to know about?'

'It's nothing to do with your perfect Christmas,' Clara assured him. 'Nothing for you to worry about at all, actually.'

'And here was me hoping it might be my Christmas

present,' Jacob said lightly, but the very words made Clara go cold.

She could almost imagine it. *Happy Christmas, Jacob! Here's your four-year-old daughter! Just what you never wanted!*

No. Not happening. Not to her Ivy.

'Not a present,' Clara said shortly. 'Just something I need with me this Christmas.'

'Intriguing.'

'It's really not.'

Jacob was silent for long minutes and Clara almost allowed herself to hope that he might let the rest of the journey pass the same way. But then he spoke again.

'Were you planning to see your family this Christmas?' he asked. 'Before I made you change your plans, I mean.'

The question startled her. Her first instinct was to reply that she *was* spending Christmas with her family, except of course Jacob didn't mean Ivy. He meant her mother and stepfather, or father and his girlfriend of the week, and all the little half-siblings that had replaced her on both sides.

'No. Why would I?'

'I know things were difficult between you—' But he didn't really know, she realised belatedly. She might have hinted that they weren't close but she'd never gone into detail. Never explained what her childhood had been like. Why? Had it just never come up? After all, they'd eloped to Vegas a month and a half after meeting, and she'd left him the following Christmas. There had been no wedding invitations, no seating plans. And whenever he'd mentioned meeting her relatives she'd put him off—until he'd stopped suggesting it altogether.

She supposed she hadn't wanted him to know how unlovable her own family had found her. Not when she was still hoping he really did love and want her.

And so he'd been left with the impression that her family

relationships were 'difficult'. Understatement of the year. 'Difficult' implied differences people could move past. Problems that could be solved.

Being unwanted, unnecessary—those problems didn't have easy fixes. Once her mother had remarried and started her new family, after Clara's dad had walked out, there'd been no place in her mother's life for the accidental result of a teenage pregnancy and shotgun marriage. Clara was merely a reminder of her mistakes—to her mother, her stepdad and the whole community.

Far better to let them get on with their lives, while she made her own. The Fosters had been the closest thing Clara had had to a family in years—until Ivy came along. Now she knew exactly what family meant, and Clara wasn't accepting anything less than a perfect family for her or her daughter.

'I just wondered if things had changed. Since you left, I mean,' Jacob went on, apparently unaware of quite how much she *really* didn't want to have this conversation.

'I can't imagine any circumstances under which they would,' Clara said firmly.

'You might be surprised.' Jacob sounded strangely far away, as if speaking about something he was experiencing right then, only elsewhere.

'My family have never once surprised me.' The words came out flat—the depressing truth by which Clara had lived her life since the age of seven. Until the day she'd turned eighteen and Clara had taken matters into her own hands instead. In the eight years between her mother's remarriage and her eighteenth birthday, Clara had learned a most useful truth: never stay where you're not wanted.

'Wait until you get a phone call from them one day that changes your whole life,' Jacob told her. 'Then we'll talk.'

He was thinking of his father, Clara realised, almost too

late. The way *life* changed, never mind relationships, when days became sharply numbered.

That phone call would never come for her—just like she'd never make it. She didn't even have contact numbers for her parents any more. But that was *her* decision—made moments after Ivy was born, and Clara had known deep in her bones that this tiny scrap of a baby was all the family she would ever need. She'd vowed silently, lying in her hospital bed, that Ivy would always be loved, wanted and cared for. She didn't need grandparents who were incapable of doing that.

But that call *had* come for Jacob.

'When did you find out?' she asked. 'About your dad, I mean.'

'Six months ago. I was in New York on business when he called.'

'And you flew home?'

'Immediately.'

She smiled. That was further evidence that Jacob was beginning to realise the importance and the power of his family. The Fosters were the sort of family that stuck together through everything, because they were glued together with the sort of love that ought to come with a birth certificate…but sometimes didn't. She didn't understand how someone who'd grown up with all of that could be so against the idea of having it for their own family, their own children.

She'd been jealous of that kind of love, once. Even when they were married, she'd always felt on the outside. Now she could only imagine the kind of words they used to describe her in the Foster family.

But she'd been right to leave, Clara knew, and right to stay away. Even if she had been wanted in Jacob's world— and if she'd been sure of that she'd never have felt she had to walk away in the first place—she knew that Ivy wasn't. She wouldn't put her daughter through that, not for anything.

'Dad sent me back to the US,' Jacob went on and Clara turned to him, surprised.

'Why?'

'Because he didn't want his personal ill health to impact on the health of the business.' That was a quote from James Foster, Clara could tell, even though she hadn't seen the man in five years. Success mattered to the Fosters almost as much as family, she'd always thought.

Now she wondered if, sometimes, it might matter even more.

Still, she'd always been very fond of James Foster. A self-made millionaire who had made his fortune by inventing a medical instrument Clara didn't even truly understand the application of, James had all of Jacob's charm, good looks and determination. But it was his son who had taken the company—Foster Medical—to new heights. It was his business brain that had seen the opportunities in a shrinking market, and the path they needed to take.

And James had trusted Jacob to do just that. Not many fathers, Clara thought, would have so happily surrendered the reins of their life's work to their son. She'd always admired James for making that decision.

Of course, he'd been repaid handsomely since then—in money, prestige and the simple pleasure of watching the company he'd founded go from strength to strength. Watching his son succeed, over and over again.

'How is the *business*?' she asked, trying not to sound bitter just speaking the word. She knew for a fact that business success had mattered more than *her*.

'Booming. As is yours, by all accounts.'

That knowledge surprised her, although when she thought about it she realised it shouldn't. He was hiring her company, not just her. Of course he'd look into how well they were doing.

'Merry and I have worked very hard at building up Perfect London,' she said.

'I could tell.' Jacob glanced across at her from the driver's seat. 'I'm glad everything worked out for you.'

'Really?' Clara raised her eyebrows. 'Remember, I was married to you. I'm pretty sure there's a part of you that wishes I'd failed miserably so that you could have swept in and told me you told me so.'

'I never told you so,' Jacob said, frowning. 'I never even realised that you wanted to run your own business. If I had, I'd have helped you. Maybe we could even have worked together.'

Had she even known herself? All she knew for sure was that Jacob had never thought she wanted anything more than he could give her—and that she hadn't known *what* she wanted to do with her life.

Had they really known each other at all? Their whole relationship—from meeting to the moment she'd left—had lasted a year and two days, and it seemed that they'd never talked about the things that really mattered until it was too late. All Jacob had known was the person Clara had shown him—a person so starved for love and attention that she'd done everything she could to be what he wanted.

She'd escaped her family, found a job and a flat-share with a friend, and thought that was all she needed until she'd met Jacob in a London bar one Christmas Eve. Then, all too quickly, really, she'd found love and friendship and family and marriage and for ever…and suddenly she was twenty-one, a wife, and still had no idea what she wanted for herself beyond that.

She hadn't found herself until she'd left him, Clara realised. How sad.

Now she didn't need his approval, his attention. Not just

because she had Ivy and Merry in her life, but because she knew who she was, what she wanted—and she believed she could achieve it all. Realising how she'd changed over the past five years made her want to weep for the girl she'd been.

Turning away, Clara stared out of the window at the passing countryside and wondered what else spending twenty-four hours preparing the perfect Foster family Christmas would teach her about her marriage.

Clara hadn't thought she'd actually be capable of sleeping, not with Jacob in the car next to her, and certainly not the whole way to Scotland. But she'd figured it would at least curb the disturbing conversations if she *pretended* to be asleep, so she'd kept her head turned away, her breathing even, and hadn't even stirred when they stopped for petrol fifteen minutes later. But somehow when she next opened her eyes the scenery around her was decidedly more Highland-like in appearance.

'Sorry about the bends,' Jacob said, his eyes never moving from the road, and Clara realised what had woken her up. 'The satnav seems certain it's this way.'

The car turned another nausea-inducing curve and Clara looked up to see an imposing stone building looming ahead. Crenellations, thick grey stone, arrow slit windows… 'I think that's it!'

'Thank God. Hang on.' Jacob swung the car onto the side of the road and pulled to a stop. Pulling his phone from his pocket, he angled himself out of the car and held it up to capture the view. Clara watched him snap a few shots, then climb back into the car and start the engine again.

'I don't remember you being much of a photographer.' It was an easy subject, at least. With the castle so nearly in sight, and the realisation that she still had the rest of the day and most of tomorrow to spend in his company, at the least, Clara was very grateful for that.

Jacob shrugged. 'It's for posterity. I want Mum and Heather to have something to remember this Christmas by for the rest of their lives.'

'I'm sure they wouldn't forget,' Clara murmured. 'But the photos will be lovely.'

It struck her again what a big thing this was for Jacob to do. Not in terms of money—that was nothing to him, she was sure. No, Jacob had poured something far more valuable into this Christmas weekend. His time, his energy and his thoughts. Jacob was a busy man; Clara knew that better than most. Usually, showing up in time for Christmas lunch and staying long enough for pudding was an achievement for him. This year, not only was he giving his family a whole weekend, he had also helped with the preparation. Well, after some nudging, anyway.

He wasn't just giving his father a perfect last Christmas; he was giving his whole family memories of James that they'd treasure always.

Clara stared up at the castle and pretended the stone walls weren't a little blurry through her suddenly wet eyes.

Maybe Jacob *had* changed, after all. She knew beyond a shadow of a doubt that the man she'd walked out on would never have even thought of arranging a Christmas like this one, let alone being so involved in making it happen.

But could she trust him with her daughter's heart—when he'd already broken her own?

CHAPTER EIGHT

JACOB PULLED THE CAR to a halt just outside the imposing wooden doors of the castle and got out to take a closer look at the location of his Perfect Christmas.

'It doesn't exactly say *homely*,' he said, staring up at the forbidding grey Scottish stone.

'Nor do any of your homes.' Clara slammed the boot closed, their suitcases at her feet, and he winced at the noise.

'My homes are…' he searched for the words '…state-of-the-art.'

'They're all white.' She'd always complained about that, Jacob remembered now. But he couldn't for the life of him remember why he hadn't just told her to decorate if it bothered her that much.

Probably because white was what his interior designer had decided on—what she'd told him was current and up-market and professional. In fact, he distinctly recalled her saying, 'It screams success, darling. Says you don't need anything to stand out.'

Jacob wondered if Clara would have stayed if the walls had been yellow. Or covered in flowers.

Probably not.

'My parents' home isn't white,' he pointed out instead. 'Honeysuckle House is officially the colour of afternoon tea and Victoria sponge.' His mother went out of her way to make their house, by far the largest in their village, appear just like all the others—at least, inside the security gates. As if they didn't have eight times the money of anyone else in their already very affluent surroundings.

'So, somewhere between brown and beige, then?' Clara asked.

'I meant it's homely,' Jacob replied, taking his suitcase from her.

'It is,' Clara admitted. 'I always loved Honeysuckle House.'

'You should go and visit. Dad would love to see you.' The thought of Clara in that space again, the place where he'd grown up, made Jacob's spine tingle. As if his past and his present were mingling and he didn't know what it might mean for his future.

It was something he'd been contemplating on the drive, while she'd slept, merrily scuppering his plans to talk her into staying for Christmas Day with his family. Organising this Christmas had brought Clara back into his life and he couldn't help but think that couldn't just be the end of it. After five years of only communicating through lawyers, they were here together, being civil—friendly, even.

Maybe there wasn't any hope for their marriage, but could they manage to be friends after this? People did become friends with their exes sometimes, didn't they? And the thought of going back to a world without Clara in it… It felt strange. Unwelcoming.

Distinctly unhomely.

Clara ignored his suggestion about visiting his father and instead hefted her handbag onto her shoulder and extended the handle of her tiny suitcase to drag it along behind her. He assumed that she'd sent most of her stuff up with the courier, or poor Merry, because there was no way she had more than the bare essentials in that bag. It was another sign, as if he needed one, that she didn't plan to stay any longer than necessary.

Well, he had the whole of Christmas Eve to work on that. And perhaps her fondness for his father was his way in. After all, it had persuaded her to take on the job in the first place. What was a couple more days at this point?

The thought that he might actually end up paying his ex-wife to spend Christmas with him caused him to frown for a moment, but if that was what it took to give James Foster his dream Christmas then Jacob knew he'd swallow his pride and do it.

Clara pulled a large metal key from her pocket and opened the doors, using her shoulder to help shove them open. Jacob couldn't help but feel that fortifications didn't really scream cosy Christmas, but Clara had said this place was just right so for now he was inclined to trust her.

'Okay, so this is your grand hall,' she said, turning around in the expansive space just beyond the doors.

'There's a suit of armour.' Jacob crossed the hall to touch it. It was real metal armour. 'Are you planning on festooning it with tinsel?'

'I'm planning on putting the tree—which should be arriving this evening, incidentally—here at the bottom of the stairs. I guarantee that by the time I've finished decorating it, no one will be looking at the armour.' He turned to see where she was pointing and clocked the massive staircase that twisted its way up to the first floor. He could almost imagine his mother and Heather descending it, dressed in their Christmas finery. Another photo for the album.

'Besides,' Clara went on, 'I rather thought your father would enjoy the armour. Doesn't he have a thing about medieval military history?'

Jacob blinked. How had he forgotten that? 'Actually, yes. Okay, I'll give you the armour. Now, how about the grand tour?'

'Absolutely.' Clara nodded and, leaning her suitcase against the wall, disappeared down a passageway.

Jacob followed, wondering whether medieval castles also came with central heating.

Clara headed for the kitchen, her heart racing. Okay, so maybe she'd underestimated quite how…*castley* this place was. Still, she could already see it, decorated for Christmas, with the scent of turkey wafting out from the kitchen, presents under the tree…and a couple of glasses of something down everyone's throats. Then it would be perfect.

But first she had to convince Jacob of that.

He'd said that the original perfect Christmas had been spent in a cottage in the Highlands, so she started with the kitchen. She knew from the photos the owner had sent over that it had a large farmhouse-style kitchen table that would be ideal for breakfasts or board games or just chatting over coffee. Between that and the Aga, hopefully Jacob would start to get the sort of feel he wanted from the place.

'This is nice,' he said as he ducked through the low doorway behind her. Rows of copper pots and pans hung from the ceiling and the range cooker had been left on low, keeping the room cosy and warm.

'The owner did the whole place up a year or so ago, to hire out for corporate retreats and the like. It must have cost him a fortune to finish it to this kind of standard but…' She remembered the rates that she—well, Jacob—was paying, and why she'd been so desperate to fill the castle and not have to pay her cancellation charge. 'I guess he figures it's worth the investment.'

'He's done a good job,' Jacob admitted, running his fingers across the cascade of copper on the ceiling. 'So, what is he—some sort of displaced laird, trying to make money from the old family pile?'

'Something like that,' Clara replied. 'Do you want to see the rest?'

Jacob gave a sharp nod and Clara took off through the other door into the next part of the castle. That was another reason why she really wished she'd been able to get up here first and alone. She'd have been able to get the lie of the land, get her bearings. She had a feeling that studying the castle floor plans the night before might not totally cut it.

Still, Jacob seemed impressed by the pantry, already filled

with the food she'd ordered for the festivities. And, once they found their way back into the main part of the castle, the banqueting room, the snug, the parlour and sunroom all went down well. Whilst Jacob managed to make a cutting comment about each, Clara could tell that he was secretly impressed.

So was she. And relieved.

'I still say that nowhere in Scotland needs a sun anything,' Jacob grumbled as they made their way back through the grand hallway to the staircase.

'Ah, but imagine the views from the sunroom if the sun did actually come out,' Clara said. 'And I know you think the banqueting hall is too large—'

'It has a table that sits thirty,' Jacob interjected. 'There's going to be four of us. Five if you agree to stay. You should, you know, just to make the numbers up.'

'But it won't feel big once I've finished decorating it. Well, not so big, anyway,' Clara said. 'And I'm not staying.' He was joking, right? The last place she wanted to spend Christmas was here with her ex-in-laws.

But the look Jacob gave her told her that she was missing something. What on earth had he got planned now? He couldn't really be expecting her to stay, could he? If so, she really needed to nip that idea in the bud.

'We'll see.' Jacob started up the stairs before she could reiterate her determination to head back to the hotel for Christmas Day.

Oh, he was infuriating. Had he been this infuriating when they'd been married? Most likely; she had left him, after all. And if it hadn't been so obvious before their elopement, it was probably only because they'd spent so much of their time together in bed.

A hot flash ran through her body at the memories, making her too warm under her knitted dress and thick tights. Clara bit down on her lip. There was absolutely no time for thoughts like that. Not any more.

She was spending Christmas with Ivy and Merry and that was all she wanted in the world. She followed Jacob up the stairs, ignoring the small part of her mind that pointed out that her Christmas with Ivy could be all the more perfect if Jacob was there too. She needed to time things right. There was too much at risk to just rush in and tell him.

'Now, this room I definitely approve of,' Jacob called out, and Clara hurried towards his voice to find out where he'd got to.

Predictably, he'd found the master bedroom—complete with its antique four-poster bed that looked as if it could sleep twelve and the heavy velvet hangings that gave the room a sumptuous, luxurious feel. This, she could tell from the moment she entered, was a room for seduction.

But not this Christmas, thank you very much.

'This is the room I'd earmarked for your parents,' she said, stopping him before he got too carried away with thoughts of sleeping there. 'It's the biggest, has the easiest access to the rest of the castle and has the largest en suite bathroom. It's also the warmest, thanks to the fireplace.'

Jacob looked longingly at the bed. 'I suppose that makes sense,' he said.

'Come on. I'll show you the rest.'

The other bedrooms were all impressive in their own way but, Clara had to admit, none had quite the charm of the four-poster in the master bedroom.

By the time their tour was finished, Jacob looked much happier with the set-up at the castle.

'Okay,' he said, rubbing his hands together. 'This is going to work. So, what do we do next?'

'*I* need to do some final checks before I have to head to the hotel for the night. I'll do the decorating and so on tomorrow, before your family arrive. They get in at four, right?'

Jacob nodded. 'Yeah. But why don't you just stay here tonight? It's not like there aren't enough bedrooms.'

For one blinding flash of a moment Clara's brain was filled with images of her and Jacob taking advantage of that four-poster bed.

No. Bad brain.

'I need to check in to the hotel,' she said, trying to banish the pictures from her mind. 'Besides, Merry will be arriving this evening too.'

'Of course. Merry.' What was that in his voice? Could it be…jealousy? No. She didn't remember him ever being jealous about who she'd spent her time with when they were actually properly married. It was highly unlikely he was about to start now.

'Anyway. I need to get on, so you can…settle in, I guess. Work, if you want to.' And didn't he always? She was surprised he'd made it this long without setting up his laptop. 'I can get you the Wi-Fi password if you want.'

'There's nothing I can do to help?' Again, Clara felt that strange tug on her heart as she realised how eager he was to be a real part of the planning.

'I'm mostly just checking that the local supplies I ordered have been delivered, and waiting for the courier company to arrive and unload the boxes. Then I'll grab a taxi down to the hotel and make a few calls to confirm the bits being delivered tomorrow—fresh greenery, fresh food, those sort of things. After that, everything can wait until tomorrow. I've got it all in hand. You really don't need to worry.' It was all there on her time plan.

She checked her watch. In fact…

The knock on the door, precisely on time, made her smile.

'That will be Bruce,' she announced.

Jacob frowned. 'Who is Bruce?'

'Bruce the Spruce,' Clara said with a grin. 'Your perfect Christmas tree.'

CHAPTER NINE

It WAS EASY to busy herself in getting the castle ready for Christmas. All she needed to do was stick to her schedule, count the courier boxes that had arrived and ignore Jacob hovering near her shoulder, checking up on everything she was doing. At least then she had a chance of making it to the hotel before Ivy's bedtime. Maybe she could stay up a bit later than normal…

'I do know how to do this, you know,' she snapped finally, when she turned to put the box with the Christmas lights in by the tree ready for the morning and almost crashed into him. 'It's my job.'

Jacob stepped back, hands raised in apology. 'I know, I know. I just feel like I should be doing something to help, that's all.' Clara bit back a laugh. All those months of marriage she'd spent complaining that she wanted him to stop working and spend time with her, and the one time *she* wanted to be left alone to work she couldn't get rid of him! Even Clara could appreciate the irony.

But their conversation in the car had got her thinking. Maybe that had been part of the problem—she hadn't had anything except him in her life so she'd clung too desperately to him. She'd been lopsided, like a Christmas tree with decorations only on one side. She needed decorating all the way around. And now, with Perfect London, and Ivy and even Merry, she had that. Well, almost. There might be a few branches still in need of some sparkle. Or some love…

Could Jacob provide that? Did she *want* him to? Clara had been so focused on what he might mean to Ivy, she had barely paused to consider what it might mean for *her* to have him back in her life.

'Can't I start decorating Bruce or something?' Jacob asked, bringing her attention back to the cold, undecorated castle hallway.

'Bruce needs to settle in overnight,' she explained. 'To let his branches drop, and let him suck up plenty of water to keep him going. I'll decorate him in the morning.'

'Then what *can* I do?' Jacob asked.

'I told you—go do some work or something.'

'I don't want to.'

Clara stilled at his words. What she would have given to hear him say that about work when they'd been married. Now it just made her suspicious. What was he playing at?

'I don't need you dancing attendance on me, Jacob. I'm not your guest—I'm here to work. You're not responsible for me, you know.'

Something flashed across Jacob's face. Was it…relief? Relief that he could get back to work, she supposed.

But he surprised her. 'Fine. But this is still my Christmas. I want to help. Give me something to do.'

Clara shrugged. If that was what he wanted… Flipping through the stack of paper on her clipboard, she pulled off a sheet and handed it to him.

'Box Seventeen?' he asked, reading the title.

'It's that one over there.' Clara pointed to a medium-sized brown box liberally labelled with the number seventeen on all sides. 'Check through it and make sure that everything on that list is in there.'

'Didn't you check them when you packed them?' Jacob slit open the box and Clara tried not to stop breathing as the scissors went a little deeper through the tape than she liked.

'Three times,' she confirmed. 'And now we check them again.'

'Were you always this hyper-organised?'

'I may have got worse since starting Perfect London,' Clara admitted. 'But pretty much, yes.'

Another thing that had set her apart from her own family. Her mother had always been the spontaneous, play-it-by-ear type. The day Clara had left for university—a date circled in red on the calendar for months in advance—her mother had decided to take the rest of the family on an impromptu trip to the seaside. Leaving Clara to find her own way to university with whatever luggage she could carry on the train.

Conversely, the only spur-of-the-moment thing Clara had ever done was marry Jacob.

'So, I guess this must be pretty weird for you,' Jacob said, looking up from his box.

'Weird? Working with a client?' Clara said. 'No, not at all. I mean, it's not the way we usually—'

'I meant setting up Christmas with your ex-husband,' Jacob interrupted her.

'Oh. Well, yes. That is a little more unusual,' she admitted. 'I mean, it would have to be, wouldn't it? I've only ever had the one husband. And technically you're not even officially my ex yet.' Great. Now she was waffling, and drawing attention to the fact that he'd spent five years not agreeing to a divorce, just when he was finally offering to do exactly that. And she was starting to wonder if she really wanted him to... *Could* he be the father Ivy needed?

And what about the husband she needed? Surely that was a dream too far.

'Yet,' Jacob repeated, his voice heavy. 'Actually, that's one of the reasons I wanted you to travel up with me, so I could talk to you.'

'Oh?' That really didn't sound good at all. 'What about?'

'My father... He's very sick.' The words came haltingly, as if Jacob was still only just admitting this truth to himself.

'So I understand.' That was, after all, the only reason she was in this mess at all. And they'd already spoken about it.

This wasn't news, which meant there had to be something more. Something worse.

'He was always very fond of you,' Jacob said.

'I was always very fond of him too,' Clara admitted with a small smile.

'Fonder than you were of me, as it turned out.' Jacob flashed her a quick, sharp grin to show he was joking, but the comment sliced at her heart anyway.

'That was never the problem,' she murmured, and regretted it instantly. She'd just given him an opportunity to ask her again why she'd left. He wasn't going to leave that just hanging there. Not if she knew Jacob at all. And, as her dreams reminded her on dark, lonely nights, she had really thought she did.

'I always thought you were going to come back, you know,' he said after a moment.

So did I. But that had been before a positive pregnancy test had changed her life forever.

Clara would never regret having Ivy in her life, not for a single moment. But she knew falling pregnant had cost her Jacob, and that thought still haunted her sometimes.

'Your note said you needed time to think,' Jacob went on when she didn't answer.

'I did.' She'd thought and thought, working her way through every possible outcome, every potential reaction that Jacob might have to her news. But she'd always come to the same stark conclusion.

Jacob Foster didn't want kids. Not ever.

'So you thought. And…?'

'And I realised that our marriage was never going to work,' she said, as simply as she could. 'I wasn't happy, and you weren't in a position to make me happy.'

It was only later that she'd realised that no man could ever make her happy. She had to find that happiness in herself. And she had—by building her own career, her own family, her own *life*. Finally, she relied on herself, not others, for her own happiness.

But sometimes, alone at night, she couldn't help but wonder if she'd become a little *too* self-reliant in that area.

'I seem to recall making you pretty ecstatic more than once,' Jacob joked, but there wasn't any levity in his words. She could hear the concern underneath and that mantra she knew he lived by: *What did I do wrong? How can I fix it? I will not fail at this...*

It was an exhausting way to live. And it had been just as exhausting being the one he was trying to fix, the person he wanted to win, to succeed at being with, all the time.

'That was sex, Jacob. Not life.' Except, at the time, it had felt like both. It had felt as if their entire existences were tied up in the way they moved together, the way she felt when he touched her, his breath on her skin, her hair against his chest... It had been everything.

Until suddenly it hadn't been enough.

'Maybe that's where we went wrong,' he said. 'Too much sex.'

Clara laughed, even though it wasn't funny.

'Maybe it was,' she said. 'Or rather, too much time having sex, not enough talking.'

'Talking about what?' Jacob asked.

Clara rolled her eyes. 'Everything! Anything! Jacob, we met in a bar on Christmas Eve and we barely came up for air until March.'

'I remember.' The heat in his voice surprised her, after all this time. Did he still feel that connection? The one that had drawn them together that night and seemed to never want to let them go.

She bit her lip. She had to know. 'Do you? Do you remember how it was? How we were?'

'I remember everything.' Clara's body tightened at his words. 'I remember how I couldn't look away from your eyes. They mesmerised me. I remember I was supposed to go home for Christmas the next day but I couldn't leave your bed. Couldn't be apart from you, no matter what day it was. I thought I might go insane if I couldn't touch your skin…'

So he did remember. She'd thought she might have embellished the memory of that connection over the years, but he described it just the way she remembered it feeling. Like an addiction, a tie between them. Something she couldn't escape and didn't even want to.

'What went wrong for us, Clara?' Jacob asked softly.

She shook her head, the memory dissipating. 'That connection… It wasn't enough. We didn't ever talk about our lives, about what we wanted, about who we really were.' All these years, she'd thought their problems had been simple: Jacob had loved work more than her, and he had never wanted a family. She'd wanted his love, his attention…and his baby. They were just incompatible. But now…she wondered if she'd had it wrong all along. Maybe they would have had a chance if they'd built on that connection to really get to know each other instead of burning it up in passion. 'How did we expect to build a life together when we didn't even know what the other person wanted, let alone if we could give it?'

'I couldn't give you what you wanted—is that what you're saying?' He sounded honestly curious, but Clara knew he'd be beating himself up inside.

'I'm saying that I didn't know what I wanted when I married you,' Clara explained. 'And by the time I did…by the time I realised I wanted more than just fantastic sex and nice parties and too many houses…it was too late.'

'I wanted more than just that, you know. I wanted forever with you.'

Clara's heart contracted. How had this happened? How had she ended up somewhere in the Highlands having this conversation with her ex-husband? A conversation she'd been avoiding for five long years.

'I know,' she admitted. 'And I wanted that too.' She couldn't tell him that, sometimes, she still did. Because having forever with Jacob would mean not having Ivy, and that was simply not possible.

This was her moment, her chance to tell him about his daughter. Her hands shook as she turned back to the box she was unpacking, trying to focus on the exquisitely wrapped gifts and shiny paper. She needed to tell him. But his family would be arriving tomorrow and she had work to do and… She could make excuses forever. The truth was, she was scared.

She took a breath, trying to slow her heart rate. January; that was the plan. She needed to stick to her plan. The New Year would be on them soon enough.

'You were talking about your father,' she said, suddenly aware they'd been diverted from his original topic. 'Was there…? It seemed like there was something more you wanted to say about him.'

'Yes.' Jacob glanced over at her, long enough for her to see the indecision in his eyes. What on earth was he going to ask?

Much as she dreaded it, Clara had to know. 'So…?'

Jacob set his list aside, abandoning Box Seventeen completely. 'Like I said, he's always been fond of you. I think… I know that he'd really like it if you could be here for this, his last Christmas.'

'Here…at the castle? With you?' She'd really hoped he'd been teasing when he'd mentioned it earlier. The idea didn't bear thinking about. 'It's your family Christmas, Jacob. I'm pretty sure ex-wives don't get invited.' Not to mention the fact that there'd be a distraught little girl at a hotel a couple of miles away, wondering where her mother was on Christmas morning.

'Ah, but as you pointed out, we're not actually exes yet. Not officially.' Her own words were now coming back to haunt her. Great. As if the Ghost of Husband Past wasn't enough of a Christmas present.

'We haven't been together for five years, Jacob,' she said. 'I think we qualify under these terms.'

'Still. You're putting together this perfect Christmas. Don't you want to stay and enjoy it too?'

No. She wanted to have her own perfect Christmas, with Merry and Ivy. With a new bike and champagne at breakfast and maybe a snowball fight after lunch.

She did *not* want to spend Christmas with Jacob's mother and sister glaring at her over the turkey.

'I don't think that would be a very good idea,' she said in what she hoped was a diplomatic manner. It occurred to her that this would all have been a lot easier if she'd just told him about Ivy the day he'd walked back into her life. He'd probably have run for the hills and she wouldn't be in Scotland at all. 'I mean, I'm sure your family aren't so fond of me any more. I can't imagine they've forgiven me for walking out on you.'

'Maybe not,' Jacob conceded. 'I mean, you broke my heart. Families tend to get a little upset about that sort of thing.'

'I imagine so.' Not that she'd really know herself. 'Most families, anyway.' She'd never even told hers she was getting married in the first place, let alone that she'd left Jacob.

'Not yours?' His gaze flicked towards hers, then back down again. Clara shook her head. If she'd managed to not discuss her family with Jacob when they were actually together, she wasn't going to start now.

'So, probably not a good idea,' Clara said. 'We're agreed.'

'Well, I agree it wouldn't be a good idea if they still thought you broke my heart.' Clara's breath escaped her. What did he mean? That he'd found someone new so he wasn't heartbroken any more? Because on the one hand she really wanted to be the bigger person and be happy for him. But on the other... There wasn't a chance she was spending her Christmas with Jacob, his family and his *new girlfriend,* no matter how ill his dad was.

'Don't they?' she said, wishing she could breathe properly again but knowing it wouldn't be possible until she had her answer.

'They won't if we pretend we're back together,' Jacob said, and Clara lost the ability to breathe altogether.

'I...I don't...'

Jacob didn't think he'd ever rendered Clara so speechless before. Well, maybe once. That night on the balcony of the Los Angeles house, after that party, with her only half wearing that gold dress...

But that wasn't the point.

'It would make the old man's Christmas just to think we were even trying to make our marriage work again,' he said, pushing home with the guilt. He needed her to agree to this. Surely she *owed* him this. He'd given her the world, and she'd given him a note asking for time to think and then divorce papers, two months later. All because they hadn't talked enough? That, Jacob had found, was usually more easily solved by *staying in the same country as someone.*

Clara owed him more than a fake relationship for Christmas.

'But it wouldn't be real,' she said. Clara's eyes darted around desperately, as if she were searching the castle for secret passageways she could escape through.

'No. We'd just play happy families for Dad's sake.'

'Until...' She trailed off, and he realised she was avoiding saying the words *Until he dies?*

'Until after Christmas,' he clarified. 'All he wants is to know that there's a chance. That we're trying.' And if it delayed the inevitable divorce until it was too late for his father to worry about it that would be a bonus.

'I can't… I can't stay for Christmas Day, Jacob,' she said, finally finding the words. 'No. I'm sorry.'

She didn't sound very sorry. She sounded like this was a punishment he was somehow inflicting on her, instead of spending Christmas with people who had once been her family.

'Just think about it,' he said. 'That's all I ask.'

'There's no point,' Clara said. 'I can't do it, Jacob. I have…other obligations.'

Other obligations. Jacob's mouth tightened. He could only imagine what they might be. Through all their conversations she'd conspicuously failed to rule out another man in her life. And what was Merry transporting up here on the train? Some perfect gift for Clara's perfect man?

'You never said,' he bit out. 'Where are you spending Christmas?'

'Merry and I have booked into a hotel a couple of miles away,' she said, not looking at him. 'Roaring fire, haggis for breakfast, that sort of thing. I wasn't sure we'd have time to get back to London after all the set-up on Christmas Eve, so this seemed like the best option.'

'Just you and Merry?' he asked, dreading the answer.

'I think the hotel is fully booked, actually. We only just managed to get the last two rooms.'

Two rooms. But who was Clara sharing hers with? That was what Jacob wanted to know.

'That's not quite what I meant.'

'Really? Then I can't imagine what you did mean.' Clara turned to look at him at last, her eyes fierce. 'Since my life, my Christmas and who I choose to spend it with are absolutely none of your business any more.'

She was right; that was the worst thing. He wanted her to be wrong, wanted to claim that the piece of paper that announced they were still technically married meant it *was* his business. But that was a low move, even he knew that. Five years apart. He couldn't honestly have expected her to stay celibate that whole time.

He just wanted to know…

'Look, all I'm asking for is a couple of days,' Jacob said, aware he was getting perilously close to begging. 'Just stay and make Dad happy. Make me happy. Then I'll give you your divorce.'

'No. A wife is for life, not just for Christmas, Jacob.'

'Really? Where was that bit of trite philosophy when you walked out on me?'

'Where were you?' she asked. 'It was Boxing Day, for heaven's sake. The day after Christmas Day. And you hadn't been home in sixteen hours by the time I left. If you're suddenly all about Christmas being a time for family, answer me this—why weren't you there to spend it with me?'

'I…I had to work.' It was the lamest excuse in the book, and he knew it. But it was all he had.

Clara sighed. 'Jacob, you've made it very clear you don't want *me* at all. Just the appearance of a wife to prove to your father that you've got your life in order.'

'Hey, you're the one who left me,' he pointed out. 'If anyone has made it clear they wanted out of this marriage, it's you.'

Clara shook her head. 'I thought…just for a moment, I thought you might have changed. Grown up. But it's all still an act to you, isn't it? Be honest. You married me because all the other top-level businessmen you worked with had the perfect wife at home and you wanted it too. The sex was just a bonus. You never even *asked* what I wanted out of our relationship. And I was so stupidly desperate for any affection at all that I didn't even question it. Our marriage wasn't a relationship—it was a business merger.

You sealed the deal then went back to work, and left me wondering what I was supposed to do next.' She grabbed her bag and threw her coat over her arm.

'I won't be in another fake relationship with you, Jacob,' she said and for a moment his heart clenched the same way it had five years ago, as he'd read her note and realised that she had left him again. 'All we have left now really *is* business. I'll see you tomorrow.'

And then she was gone.

CHAPTER TEN

CLARA WRAPPED HER COAT tighter around her shivering body as she scanned the darkening road down from the castle towards the village for any sign of headlights. The taxi she'd called had promised it wouldn't be long. She checked her watch. If it made it in the next ten minutes she could be at the hotel waiting to greet Merry and Ivy when they arrived.

That was what she was focusing on. *Her* family. *Her* perfect Christmas. Not Jacob's.

She couldn't think about him now. Couldn't let herself stop and absorb the realisation that all she'd ever really been to him was a useful accessory, like a laptop or a briefcase. She'd felt neglected when they were married, sure. Even unwanted, or unloved towards the end. But she'd never felt as unimportant to him as she did today—at the very moment when he was telling her he needed her to stay.

But not for herself. Not for Clara. For what she represented—his own success. To show his dad that he wasn't a failure. That was all.

He'd made her think he wanted her. For one fleeting moment, she'd almost believed that he still loved her. But it was all still just a game to him, the same way their whole marriage had been. It was the game of life—a game Jacob was bound and determined to win.

She'd asked him why he hadn't stayed for that Christmas night, but she'd known the true answer before he'd spoken. He'd said he had to work, of course, but she knew what that really meant, now.

He hadn't considered her part of his family. Just like her own parents hadn't, in their way. Just like her stepdad hadn't. She hadn't been important to him either—certainly not as important as his work, or her stepbrothers. She hadn't mattered at all.

But she mattered to Ivy. She mattered now. And he could never take that away from her.

How could she have thought that he'd changed? That he might be *worthy* of knowing his incredible daughter?

Jacob Foster would never know the true value of love, of family, of relationships—of her. Not if he was willing to use her just to prove a point to his father.

Ivy didn't need that kind of person in her life. She didn't need a father who would swoop in and show her off when it benefitted him and ignore her the rest of the time. She needed someone who would show her that she mattered every day of her life.

And so, Clara realised as she finally saw the taxi's headlights approaching, did she.

Alone in the castle that evening, Jacob stared up at the monstrously large Christmas tree in the hallway, obscuring the suit of armour, and wondered if this whole thing had been a massive mistake.

Not Christmas in general, or even bringing his family together for this last perfect Christmas. But asking Clara to organise it.

He couldn't have done it all himself, he knew. He had many skills and talents but organising the details of an event like this weren't among them. Clara, on the other hand, seemed to thrive on such minutiae. He'd caught a glimpse of her clipboard while she was debating the exact position of the tree, and discovered that she had everything planned down to the minute. She knew exactly what needed to happen every hour of every day until Christmas was over. She'd probably leave them a timetable for festive fun when she headed back to the hotel tomorrow.

She'd even named the Christmas tree. Who called a tree Bruce, anyway?

No, he couldn't have done it without her, but still he wondered if he should have asked someone else. Or if she should have said no. If seeing her again was only going to make things far worse in the long run.

Maybe he should just have given her a divorce five years ago, when she first asked, and skipped this current misery.

Had she really meant everything she said? That he'd not just neglected her but *used* her? And he'd been thinking she owed him for walking out. Perhaps he owed *her* more than he thought.

Sighing, Jacob sank down to sit at the bottom of the stairs. He'd known all along that the chances of him being a good husband—a good man—were slim, no matter how hard he tried. He'd proved that before he'd even turned eighteen. That disastrous night… Burned into his mind was the memory of his mother's face, wide-eyed with horror and disbelief, and the stern, set jaw of his father that night, all mingled with the sound of the ambulance tyres screeching up the driveway on a winter night…

But worse, far worse, was the image of Heather's tiny body, laid out on a stretcher, and the sobbing wrenched from his own body.

He forced it out of his mind again.

He should never have got married in the first place. He should have known better. He'd let himself get swept away in the instant connection he'd felt with Clara and had told himself what he needed to hear to let the relationship carry on far past the point he should have ended it. It should have been two weeks of intimacy, a wonderful Christmas holiday memory to look back on years later.

Because he didn't deserve anything more, anything deeper than that.

He'd reassured himself that Clara was an adult, that she

could take care of herself. But it seemed a heart was even easier to break than a body.

Jacob buried his head in his hands, his fingers tightening in his hair. His father had known, he realised. James had known that marriage was beyond him—he'd practically said it when Jacob had brought Clara home to meet the family! All his talk about responsibility... What he'd meant was: *Do you really think you can do this?*

And Jacob had proven he couldn't.

He'd been all Clara had, it dawned on him now, too late. He'd been given the gift of her love and all he'd had to do in return was take care of it. She was wrong about one thing, at least—he *had* loved her. She'd never been a convenience, an accessory, even if apparently that was how he'd treated her.

He'd broken her. Let her down. He'd pulled away because he'd been scared—scared of how deeply he felt for her, and scared of screwing it up. That he wasn't up to the responsibility of being a husband.

Maybe he still wasn't. But he liked to think he was a better man at thirty-one than he'd been at twenty-five, and a world better than he'd been at sixteen. He was improving, growing. He might never be a good man, but he could be a *better* one.

And a better man would apologise to the woman he'd hurt.

Jumping to his feet, Jacob grabbed his car keys and his coat and headed out to find Clara's hotel.

It wasn't hard to find; the twisting road down from the castle didn't have much in the way of buildings along it and the Golden Thistle Hotel was the first he came to.

Swinging the door open wide, he stepped inside and... promptly realised he had no idea what he was going to say. Clara hadn't answered him when he'd asked who she was staying with. What if she really was there with another man? The last thing she'd want was her ex-husband storming in, even if he was there to apologise.

'Can I help you?' the teenage girl behind the reception desk asked.

'Um...' Jacob considered. He was there now, after all. 'Are you still serving food?' At least that way he'd have an excuse for being there if Clara stumbled across him before he decided on his next move.

The receptionist cheerfully showed him through to the bar, where he acquired a snack menu and a pint and settled down to study his surroundings.

It wasn't entirely what he'd expected. Not that he'd given it a huge amount of thought. But he'd imagined Clara to be staying in a wildly romantic boutique hotel, with no kids and plenty of champagne and roses. The Golden Thistle Hotel, while lovely, seemed a rather more laid-back affair. The roaring fires were cosy and the prints on the stone walls were friendly rather than designer. The low, beamed ceilings and sprigs of holly on the tables made it feel welcoming, somehow, and somewhere in the next room someone was belting out carols at a piano.

But there was no sign of Clara, or Merry. And the longer he sat there, the less inclined Jacob was to look for them. How would he find them, anyway? Explain to the nice receptionist that he was looking for his estranged wife? That was likely to get him thrown out on his ear if the woman had any sense.

He shouldn't be here. She had been right. It wasn't any of his business who Clara chose to spend Christmas with. Not any more. And maybe she'd been telling the truth; maybe it really was just her and Merry. Perhaps she just wanted to get away from him. And, given his current actions, who could blame her?

She'd left him once. He really shouldn't be surprised if she kept trying to repeat the action.

Jacob drained the last of his pint and got to his feet. Never mind the bar snacks, or his wife. He'd head back to the castle, eat whatever had been left in the fridge for him and go to bed. And tomorrow he'd be professional, adult and considerably less of a stalker.

He'd apologise when she arrived for work. They'd get through Christmas and they'd be divorced in the New Year. He'd give Clara her life back, at least, to do whatever she wanted with it.

Without him.

Glancing into the next room on his way past, he saw a small girl standing on the table, singing 'We Wish You A Merry Christmas' at the top of her lungs and turned away. A perfect Christmas—that was what he was here for. Not to reconcile with his wife, or even exact some sort of revenge on her for leaving him. This weekend was about his family, not his love life.

Clara was his employee now, not his wife. And once this Christmas was over, she wouldn't be his anything at all.

He had to remember that.

Clara arrived at the castle bright and early on Christmas Eve, wrapped up warm and in full warpaint make-up, ready to be professional, aloof and totally unbothered by Jacob Foster. Today, he was her client, not her ex, and all they had to discuss were Christmas plans and decorations. Nothing to do with their marriage—and definitely nothing to do with Ivy.

She'd caught a taxi up to the castle, loaded full of the last few essentials that her friend had brought up herself, not trusting them to the courier company. Namely, the Foster family antique decorations and Jacob's Christmas presents to his family. Everything else she figured she could replace or improvise if the courier company let them down.

But they hadn't. All the boxes had arrived, just as they'd

packed them. The tree was in place, the final food delivery was expected within the hour from the local butcher and deli. All she had to do now was 'Christmasify' the castle. And that was Clara's favourite part.

Normally, she'd have Merry along to help her, but today her business partner had taken Ivy off into the local town to do some last-minute Christmas shopping in the hire car Merry had picked up at the station the day before. Hot chocolates had also been mentioned. Clara was trying very hard not to feel envious; she needed to work and Ivy understood that. Plus, spending time with Aunt Merry was always a special treat for her daughter.

At least they'd all managed to have a wonderful evening together last night at the Golden Thistle Hotel, when she'd finally got done at the castle. She hadn't been completely sure when Merry had suggested the place, but it was the closest and easiest hotel on offer. As it turned out, though, it was wonderful. The staff had welcomed Ivy in particular with open arms, and they'd spent the evening eating chips and then mince pies in the bar while one of the locals played Christmas carols on the old piano there. It hadn't been long before Ivy had been singing along too, much to everyone's delight. All in all, the evening had been the ideal respite after the hideous few hours with Jacob at the castle.

Had he honestly believed that Clara would spend Christmas there, just to make his father a tiny smidgen happier? He couldn't honestly believe that James would care all that much about his ex-daughter-in-law being there, could he? Clara was pretty sure that as long as Sheila, Jacob and Heather were there, everything would be perfect as far as James was concerned.

And as long as she had Ivy and Merry, Clara knew the Golden Thistle would be perfect for her too. In fact, she couldn't wait to get back there this evening and spend Christmas Eve with her girl. The owners had already said that Ivy was welcome to hang her stocking by the main fire, to make it as easy as possible for Father Christmas to find her that night. Ivy had positively vibrated with excitement at the thought.

Yes, Christmas was here and it was wonderful. All Clara had to do was hope that Jacob had come to his senses, get through a few more hours of setting up the castle for the Fosters, and then she could start enjoying herself. This year, she'd decided, would be the one to make up for all those miserable childhood Christmases—not to mention the last lonely one with Jacob.

She shivered as she stepped out of the car onto the frosty castle driveway. There was no snow yet, but the forecast said there would be overnight. All the more reason for Clara to get the job done and get out. The air around her was bitterly cold, cutting into every centimetre of exposed skin, and Clara was thankful for her scarf and gloves, and even the woolly hat Ivy had pushed onto her head before she'd left.

'You don't want to catch a cold, Mummy,' she'd said sternly, and Clara had given up worrying about what it might do to her hair.

Letting herself in to the castle, a box of decorations balanced on one hip, Clara wondered whether she should call out to Jacob. He could be sleeping, she supposed, or working. Either way, she probably shouldn't interrupt him. Besides, she'd work quicker on her own.

By the time he appeared, dressed in jeans and a jumper and heavy boots, she'd already brought in all her boxes and waved the taxi off, unpacked the fresh food delivery, and twined freshly cut greenery all the way up the twisting banister. She was just adding the ribbons and baubles to the stair display when she heard his voice.

'What are you doing?' he asked from the top of the stairs. He sounded amused, which she hoped meant that he planned to ignore the way they'd parted the day before too. The only thing for it, as far as Clara was concerned, was to get back to being client and organiser as soon as possible.

Clara glanced up, one end of the ribbon she was tying still caught between her lips. 'Decorating,' she said through clenched teeth. It came out more like 'Echoratin' but he seemed to get the idea.

'Need a hand?' He jogged effortlessly down the stairs and Clara allowed herself just a moment to appreciate the way his lean form moved under his winter clothes; the clench of a thigh muscle visible through his jeans, the way his shoulders stretched the top of his sweater. Call it a Christmas present to herself.

Then she turned her attention back to her ribbon before he caught her ogling. The man's ego did not need the boost, and she didn't need him thinking he might be able to find a way out of their divorce agreement.

'You could start on Bruce, I suppose,' Clara said doubtfully. Then she realised that Jacob Foster probably had no idea about the right way to decorate a tree and changed her mind. 'Or maybe the table decorations.' They, at least, were already made up and just needed putting in place.

'Or I could make you a coffee and fetch you a mince pie?' he suggested. 'As an apology for yesterday. And, well, our entire marriage.'

'Tea,' she reminded him. 'But actually, that sounds great.'

He returned a few minutes later with a mug and plate in hand. Clara took them gratefully and sat down on the nearest step to eat her mince pie. The early start had meant forgoing breakfast at the hotel, and she realised now that might have been a mistake. Decorating was hungry work.

'I *am* sorry,' he said, standing over her. 'About everything. Not just asking you to fake a relationship for the sake of my pride, but for not giving you what you needed when we were married.'

Clara shrugged, swallowing her mouthful of pastry. 'Forget it. I guess it was inevitable that some old thoughts and habits would come up with us working together. But in a few hours I'll be out of your hair and you can get on with your Christmas and forget all about me.' Now she said it out loud, the thought wasn't actually all that appealing.

'I don't want to forget about it,' Jacob replied. 'Not yet. I…I wasn't made for marriage. I should have known that and not let myself give in to what I wanted when I'd only hurt you in the long run.'

Not made for marriage? Because he cared more about his work than people? Clara supposed he might have a point. Still, she couldn't help but feel a little sad for him, if work was all he'd ever have.

'I should have talked to you more,' she admitted. 'Explained how I felt. But it was all tied up in my family and I…'

'Didn't want to tell me about them,' Jacob guessed. He sat down on the step below, those broad shoulders just a little too close for comfort. Clara could smell his aftershave, and the oh, so familiar scent sent her cascading back through the years in a moment. So much for forgetting. As if that was even possible. If she hadn't forgotten him throughout those five long years apart, why would she begin now, just because he finally signed a piece of paper for her? 'Why was that?'

Clara looked down at her plate. Suddenly the remaining half of her mince pie seemed less appealing.

'You don't have to tell me,' Jacob added. 'I know it's none of my business any more. I'd just like to understand, if I can.'

'My mother… She fell pregnant with me when she was sixteen,' Clara said after a moment. Was that the right place to start? *I was born, I wasn't wanted.* Wasn't that the six-word summary of her life? 'I was an accident, obviously. Her parents demanded that she marry my dad, which was probably the worst idea ever.'

'Worse than our marriage?' Jacob joked.

'Far worse. At least we had a few months of being happy together. I don't think they even managed that.' She sighed, remembering the fights, the yelling. Remembering the re-lief she'd felt, just for a moment, when her father had left and her mother met someone else. Until she'd realised what that meant for her place in the family. 'My mother always said that I was the biggest mistake she'd ever made in her life.'

Jacob's sharp intake of breath beside her reminded her exactly where she was, who she was talking to. A client, not her ex.

She flashed him a too bright fake smile. 'Anyway. Need-less to say, they don't miss me. My father left when I was seven, my mum remarried a few years later and started a new family. One she really wanted. I became…surplus to requirements. That's all.'

'Clara…I'm so sorry. If I'd known…' He trailed off, pre-sumably because he knew as well as she did he wouldn't have done anything differently. Except maybe not marry her in the first place.

She shrugged. 'I'm a different person now. I don't need them.' *Or you.* 'I have my own life. I'm not the girl I was when my dad left, or the teenager being left out by her new family. I'm not even the person I was when I married you. I don't even drink coffee any more!' She tried for a grin, hoping it didn't look too desperate. Anything to signal that this part of the conversation was over. She didn't need Jacob feeling sorry for her.

He took the cue, to her relief. 'So what turned you off coffee, anyway? Some sort of health kick?'

'Something like that.' Clara gave him another weak smile. Why on earth had she chosen that as her example? She couldn't exactly explain about the morning sickness, or the fact that caffeine was bad for the baby, could she? 'I guess I'm just out of the habit now.'

'Funny. You used to swear it was the only thing that could get you going in the mornings.' At his words, another memory hit her: Jacob bringing her coffee in bed before he left for work in the morning and her distracting him, persuading him to stay just a few more minutes... She bit her lip, trying not to remember so vividly the slide of her hands under his shirt, or the way he'd fallen into her kisses and back into her bed.

She couldn't afford to let herself remember. Couldn't risk anything that could lead her back there, back to the girl she'd been when she married him. She'd moved on, changed. And Ivy needed her to be more than that girl. She needed her to be the Clara she'd grown up into. Ivy's mother.

And she couldn't take the chance of Jacob seeing how much of him she still carried in her heart either. She had to shut this conversation down. Fast.

'Now I get up excited to live my life,' she said bluntly and lifted her mug to her lips to finish her tea. It was time to get back to work. 'Things are different.'

'Yeah,' Jacob said, his expression serious, his eyes sad. 'You're happy.'

Clara's heart tightened at the sorrow in his words. But he was right; she *was* happy in her new life. And she needed to cling on to that.

So she said, 'Yes, I am,' knowing full well that she drove the knife deeper with every word.

CHAPTER ELEVEN

HOW HAD HE not known? How could he have loved a woman, married her even, and not known how she had grown up? That her biggest fear had been being unwanted, unloved?

This was why he couldn't be trusted with people. He'd had a whole year with Clara and he'd never learned even this most basic truth about her. And he'd hurt her deeply because of it.

The Foster family prided itself on success, on not making the stupid sort of mistakes others made. And in business Jacob was the best at that.

In his personal life… Well, all he could do now was try and avoid making the same mistake twice. He didn't imagine that would be much of a problem. Since Clara had left, there'd never been another woman he'd felt such an instant connection with. There'd never been anyone he'd been tempted to stray from his limits for. He couldn't honestly imagine it happening again.

He'd had the kind of love that most people searched a lifetime for and he'd ruined it. The universe wasn't going to give him that kind of luck twice.

Perhaps it was all for the best. This Christmas project had given him a chance to know his wife in a way he never had when they were married. He knew now for sure that she was happier without him. Yesterday, when they'd talked, for a moment he'd seen a hint of that old connection between them, the same heat and desire he remembered from their first Christmas together. But today Clara was all business, and all about the future. She'd moved on and it was time for him to do the same.

As soon as they made it through Christmas.

Clara drained the last of the tea from her mug and jumped to her feet again.

'Back to work,' she said. 'I'm about to add your family baubles to the tree, if you want to help.'

'Is that at all like the family jewels?' Jacob jested, knowing it wasn't funny but feeling he had to try anyway. Had to do something—anything—to lighten the oppressive mood that had settled over them. 'Because if so…'

'Nothing like it,' Clara assured him. He took some small comfort from the slight blush rising to her cheeks. 'Come on.'

The tree—Bruce, as Clara had christened it—was magnificent, rising almost the whole way to the ceiling even in the vast castle entrance hall. He smiled, remembering the trees they'd had as children. Heather had always insisted that the tree had to be taller than her, so as she had grown so had the trees.

He suspected his parents had been secretly pleased when she'd finally stopped growing, just shy of six foot.

'Do we have a ladder?' Jacob asked, staring up at the topmost branches.

Clara nodded. 'I think I saw one in one of the cupboards off the kitchen. I'll fetch it.'

She was gone before he could offer to help.

That was another change, he mused, pulling out the box of baubles he'd retrieved from his parents' house for the occasion and starting to place them on the tree. Not that Clara had ever been particularly needy or helpless, but he didn't remember her being so assertive and determined either. Whenever anything had come up throughout the planning process—even choosing Christmas presents—she'd taken charge as if it were inevitable. As if she were so used to having to deal with everything alone—make every decision, undertake every task—that it had become second nature.

The bauble he picked out of the box now caught the

lights from the tree, twinkling and sparkling as he turned it on its string. Those baubles had hung on his family's tree for every Christmas he could remember. As far as he knew, they weren't particularly expensive or precious. But they signalled Christmas to him.

And this would be his father's last one. He needed to focus on the real reason they were here—not dwell on his past failures as a husband.

Jacob hung the bauble in his hand on one of the lower branches and stood back to admire his small contribution to the decorations. And then he headed off to help find that elusive ladder.

The least he could do for Clara was decorate the stupid tree. Even he couldn't screw that up.

Clara swore at the bucket as her foot got stuck inside it, then at the broom as it fell on her head. She had been so certain there was a ladder in this cupboard somewhere, but so far all she'd found had been murderous cleaning utensils.

With a sigh, she hung the broom back on its hook, disentangled her foot from the bucket, ignoring the slight throb in her ankle, and backed out of the cupboard. Carefully.

Well, there had to be a ladder somewhere. She'd seen one. Unfortunately, since she'd explored every square inch of the enormous castle the day before, exactly *where* she'd seen it remained a mystery—and a mystery which could take quite a lot of searching to solve.

She could ask Jacob for help, she supposed, but even the idea seemed a little alien. She was just so used to doing things herself these days, not just at work but at home too. At four, Ivy was becoming a little more self-reliant, but she still needed her mummy to take care of the essentials. After four years of tending to another person's every need—and knowing that you were the only person there to look after them—doing what was needed had become more than second nature. It was just who she was now.

She hadn't been like that when she was married to Jacob, although that was only something she'd realised later. Shutting the cupboard door, she tried to remember that other person, the one Jacob had married, but it was as if that woman, that other her, was a character in a play she'd acted in once. A person she'd pretended to be.

Clara knew without a doubt that the person she was now—Ivy's mother—was the one she'd been meant to be all along.

But that didn't help her with the ladder. With a sigh, Clara set about checking all the other cupboards off the kitchen and then, when that didn't get her any results, extended her search to the rest of the ground floor.

She was just about to give up, head back to the hall and try upstairs, when Jacob found her.

'Did you find a ladder?' Jacob's words made her jump as they echoed down the dark stone-walled corridor.

'Not yet,' she said, her hand resting against her chest as if to slow her rapidly beating heart.

'Don't worry. I found one.'

Of course he had. Because the moment she was congratulating herself on being self-reliant was exactly the time her ex-husband would choose to save the day.

It's a ladder, Clara, she reminded herself. *Not a metaphor.*

Unless it's both.

She followed the sound of his voice back down the corridor, through the dining room and back into the hallway.

'What do you think?' Jacob asked, beaming proudly at the half-decorated tree. Apparently he'd found the ladder early enough to have hung the rest of his family's decorations haphazardly across the huge tree. Clara thought of her carefully designed tree plan and winced. Still, it was *his* perfect Christmas…

'It looks lovely,' she lied. 'Help me with the lights? Then we can add the rest of the decorations I brought.'

Crossing the hall, she reached into the carefully packed boxes and pulled out the securely wrapped lights; they'd been unpacked for testing back in London, then rewrapped so they'd be easier to set up once she arrived. Merry had also added a bag of spare bulbs and two extra sets of fairy lights, just in case.

And, underneath those, was the apple-green project folder she always brought with her. The one with the Wi-Fi password on the front, apart from anything else. But there was one more note she didn't remember adding. Clara pulled the file out and read the stocking-shaped note stuck on the front: *For when it's all done!*

Frowning, Clara opened the file. On top, before all the contract information and emergency contact details, sat her divorce papers, just waiting for Jacob's signature. Of course. That would be Merry's idea of a brilliant Christmas present.

But for Clara it was growing harder and harder not to imagine both futures—the one she could have had with Jacob and the one she was living now—and wonder what the first would have been like if they'd ever really opened up to each other. She accepted now that she'd never let him in, had never wanted to open herself up that way. What if he had been doing the same? She'd always known Jacob had held his own secrets close to his chest. There were some things they just didn't talk about and she'd accepted that, not wanting to push him and have him push back.

She'd never told him why his behaviour hurt her so much. And she'd never asked him *why* he didn't want children. Was it just a knee-jerk reaction, the fear of a young man, which he might grow out of? Or had there been something deeper there? His reaction to her pregnancy scare told her there was. Was it too late to find out what that problem was?

And would it make a difference when she told him about Ivy?

She needed to tell him. And she was starting to think it couldn't wait until January.

Maybe it was just the Christmas sentimentality getting to her. Didn't every single person have a wobble around the festive season and start wishing that maybe they had someone to share it with?

Well, everyone except Merry. Her best friend was very firmly anti-relationship. Something that worked very well alongside Clara's resolve to give Ivy a stable, secure and loving upbringing, even if that meant being a one-parent family rather than introducing her to potential step-parents who might not hang around.

Could Jacob give her that security? Clara still wasn't sure. But she realised now she wouldn't ever be sure unless she opened up to him.

'Everything okay with the lights?' Jacob asked from just over her shoulder.

Clara slammed the folder closed and shoved it back into the box, hiding it under some emergency ribbon for the tree.

'Fine.' She grabbed the fairy lights and turned, stumbling back slightly on her heels as she discovered Jacob was even closer than she'd realised.

He reached out to steady her and Clara could feel the warmth of his hands even through her light sweater. She bit the inside of her cheek and stepped away.

She'd let her guard down. Let herself appreciate the way he looked at her—the way he looked in his jeans and jumper. She'd let her imagination enjoy the moment. And she couldn't afford to do that, not any more.

Especially not when he had that hot look in his eye. The one she remembered all too well from their wedding night.

She had to focus on getting the job done and getting out of there. The connection between them might still be there, but giving in to that attraction was exactly how they'd ended up as man and wife without knowing the most basic things about each other. She couldn't let that happen this time. She needed to tell Jacob about Ivy before she could even *think* about what it might mean for their relationship.

Swallowing, Clara found her voice again. 'Let's string some lights.'

CHAPTER TWELVE

JACOB FLICKED THE SWITCH on the lights again, smiling when every single bulb lit up. Clara's excessive testing at least meant he didn't need to hunt for the missing ones and replace them, like he always found himself doing at home.

Maybe it truly was a perfect Christmas.

The thought soured even before he appreciated it as he remembered the folder in the decorations box. She'd been fast to close it, but not so quick that he hadn't seen enough to know what it contained.

Divorce papers. The very ones he'd been avoiding signing for five years.

Who brought divorce papers to a Christmas celebration?

But this wasn't *Clara's* celebration, no matter how much he'd tried to convince her to join it. For her, this was still work. And his signature on those papers was part of her payment.

She'd earned it. More than earned it. She deserved to be free of him.

Except... The hardest thing was knowing how good things *could* be between them. Yes, their marriage had lasted less than a year, and yes, he'd screwed up. And Clara was right—they'd spent more time in bed than they had talking. They hadn't known each other the way they'd needed to.

But that time in bed... He'd been working so hard to forget it, until the moment she'd stumbled against him and it all came flooding back. The feel of her body pressed against his, however fleeting, had been so familiar, so right, his own had immediately reacted the way it always did when Clara was near.

And now all he could think about was that four-poster bed, going to waste upstairs.

But no. He needed to keep his distance. Set her free. Sign her blasted papers.

It was just that it had been five years. Five long years he'd hung in there, not quite letting her go. Now he just couldn't imagine saying goodbye without kissing her one more time. Without showing her that however much she'd thought he hadn't wanted her when they were married, he had, and he still did. For all the distance he'd put between them, trying to keep her safe from him, he wanted to stride across it now and hold her, kiss her, touch her.

Love her, one last time.

'Just a few more decorations and I think we're done here,' Clara said, unnecessarily cheerily, in his opinion. 'I'll be able to leave you to enjoy Christmas with your family.'

Jacob checked his watch. His parents and Heather were due at four, only another hour away. Clara was cutting it fine and, from the way she scurried around the tree adding decorations, she knew it. She'd already packed up everything else. Clearly, she planned on making her escape the first chance she got.

Only he wasn't sure he could let her go. Not forever. Not like this.

'Are you sure you won't stay?' he asked. 'Not even for a sherry and a mince pie?' That was the polite, proper thing to do on Christmas Eve, wasn't it? And Clara wouldn't want to be impolite… 'I know my family would like to see you again, however briefly. To thank you for everything you've done setting up this weekend, if nothing else.'

Clara paused, halfway through hanging a silver bell on the tree. 'You told them you were working with me on this project?'

'Of course I did.' Maybe not entirely intentionally, but he'd told them. Jacob wasn't one of those people who told his parents everything that was going on in his life and he was pretty sure they wouldn't want to know. But when it mattered, he kept them informed. Mostly.

'And they weren't…weird about it?'

'Why would they be?'

Clara raised her eyebrows at him and Jacob interpreted the look as meaning: *Ex-wife. Remember?*

'They were fine,' he said, skipping over his mother's concern. Mothers worried.

'Really?' Clara asked, disbelief clear in her voice.

Jacob sighed. He'd never been able to get away with lying to her when they'd been married either. He'd thought that made them a great match, at the time. But clearly Clara had been much better at hiding the truth. Otherwise he'd have realised how unhappy she was long before she'd left.

He'd honestly thought she was coming back. That it had been just another of their spats—a minor retaliation for the fact he'd had to work on Christmas Day. He hadn't believed she'd really meant it.

Not until she still hadn't come back a month later.

No wonder his mother worried. He'd been the poster child for denial at the time.

'They just want me to be happy. And I want them to be happy. And you staying for sherry and a mince pie would make us all very happy.'

With a small, tight smile on her lips, Clara shook her head again. 'I'm sorry.' Reaching down, she picked up her bag.

She was actually leaving him. Again. And this time he was under no illusions that she would come back.

He had to let her go. But not like this. Not when he was so close to understanding everything that had gone wrong between them. To knowing her the way he never had before. Maybe it wouldn't have made a difference, but maybe it would. And he just knew, deep down, that there was more here. Something she wasn't saying.

This was his last chance to find out what that was.

Jacob swallowed his pride.

'Please. Stay.'

'I can't.'

Those words again. He hated those words.

He stepped closer. 'Why?'

'I told you,' she said, frustrated. 'Merry is waiting for me at the hotel.'

'Merry. I don't buy it.' He didn't want to have the same argument again. Wasn't that the definition of insanity—doing the same things and expecting different results? But then, Clara might actually be driving him insane. Even if she left again, even if they finally got divorced, even if he never had another chance with her…he needed to know the truth. The truth about it all. He now knew why she'd left but not why she hadn't come back. He knew now how he'd hurt her but there was more, he could tell. He wanted to know everything.

Starting with why she wouldn't stay.

'Merry wouldn't be enough of a reason for you to be this determined not to stay,' he said. 'Tell me the truth, please. I'm not asking to start a fight, or to judge you or anything else. I just need to know. Is there someone else? Is that what you're not telling me? Are you afraid I won't give you the divorce if there is? Because we had a deal.' It might break his heart into its final pieces but if she was truly happy with another man he'd give her the divorce. She'd made it clear that he couldn't make her happy and goodness only knew somebody should. Clara deserved all the happiness in the world.

She stared back at him, her beautiful dark eyes so wide he could almost see the battle going on behind them. Would she tell him the truth? Or would he face more evasion?

Eventually, she shook her head. 'That's not it. I almost wish it was.'

Jacob frowned. 'What do you mean?'

'It would be so much easier to just lie. To tell you I'd fallen in love with a lumberjack from Canada or something. Because the truth is...' She sighed. 'There's no one else, Jacob. There never has been. It's only ever been you.'

Jacob reeled back as if he'd been hit. Five years. Five years he'd spent trying not to imagine her with other men, and failing miserably. Five years torturing himself with thoughts of her falling in love again, of her pressing him for divorce because she wanted to remarry. Five years of thinking he hadn't been enough for her, that she'd needed to go and find something else, someone better. And all this time...

'No one,' he repeated. 'There's been... You mean, you haven't...'

That was a game changer.

Clara's cheeks were bright red. 'I shouldn't have told you that.' She brushed past him, heading towards the door, and he grabbed her arm to stop her.

'Yes. You should.' Because that meant something, didn't it? It had to. Five years, and no one else. That wasn't nothing. Those weren't the actions of a woman who was desperate to get away from him.

'Why?' she asked, sounding anxious. 'Why does it even matter now?' She pulled her arm away but he reached out and took it again, more gently this time—a caress rather than a hold.

'It matters.' The words were rough in his throat. He couldn't even put a name to his emotions but he knew it mattered. Knew he cared, still. Knew that the sense of relief flooding through him as he realised there really wasn't another man waiting for her at the hotel meant something.

No other man had touched her. No one had run their

hands over that pale, smooth skin the way he had. She'd been a virgin when they'd met, when she was twenty-one and he twenty-five, so he knew now that he was the only man she'd given herself to. Ever.

And that definitely meant something. The primal urge to take that again rose up strong within him.

Clara shook her head, looking down at the stone floor. 'It's over, Jacob. None of it matters any more.' Her voice was small, desolate and, despite her words, he didn't believe it.

'It doesn't have to be.' For the first time he was almost convinced. He knew her now in a way he hadn't before. He was older. Better. Maybe this time he could make her happy.

Stepping closer, he ran his hand up her arm, wrapping his other arm around her waist. 'Stay, Clara.'

'I can't.' Always those words. He was starting to wonder if they really meant what he thought they did.

'Because you don't want to?' Raising his hand to her chin, he nudged it up so she had to look at him and her eyes were wide and helpless as they met his.

She wanted to. He could see it. So what was stopping her?

'No,' she admitted, swallowing visibly. At least she wasn't lying to him now. It was a small victory, but he'd take it.

'Then why?'

She bit her lower lip, her small white teeth denting the plump flesh. Oh, how he wanted to kiss her…

'You can tell me,' he assured her, shifting just a little closer.

Her gaze dropped again as she gave a small hollow laugh. 'I really, really can't.'

'If you don't tell me, I'll be forced to guess.' He tried to make it sound like a joke, but it really wasn't. Not knowing was driving him crazy.

Looking up, she rolled her eyes at him. 'Fine. You want to know the real reason? Because our marriage is over, Jacob. I have the divorce papers in my bag, ready for you to sign. And I know you. If I stay, you'll try and convince me to give things another shot.'

'And you don't think you'll be able to say no?' Something wasn't right here. Apart from the fact he knew full well that Clara was of course capable of saying no to him—and she knew he'd respect that—the bitter, hard words didn't match the desperation in her eyes. She was making excuses.

She *was* still lying to him.

Clara looked up and met his eyes. 'Of course I can say no. *I left you*, remember?'

As if he could ever forget. 'And why am I starting to think that maybe you regret that decision?' It was a stab in the dark, a wild guess. But there hadn't been anybody else... What if she really did still have feelings for him? *Could* he make it work this time? Could he be the husband she needed?

'It was the best decision I ever made.' Her words were clear, bright and true, echoing off the walls of the castle. She meant every word, Jacob could tell.

The hurt in Jacob's eyes was palpable as his arms fell away from her and Clara regretted the words as soon as she'd spoken them. It was true, of course—if she hadn't left Jacob, then Ivy wouldn't have been born into a loving home, even if that home only had one parent.

Leaving had been the right decision—for her, for Ivy and even for Jacob, although he didn't know it.

But that was the point. He *didn't* know. And without that context her words were harsh, hurtful. Cruel.

And Clara tried hard never to be cruel. Cruelty was

something she knew too much about to knowingly inflict it on another person.

She had to tell him the truth. Now. But how?

This wasn't the plan. The plan was to get the job done then meet him privately in London, somewhere public but discreet, and have the conversation. Not in a secluded castle in the middle of nowhere with his family due to arrive within the hour!

But how could she not tell him now?

Swallowing, she stepped forward and placed a hand on his arm. 'I'm sorry. I didn't mean…'

'Yes,' he said, the word coming out raspy. 'You did. I can tell when you're lying to me, Clara. And you meant that.'

Hysterical laughter bubbled away in her throat. If he really could tell when she was lying then they were both doomed. 'I… Being married to you… For a time, it was the best thing that had ever happened in my life.'

'But not for long enough.'

'It took me a while,' she said, feeling her way to the right words. 'But I realised that we both wanted different things.'

'You never told me what you wanted!' Frustration flew out from Jacob's words, and the tension in his shoulders and the tightness of his jaw. She was doing this all wrong. 'If I'd known you wanted to run your own business, I'd have helped you! We could have worked together. And if I'd known about your family—'

'I know, I know. I should have told you, should have opened up to you more,' Clara said. 'But Jacob, that's not what I'm talking about.'

'Then what? If not that, then what on earth did you want that I couldn't give you?'

'A baby.'

Jacob froze, his eyes wide and scared, his face paling by the second as if he was turning to ice. 'You…you never said,' he stuttered eventually.

'Because I knew how you felt about kids.'

'I can't have them.' As if he needed to confirm it all over again now. 'I can't.'

'Can't?' Clara asked, eyebrows raised. From her experience it seemed to be much more of a *won't*.

'I'm not meant to be a father, Clara.' Jacob scrubbed a hand over his hair. 'Jesus. You're right. We really should have talked more. I always assumed that you were happy with it just being us. But if you really wanted…that. Then yeah, I get why you left. Finally.' He gave a small, sad half laugh then looked up at her, his eyes narrowing. 'Wait. If you wanted a baby, why haven't you done anything about it? Five years, Clara. You could have met someone else in that time, started a whole tribe if you'd really wanted. You're gorgeous, caring, wonderful… Don't tell me you didn't have offers.'

And this was it. Confession time. Clara sucked in a deep breath.

'I didn't need them. You see, when I left you…I was already pregnant.'

This time, Jacob didn't freeze. He was all movement—staggering back away from her, his mouth falling open. 'You…'

'I should have told you, I know. But I knew how you felt. When I left, I thought I'd come back again, same as every other time. But then I took the pregnancy test and I knew…you wouldn't want me if I did. You wouldn't want her. And Jacob, I couldn't let my daughter—she's a girl… we had a girl… I didn't say—and I couldn't let her go through what I did, growing up with a parent who didn't want her. I couldn't.' The words were tumbling out of her mouth, too fast for her to think them through. 'But I always meant to tell you eventually. And when you came back… I thought this would be my chance to see if you wanted to get to know her.'

'To know her?' he echoed, sounding very far away.

'Ivy. I called her Ivy. And she's the best person on the planet.' If Jacob only ever knew two things about his daughter, it should be those.

'I don't…' He shook his head as if he were trying to shake away this new reality he found himself in. 'I can't…'

Clara nodded. 'I know—it's a shock. And I'm sorry. I'll go. Let you… Well… I'll just go.'

She stumbled backwards, fumbling for the door handle and yanking the door open. As she did, there came a sound like a feather mattress falling to the floor with a *whoomp*. Suddenly Clara was pulled back and she came to the realisation that Jacob's arm was around her waist, tugging her safely out of the range of the huge bank of snow that had fallen from the castle's crenellations. It must have been building up all day, Clara thought, amazed. She hadn't even known it was snowing out there.

But now, when she looked out of the door, she saw a blanket of snow covering the land—deep and crisp and even.

But mostly deep. Really, really deep.

CHAPTER THIRTEEN

'LOOKS LIKE YOU might be spending Christmas with me after all,' Jacob said, his voice faint even to his own ears.

She'd lied to him for five long years. She'd let him believe that he'd screwed up—and maybe he had, but not in the way he'd always believed. She'd planned to come back. She'd planned to keep trying. Until she'd found out she was pregnant.

He was a father. How could that even be possible? Why on earth would the universe *allow* him to father a child?

He stared out at the snow. Somewhere out there, in the dark and the cold—well, actually she was probably nice and warm at the hotel, but that wasn't the point—somewhere out there was a little girl who belonged to him. That he was responsible for.

Just like he'd been responsible for Heather.

The thought chilled him far more than the weather ever could.

'I have to get out of here.' Clara spun on her heel and stared at him with wide, panicked eyes. 'I have to get back to Ivy. We can dig your car out. I saw a shovel somewhere...'

Probably in the same place as the mythical ladder she hadn't been able to find. And, given that he could only just make out the windows of his car and the tyres were completely snowed in, he thought she was being a little optimistic. The snow was coming down faster than they'd be able to shovel.

'Wait, Clara. You can't. You need to—'

'What? Stay here with you?' She gave a high shrill laugh. 'Not a chance. I know that look, Jacob. That hunted, panicked look. I recognise it distinctly from the first time

I thought I was pregnant, thanks. It's fine—you're off the hook. Ivy doesn't know you exist and now she never has to. You never even have to meet her—but you *do* have to help me get home to her *right now*!'

She was losing it, Jacob realised. He needed to calm her down. He could have his own breakdown about being a father later. He'd waited five years, apparently. Why rush it now?

'How do you plan to do that?' he asked, ignoring the rest and focusing on the part that was clearly making her crazy right now. 'That road back to the hotel isn't going to be passable even if we could dig out the car.' He remembered the steep stretches and sharp turns. There wasn't a chance of either of them driving it in this weather.

'Then I'll walk,' she said. She was so stubborn. How had he forgotten that?

'In those shoes?' The fur-lined boots she was wearing looked warm enough but, unless he was mistaken, they were suede and the soles looked too thin for any decent grip. Definitely fashion items rather than practical.

'There might be some boots around here somewhere.' Clara cast a desperate glance around the hall as if she was expecting Santa himself to appear and furnish her with some, but even she had to know her arguments were growing weaker and weaker.

'If we didn't find them looking for that ladder then they're not here,' Jacob pointed out. 'Look, Clara, it will be fine. Your...' he swallowed '...*our* daughter, she's with Merry, right? At the hotel?' She nodded. 'Then she's safe. And we're safe. That's the important thing. The moment they clear the roads, I'll drive you back, I promise. But for now...you're stuck here with me, I'm afraid.'

Clara glared at him. 'You do realise that if I'm trapped here, there's no way your family can get here either.'

A chill settled over him that had nothing to do with the

snow. He'd been so busy focusing on Clara that he'd forgotten, just for a moment, what the weather would mean for his parents and Heather.

'They'll get here.' They had to. It was their perfect Christmas. One way or another they had to make it to the castle, or everything would have been for nothing. He'd have failed his father one last time, and he might never get the chance to put it right.

That was unacceptable.

'How?' Clara asked, incredulous. 'If I can't drive or walk out of here, what have you got planned for your family?'

'Helicopter,' Jacob suggested desperately. 'I'll make some calls…'

'They won't fly in this weather.' Clara tilted her head as she looked at him, as if she was studying his reactions. 'You know that. Are you sweating? Jacob, it's zero degrees out there.'

'I'm not sweating.' But he was. He could feel the cold clamminess of the moisture on the back of his neck, under his jumper. Like always, it was all about his father. 'I'm thinking.' Thinking *How can I put this right?* And *How am I going to tell him I got Clara pregnant?*

Given his father's reaction to the news of Jacob's marriage, and his emphasis on responsibility, Jacob could only imagine how James Foster would take the news that he was now a grandfather—and that Jacob had taken no responsibility so far at all for his daughter.

'Well, when you figure out a way to get them here, we can use the same method to get me out. I've got my own Christmas I need to get to. Mine and Ivy's.'

One he hadn't been invited to share. One he was pretty sure he didn't want to share.

But he couldn't help but wonder… *Does she look like Clara or like me?*

Hands visibly shaking, Clara held up her phone. 'I need

to find some reception in this place and call Merry. I need to know that Ivy is okay.'

She disappeared up the stairs, as quiet as the falling snow. Jacob waited until he knew she must have reached the bedrooms, then sat heavily at the foot of the stairs.

He was trapped in a castle with his ex-wife, he'd just discovered he was a father and the perfect Christmas he'd worked so hard planning was ruined. What would his father be thinking now? He wouldn't blame Jacob for the weather—the man wasn't irrational. But that didn't change the fact that in the annals of Foster history this would go down as his mistake. Jacob's failure. He had been the one who'd decided to host Christmas in the Highlands, after all. *Ha!* He'd even asked Clara for a white Christmas.

Seemed like she couldn't help but deliver, even when she didn't want to.

His shaky laugh echoed off the lonely stone walls and he dropped his head into his hands, his fingers tugging at his hair as they raked through it.

The difference was that, this time, there'd be no years to come for his father to bring this up, to tease him for his stupid plan. This was going to be his last Christmas and Jacob had ruined it.

His throat grew tighter as he remembered that long-ago Christmas, and another screw-up. One that no one ever mentioned, especially not as a joke. One that he never needed to be reminded of anyway.

He had a clear visual every time he saw the scars on Heather's arms. He knew just how badly he'd failed his family in the past.

And now he'd done it again.

What could he do now?

Clara made sure the master bedroom door was closed behind her before she let her shaky legs give way. The fire she'd lit in the grate earlier burned bright and merry but she couldn't stop shivering. She couldn't think of anything except Ivy, stuck in a strange hotel with her aunt Merry, waiting for her mum to arrive for hot chocolate and Christmas presents.

Except Clara wasn't going to be there.

Damn Jacob and his stupid perfect Christmas. How had she let herself get dragged into this in the first place? A ridiculous desire to prove to her ex-husband that she was better off without him, she supposed. To prove it to herself too.

If only she'd stayed in London with Ivy, where she belonged, she wouldn't be in this mess.

And she'd told him. She'd told him everything—although how much he'd taken in, what with the shock and the snow and everything, she wasn't sure. They'd have to talk again later, she supposed.

If they really were snowed in for the duration, they'd have plenty of time for that conversation.

She made a sound that was half sob, half laugh as she realised there was another, more pressing, conversation she needed to have first.

Clara fumbled with her phone, holding it up towards the window and praying for reception. There it was. Just a single bar, but hopefully enough for her to reach Merry.

She dialled, held her breath and waited.

'Clara? Where are you? I've been trying to call all morning, ever since the snow started, but I couldn't even get through to your voicemail.' Merry sounded frantic. Clara didn't blame her.

'I'm so sorry. Reception here is terrible. And I was so busy getting things ready…I didn't notice the snow.' If she had, she'd have called a taxi and headed straight out of the castle before the roads became impassable. 'Is Ivy okay?'

'Wondering where you are. Clara, are you even going to be able to get back in this? The roads look bad.'

Clara's heart hurt at the idea of her little girl watching out of the window of the hotel, waiting for her to come home. This was exactly what she *never* wanted Ivy to feel— as if she'd been abandoned for a better option. That there was something else that mattered more than her. Because there really wasn't, not in Clara's world.

'They look worse from this end,' she admitted, her throat tight. 'We can't even dig Jacob's car out, Merry. And the road…' She stared out of the window at a vast blanket of white. 'I can't even see where it should be.' Somewhere in the distance, beyond all the falling flakes, was the Golden Thistle. Clara wished more than anything in the world that she could be there now.

'Hang on,' Merry said. Clara heard her murmuring something, presumably to Ivy, then the sound of a door closing. 'What are you going to do? It's Christmas Eve!'

'I know!' Clara rubbed a hand across her forehead and tried to blink away the sudden burn behind her eyes. 'I wanted to walk but I don't fancy my chances. And Jacob's family can't even get here. He was talking about trying to find a helicopter or something but… I think I'm stuck here. And Merry…that's not the worst of it.'

Her best friend must have sensed that Clara was on the edge because suddenly the note of panic was gone from Merry's voice and she became all business again. They had a rule at Perfect London: only one of them could fall apart at any given time. And it was definitely Clara's turn.

'Tell me what happened,' she said briskly. 'Tell me everything, and I'll fix it.'

Clara let out a full-blown sob. 'Oh, Merry, I'm so sorry. But I have to tell you something. Something I should have told you years ago.'

'That Ivy is Jacob's daughter?' Merry guessed, calm as anything.

Holding the phone away from her ear, Clara stared at it

for a moment. Then she put it back. 'How…how did you know?'

'It doesn't take a rocket scientist, Clara. Not when you've seen the two of them. She's very like him.' Merry gave a low chuckle. 'Besides, you never were the one-night stand type. So I always wondered… Did you tell him?'

'Yeah. It went…badly.'

'Then he's an idiot,' Merry said simply. 'Ivy is the coolest kid in the world. He should be so *lucky* as to have her as a daughter.' Clara relaxed, just an inch. Maybe Ivy didn't need a father at all. Not when she had an Aunt Merry.

As long as Aunt Merry forgave Mummy for lying to her, of course.

'Are you mad?' Clara asked in a tiny voice.

Merry paused before answering, and Clara's heart waited to beat until she spoke. 'I understand why you wanted to keep it a secret, I think. I hope you know that you could have trusted me with it but…I guess we all have our secrets, don't we? So no, not mad. But I *do* want a full retelling of everything, with wine, the moment we get you out of there.'

'*If* we get me out of here,' Clara muttered, but she couldn't help a small, relieved smile spreading across her face. Despite everything, she still had Merry. Her best friend still wanted to be exactly that.

'Okay, let's fix that first,' Merry said, businesslike once again. 'How stuck is stuck? And what do you want me to tell Ivy?'

'I don't know.' The words came out practically as a wail.

'Let me check the weather forecast. Hang on.' Clara heard the tapping of laptop keys in the background. 'Okay, it's deep and treacherous right now, but there's no more snow due overnight. Snowploughs will be out as soon as it stops, then we can look at getting you out of there. So tomorrow morning, if we're really lucky. The next day if we're not.'

'But tomorrow is Christmas,' Clara whispered. Oh, poor Ivy. How was she ever going to explain this to her?

'Not this year it isn't,' Merry said firmly. 'This year, Santa is snowed in up at the North Pole too, and will be coming tomorrow night. Then we'll celebrate Christmas once you're back here.'

'I'm pretty sure Father Christmas can't get snowed in,' Clara said dubiously.

'Well, as long as your daughter doesn't know that, we should be okay,' Merry replied. 'Look, I'll fix it, okay? You've fixed things for me often enough—our own business, as a case in point. Let me fix this for you.'

She sounded so sure, so determined, that Clara almost began to feel a little better. 'What are you going to do?'

'I'm going to talk to the staff here, and the other guests,' Merry explained. 'I reckon they'll all buy in to postponing Christmas until Santa—and you—can get here.'

'But it's their Christmas too,' Clara protested. 'Some of them were only staying until Boxing Day night. We can't ruin it for them just because I screwed up.'

'You didn't screw up—you were doing your job. Besides, we can have a practice Christmas tomorrow. As long as Ivy believes that the real deal is the next day, it doesn't matter anyway.'

'Do you really think you can pull it off?' If Merry managed it, then Clara would still have Christmas with her daughter. It might not be perfect, but it would be pretty wonderful all the same.

For the first time ever, Clara cared a whole lot less about perfect. She just wanted to be with Ivy for Christmas. Whatever day they decided that was.

'I can do it,' Merry promised her. 'Just leave it with me. Now, do you want to speak to Ivy?'

'Please. And Merry…'

'She can't know about Jacob. I know.'

Clara waited until she heard her daughter's high-pitched voice coming closer, feeling her heart tighten with every second.

'Mummy?'

'Hi, sweetheart. Everything okay there?' Clara tried her best to sound light-hearted. She knew from past experience that Ivy would pick up on any slight tension in her voice.

'It's brilliant here. Auntie Merry and I went shopping and we bought you—' Clara heard a shushing noise from the background '—something I'm not allowed to tell you about yet. And then we went for hot chocolates.'

'Sounds wonderful. I wish I could be there.'

'Are you coming home soon?' Ivy asked. 'It's really, really snowy out there.'

'I know. And I'm afraid the snow is very deep where I am too. It's half way up the door!' She made it a joke, even though it meant that no taxi would drive to the castle in this, and she had no means of escape. The most important thing was that Ivy continued to believe this was all one big, fun adventure.

Ivy let loose a peal of laughter. 'How are you going to get home?'

'Well, it looks like I might have to wait for the snowploughs to clear the roads.' Now came the tricky bit.

'Will you be home before Santa comes?'

'Actually,' she said, dropping her voice to a secretive whisper, 'I just heard—Father Christmas is snowed in too!'

'Nooo…' Ivy breathed, amazed.

'Yes. So he's postponing Christmas! I can't remember the last time that happened!' Because it never had. But Ivy didn't know that yet.

'Does that mean he won't be bringing my presents?' Ivy asked, obviously anxious.

'Of course he will! You've been such a good girl this year, he wouldn't not bring you presents. It just means that he might have to come tomorrow night instead of tonight. And I'm sure I'll be back by then.' If she and Jacob hadn't killed each other before Boxing Day.

'What are we going to do tomorrow then?' Ivy sounded confused but hadn't expressed any disbelief yet. Clara took that as a good sign.

'Have a practice Christmas, of course!' She injected as much fun as she could into the words. 'You and Auntie Merry can practise opening a few presents, eating Christmas dinner, pulling crackers, wearing the hats and telling the jokes…all the usual things. Then, when I get home, we can do it all again for real, once Santa has been!'

'So I get two Christmases this year?'

Clara let out a small sigh of relief at the excitement in her daughter's voice. 'Exactly!'

'Brilliant!' There was a clunk, the familiar sound of Ivy dropping the phone as she got bored and wandered off. In the distance, Clara heard her excited chatter. 'Auntie Merry! I get two Christmases this year! Did you know? Santa's stuck too!'

Clara waited, listening to the plans for the Christmas she was missing, and wiped a rogue tear from her cheek. She didn't have time to break down now, not with Jacob here.

Although, until those snowploughs made it up here, she had nothing *but* time.

Eventually, Merry came back on the line. 'Okay?'

'Seems to be.' Clara sniffed. 'Tell her I love her, yeah? And you'll be okay tucking her in? You know she likes to sleep with—'

'Blue Ted,' Merry finished for her. 'I know. I've babysat for her a hundred times. We'll be fine.'

'I know you will. I just wish I was there.'

'And you will be. Really soon,' Merry said soothingly. 'Now get off the line so I can phone whoever is in charge of snowploughs around here and work out how to post-pone Christmas.'

'Thank you, Merry.'

'For you, anything. Go and make your ex-husband and the father of your child miserable. That should cheer you up.'

Clara gave a watery chuckle. Merry had all of the best ideas.

CHAPTER FOURTEEN

JACOB STARED AT THE bottle of brandy. It stared back. Well, probably it didn't but he'd drunk a good quarter of it now so it felt as if it might.

'So...your latest solution to the snow issue is getting drunk?' Clara's voice from the doorway made him spin round—too fast, as it turned out. It took a good thirty seconds for the rest of the room to catch up.

'I called Heather,' he informed her. 'Before the brandy.'

'Are they all okay?' Sitting down across the table from him, she poured herself a small measure into a clean tumbler. She'd never been a big drinker, he remembered. Apparently being snowbound in a castle with him was driving her to it.

'Fine. They're actually in a hotel in Inverness at the moment. They're hoping to travel up tomorrow morning, meet us here if the snow has cleared enough.' So his father would be spending his last Christmas driving on treacherous Scottish roads, trying to save his only son from his own stupidity. Just the way he wanted it, Jacob was sure.

Time for another brandy.

Clara moved the bottle out of his reach as he moved across the table to grab it. 'You're a terrible drinker, Jacob. You're plastered after about two pints.'

'I might have changed.' As he said the words, he thought of all the ways he had changed, or might have changed since she'd left. Drinking wasn't one of them but she didn't know that.

'Apparently not.' The certainty in her voice told him she wasn't just talking about alcohol. 'But anyway. Here's to a perfect Christmas.' Clara raised her glass and took a long swallow. 'Somehow I don't think you're going to be giving me a top recommendation after this.'

'I don't blame you for the snow, Clara,' he said. For many other things, sure. But not the snow.

'But I bet you're blaming yourself, aren't you?' Her eyes were too knowing, and she saw too deep. He glanced away the moment her gaze met his. How did she always manage to do that? Pick up on his biggest insecurity and dig right in to it?

'I was the one who wanted Christmas in the Highlands. The part of Britain voted most likely to get snow at Christmas.' It was his fault. His failure.

'And I was the one who brought you to a castle on top of a hill,' Clara countered. 'Place least likely to get its roads gritted, or cleared by the snowploughs first.'

'It's what I asked for.'

'What if I told you I had an ulterior motive for bringing you here?' Clara asked.

Suddenly, Jacob's mind filled with exotic scenarios. Had she brought him here purposefully to punish him? Or, more likely, to tell him about his daughter… 'What ulterior motive?'

'I'd booked this place for another client.' Clara took another sip of brandy, her eyes warily peering over the rim of the glass, watching to see how he'd react. 'They pulled out and left me liable for the reservation fee, thanks to a contract screw-up. Holding your Christmas here meant I wasn't out of pocket after all.'

'I see.' It wasn't what he'd expected but part of him had to admire her business sense. 'So it really *is* your fault that we're snowed in and stranded in a castle at the top of a hill.'

'Hey, you asked for a white Christmas.'

Jacob couldn't help it; the laughter burst out of him before he could think. Somehow, tossing the blame for their predicament back and forth had defused some of the awful tension that had been growing between them since they'd arrived. After a moment Clara joined in, giggling into her brandy. Jacob marvelled at her. For once, she looked just like the Clara he remembered. The woman who, he knew now, had fought back against a childhood that could have left her bitter and cruel and instead had chosen to find joy in the world. He'd been scared that being married to him had taken that away from her.

He'd always thought her capacity for joy the most beautiful thing about her.

'I'm sorry,' she said once she'd calmed down again. 'Believe me, I really never intended for this to happen.'

'Oh, I believe you,' Jacob said with a half-smile. 'After all, you've made it very clear you'd rather be anywhere else than here with me.'

'Not anywhere.' She gave him an odd look, one he couldn't quite interpret. 'I just… I'm supposed to be elsewhere tonight. That's all.'

'With Ivy.' It was the child-sized elephant in the room.

'That's right.'

'She must be…four now?' Even simple mental arithmetic was proving tricky. 'Is she okay? With Merry?'

Clara raised her eyebrows. 'Suddenly concerned for the child you didn't know existed an hour ago? The one you made it rather clear you don't want in your life?'

'I didn't say that.' His reaction might have strongly hinted at it but he hadn't actually said the words. 'And you're worried about her. I'm just worried about you.'

'Don't.' Clara sighed. 'Ivy's having the best slumber party ever with one of her favourite people in the world and, thanks to a story about Santa getting snowed in, is potentially having two Christmases this year, if we don't get out of here in time. She might be missing me but she's fine.'

She was a good deal better than Clara was, by the sound of things.

Jacob reached across, took the bottle of brandy and poured a small measure into both of their glasses. 'Since we're stuck here...we should talk about it. Her, I mean.' Clara pulled a face. 'We're never going to get a better opportunity than this,' he pointed out.

'I know. And you deserve to know everything. I realised this week...it wasn't just that we didn't talk when we were married. We didn't let each other in enough to see the real people behind the lust.' She waved her glass in the air as she spoke. 'We thought we had this epic connection, this unprecedented love. But we never really knew the true heart of each other. We never opened up enough for that.'

Jacob stared down at the honey-coloured liquid in his glass. She was right, much as he hated to admit it. He'd wanted to believe that he could be a success as a husband, that he could be what she needed, so he'd only let her see the parts of him that fitted his vision of what that meant— working hard, taking responsibility, earning status, being a success. Everything his father had always done.

He'd hidden away the other parts, the bits of him he wanted to pretend didn't exist. All the parts that made his family ashamed of him.

Would it have made a difference if he'd shown them to Clara? Or would they just have made her leave him sooner?

'I always knew,' he said slowly, 'that something was different the last time you left. I just never guessed it could be this. I always thought that it was me and that I'd let you down. And I had, I know. But that's not why you didn't come back to try again. That was because...'

Clara finished the thought for him. 'Ivy mattered more.'

'And that's why I could never have children.' Jacob gave her a wonky smile then tilted his glass to drain the last few drops. 'I never did seem to grasp the concept of other people mattering more.'

'What do you mean?' Clara asked, frowning. 'Do you

want me to tell you you're selfish? Because you are a workaholic who often forgets there's a life outside the office…or at least you used to be. I think this Perfect Christmas project of yours shows that you're definitely capable of thinking of others when you want to.'

Jacob's mind raced with warnings to himself. With all the things he'd never told Clara—all his failures, the acts and mistakes that would strip away any respect she'd ever had for him.

Why tell her now? Except it was his last chance. The last opportunity he might ever have to explain himself to her and to make her understand the sort of husband he'd been and why.

Should he tell her? He gazed into her eyes and saw a slight spark there. Was he imagining the connection that still existed between them? The thread that drew them together, even after all these years?

Would the truth be the thing that finally broke it? Or maybe—just maybe—could it draw her in to him again?

'I made a mistake once,' he started.

'Just the once? Jacob, I've made hundreds.' She was joking, of course, because she couldn't know yet that this wasn't a laughing matter. Not for him and not for his family.

'Only once that counts,' he said and something in his tone must have got through to her because she settled down in her chair, her expression suddenly serious.

'What happened?'

'My parents… They left me in charge of Heather one evening while they were at a friends' Christmas party. I was sixteen. She was six. I resented it. I wanted to be out with my friends and instead I was stuck in, babysitting.' Across the table, Clara's eyes were wide as she waited, even though she had to know that the story ended as well as it could. Heather was still with them.

Just.

'I was messing around in the kitchen,' he went on, hating the very memory. He could still smell the scent of the Christmas tree in the hallway, the mulled wine spices in the pan on the stove. 'I was experimenting. I used to think I wanted to be a scientist, did I ever tell you that?'

Clara shook her head. 'No, you didn't. Like your father, you mean? What changed?'

'Yeah, like my dad.' That was all he'd wanted: to be like his father. To invent something that changed people's lives for the better. At least he had until that night. 'And as for what changed...' He swallowed. 'I sent Heather up to bed early because I didn't want her getting in my way. I was trying some experiment I'd read about—a flame in a bottle thing—when the phone rang. I turned towards it, moving away from the table.' The memory was so clear, as if he was right there all over again. A familiar terror rose in his throat. As if it were happening again and this time he might not be able to stop it...

'I was far enough away when I heard the explosion. And then I heard Heather scream,' he went on, the lump in his throat growing painfully large. But still he struggled to speak around it. 'The experiment... The fire should have been contained in the bottle, burning up the methanol. But I screwed it up, somehow. It exploded. And when I turned back...Heather...'

'Oh, Jacob,' Clara whispered and reached out across the table to take his hand. He squeezed her fingers in gratitude.

'She'd come downstairs to see what I was doing,' he explained. 'She was right by the table when it happened. Her arms...'

'I'd seen the scars,' Clara admitted. 'I just never thought... She always kept them covered, so I didn't like to ask. I should have.'

'No, you shouldn't. We don't... Nobody in my family likes to talk about it. We like to pretend it never happened.'

Even though there hadn't been a day since when Jacob hadn't thought about it, hadn't wished he'd acted differently. 'Dad only ever refers to it as our lucky escape. Heather put her arms up to protect herself when the bottle exploded but her pyjamas caught fire. I grabbed a throw blanket and smothered her with it to put the flames out but...' He swallowed. This was the part of the memory that haunted him the most. 'The fire chief said that she would have been burnt beyond recognition if I'd been a moment slower, if her hair had caught fire. It could have taken her sight too. And she might have...'

Clara's fingers tightened around his. 'But she didn't. She's fine, Jacob. She's out there right now with your parents, waiting for this snow to clear. She's fine.'

She's alive. Some mornings, that was the first thing he said to himself. Whenever he worried about the day ahead, about a deal that might go wrong or a business decision he had to make, he just reminded himself that Heather was alive, and he knew anything was possible. But nothing had ever been the same since. His parents had never looked at him the same way. They loved him, he knew. Forgave him even, maybe. But they couldn't love him the same way they had before he'd hurt their baby girl. And they couldn't trust him, not with people.

He'd been lucky—far luckier than anyone had any right to be, his father had said. But Jacob knew he couldn't ever rely on that again. He'd used up his allocation of good luck and all he had left was hard graft and determination.

A determination never to let his family down like that again. A resolution never to put himself in a position where he was responsible for a child again.

He couldn't be trusted. He should always focus on his own dream, his own ambition, instead of another person's welfare. He couldn't take the risk of hurting another kid that way again.

He'd thought that maybe he could manage marriage, as long as it was on his terms. And when he'd met Clara he'd known he had to try.

But in the end he'd only let her down too. He'd neglected her the way he'd neglected Heather that night, but the difference was that Clara had been an adult.

When he'd hurt her, Clara could leave, and she had done exactly that.

And he couldn't ever blame her.

Clara held Jacob's hand hard and tight, her whole being filled with sympathy and love for that younger version of her husband. A teenage boy who'd been acting exactly like sixteen-year-old boys always would—foolishly—and had almost destroyed his family.

'It wasn't your fault, Jacob,' she said and his gaze snapped up to meet hers.

'How can you say that? It was entirely my fault. Every last bit of it.'

The awful thing was, he was right. 'You were a child.'

'I was sixteen. Old enough to be responsible, at least in my parents' eyes. I let them down.'

And he'd never forgiven himself, Clara realised. He'd held this failure over himself for years and it had coloured every single thing he'd ever done since.

Even his marriage to her.

Clara sat back, her fingers falling away from his as the implications of that washed over her. In her mind, a movie reel replayed their whole relationship with this new knowledge colouring it.

Suddenly, so many things made sense in a way they never had before.

This—*this* was why he was so determined to succeed, every moment of every day. Why he'd worked so hard to never let his father down, ever again. Why he did everything he could to bring glory and money and power to his family—to try and make up for the one time he'd got it wrong.

Finally she understood why he was so adamant that he never wanted children. Because the one time he'd been left in charge of a child something had gone terribly, almost tragically wrong.

He'd spent almost half of his life carrying this guilt, this determination not to screw up again.

Clara knew James Foster. He was a good man, a good father—but he demanded a lot. He was an innovative scientist who'd achieved a great deal in his lifetime and expected the same from his children.

She could only imagine how that sort of expectation, weighted down by his own guilt, had driven Jacob to such lengths to succeed.

She focused on her almost-ex-husband again, seeing him as if through a new camera lens. Suddenly, the man she'd thought she'd known inside out had turned out to be someone else entirely.

Someone she might never have had the chance to get to know were it not for an ill-timed snowfall and a castle in the middle of nowhere.

He was the father of her child. The man she'd always believed had no interest in kids or a family because he had other priorities—namely, chasing success. But that was only half of the truth, she realised now.

He wasn't chasing success; he was running away from failure. Because Jacob Foster was scared. Deathly afraid of screwing up. That was why he'd worked so hard to show her the trappings of success, not knowing that what she really wanted was to have her husband with her. This was why he'd avoided a family, not realising what Clara herself had only learned once Ivy had come into her life: that children, family and the love they brought were what made failure bearable, what made every setback something you could recover from.

Jacob had missed out on four years of Ivy's life. But, if Clara was right, if she could convince him that one teen-age mistake didn't have to ruin his whole life, was there a chance that he might not have to miss any more?

And did she have the courage to find out? She wasn't sure.

'All these years,' she said slowly, choosing her words with great care, 'you've been blaming yourself for this?'

'It was my fault,' Jacob reiterated. 'Of course I have.'

'Does Heather hold it against you? Your father? Your mother?' Clara knew the family, and she thought she knew the answer to two of those questions. But she wasn't quite sure about the third.

'Heather… I'm not even sure how much she remembers. And Mum won't talk about it, ever, so I don't know how she feels.' Clara felt sure that they would have forgiven him long ago. But that wasn't enough, not if Jacob hadn't forgiven himself. And if Sheila wouldn't talk about it… Clara could understand that. Of course Sheila would want to protect her daughter, and try to block out the memories of her being hurt. But, by refusing to talk about it, she might not have realised how badly she was hurting her son.

'What about your father?' James Foster was a fair man usually, but one with exceptionally high expectations. Why else would Jacob have gone to such trouble putting together a perfect Christmas for him?

'I… Like I said. He calls it our lucky escape,' Jacob said. 'I think it reminds him of how quickly things can change. Once Heather was home from the hospital…he made me make him a promise. A promise to never screw up like that again. And I haven't.'

He'd lived his whole life trying not to fail. What would that do to a person? What had it done to Jacob?

'At least, not until you walked out that last time,' he added.

The words flowed like cold water over her. He considered their marriage his personal failure. Well, of course he did; she could see that now. But before today…she hadn't been sure he had cared that much at all.

'Me leaving…that wasn't just *your* failure, Jacob. We were too young—we wanted different things. That's all.' Except now she was imagining the life that they maybe could have had, if she'd known his secret sooner. If she'd understood, been able to convince him that blaming himself wasn't getting him anywhere… Was it too late for that now?

'I really thought we were supposed to be together, you know.' The wistful tone of his voice caught her by surprise. 'That's the only reason I risked it. I knew I couldn't take responsibility for a child again, but I thought that maybe, just maybe, I could take care of you. But I was wrong.'

Clara's heart twisted. She couldn't leave him like this, believing this. She had to help heal Jacob's heart, even if it was the last act of their marriage. But dare she try to show him another life, one where he didn't have to be so scared of failure? Where love could be his, no matter what went wrong? Where forgiveness was automatic?

Did she even believe that love was possible any more?

She wasn't sure. But, for Ivy's sake, she knew she needed to find out for certain.

One night. That was all she had to give. One night to find out if there really could possibly be a future in which Jacob might choose to be a part of his daughter's life and maybe even forgive Clara for keeping her existence a secret from him.

One night to find out if their marriage had a future after all.

By the time the snow cleared she needed to know for certain, one way or the other.

She was almost scared to find out which it would be. But, for her daughter, she'd take the risk.

Clara swallowed around the lump that had formed in her throat.

'Come on,' she said. 'I've lit the fire in the main sitting room. Let's take some food and drinks through there where it's more comfortable. We've got a long, cold night ahead of us.'

CHAPTER FIFTEEN

JACOB SCRUBBED A HAND over his face as he stared at his reflection in the bathroom mirror. He needed to get a grip. Clara was waiting out there, probably with a glass of something, definitely with a romantic fire lit and festive food. He needed to focus. He needed to figure out how not to mess up whatever happened next.

It was too late for Heather. The scars he'd caused would be with her for life; he'd accepted that long ago. He was just thankful she was here. And as for his father... Jacob had limited time. He would never be able to make up for the mistake of his youth, and he couldn't personally change the weather forecast, as much as he might want to right now.

All he could do was work with what he had. And right now that was...Clara.

Why had he never told her about Heather before? Perhaps because he didn't want his wife to know his deepest regrets and mistakes. She'd always looked at him with such love and adoration before their marriage. Awe, even.

It was only once the vows had been spoken that she'd discovered exactly the sort of man he was. And she'd left him, without even knowing his deepest shame.

Maybe she'd always had a better understanding of who he really was than he'd given her credit for.

Could he change that?

He needed to ask her about Ivy, he realised. It was strange; he'd only known that he was a father for a couple of hours but already that knowledge was buzzing at the back of his head, every moment, colouring his every thought. He just didn't quite have a handle on how he felt about it yet—at least, not beyond the initial terror.

At least Clara understood at last why he couldn't be a father.

And now…what? What did Clara want from him now?

And would he be able to give it?

It was time to find out.

'I've put the oven on for some nibbles,' Clara said, smiling at Jacob as he opened the door. 'Remind me to go and put them in to cook when my phone buzzes?'

'Sure.' He took the glass of wine she offered him and returned her smile as well as he could.

'I figured that maybe we should go for something a little more easy-going than the hard spirits, seeing as it is still only barely half past four,' she said.

'Ah, but it is Christmas Eve,' he pointed out. 'Everyone knows that wine o'clock comes earlier on Christmas Eve.'

'Which is why we're having wine. Not brandy.'

'Fair enough.'

She grinned, raised her glass, and the last of the tension he'd felt lingering from the emotional exchange in the kitchen evaporated. How did she do that? Clara had always been able to make him relax, but usually it had involved a rather different range of techniques. But now he was starting to think it had just been her, that the massages or the sex or even the wine had just been accessories, a mask, even, that was hiding the truth.

Clara just made him feel better.

How had he forgotten that over the past five years? How had he forgotten how it felt to be the centre of her world? To have her focus all that love and attention on him?

And, more to the point, what had he done to earn it back now?

'So, we're stuck here,' Clara said, settling onto the sofa in front of the promised roaring fire. 'At least until tomorrow at the earliest.'

'Are you okay with that?' he asked, suddenly more aware

that this wasn't just his own personal disaster. Clara had Christmas plans that had been ruined too. It might have taken him a while to catch up, but now he needed her to know that he wasn't just thinking about himself.

'Not really.' Clara plastered on the most falsely cheery smile he'd ever seen. 'But it's the situation, and we can't change that. So we just need to figure out how to make the most of it.'

Her smile settled into something a little sadder but more real. Something more familiar too. And suddenly he had an idea of exactly what they might do to pass the time…and it wasn't very in keeping with their divorce plans.

'What did you have in mind?' he asked, clearing his throat as he tried to disperse the images filling his head. But really… Secluded castle, snowed in, roaring fire… There was even a sheepskin rug in front of it, just waiting for naked bodies.

But not his and Clara's bodies. Because that would be wrong. Somehow.

Why would that be wrong again?

Clara's teeth pressed against her lower lip before she answered, and Jacob's mind wandered on a little field trip again.

'I thought maybe you might want to hear a little about Ivy.'

He swallowed, hard. *Ivy.* His daughter. Fear rose in his throat once more at the thought. 'I'd like to know a little more about what happened. After you left, I mean.' Facts, those he could control, could understand. So he'd focus on the events—what happened and when. 'What did you tell people?'

'What people?' Clara asked with a half-smile. 'Once I left you…I didn't have anyone. Until Ivy came along, and until I met Merry.'

He hated the thought of her all alone in the world. But

it had always been her choice. 'What did you tell Merry? The truth?'

Clara shook her head. 'I told her that I'd had a one-night stand after I left you, and that he didn't want anything to do with the result.' *The result. A daughter.* 'That's what I told anyone who asked about Ivy's dad.'

'What did you tell her?' He swallowed. 'Ivy.' *His* daughter.

'That I loved her father very much but he couldn't be with us.' Her gaze locked onto his. 'So, the truth. That's why I couldn't come back. I took that pregnancy test and…I knew I couldn't have both. I could have you or a baby. And I chose Ivy.'

Of course she had. Wasn't that what any reasonable human would do? Any loving mother?

'You chose to lie to me,' he said, his voice hard. 'You chose to take away *my* choice. To take away the rights of my parents to see their grandchild, to even know that they had one. You made a decision that wasn't just yours to make.' It didn't matter that her choice had been the right one. It should have been his too.

'It was my body. My choice.'

'My daughter.' Hearing it out loud was even more frightening. 'Five years, and you never even told me she existed.' Never gave him the chance to understand what had really happened between them.

'You didn't want a family—you made that crystal-clear to me from the outset. Or at least once we were married, when it was too late for me to do anything about it.'

'So what? I'm allowed to make that choice. What did you think I would do? Did you think I'd order you to get rid of the baby?' Even the thought made his skin crawl. If she truly believed that about him, then she'd never known him at all. Their whole marriage had been a mistake.

'No!' Clara's eyes grew wide with shock. 'I didn't… I

knew you wouldn't do that. No, Jacob. It wasn't that.' He shouldn't feel relieved—everything was still such a mess. But a very small part of him relaxed just a little bit at her words.

'Then what? Why didn't you talk to me at the time?'

Clara ran a shaky hand through her dark hair. 'I didn't find out until after I left. I took a dozen pregnancy tests in a hotel bathroom, just to be sure. But… I'd already left you, Jacob. Again. And I realised that was all we'd been doing since the day we'd got married: pulling apart until we snapped back together again. Everything would be perfect, then you'd get caught up in some project and I wouldn't see you for weeks. I'd get lonely, I'd walk out to get your attention…and then you'd win me back and it would be all flowers and romance. But only for a while, until it started all over again.' She sighed. 'I knew that even if by some miracle you changed your mind about having a family—which you wouldn't have done—we couldn't have brought up a child like that. So I made the decision not to come back.'

'And since then?' He didn't want her answers to make sense. And even if they did, he was still furious. Not because she was wrong—he couldn't say he would have changed his mind about wanting a family. He still hadn't, even though he apparently had one. But because she'd taken away his chance to decide. She'd made him powerless. He felt the same helplessness he'd felt the night Heather had been hurt. And he couldn't forgive that. 'It's been five years, Clara. Did you really at no point think, "Ooh, maybe I should let Jacob know about *our child*"?'

'Of course I did!'

'Then what stopped you?' Because that was the part he really couldn't understand. Maybe a child meant that they couldn't be together any longer; maybe she was right that their marriage couldn't have taken that. But that was still no reason not to tell him.

'You did.' Her words were soft but heavy. Full of meaning. And he understood them instantly. He hadn't been good enough. He'd failed as a husband and Clara had known he'd fail as a father—and so had he! That was exactly why he'd been so adamant about not becoming one.

But hearing her say it out loud, seeing it come from those same lips he'd been thinking about kissing… Jacob felt his heart break, just a little.

'I see.'

'I'm not sure you do.' Clara twisted her hands together as she stared up at him. 'I knew you didn't want a child. Knew that Ivy was the last thing you wanted in your life. You'd made that very clear.'

'So you were sparing me the knowledge? It was for my own good?' he asked, incredulous. Not even Clara could believe that.

'No. It was for Ivy's. I couldn't let you reject her, and let her live her life knowing that she wasn't wanted. I wouldn't do that to her. Not even for you.'

Jacob looked away. 'I can understand that, I guess. And…as much as I hate it, you made the right decision. For both of us.'

'Did I?' His gaze snapped to her face as she spoke. 'I always thought so. But after this week…I'm not so sure.'

'What do you mean?'

'I mean…I thought it was all over for us, the moment I left.' Clara's gaze met his and he felt it deep in his soul. He was missing something here. And he had a feeling he couldn't afford not to listen to her this time. 'But you never would sign those divorce papers.'

It was a risk. A calculated one, but a risk nonetheless. Still, the more she thought about it, the more she wondered. Yes, it had been five years. And yes, she understood now that Jacob's fear of failure must have played into his reluctance to actually give her the divorce. But surely the easier choice would have been to move on, to start over and succeed with someone else, if that was all it was.

There had to be something more. A bigger, better reason why he'd never really moved on from their marriage. From loving her.

Clara knew she had the advantage there. She'd never been able to move on completely, or leave Jacob behind, because his eyes had stared at her every day over the breakfast table, looking out from their daughter's face. She could never cut him out of her memories, even if she'd done her best to cut him out of her life.

But Jacob… Once they left here, that could be it for him. As soon as the snow melted, he could sign those papers and walk away for ever. Never see Ivy. Never see Clara again.

If that was what he really wanted. But she was starting to suspect it wasn't.

'What do you want from me?' Jacob asked, pulling back to put a little more distance between them. 'I've given you all of my secrets now. You know everything. So, what do you want?'

'I want you to know you have a choice,' Clara said slowly, thinking it through as she spoke. 'You have a daughter, and you know that now. You can choose to ignore that fact, but you can't deny that you know it. So you have to decide—do you want to be a part of Ivy's life?'

She held her breath while she waited for his answer.

'You'd let me? If I wanted?'

'Of course.' Clara nodded. 'But there are conditions.'

'I thought there might be.' He folded his arms across his chest. 'Go on, then.'

'If you want in, you have to be one hundred per cent sure. Because once she meets you…you're her father. You have to be there for her, for everything she needs. You can't let her down.'

'And if I can't commit to that?'

'Then you walk away now and Ivy will never know that you exist.' It was just what she'd planned, the way she'd lived for so long. So why did the idea feel like such a wrench to her heart now?

'What about you? You'll always know. And what about us? Is our marriage part of this deal?'

Clara shook her head. 'I don't know. It depends.' She couldn't think beyond Ivy right now.

'Depends on what?'

She looked up and met his gaze again. 'On why you never signed the divorce papers.'

He made a huffing sound that was almost a laugh and put his wine glass down on the table. Clara watched the firelight dancing across his skin and wondered if she really could let him go again without touching him one more time…

'If I signed them,' Jacob said, the words slow and precise, 'I knew, once they were signed, that there was no chance of you ever coming back. And I wasn't ready to face that.'

'Because it would have meant you'd failed?'

'Because I couldn't imagine my life without you in it, even when you weren't there.'

The breath caught in Clara's throat. Had he spent the past five years the way she had, imagining a parallel life in which they were still together? Another universe where they were happy?

'I couldn't let go of us either,' she admitted quietly. 'That's one of the reasons why I never pushed back when your lawyers put obstacles in my way.'

'I wondered.' Jacob shifted closer, just near enough so that his sleeve brushed against hers. Barely touching, but still she felt it like a lightning strike through her body. It was as if everything she'd ever been missing was finally coming home. 'I hoped.'

'I guess it's not as easy as all that to just leave a year of marriage behind,' she said, swallowing hard as she saw the heat in his eyes.

'Oh, I don't know. The marriage part was only ever a piece of paper. It was *you* I couldn't bear to be without.' Not the status. Not the band on his finger that showed his clients that he was serious, grown up, able to take care of business.

Her. Just Clara.

He wanted her, the way that her own family never had. And even if he decided to walk away tomorrow, she owed herself one more night of being wanted like that.

She knew now the real reason why she'd never signed those papers either. Because she still wanted him too. She'd been waiting for him to confirm that it was over.

And suddenly it wasn't. It wasn't over at all.

She couldn't say which of them moved first, but in a blink of an eye the distance between them disappeared and she was close enough to feel his breath against her lips. Her tongue darted out to run over them, as if she could taste him there already.

Jacob groaned, low, in the back of his throat, and then the millimetres between them vanished altogether.

The kiss felt just as Clara remembered—like love, and home, and warmth—and she wondered how she'd lived without this for five long and lonely years. How she had ever believed, even for a moment, that things could be over between them.

She knew now, in that instant, that things could never be truly finished between her and Jacob. Whatever happened next, however large the distance between them might grow, it would never be the end. She would always be connected to this man, in a way far more elemental and real than a mere marriage certificate. It wasn't even only Ivy who held her tied to him; it was her own heart.

And that, she'd discovered, she couldn't organise and order into submission. Her heart had a life of its own, a love of its own, and it had chosen Jacob six years ago and had never let go.

She knew now it never would.

Jacob pulled back, just enough to look into her eyes, his forehead resting against hers and his breath coming as fast as her own.

'Okay?' he murmured.

'Just fine,' Clara replied, her mouth strangely dry.

She knew there were questions to be answered, things to consider and decisions to be made, eventually. But, right in this moment, her world had shrunk to little more than just the two of them and the snow falling outside that had kept them together on Christmas Eve, six years to the day after they met.

Then her phone buzzed and she remembered the oven warming and the food waiting to be cooked. She pulled back but Jacob's hand shot out and he wrapped his fingers around her waist.

'Ignore it,' he whispered.

'Aren't you hungry?' Clara asked.

'Not for anything you can cook.' Jacob gave her a slow, hot smile and Clara knew that dinner would be several hours away.

And by that time she would be ravenous.

This time, it was Clara who leant in to kiss him first and that kiss led to many, many more, each more wonderful than she'd remembered, or ever dreamt she'd feel again.

CHAPTER SIXTEEN

JACOB STRETCHED OUT across the sheets of the four-poster bed, luxuriating in the warmth of the fire burning in the grate, the wonderful ache in his muscles from a night of loving his wife and the feel of Clara's smooth, bare skin beside him.

Well.

That wasn't quite what he'd had in mind when he'd envisioned the perfect family Christmas, but now it was here…

He'd forgotten how in tune they were, physically. They might not have been able to communicate all the issues they had between them in their marriage, and in their pasts, but physically they'd always been able to express themselves totally. The way their bodies moved against each other, the way their fingers sought out sensitive places, the way their mouths moved across skin… That was beyond conversation, beyond language, even. It was innate. It was special.

It was something Jacob knew he'd never find with another living soul, no matter how hard he looked.

Maybe that was the real reason he'd held up the divorce. Maybe it hadn't been his need not to fail, or to prove something, or to make Clara as miserable as she'd made him by leaving.

Maybe it had been as simple as knowing that Clara was his only chance at true happiness.

Only an idiot would give that up without a fight. But when Clara had left she'd denied him that fight, taking the battleground far away, somewhere he couldn't reach.

But now he had his opportunity.

His last chance to win back his wife.

But if he wanted that chance, he had to make a decision—

the biggest he might ever make. He couldn't rush it, just because sex with Clara was so good. This mattered—Ivy mattered. Even if he couldn't be her father, he still knew she mattered more than anything, especially to Clara. So he had to get this right. He wouldn't hurt another child—physically or emotionally.

One night with Clara wasn't enough to brush away all of his fears, and he'd be an idiot if he thought it could. But Clara believed in him. That counted for something.

It counted for a hell of a lot, in fact.

But was it enough?

Only Jacob could make that decision. And he wasn't sure where to start.

Clara woke to the glorious pressure of Jacob's lips against her skin and let herself just enjoy the moment for almost a full minute before reality came crashing down around her.

She'd slept with her ex-husband. She'd let herself get carried away by the connection between them before they'd come to any decision about Ivy—just as she'd promised herself she wouldn't do.

She hadn't even worked on persuading him that having a child in his life would not be the terrible, horrible thing he imagined.

She'd done nothing to convince him that Heather's childhood accident shouldn't affect his whole life, or to deal with the issues that had spanned their marriage and led to her leaving in the first place. Instead, she'd just taken what she'd wanted, selfishly and greedily, and without thinking about what would happen in the morning.

But now it was morning.

She sighed, puffing air out into the pillow. They had talked, they'd covered all sorts of secrets and she'd given him her terms. That wasn't nothing. She understood him a lot better now. She'd just have to hope it was enough and that he knew what he was committing to if he chose to be part of Ivy's life.

Jacob's hands ran up the length of her body, his fingertips skimming her skin and making her shiver. She almost didn't want to move, didn't want to give any sign that she was awake, because the moment she did the night would be over and they would have to deal with the hard decisions to be made in the cold light of day. If Jacob said no, if this really was the end for them, she just wanted one more moment in his arms...

But Ivy was out there waiting for her.

Opening her eyes, Clara realised that they hadn't even managed to close the curtains before falling into the massive four-poster bed the night before, and the winter sun that Jacob had been so sure that Scotland never saw was streaming in through the glass.

'It's stopped snowing,' Clara said, blinking in the light.

'Mmm-hmm,' Jacob murmured, his lips busy working their way across her neck. 'So it has.'

Suddenly, Clara's mind overruled her body and she twisted around in his arms to face him, even as her skin called out for more. 'If the snow has stopped they might be clearing the roads.'

Jacob's hands fell away from her. 'Are you still that keen to get away from me for Christmas?'

'No! I just...' *I'm desperate to get back to our daughter.* 'Ivy will be waiting. Besides, I put a lot of work into setting up your perfect Christmas, you realise. I want your family to be able to enjoy it, if at all possible.' She tried to insert some levity into her words, even though inside, her heart ached.

With a groan, Jacob rolled out of bed, naked despite the cold morning air, and crossed to the window. 'I think I can see the ploughs working their way up from the bottom of the hill.'

Clara swallowed. That meant that she'd be able to get home to Ivy soon, and the relief she felt at that realisation was huge. She just wished it wasn't also tinged with the sadness of having to leave Jacob.

'So,' he asked, sitting on the edge of the bed and pulling the blanket back over him. 'You're the planner. What happens now?'

Nothing like an approaching snowplough—and ex-in-laws—to get the brain working fast in the morning.

'Well, if they're still at the bottom of the hill we probably have an hour or more before the roads are clear enough to drive. You should call your family, see where they are and if they're willing to drive over now. I can get things going downstairs—get the turkey in the oven and so on. Most of the food is ready prepared so it won't take too much effort to get the meal cooking. I can't imagine the staff I hired are going to make it here now, anyway, but we can do it between us, I'm sure.' She wished she had her handbag with her, with her planner inside. She needed her lists. But they had been the last things on her mind when she and Jacob had retired to the bedroom the night before... She checked her watch. 'Lunch is going to be rather later than is traditional at this point, but at least it will happen. The presents are all ready, under the tree, and the... What?' she asked, suddenly aware that Jacob was barely containing his laughter. 'What's so funny?'

'You,' he said, grinning. 'You sitting there, naked, in total professional mode.'

'You think me being professional is amusing?' Clara asked, bristling.

'No, I think it's hot as hell,' he admitted. 'But when I asked what happens now... I wasn't talking about the perfect Foster family Christmas. I was talking about us.'

His grin faded away as he finished speaking, and she stared down at her hands to avoid his gaze. Talking about work was *so* much easier than discussing their mess of a relationship. Of a marriage.

'Unless you already knew that and were avoiding the subject.' There was no laughter in Jacob's voice now.

'No, I wasn't. It's just that whatever happens next... It's up to you, Jacob.' Apparently there was no putting it off any longer. 'I know you haven't had much time, and we were, well, busy for a lot of it. But have you thought about whether you want to meet Ivy?'

Jacob blew out a long breath. 'Yeah. It's pretty much *all* I've been thinking about since you told me. Well, on and off.' He flashed her a smile that told her she'd been a pretty good distraction.

'And?'

'Honestly? I'm scared, Clara. I never planned this. I didn't even get the usual nine months to get used to the idea.'

'I know. I'm sorry.'

'But...' She held her breath, waiting for him to continue. 'I'm not willing to give this—us—up. Not yet. Not without trying.'

But trying wasn't good enough. 'Jacob, if you step into her life you can't just—'

'Step out again, I know,' Jacob said. 'But I've got an idea, if you're willing. A compromise.'

Clara gave a slow nod. 'Okay. Go on.'

He wrapped an arm around her bare waist and pulled her close. 'Bring Ivy and Merry up to the castle for Christmas. We don't need to tell her, or my family, anything just yet. Just...give me a chance to meet her, spend time with her. See if I can manage that without a full-blown panic attack.' He made it sound like a joke but Clara suspected it wasn't. Not entirely, anyway. 'Break me in gently. Then we can decide if we should tell her.'

We. We can decide. Clara liked the sound of that. The two of them. Just like it should have been from the start.

She nodded. 'Okay. I'll call Merry.'

'In a moment.' Jacob darted forward, capturing her lips with his own again. 'How long did you say we had until the roads were clear?' he asked between kisses.

'Sadly, not long enough,' Clara said.

He kissed her one last time, hard and deep and full of promise. Then he pulled away with a groan. 'Then I suppose we'd better make ourselves respectable.' With a wink back at her, he strolled towards the bathroom, whistling.

Clara gave herself one whole minute lying back in bed, replaying the events of the last day in her head. Maybe, just maybe, this could all work out okay. Maybe she didn't have to choose between her two futures any more. Maybe they could be a real family at last.

She smiled to herself. Maybe this would be the best Christmas ever, after all.

Then she sat up and called Merry.

CHAPTER SEVENTEEN

JACOB STOOD AT THE open front door of the castle and watched as the large SUV his father had hired weaved its way up the hill towards him. Heather had texted earlier to say they were waiting at the hotel down the road for the snowploughs to finish clearing the way, and that they had coffee and Christmas cake and carols so Christmas was off to a brilliant start. He wondered if they'd met Merry and Ivy already.

Somehow it seemed that, despite the huge odds stacked against it, he might actually pull off the perfect Christmas after all.

Perfect for more than just his dad, now that Clara was there too. Jacob was apprehensive still, about meeting Ivy. But Clara had promised to introduce him just as 'Jacob'—no pressure, no expectations, just a chance to get to know the little girl he'd helped to make, if not to raise.

And if that went well...who knew? If Clara thought he could be a father, a real husband again, maybe it was possible.

For the first time since his father's diagnosis, the future looked like a place he could bear to live in, even if he knew the inevitable losses coming his way would still be soul-destroying. With Clara at his side, he had faith that he could make it through them.

Everything seemed possible when Clara was with him.

'Are they nearly here?' Clara appeared from the kitchen, a festive apron still wrapped around her waist, and she wiped flour from her hands onto it. 'Have I got time to wash up?'

'Nope.' Jacob pointed down the path. 'That's Dad's car.

They'll be here any moment.' The excitement thrumming through his veins was only partly to do with the festivities and pulling off the whole plan. Mostly, he suspected, it had something to do with Clara standing beside him, smelling of cinnamon. He hadn't felt this kind of excitement at Christmas since he'd been about ten.

'Oh, no. I look a state.'

'You look beautiful.' He snaked an arm around her waist and kissed the top of her slightly floury hair. 'What have you been making?'

'Last-minute mince pies,' she said, absently. She peered out of the door. 'There's Merry's hire car too, just behind them.'

Merry. And Ivy. Jacob's chest tightened and he focused on breathing in and out, creating steam in the frosty air. He could do this. 'Nearly time, then.'

'For our perfect Christmas.' Clara's small hand sneaked into his and he felt her warmth throughout his body.

'Ours,' he echoed.

The SUV pulled up onto the driveway with a crunch of snow. 'And here they are! Merry Christmas!' Stepping out into the glorious winter's day, he helped his mum down from the car and held her tightly before hugging Heather and shaking his father's hand.

'We made it!' Heather said, beaming. 'Jacob, this place is incredible!'

'Isn't it? Come on in. Clara's waiting to see you all!' He realised that the second car had pulled up beside the castle too. 'And we've got some other special guests today too.'

Clara's business partner, Merry, stepped out of the car. And behind her walked a small girl. The girl who must be Ivy. His daughter.

A chill settled into Jacob's bones as he watched her smile and bounce out into the snow.

She looked exactly like Heather had as a child.

* * *

'Mummy!' Ivy yelled and raced across the snow into Clara's arms. Dropping to her knees, Clara held her daughter tight and, just for a moment, refused to think about what might happen next. It was Christmas morning and she was with her daughter. That was all that mattered.

'Hello, sweetheart,' Clara murmured. 'I'm so happy to see you.'

'Clara?' Jacob asked, and she could hear the nervousness in his voice.

'We should get everyone inside the castle. It's cold out here,' she said, straightening up to stand again. 'But first… Ivy, this is Jacob. He's the one who planned this whole Christmas in a castle for his family and for us.'

'And then your mum organised it all,' Jacob said, still standing a metre or so away.

Ivy turned her big, blue eyes on him then stuck out a hand. 'I'm Ivy.'

Clara watched Jacob's jaw tighten as he reached out to take his daughter's hand. 'Hi, Ivy. It's brilliant to meet you.'

A bubble of hope floated up inside her. Maybe, just maybe, this might all work out.

Christmas dinner went as well as she could have hoped. Merry kept up a constant stream of inconsequential conversation, for which Clara was eternally grateful. And when James turned to her over Christmas pudding and said how pleased he was to see her again, and how he hoped she'd become a permanent fixture of the family once more, Clara even managed a polite smile.

'It's very kind of you all to let us impose on your family Christmas,' she said. 'Especially since we were caught here by the snow. I know it's been very special for Ivy.'

'It's been very special for us spending time with Ivy too.' James's pointed look was knowing, but Clara ignored it.

She didn't want to give anyone false hope about the future of their families.

Least of all herself.

'Time for presents!' Heather announced, jumping to her feet, seeming more like a child than a twenty-something.

'But I thought Father Christmas got snowed in at the North Pole,' Ivy piped up and Clara winced.

Heather smiled down at the girl and Clara realised that Merry must have primed everyone on the story they'd told her. 'Well, if the roads here got clear enough for us to make it to the castle for Christmas, maybe Father Christmas was able to get out too. If he's been, I reckon there'll be more presents by the fireplace next to the tree. Shall we go and check?'

'Okay.' Ivy reached up to take Heather's hand and followed her into the hallway. Moments later, they all heard a gasp, and Ivy came racing back into the dining room. 'Mummy! Mummy! He's been! He must have come while we were eating dinner!'

'Really? Fantastic!' Clara caught Merry's eye over Ivy's head and mouthed *Thank you,* but Merry just shrugged.

They all made their way into the hall, where seven red stockings hung by the fire, each with a name tag hanging from it.

'It's a Christmas miracle,' Jacob said drily, but he squeezed Clara's hand when no one was looking. She squeezed back. Really, he was coping surprisingly well. A lesser man might have been driven to distraction by Ivy's many questions over the dinner table, but he'd answered every one thoughtfully and patiently. He'd even lost some of the slightly panicked air that had surrounded him since Ivy had stepped out of the car.

Clara had seen photos of Heather as a child; she knew exactly what he must have been thinking. But that was why today was so brilliant an opportunity for them to meet.

Heather was right there with them, happy and whole and alive.

The whole set-up was just asking for a happy ever after.

Clara smiled to herself as she watched Ivy dig through her stocking. She unwrapped the bike lock, helmet, knee and elbow pads that Clara had bought for her, then reached into the bottom to find an envelope. She tore it open, then frowned at the ornate letters printed on the card. Merry leaned over her shoulder.

'It says *Look outside.*'

Ivy dropped her haul and dashed out of the front door, squealing with delight. 'It's a bike! A purple bike, just like I wanted!'

'How on earth did you get that up here without her noticing?' Clara asked as they followed her outside.

'Trade secret,' Merry replied, tapping the side of her nose. 'Plus we bumped into Jacob's family at the hotel before we drove up. That helped.'

'Mummy! Come see!' Ivy called, and Clara went to watch her daughter wobble across the snowy ground on her new bike. Then Ivy yelled, 'Jacob! Come watch me ride!'

But Jacob wasn't there. Clara frowned; he'd been beside her before they'd come outside. What had happened to him?

'I'll go find him for you, sweetie,' she told Ivy and, leaving Merry in charge of supervising the bike riding, headed back through the giant wooden doors into the castle.

'All I'm saying is, Clara has taken on a lot of responsibility, raising that child alone.' James Foster's voice echoed off the stone walls, and Clara's frown deepened as she followed the sound. She didn't like the idea of her father-in-law discussing her in her absence—especially when it involved a subject he knew nothing about.

'Dad, I know that. And if…well, if things had been different…' Jacob sounded more stressed than he had since the moment they'd realised they were snowed in the day before. Clara disliked that even more.

Stepping through the doorway into the kitchen, she coughed loudly to announce her presence. 'Jacob?' she added for good measure. 'Ivy's looking for you. She wants you to see her riding her bike.'

Jacob spun round, apparently surprised to see her there. 'Right. I'll be right there.'

But his father's hand was already on his arm. And James was murmuring something more, something she couldn't hear.

She'd always been fond of Jacob's father. But, right now, she wondered if she hadn't paid enough attention to James's relationship with his son.

Jacob nodded and stepped away, taking Clara's hand and turning her back the way she'd come. 'Come on then,' he said, flashing her a smile that didn't reach his eyes. 'Let's go see your girl cycle.'

Clara has taken on a lot of responsibility.

His father's words echoed through his head as he watched Ivy gleefully cycling up and down the same stretch of driveway. The snow was still piled up in banks on either side, but they'd cleared enough that she could ride in one big circle around the cars.

Raising that child alone.

He'd wanted to explain—tell him how he hadn't known about Ivy. How, if he had, he'd have done things differently. But the truth was, he didn't know for sure if that was the truth.

Today had been wonderful. He'd honestly enjoyed Ivy's company, loved hearing her questions and answering them as best he could. He'd loved watching the pure joy on her face as she'd opened her presents. Loved standing with Clara, seeing her bursting with pride for her girl.

Their girl. Their child.

But Christmas Day wasn't like any other day, was it? And life wasn't all Christmas Days. It was balancing work and family, and looking after each other, and too many other everyday things he didn't even know how to imagine yet. Could he do *that?* He didn't know.

He wouldn't know unless he tried.

And now that you're in that child's life? his father had asked in a murmur, while Clara had stood waiting. *I hope that you will live up to your responsibilities, Jacob.*

Could he? And could he risk it, not knowing for sure?

He wanted to; he knew that much. He wanted to try, for the first time since Clara had walked out. He wanted to try for something he wasn't sure he could succeed at, something he was certain he didn't deserve. But did that make it the right decision?

'Look at me, Jacob!' Ivy called out to him and he waved to show her he was watching. Taking in every second of her gleeful, happy ride.

Could he walk away from this? Maybe that was the question he should be asking.

When it happened, it happened in slow motion.

Ivy was still waving back, riding one-handed as she wobbled along on her stabilisers, not looking where she was going. She couldn't have seen the rock, hidden under the snow bank. As he watched, her front wheel bashed into it, jerking her to a halt, sending Ivy flying over the handlebars into the snow.

Jacob darted forward but he was a full second behind Clara, too slow to reach Ivy first. And too slow to warn them about the wedge of snow, dislodged from the castle walls above as it slid down towards them.

He shouted to them to move, but Clara was too busy pulling Ivy up out of the snow bank, holding her close as she cried. Without thinking, he dived forward and yanked them both aside, shielding them with his body as the snow landed, hard and cold and wet against his back, even through his coat.

'What… Where did that come from?' Clara asked. 'The roof?'

Jacob nodded, too winded still to speak.

'You saved us.' Ivy stared up at him, her eyes wet with tears, but filled with a look of trust and hope that was all too familiar. Jacob felt it like a stab wound to the heart.

That was how Heather had looked at him when she was a child. Before the accident.

He didn't deserve Ivy's trust. And he'd only betray it in the end if he stayed. He couldn't let her believe otherwise, not when he knew how badly he could fail.

He couldn't be her father.

He stumbled backwards, almost losing his footing on the snow. 'I need to go…dry off.' Turning away, he headed back into the castle, head down.

He needed to escape. He needed to get away from those eyes. From that faith and expectation and responsibility.

From everything he'd always failed at before.

'Ivy's fine.' Clara leant against the bedroom door frame, watching Jacob towelling off his hair. 'Your mother is feeding her mince pies and hot chocolate. She's been so spoilt today she's never going to want to leave, you realise.'

But they were going to have to leave. They had to go back to London, to the real world and their real lives.

And, from the way Jacob had just run from them, Clara had a horrible feeling they'd be going alone.

Jacob looked up, guilt shining in his eyes. 'I'm glad she's not hurt.'

'Thanks to you.'

He shook his head. 'I should have got her out of the way sooner. Or stopped her from falling. Told her to keep both hands on the handlebars, watch where she was going. Something.'

'She's a child, Jacob,' Clara said, sitting on the edge of the bed. 'Children have accidents all the time. It wasn't anyone's fault.' Never mind that her own heart had stopped for a moment as she'd watched it happening. She couldn't let Jacob blame himself for this.

'Maybe not. But that just makes it worse.'

Clara frowned. 'How?'

'I couldn't keep her safe, Clara. She was my responsibility for half a day and she got hurt. I wasn't paying enough attention.'

'You know how crazy that sounds, right? It was an accident, Jacob, that's all.' She reached out to touch his arm but he pulled it back, out of reach.

'I can't do this Clara.'

And there it was. The words she'd dared to believe might not be coming. But there they were, out in the world like a final sentence. His last words.

'Because of one stupid accident?'

'Because I'm not the right person for this. I never was. I thought… When I married you, I convinced myself that I could be a good husband just because I *wanted* it so much. Wanted *you* so much.' He ran his fingers through his damp hair, a look of agony on his face. 'And I almost made the same mistake again. I wanted to be with you, with Ivy, so much I thought I could be what you need. But I can't. And it's not fair to Ivy to take that risk. She deserves everything—including a wonderful father. And that's just not me.'

'You're giving up,' Clara said quietly. 'Giving in. Because you're scared.'

'You're right I'm scared. I'm terrified, Clara. And that's a sign. I shouldn't be doing this.'

Anger rose up inside her, the flames licking her insides.

'You're wrong. If you're scared, it's a sign it's worth fighting for.'

Jacob laughed, and it came out harsh and bitter. 'Like you fought for us? You walked out without a backward glance, Clara. And you know what? *You were right.* I admit it. So now it's my turn to do the same.'

'And you never came after me! You wouldn't let me go, wouldn't divorce me, but you wouldn't come after me either. Why was that, Jacob? Because you were too scared to lose me—but too scared to love me too. Too scared to let me in, let me close.'

'And you weren't?'

'Maybe I was. But you know what? I've grown up. I've opened up to you, told you everything. And I took a risk; I gave you a chance. A chance at the best thing you could ever have—being Ivy's father. And you're turning it down?' She shook her head sadly. 'You're an idiot.'

'Maybe I am,' he said, his voice soft. 'But Clara, I'd rather hurt you both now than risk breaking you later.'

She stared at him. He was really doing this. After everything they'd shared, said and done, he was pushing her away again.

'One day you're going to realise,' she said. 'Keeping people at arm's length doesn't keep them safe, Jacob. It only keeps them lonely.'

He didn't answer.

Clara turned and left, closing the door behind her, alone once again. Alone, not because he didn't want her, or even because he didn't love her, but because he didn't have the courage to be with her and Ivy.

She wasn't sure if that was better or worse.

'So that's that, then?' Merry asked, and when Clara looked up she saw her best friend standing a little way along the corridor.

'You heard?'

'Enough,' Merry confirmed. 'What do you want to do now? Sheila has invited us to stay here for the night, and Ivy looks close to falling asleep on her feet.'

'I know.' Clara chewed her lip. Part of her wanted to get out of there the first chance they got, but another larger part didn't want to do anything to ruin Christmas Day for the others. She couldn't stay but she couldn't run either. Not just yet.

'Let's put Ivy to bed,' she decided. 'Then we can clear up down here.'

'And then?'

'Then, the moment everyone else goes to bed, we get Ivy in the hire car and drive back to London,' Clara said.

Christmas was nearly over.

It was time for her new life to begin again.

CHAPTER EIGHTEEN

'I ONLY ASKED if you'd spoken to her,' Sheila said, throwing up her hands defensively. 'There's no need to snap.'

'I didn't snap,' Jacob said, knowing full well that he had. But really, it had been four days. No, he hadn't spoken to Clara. And no, he had no intention of doing so.

His family hadn't taken Clara's departure in the middle of the night well, or the note that she'd left explaining that she and Merry had work back in London they needed to return to. Jacob, who was more used to being walked out on in the middle of the night, had simply crumpled the note up and thrown it on the fire.

He'd made his decision. He couldn't blame her for abiding by it. Not this time.

'Is Dad in his study?' Jacob asked, looking past his mother down the hallway at Honeysuckle House. The Christmas decorations were still up and he wanted nothing more than to tear them down. Wasn't it New Year yet? Couldn't they move on?

He was ready to start his new life, without Clara. Without Ivy. He just needed the world to stop reminding him of them both.

Both. That was the biggest surprise. He'd expected to be haunted by Clara's memory—he had been often enough over the past five years to have grown almost used to it. But Ivy... Jacob had spent less than a day with her, and yet everywhere he turned he seemed to find reminders of her. A girl on a bike, a small red coat, a too bright smile, a Christmas cracker like the ones she'd insisted on pulling with everyone. Even the Christmas lights made him think of her.

Clearly he was losing his mind.

'Yes, he's upstairs, I think,' Sheila said, answering the question Jacob had almost forgotten he'd asked.

'Right.' He made for the stairs, his mind still occupied by thoughts of an empty castle, and a note he never wanted to see again.

He'd hoped that a business conversation with his father would take his mind off things, as well as giving him a chance to check on James's health after the trek to Scotland and back. But, instead, he found his dad in a pensive, family orientated frame of mind. Which was the last thing Jacob wanted.

'Come in! Sit down!' James motioned towards the visitor's chair. 'Pull it up over here. I'm just looking through some old photo albums.'

Jacob's stomach clenched as he saw the open page, filled with photos of Heather as a little girl, through from babyhood to a final one of her with bandages wrapped around her arms and scratches and cuts on her face. Why had they even taken that picture? Who wanted to remember that moment in time?

He reached across to try and turn the page but James stopped him with a gentle hand on his wrist. 'She really did look uncannily like Ivy, don't you think?'

'Yes. And no, before you ask, I haven't spoken to them.'

'Why?' James asked. 'Really, Jacob. Why haven't you gone after them?'

'Because we decided it would be best for Ivy if I wasn't part of her life.' The truth was always easier than a lie. 'I can't commit to being a father right now.'

'And whose decision was this, exactly? Yours or Clara's?'

Jacob looked away. 'Does it matter? She kept Ivy's very existence from me for five years. I think we can assume that Clara agrees I'm not the right person to be a father.'

'I think she was scared. Maybe even as scared as you are right now.'

Jacob looked up to meet his father's gaze and found a depth of knowing and understanding there that shocked him to his core.

'When your mother first told me she was pregnant with you, I was terrified,' James admitted, flipping to the next page of the album as if his words were of no consequence. But Jacob clung to them anyway. 'I had no idea how to be a father—I was a scientist! An academic, at that point. I was the only child of an only child, so there had never been any babies around when I was growing up. I hadn't the first idea what you should do with one.'

'So what did you do?'

'I learnt,' James said bluntly. 'Because I knew that being a father was the one thing in life I couldn't afford to fail at. So I learnt everything I could.'

'It worked,' Jacob said with a bitter laugh. 'You were an excellent father. Far better than I could ever hope to be.'

'No, I wasn't.'

Jacob looked up at his father in shock. 'You're wrong. I...I couldn't keep my sister safe, or my wife happy or by my side, or even stop Ivy from falling off her bike! But you, you kept our whole family together, all these years.'

James shook his head. 'It's not enough. I think maybe our fear for Heather, after the accident... We focused so hard on her, on keeping her safe, maybe we ignored your needs. I should have told you...so many things. That I'm proud of you. That no one ever blamed you for what happened. It was a freak accident. You didn't *mean* to hurt her. I should have told you that nothing you ever did could make me less proud of you.'

'Dad... You don't have to...' Jacob felt as if his heart was growing in his chest as his father spoke. As if years of armour built of fear and shame were falling away from his shoulders, leaving him lighter than he could remember feeling since he was a child.

'Yes. I do.' James reached out and took Jacob's hand. 'I'm dying. We both know that. And people say you have all sorts of revelations at the end of your life. But that's not what this is. These are all the things I should have told you years ago—that I should have been telling you every day and didn't.'

'And you've said them. Thank you.'

'But that's not all. Son, you have to know…it's okay to fail. It's okay to screw up and make mistakes. As long as you *try again*. When I was inventing, for every thing I created that worked, I made a hundred—a thousand!—that didn't. But I still didn't give up, no matter how many times I failed. That's the key to the things that matter in life. You just have to keep trying.'

'I tried, Dad, with Clara. We both did. Time and again. It just didn't work.' Whatever he did, she was always going to leave him.

'What about with Ivy? Isn't it worth trying again for her?'

'Not if I'm just going to mess it up again.' He'd seen the look on Clara's face when she'd spoken about not wanting Ivy to feel unwanted. He knew where that came from—knew how scared she was of Ivy living through what she'd had to. And maybe she was right not to take that risk.

'As long as you keep trying, you can't get it wrong,' James promised him. 'Look at me. I've been messing up your upbringing for over thirty years, and I'm still trying to make it right. So let me try. And help me succeed.'

'What do you want me to do?'

'I want you to be happy,' James said simply. 'I want you to think about the last time you were truly happy, and do whatever it takes to get you there again. And then I want you to try your best to stay there. Can you do that?'

The last time he had been happy. In bed with Clara at

the castle. Except…no. There was one more moment after that, one more second when he'd felt pure happiness.

Watching Ivy's face when she'd found her bike outside the castle.

Jacob swallowed, hard.

'I think I can,' he said. 'And I'm definitely going to try.'

James clapped him on the shoulder. 'That's my boy.'

Clara was officially pampering herself. Or at least that was what Merry had instructed her to do when she'd shown up to whisk Ivy off to see a pantomime earlier that afternoon.

'You've been working flat out ever since we got back from Scotland. You need a day to relax and get yourself ready for the Charity Gala tonight. To get ready for the new year to start and for you to begin your awesome new life,' Merry had said. 'And you can't do that while you're busy putting on a brave face for Ivy or working too much so you can pretend you haven't just had your heart broken. So we're going out. Take a bath or something.'

'But what about the gala? There's last-minute stuff to sort—'

'All delegated. That's why we have staff.'

'What about the last table? The cancellation?' One last-minute cancellation had left them with an empty table—or, at ten grand a plate, one hundred thousand pounds less money that had been raised. That wasn't acceptable—and it definitely wasn't Perfect London.

'Sorted. I sold it this morning.'

'Seriously?'

'I am a miracle worker. I have planned and fixed everything. Now, go run that bath.'

Merry probably hadn't planned on the knock on the door, however.

Clara sighed into the bubbles around her. Then, as whoever was waiting knocked again, she hauled herself out of the bath and wrapped a towel around her.

'Mrs Clara Foster?' the delivery man at the door asked.

Clara blinked. 'I suppose so.' Even if no one had called her that in five years. 'For now, anyway.'

'These are for you.' He motioned to the large stack of boxes in his arms. 'Shall I bring them in?'

Clara nodded. He set them on the table, then discreetly disappeared again, leaving Clara to open them in peace.

Fixing her towel more tightly around her, she opened the largest box, lifting out the most beautiful ballgown Clara thought she had ever seen. It was dark red velvet, sprinkled with sparkles on the bodice and overlaid with lace on the skirt. She held it against her and imagined dancing in it at the gala that night. She'd never worn anything half as beautiful. Even her wedding dress had been grabbed off the rack at the shop next to the Vegas chapel.

The next box held matching shoes, then a bag and smaller boxes with discreet silver and garnet jewellery— earrings, a necklace—and a silver bangle studded with garnets, and with a message engraved on the inside: *She believed she could, so she did...*

Someone knew exactly what she liked. Clara pulled out the card last, and held her breath as she read it.

I chose the presents myself this time.
I'll see you tonight.
Both of you.
Love, J x

She blinked. *Both of you?*

A second knock rattled the door and she dashed across to answer it, half expecting Jacob to be there himself. But instead it was another delivery man, carrying another stack of boxes, all a little smaller than the first.

'I'm looking for a Miss Ivy Foster?' the delivery man said.

Clara bit back a smile. 'She's not here right now, but I can take those for you.'

This time, she reached for the card first.

Ivy,
I can't wait to carry on our conversations at the ball
tonight. I hope your mum might still let me tell you
something very important.
Love, Jacob x

Clara grabbed her phone, hoping to catch Merry before the pantomime started. 'Who exactly did you sell the last table to?' she asked when her friend answered.

'Ah,' Merry said. 'It's a funny story…'

Clara fell into her chair and laughed, her heart lifting for the first time since she'd left Scotland.

CHAPTER NINETEEN

THE BALLROOM AT THE Harrisons' mansion was bedecked with sparkling white fairy lights. Perfectly laid tables were dressed with crisp white linen and glistening crystal chandeliers hung from the ceiling. Jacob tugged at the collar of his tuxedo and hoped, not for the first time in the last few days, that this wasn't all a huge, huge mistake.

He'd already let Clara down. He'd played right into her worst fears and walked away just when she thought she could rely on him to be there for her and Ivy. It was asking a lot to want to come back from that, and all he really had to work with was a couple of fancy ballgowns, a ridiculously expensive dinner and—he glanced behind him at the three people sitting very expectantly at a table set for ten—his family.

'This could be a huge mistake,' he told them, taking his seat. His mother pushed a bread roll towards him and Heather motioned a waiter over to bring him a glass of wine. 'I mean, she's running this event. She could actually have us thrown out.'

'She won't,' his father said, totally calm. 'Patience.'

'Where is she?' Jacob craned his neck to try and spot her in the crowd, but there were so many people filling the ballroom it was almost impossible to pick out any one person.

Of course, if she was wearing the dress he'd sent, he had a feeling she'd be hard to miss.

'She'll be here,' his mother reassured him. 'Eat some bread. You should never go into a stressful situation on an empty stomach.'

'It's not stressful!' Heather said, reaching for her own

wine. 'It's romantic. He's paid *thousands* to be here tonight to tell her he loves her and he wants to be a family again.'

'You make it sound easy.' Meanwhile, just thinking about it made his hands shake with nerves. God, what was it about Clara that could drive him to such panic? He was never like this before a big business meeting.

'It is! All you need to do is tell her, "I love you, I'm sorry, can we try again?"' Heather said.

'I think it might take a bit more than that.' Such as an entire personality change from him. Oh, no, this was *such* a bad idea.

'I think you'll be surprised.'

Before they could argue the point further, a small girl in a dark green velvet dress, complete with satin sash, came barrelling through the crowd towards them, a harried-looking Merry hurrying behind.

'Jacob!' Ivy squealed, throwing herself into his arms. 'You came! Thank you for my dress—I love it!'

Jacob let himself savour the feeling of those tiny arms around his neck, the scent of clean little girl and a sweetness he suspected had something to do with Merry sneaking her chocolate. He looked up at Clara's business partner.

'Clara's double-checking things in the kitchen and briefing the entertainment for later. She'll be here soon. Can I leave Ivy with you guys for dinner?'

'Absolutely!' Jacob's mum beamed. Then, belatedly, she looked across at Jacob. 'That's fine, isn't it, darling?'

His first parental moment, pre-empted by his mother. He supposed it was inevitable.

'Ivy will be fine here with us,' he told Merry. 'And, uh, if you see Clara…'

'I will surreptitiously nudge her in this direction.' Merry rolled her eyes. 'It's not like she doesn't know you're here, you know.'

'So she's avoiding me?'

'She's working,' Merry said, looking amused. 'I'd have thought you would have appreciated that.'

Jacob returned her wry grin. He hadn't been able to focus on work since Christmas.

But then he looked up and saw Clara across the room, the dark red velvet dress he'd chosen for her clinging to her very familiar curves, and he knew he'd never be able to focus on anything else but her again.

'Ivy? Are you okay staying here with Heather and my parents while I talk to your mum?'

Ivy, who was already pulling a cracker with Heather, nodded.

'Right. Then I'll…go and do that.' He paused for a moment.

'Go on, son,' his father said, placing a hand on his shoulder. 'You can do it.'

Yes. He could. He hadn't been sure in Scotland, but now…he knew exactly what he needed to do.

Heather's words came back to him. *All you need to do is tell her, 'I love you, I'm sorry, can we try again?'*

He could do that.

'Clara?' He crossed the ballroom towards her and lost his breath when she turned and faced him. It wasn't just her beauty—formidable though it was. It was the connection, the instant spark of recognition he felt when their eyes met. The link that told him that whatever happened, however he screwed up, they were meant to be together. Always.

Clara's smile was hesitant. 'Jacob…it was kind of you to buy the last table tonight. I know the Harrisons appreciate your generous donation. And I hope it means that maybe we can work something out between our families. I know Ivy would love to see more of Heather, and your parents.'

'But not me?' Jacob finished for her.

'Well, that rather depends on you,' Clara said, meeting

his gaze. 'And whether you've changed enough to make the commitment we need from you.'

This was it, Jacob realised. His second chance. And he might not have the perfect plan but he had a heartfelt one. One that was good enough to make a start with, anyway.

And if he screwed it up he'd just have to try harder.

Jacob took a deep breath and prepared to change his life for ever.

Clara smoothed her hand over her dress, the weight of her ballgown giving her small courage as she waited to hear what he'd say. He'd paid a lot of money to be there. It couldn't be the end of everything, as she'd thought. But could there really be a way through for them? She still wasn't sure.

And she knew it all hinged on Ivy.

She glanced across and saw her daughter pulling a cracker with Jacob's father and smiled. Her daughter had been so delighted with the dress Jacob had sent, so excited to be allowed to go with her this evening. The Harrisons had thought it a charming idea and, with Merry delegating so efficiently, Clara had very little to do at the gala but enjoy the evening.

Right then, all she could see was Jacob, gorgeous and nervous and smiling in his tux.

'I keep seeing children. Everywhere.'

Clara blinked at his words in confusion.

'There are...quite a lot of them in the world?' she said.

'Yes. But I never noticed them before. Not until I met Ivy.' He took her arm and led her to the window, out of the way of the flow of the other guests. Outside, more lights flickered in the trees, bright and full of hope for the year ahead.

Maybe Clara could be hopeful too.

'And now?' she asked.

'Now I can't stop seeing them. Can't stop wondering if they're older or younger than Ivy. What she was like at their age, or what she will be like. Whether she likes the same things. Obviously she's prettier and cleverer and more wonderful than all of them… I can't understand it, though. I only spent one day with her and suddenly she's everywhere.'

'She gets under your skin,' Clara said. 'Once I knew I was pregnant, I saw babies everywhere. And once she was born… She's my first thought every morning when I wake up, and my last thought before I go to sleep.'

'You used to say that was me,' Jacob said, but he didn't seem disappointed. More…proud?

'It was,' Clara admitted. 'You were all I thought about. But being a parent, it changes you. In all sorts of good ways.'

'You were everything to me too,' Jacob said. 'All that I could think about, any time of the day. I know you thought I ignored you and that I focused too much on work, but really I never stopped thinking about you, not for a moment. It was…everything. And terrifying. Because I didn't know if I could cope if I hurt you, lost you.'

'So you kept me at arm's length.' Just like he'd tried to do again at the castle.

'Yeah. I think so.'

'What about now?' Clara asked.

'Now…I'm still thinking about you. But not just about losing you. I'm thinking about all the possibilities we have, instead. I'm thinking about Ivy. I'm thinking about the life we could have together.'

'I thought you didn't want that.' In fact, her entire existence for the past five years had hinged on the fact that the last thing he wanted was a family.

'So did I,' Jacob agreed. 'Right up until the moment I

realised that you had gone again, and this time you'd taken Ivy with you.'

Clara grabbed hold of the window frame behind her. The world must be spinning off its axis because she felt a fundamental shift somewhere underneath everything she knew to be true. 'What are you saying?'

'I've spoken to my real estate agent. I'm selling the houses—all those white, soulless designer places you hated. We'll choose a new home together, the three of us. And I'm speaking with the board, working out a more family friendly schedule. One that will work with your business commitments too, I hope.

'Basically, I'm saying…I love you. I'm sorry. Can we try again?'

Clara shook her head. 'Jacob, we tried. So many times.'

'Yeah, but this time we've got a better reason to succeed.'

'What happened to you?' Clara asked. 'What changed? Because…I want to believe you. But I need to know why.'

Jacob stood beside her and took her hand. 'It was my father, mostly. He told me that success nearly always starts with failure. That the key is to keep trying for the things that matter. And you, Clara…you matter more than anything. You and Ivy. You're all that matters.'

'You never wanted to be a father.'

'I was too scared to be a father. Too scared that I'd screw it up.'

'Everyone screws it up. That's what being a parent is all about.' Hadn't she learned that the hard way, over the past four years?

'So my parents tell me,' Jacob said with a wry smile. 'And the thing is…I think, if we were screwing up and trying again together, if it wasn't just me on my own, scared to death of failing…if it was *us,* I think I could do it.'

'You have to be sure, Jacob. Ivy can't take maybes. She's four. She needs to know you'll always be there.'

'And will you?' Jacob asked. 'Will you be there for me, as well as her? Because if we do this…I need to know you won't leave again.'

Clara looked down at her hands, at where her wedding ring used to sit. 'I will. I realised, this time…I can't spend my life running away. I wanted to be wanted, and when I thought I wasn't, I left. But with Ivy, I'm not just wanted, I'm needed. And that's so much more important.'

'She's not the only one who needs you,' Jacob said. Clara looked up to meet his open gaze and saw the truth of his words there. 'I need you in my life, Clara. I need you there to pick me up when I fall, to hold me when things fall apart, to cheer me on when things are going well and to love me, all the time. And, most of all, I need you to let me do all those things for you too. Because I love you, more than I ever thought I could. More than I ever realised I would. You're part of me and I can't risk losing that part again. I need it. I need you.'

Clara let out a choked sob and he pulled her against him, his arms warm and safe around her. 'I need you too,' she admitted. 'Not because I can't do it on my own—I know I can. It just doesn't mean as much without you there.'

'Then I'll be there. For you and for Ivy. Whenever you need me. I promise.'

'And I'll be there too. I won't leave again.'

'And when we both screw up?' Jacob asked. 'Because I have it on good authority that we will. Things won't be perfect all the time.'

Clara shook her head. 'They don't need to be perfect. We just need to try. And when we screw up, we'll try harder. Together.'

'Together,' Jacob echoed. Then he smiled. 'Look,' he said, nudging her chin upwards. 'Mistletoe.' She smiled.

Apparently Merry had known what she was doing when she'd insisted on hanging it in all of the window alcoves.

'Well, you'd better kiss me then,' Clara said, her heart full to bursting. 'And then we'll go and tell Ivy that she just gained a family.'

'She had us all along,' Jacob said. 'I just didn't know it yet.'

'And now that you do?' Clara asked, in between kisses.

Jacob grinned down at her under the mistletoe. 'Now...' he said. 'This is officially my perfect Christmas.'

* * * * *

LET'S TALK

For exclusive extracts, competitions
and special offers, find us online:

 facebook.com/millsandboon

@MillsandBoon

@MillsandBoonUK

Get in touch on 01413 063232

MILLS & BOON

THE HEART OF ROMANCE

A ROMANCE FOR EVERY KIND OF READER

MODERN

Prepare to be swept off your feet by sophisticated, sexy and seductive heroes, in some of the world's most glamourous and romantic locations, where power and passion collide.
8 stories per month.

HISTORICAL

Escape with historical heroes from time gone by. Whether your passion is for wicked Regency Rakes, muscled Vikings or rugged Highlanders, awaken the romance of the past.
6 stories per month.

MEDICAL

Set your pulse racing with dedicated, delectable doctors in the high-pressure world of medicine, where emotions run high and passion, comfort and love are the best medicine.
6 stories per month.

 *True Love*

Celebrate true love with tender stories of heartfelt romance, from the rush of falling in love to the joy a new baby can bring, and a focus on the emotional heart of a relationship.
8 stories per month.

 Desire

Indulge in secrets and scandal, intense drama and plenty of sizzling hot action with powerful and passionate heroes who have it all: wealth, status, good looks…everything but the right woman.
6 stories per month.

HEROES

Experience all the excitement of a gripping thriller, with an intense romance at its heart. Resourceful, true-to-life women and strong, fearless men face danger and desire - a killer combination!
8 stories per month.

DARE

Sensual love stories featuring smart, sassy heroines you'd want as a best friend, and compelling intense heroes who are worthy of them.
4 stories per month.

To see which titles are coming soon, please visit

millsandboon.co.uk/nextmonth

MILLS & BOON

MODERN

Power and Passion

Prepare to be swept off your feet by sophisticated, sexy and seductive heroes, in some of the world's most glamourous and romantic locations, where power and passion collide.